# Wandering Canalside

Patricia Willers

*For Matt*
*I couldn't have done it without you.*

# Wandering
# Canalside

Patricia Willers

## *Amsterdam*

*Much too soon, it was time. As Clara brought her bags downstairs to stack in the entry, she relived her last morning in Amsterdam. She already missed the vivacious international city.*

*That morning she had gone to the market with the idea that it would be a nice quick trip. Instead, the sun, the people, and the boats cruising up and down the canals took her captive and she wandered amongst the crowds for an hour, eating cubes of young Gouda and freshly fried calamari and admiring the bustling market activity.*

*The mellow crowds at the market were amazing. Absent was the usual rush to be the first in the cheese line; instead there was an almost sedated form of happiness that could only be induced by wandering with a melting ice cream cone or sitting on the canal drinking wine or cappuccino and watching the boats drift by.*

*In one handsome, honey-colored, wooden boat an old man sat, shirt off and working on the start of what—by the end of the summer—would be a large, dark brown belly. There were wine glasses next to him, half full of a nice summer Riesling from a few hundred kilometers away across the German border. His wife was missing, probably picking up sandwiches or herring.*

*As Clara continued down the stretch past the fish men, she passed a cellist and later, a violin-playing puppet. On days like this, it was all so much like a dream that it was hard to believe that she had actually been in this city for more than a month.*

*She sometimes wondered about these memories she was collecting. Years from now, would she remember this part of her life? Or would she forget just how vivid and colorful life could be?*

*Back at her perfect canalside apartment, Clara sat at her*

*window one last time to watch the water of the canal float by—the very same water that the handsome wooden boat spent its life in.*

*Just a few months before she'd had a plain, typical, American life. She hadn't known change was coming, but it had.*

# Part 1

## *Sacramento*

### one

Clara woke up with a sigh and a smile as she stretched her arms slyly above her head. Her right hand, extending over her nightstand, nearly knocked off an empty wine bottle.

*What a night,* she thought, *what a wonderful night of ruby red port, Sinatra, photos, and sex.* It had been a trying year for her marriage, what with all the silence, indifference, and lack of sex, and until last night, she had been starting to worry that their relationship was on the downhill slope. With a deep breath, she flung off the worn tan cotton sheet and swung her legs out of bed, slipping her toes into the bright green and fuzzy clog slippers that lived on the floor immediately next to her bed. She threw on Jack's red striped polo from the day before.

*Ew, yuck,* golf sweat- maybe not. She pulled it off and chucked it into the closet and grabbed instead a yellow, flowered kimono-esque robe that, along with her slippers, completed her image as a nutty, young art teacher.

She tied the sash in a loose bow and ran her fingers through her nut brown hair and down her neck. She was beaming; she couldn't help it. She couldn't remember the last time she and Jack had made love, and this, this was probably the best ever.

To be perfectly truthful, she had stolen that phrase. She

had stolen it right out of her husband's mouth, to be precise.

"Probably the best sex I've ever had," he'd said to her just moments before they had fallen asleep—exhausted, sweaty, and satisfied.

She looked to the window where the sheer cream curtains were masking the morning sun that desperately wanted to shine into the upstairs bedroom of the Victorian that had become their home over the last nine years.

The house had belonged to a friend of Jack's family who had always adored little Jack. When the miserable but ridiculously wealthy woman passed away, she left the house to him. He'd made the most of the situation during college, hosting parties, renting his extra rooms for far too much, and likely convincing numerous women that *he* was the wealthy one. The house required some much-needed love and care by the time Clara came along. Years of college parties and forty years in the hands of a grouchy *bachelorette* tended to have a way of doing that.

Now, here they were, almost a decade later, the best ever... Finally, things were coming together.

She left the bedroom and shuffled down the charmingly creaky staircase, but paused when she noticed that her favorite painting, a colorful Georgia O'Keeffe which was obviously a relic of old lady Sanden's days, was no longer on the wall in the stairwell. After pondering for a second, she decided it was nothing and continued down the stairs to the kitchen where she hoped her recently rejuvenated lover would be making the Sunday morning dish of his college years. He called it Hazy Hash and Eggs, though nowadays, the hash wasn't hazy in the same way it used to be.

As she was about to enter the kitchen, something caught her eye. On the accent table in the entryway, leaning against a clay vase of swirling red, orange, and yellow that she'd made in college, was a familiar, crisp, cream envelope. She felt a shiver run through the hair on her arms. *For me?* She thought, and pulled out the card inside.

*Dear Clarie,* it began. He always called her Clarie when

he had something important to tell her. When he'd asked her to marry him, when he'd first gotten a real job after college, when he'd totaled their brand-new car... It didn't necessarily mean something good or bad, but something of meaning, something that would affect both of them, life-changing moments in one way or another.

She read the simple notecard. It took her either 10 seconds or 10 minutes. She looked at the envelope and focused on her name, and then read it again. One more time she read it, still unable to believe what she was seeing.

*...not working...*
it read,
*...you're not a part...*
*...leave.*

And the last line, just when she thought it couldn't get any worse,

*with Jane.*

How could this be? How could he after the wonderful night they had just had? All those photo albums they had looked through together...

He *knew*, she realized. He knew the whole time. It was all part of the plan. *Sinatra*, like their wedding night. Hours huddled on the couch, laughing and looking at pictures of their years together, and the many, many stories which went along with them. He had known the whole time that this would be the last time he'd be able to reminisce like this—with her at least.

Four words kept flashing in her mind, "Probably the best ever."

*Had he even spoken the words, or had she just imagined it?*

She focused on the one significant word: *probably*. She hadn't been insulted by it before, but she certainly was now.

*Probably!?* Who else had been better? He hadn't been the smoothest guy in college, just a normal guy. Had there been someone better that long ago? Someone who she, apparently, had been working to outdo for the last nine years? Or was there someone better than her now? *Probably.*

She understood why he had removed the huge O'Keeffe and she hated him for it. He knew she loved it, and that painting was his—just like the house, the garage, the yard, the fence. He didn't want her to have anything.

## two

Clara left the house later that same day. She hadn't showered or eaten, or even had coffee, which probably added to her catatonic state of lifelessness. She paid her neighbor's dog-walker to load everything feminine-looking or of value into his car and drive it to her friend Krista's house. She wondered what that would mean to him—a stranger, essentially, though she'd seen him every day for the last five years. And what did it mean to her? Did anything have value after your life was uprooted like this? Would anything be important enough to keep, in the end? She attempted to swallow the lump in her throat and without a glance back at her former home, stepped into the taxi she had called.

She trained her eyes straight ahead as they drove from stop sign to stop sign down to a nearby hotel. *What a note could do*, she thought. *A note*! Though admittedly, she almost preferred the note. She couldn't help but imagine what she would have done if Jack had decided to tell her in person. She would have cried. Would she have begged? She shuddered at the thought. Could her life have come to that? Begging to stay? Begging him to try to love her again? Just the thought put a bad taste in her mouth.

With very little thought, she got herself a room at the Desert Sands Motel. She needed to be alone for a while, perhaps a long while. Clara was no extrovert, and a traumatic event like this was very nearly enough to send her into hiding forever. While part of her desperately wanted to call Krista, she couldn't bring herself to pick up the phone to tell her best friend that the worst had happened. She simply couldn't bring herself to say the words.

Her marriage was over. Life as she knew it was over. She knew all the information was there in her head somewhere, but since she couldn't grasp it, when her alarm went off on Monday morning, she went to work. She lasted until just after lunch, when one of her students brought up her complementary colors project.

"This is love and hate," the girl stated simply.

It was beautifully done. The thoughtful, brown-haired fifth grader had chosen red and green as her colors. The left side of the thick 11 by 17 piece of paper had a beautiful and clearly outlined red heart in the center. Green leaves surrounded it elegantly, making it appear that the heart was in fact a blossoming flower in the spring. The happiness ended there. Flowing rightward was a string of leaves on a vine that became darker and mysteriously grotesque. Clara's chest tightened as she followed the vine, and her face grew far too warm as she saw that the vine of hate didn't stop when it reached the right side of the paper, but wound around and around in confusion, eventually leading back to the peaceful heart, about to be strangled. It was all too near and dear for Clara. She managed to nod at the young girl before waving to the aide in the room and excusing herself to head down to the principal's office.

Back at the hotel she crawled in and pulled the covers up over her head. She should have known better.

## three

It was a blur of nothingness in the dark, hot hotel room. She didn't have the energy to toggle the air conditioning, so she just accepted the stuffy heat. She had no idea how long she had been out, or if she had slept at all. Surely it wasn't long enough. Several times she found herself staring out at the moon—well, that and the glowing Desert Sands sign across the parking lot.

On Wednesday, her mother called. She hadn't actually known that it was Wednesday, except her mother always called on Wednesday. She took the call, responding in low murmurs to all the goings-on of her mother's life. She couldn't always get by with this, but every once in a while it worked out, and luckily this week it was her mother's turn to host reading group, so the entire call was filled with her mother's animated descriptions—the book, the forthcoming discussion, the menu of appetizers that would be served.

When Clara was finally able to snap her phone shut, she felt an odd sense of relief to be able to let the anger, hurt, and emptiness wash over her once again. Missing the call or having to say anything at all would have given her away, and she still wasn't ready to speak. She actually felt the tiniest bit proud of herself. She turned over and went back to sleep, wondering if she could make it to the next Wednesday, or the next; wondering, really, if she ever had to come to terms with what had happened, or if she could just go on this way forever.

She couldn't bear to tell anyone what had happened, nor could she fathom telling anyone her current state—alone in a horrible hotel, the do not disturb sign permanently in place, her only contact with the outside world a delivery of fried rice from the Chinese place down the street. All alone, she could simply close her eyes and pretend that he didn't have such a horrible, impossible request.

*Leave.*

At some point, she heard pounding on the door and eventually, Krista was there with her, watching reruns of *Grey's Anatomy.* She wondered if she had let Krista in, or if she somehow had her own key. Clara went back to sleep, somewhat aware that she was no longer alone, at least in the most technical sense of the word.

There was a dusky light filtering into the room when

Krista first spoke, asking about the last thing she'd had to eat or drink.

"Nothing," she'd responded, not remembering and not caring. Krista tried to push something on her, something white and soft, but it was no use. Clara needed a few more days of nothingness. The only thing she really wanted she would never again have.

The next time Clara's eyes opened, there was still a duskiness in the room. It occurred to her now that this meant nothing. In this part of town it could have been produced by the streetlights. However long it had been, Clara finally turned to Krista.

"How did you find out where I was?" she asked. Krista's eyes lit up in shock and she immediately muted the television. Clara hadn't noticed that it was on.

"Desert Sands?" Krista replied, smiling gently, "Come on; give me some credit for being your friend for almost 20 years." She came over to the bed and squeezed in next to Clara, not touching her, but simply being next to her. "What is it with this place anyway? It can't be the one you're dreaming about."

Clara looked sleepily around the dingy hotel room, pondering her lifelong obsession with the Desert Sands. She hadn't chosen it at random, but her exact reason somewhat escaped her tired mind at the moment.

"A nightmare, I suppose," Krista continued when Clara didn't speak. "Plus, you love those doughnuts from the shop down the street." Krista extended a pink cardboard box and flipped it open. "Ahhh, maple bars," she hummed. "Want one?" she asked enticingly. Without waiting for an answer she shoved a custard-filled maple bar into Clara's hand. "Eat up," she said sternly, "It's been a while." With one final disapproving look, she turned back to the television.

Clara's thoughts stumbled a bit, but after a few moments she realized that this was her cue to eat. Apparently there would be no more discussion until she had ingested something.

Five minutes and two doughnuts later, Clara was sitting up for the first time in days, licking sticky chocolate icing off her fingertips. It felt surprisingly good to be awake and to have her best friend sitting right next to her.

"Krista?" she asked, "Have you been here the whole time? Did you have to take vacation from work?"

"It's the weekend, Clare," Krista responded dryly, knowing that Clara had no idea whether time was passing forwards or backwards.

Clara just nodded, staring straight ahead, but seeing nothing of the *Oprah* rerun that was gracing the television screen.

"Clare? You know it's been a week?" she half asked and half stated.

"Ungh," Clara grunted.

"That's kind of a long time..." she continued, "and I talked to your mother yesterday."

Clara glanced up at the mention of her mother. *Who else knew?* She wondered.

"She didn't know a thing," Krista explained, knowing this was the piece of information that Clara was interested in. "I asked her if she had talked to you recently, and she said no... that it had been a couple of days."

"Well," Clara murmured, not really a part of the conversation, "didn't feel like talking."

"Yeah- I figured you didn't, except that then she told me she hadn't talked to you since Wednesday..." Krista looked at her with a sad and inquisitive look on her face. "Wednesday?" Krista repeated, "Clara-"

Krista never called her Clara, only Clare. She wasn't sure why, it was just something that had always been. Clara secretly thought that Krista thought *Clare* was a *cooler* version of Clara—more hip, young, chick and less Grandma Clara.

"Clara?" she repeated. "When did this happen? Because I, for one, was under the impression that it all happened on either Saturday or Sunday- *before* Wednesday. Clare, why didn't you tell her? Why didn't you tell me? Why didn't you tell anyone?"

Clara could feel eyes drilling into the side of her face, but didn't have the energy to turn and face it.

"I spoke with Delia yesterday," Krista continued, still uninterrupted, "and she said she hadn't talked to you for at least two weeks. I thought you talked to Delia all the time. I thought you told her everything. Not your mother, not your sister, not me. Why didn't you call me!?"

"I *hardly* talk to Delia," Clara said defensively. She had a civil relationship with her sister, but they certainly weren't friends, though they talked surprisingly often. "She's just that nosy. Plus," she supplied, "Delia loves Jack." Clara hadn't been able to imagine telling anyone what had happened, let alone her younger sister, who was dead-certain that Jack was *the one*.

"She doesn't *love* Jack," Krista countered, "she just likes that you were married- happily married with a cute little house and a cute little job as an art teacher… That-" she explained, "is why Delia liked you and Jack. She thought you were happy. I think maybe she was even a bit jealous."

"Delia's never been jealous of me…" Clara trailed off.

"Clare, hon- you've *got* to tell people, or at least communicate with people, you can't just cut yourself off like this!"

Clara once again had no response. It wasn't that she didn't understand this point of view, she just had no energy for it. She suddenly felt a strong urge to slip back under the covers and go back to sleep. This was exactly why she hadn't told anyone.

"What did the school say? Have you told them?" Krista was becoming quite emphatic now, "I mean, you must have, because it's been a few days, so they had to have noticed something. Are you sick? Are you taking vacation? How did you justify this? I can hardly imagine you're calling in every morning." Krista took a deep breath and adjusted herself so she was sitting across from Clara rather than next to her. "Hello!?" she barked, glaring right into Clara's eyes.

11

"I'm on a leave of absence," Clara stated glumly.

"What? Really?" There was a long pause as Krista examined Clara's eyes. "Shit. Didn't expect that."

Clara gave her one short, slow nod.

"So you planned this? You knew you were going to come here and wallow for a week?"

"No!" Clara defended herself, "I didn't know what I was going to do; I obviously hadn't *planned* on having to do this." She callously emphasized the word, stinging Krista for her choice of words.

Krista waved it off. There was no stopping her. "What are your *plans* for tomorrow and the next day and the next, and the next *Wednesday* when your mother calls and you pretend that nothing has changed, and that you're still going to work and living with Jack and that you have a life. Are you just going to stay in this hotel room forever and wallow?"

"Fine!" Clara yelled, "I am going to wallow. I like to wallow! It's comforting. You would wallow, too. I know you would. Who wouldn't!?" she shrieked, "He kicked me out, Krista! I am alone and broken-hearted. There is absolutely nothing to do but wallow!" Clara's shoulders shook with the grief and pain of it all, but there were no tears. She liked to think that she wasn't allowing herself to cry because she was that angry, but it wasn't that. There were just none. It was all too stunning.

Krista frowned at Clara's words and pulled her into her arms. "Comfort, yes, fun, no. Doing this forever is not a possibility. You'll turn into one giant slug and never have a normal life again- you have to get out of here. You have to *find* something else, something that's motivating and uplifting and fun, and get your life back!"

"He kicked me out of my house, Krista!" She was standing, something that she couldn't remember actively doing for days. "He listened to Sinatra with me, he danced with me, he drank wine with me, he had sex with me, and then he left me a *note*- on the entry table, by the way, where we would leave notes reminding each other to pick up milk or toilet paper. He kicked. Me. Out!!!"

Krista stood up slowly, taking Clara's shoulders, "I know, honey and I'm so sorry, but still, you can't go on like this forever!"

"We hadn't had sex for a year!" Clara shrieked.

The silence that followed was thick with disgust.

"What?" Krista asked sharply, "What?"

"A year, Krista," Clara repeated. "He hadn't had sex with me for over a year. And this is what came of it."

Krista looked down at the floor, maybe shocked by the information she had just received, maybe just examining the bizarrely modern black and green patterned carpet.

"How- Wh- Were you guys..." she paused, choosing her words carefully, "Were you guys talking? I mean- was he still living there? Was he still coming home? How could you be sleeping in the same bed for a year and not have sex... at least once... Come on, a year?"

"A year," Clara repeated, as if this explained it all, which it kind of did. Things were just much worse than she had ever admitted. For years they had been cohabiting and nothing more. It was all meaningless, automatic. Not forced, because they didn't even put that much effort into it—just automatic, until something better came along. Something better in the form of *jane*, in his case. Clara cringed at the thought, but didn't mention it. She wasn't ready to speak the other woman's name, even to Krista.

At that moment, there was an unfortunate pounding at the door—much louder than housekeeping would ever dare to knock—and in a steady rhythm that could only mean one thing.

"Did you *tell* my mother?" Clara demanded.

"No," Krista responded, "Definitely not."

Clara glared at her skeptically.

"No!" Krista repeated, "I seriously didn't! I talked to her for a bit, asked when she had last talked you, asked whether or not she had talked to Jack-"

"Jack- there it is—she knows." Clara interrupted. "You

bitch." She shook her head angrily. "Now look what happened. My mother is here, at the door, and *you* have to answer it."

"Why would I have to answer it? She's your mother."

"Because you provoked it! She would never have come here if you hadn't called her and been all suspicious asking about me and, and Jack, and phone calls, and messages, and call time…"

"I didn't ask about call time-"

"Yeah, I'll bet you didn't. Just go tell her to go away." Clara ducked back under the giant flowered comforter, popping back up almost immediately, "*Don't* let her in. I don't want her here. I *can't* have her here. It'll kill me, I swear."

Krista shook her head, rolled her eyes at the dramatic turn Clara's words had taken, and went to answer the door. She knew, as any daughter knew, that Clara's mother would be coming in.

four

"Clara Jean Mason!"

Her mother stormed into the room the minute Krista opened the door. Krista was prepared and quickly pulled the door open and backed up against the wall. She'd visited the Mason household enough times to know not to get in the way of an angry Mrs. Mason.

"Young lady, what is going on!? This is a *horrible* way to treat your mother."

*Yeah, what a way to treat someone*, Clara thought. *Calling her by her maiden name, ouch.* That in itself would take a month to recover from. From under the covers, Clara watched Krista walk over to join her on the bed. *Yes, this is what friends were for*.

"Clara!" Mrs. Mason began again, "get out from under that blanket and let me see your face! You are a grown-up!"

Krista snorted quietly, and then looked away, trying to

avoid Mrs. Mason's laser eyes.

"You could be handling this a bit more gracefully, don't you think!?"

Krista couldn't help but snort again at the word *gracefully*. Clara winced under the covers. Her mother sure as hell wouldn't be doing anything *gracefully* if she were in the same position.

"Clara!"

"Go awaaaay!" Clara suddenly wailed from under the blankets.

"Oh, Clara!" her mother cried in despair, apparently under the impression that Clara's words were a cry for help. She went straight to Clara's bedside, sat on the edge, and pulled back the stale comforter.

"Clara, you look just horrible!" she exclaimed, leaning away from her as if she had accidentally pulled back the sheet to find a rotting pumpkin rather than her oldest daughter.

"Why, you're not taking care of yourself at all! Have you even showered!?"

Only silence came from Clara.

Mrs. Mason huffed. "Clara, dear, have you called Jack?"

Clara groaned but said nothing else.

"You should call him Honey, he needs you right now."

Several things happened at once. First, Krista choked out a cough and dropped the cup of coffee she was holding, spilling it all over the table and the floor. On the tv in the background Jerry Springer turned to his guest and asked dramatically, "Did you know your husband cheated on you with over a hundred women?" Clara threw back her covers and sat up in bed. Dust noticeably puffed from the bedspread as she did so.

"Get. Out! Mother!"

"Cla-ra," Mrs. Mason spoke her name in two disapproving and condescendingly pitched syllables. Krista was practically pawing the carpet in anticipation of throwing Mrs. Mason out of the room.

"No, Mom, I need him. He doesn't need me. That's the

point. I need him to call me. I need him to comfort me. I need him to love me, but he doesn't. Doesn't need me, doesn't," she choked, "want me... Now get out. I want to be alone."

"Cl-"

"Get out!" Clara screeched.

Mrs. Mason stood up in shock and hesitantly took a step toward the door. Even Krista was taken aback by the volume of the scream.

"Both of you," Clara added, looking down at her intertwined fingers, wringing her hands before covering her eyes and rubbing her temples.

Mrs. Mason looked hurt by the command, though possibly more surprised about Krista's ejection than her own. Krista, however, seemed unfazed.

"Go on, Mrs. Mason," said Krista. "I have to gather my things. We'll see you soon."

"Yes, dear," she replied softly, "You take care." She looked sadly towards her daughter as she said it.

"Yes," Krista replied softly, knowing that the well-wishes weren't for her at all, but for Clara.

As the door closed behind Mrs. Mason, Krista settled into a chair, picking up the remote and a chocolate sprinkled doughnut. Clara turned and looked at her, but Krista didn't return her blinking stare. She increased the volume and mumbled quietly but confidently, "You think I'm leaving you've got another thing coming."

Clara blinked again.

"Somebody's gotta monitor the wallowing."

Clara got back in bed and pulled her covers up over her head to try to drown out the lively and spirited confrontation that was now taking place on the daytime television show.

*No*, she found. The woman had not known that her husband had cheated on her with over a hundred women. In fact, she had not known about even one.

## five

The next morning, Clara woke up smelling something very much like maple syrup in her hotel room. She sniffed the air a bit, searching for the source, and found Krista sitting at the round little table by the window with a fork in her hand.

"French toast?" Clara asked timidly. Krista really knew how to get her up and out of bed. Krista's knowledge of her behavior was based on nearly two decades of friendship, including four years of attending college together at Sacramento State. Only Krista had known that every Tuesday morning for four years Clara had been present for French toast day at the school cafeteria, whether she had a meal plan or not. While others thought them soggy and unappetizing, Clara found the Texas toast that they used to be the perfect thickness and texture for a nice college breakfast.

"Texas toast?" she inquired, now peeping out from under the blankets.

"You'll have to come to the table and see," Krista taunted.

This made sense; she was being lured out of bed with take-out French toast. She thought about it for a minute and realized that it just might work. She'd hardly been out of bed at all besides the direct route from the bed to the bathroom, and even those trips were rare considering that she was still more or less on a hunger strike. Despite her mother's accusations, she *had* showered. Well, she had at least allowed water to pour on her head, soap may or may not have been used.

Clara sat up and rubbed her hands through her hair and took a minute to redo her ponytail. She glanced across the room at the mirror and decided she didn't look all that terrible. Yes, her hair had a certain shimmer of grease to it, but with it pulled back into a smooth ponytail, it wasn't half bad. Since she had yet to cry a tear, her face looked more or less normal as well, a little dead in the eyes, but what more could you expect in this sort of a situation? She turned back to Krista and found her watching Clara's strange self examination. She, too, seemed pleased as she examined Clara's attire.

"Feelin' scumfy?" Krista asked. Clara almost laughed aloud.

"I was just thinking that," she admitted, "and yes."

Clara was wearing an outfit of entirely forest green Sac State sweats. She and Krista had coined the word *scumfy* back in college when they were first discovering the joys of dorm living. There was nothing like a comfy level of scum on rainy winter weekends of college term papers. It was likely that Clara was wearing the exact outfit she had on the day they coined the word.

In a sudden glimmer of confidence, clearly induced by Krista and food, she threw the comforter back and swung her legs out of bed.

*Yum*, she had just gotten a whiff of bacon, too. She wondered if Krista had gotten her signature omelette o' onions, which was about as standard a meal as Clara's French toast.

"Okay," Clara conceded as she walked the three steps to join Krista at the table, "I'll join you." She looked down at a stack of buttery French toast and then up at Krista. "Yum. Thank you friend."

"Anytime, dearie, that's what I'm here for. I lie around and watch reruns of old sitcoms on TBS and eventually get your ass out of bed and filled with junk food," she explained.

"Well, nice choice," Clara noted.

"I do what I can."

They ate for a few minutes in silence, both enjoying their special meal. Clara looked around. She really hadn't taken in her surroundings at all since she arrived. Krista had opened the thick curtains, causing the slightly startling aroma of smoke to float around the room, and Clara could now see the sad, empty, deserted pool that was oddly situated in the parking lot.

"You know," Clara started, looking around the room, "this place is nothing at all like my Desert Sands dream."

Krista nodded her head enthusiastically, "I completely agree. That comforter gets uglier every day, I swear. And this carpet! When was this place built?"

The carpet was so poorly matched with the rest of the depressingly outdated attempt at swankiness that it almost made her dizzy to consider the room as a whole.

"So what is the basis for this Desert Sands obsession anyway, Clare? Have you actually been to a *nice* Desert Sands? Or is this all a figment of your imagination?"

"No, no, it's not a figment of my imagination. It's kind of stupid though, just something from when I was a kid. It's nothing."

"Okay..." Krista said slowly, "well, since I was a kid then too, why don't you elaborate a bit for me."

"Nah, never mind."

"Clare, come on. I've been sitting with only the tv for company for days. Give me something."

"Uh, well," Clara felt a tinge of embarrassed tint her face, "do you remember," she paused, looking away and out the window, "Jessie Spano?"

"From *Saved by the Bell*?"

"Yeah, well her dad owned or ran or managed or something- the Desert Sands Resort in Beverly Hills. It always sounded cool. Remember when they all stayed there? During that episode when Zach proposes? Or was it for their graduation?"

Krista's mouth was hanging open and her expression was something in between shock and gut-wrenching laughter.

"Wait," she said, "so this whole dream is based on the hotel that someone's dad owned in *Saved by the Bell*!? You have got to be kidding me!"

"What!?" Clara defended herself, "*Saved by the Bell* was great! And I really liked Jessie; she was cool."

"Cool? Oh, my God, Clara, you are such a dork."

"I am not! I just liked the show! And so did you, may I remind you."

"Yeah," Krista laughed, "so did I... but that love affair ended about a decade ago."

"Shut up."

"Might have been a decade and a half."

"Shut up."

This caused Krista to laugh even harder, so Clara went back to her French toast, adding a bit more whipped butter and syrup. It really had been a while since she'd had a good meal. Even Krista's crazy omelette looked and smelled great to Clara today. A couple of eggs, and stuffed with green, red, white, and yellow onions, tons of cheese, and a healthy dose of pico de gallo, *Yum, maybe she would try that tomorrow.*

"Where's this stuff from anyway?" Clara asked.

"Cap Garage."

Clara nodded back in obvious understanding. "Should we get more tomorrow?" she asked hopefully.

"Um," Krista hesitated. She looked disappointed in what she was about to say. "I think I have to work tomorrow, Clare... But I'll come back right after work okay? I'll even bring some clothes and stay the night."

There was no way Clara could fake it. With Krista's words, she was already feeling the emptiness sweep back over her. She wasn't sure if she could make it out of bed tomorrow without Krista there, "Yeah, that's fine," she began, but picked up her plate with the intention of going back to the bed.

"No, no, no! Stay here! I'll just work for a few hours and then I think Rog will let me work from home, so-" she thought for a second, "I'll be here by 11 for sure, you'll hardly be out of bed."

Clara looked at her skeptically when she said *out of bed.*

"Okay, so you won't be out of bed. So no worries... okay?"

Clara pondered. Krista was, no doubt, worried about having to start this whole process over again.

"Okay?" Krista confirmed again, looking warily at Clara, who seemed to be staring intently into nowhere.

"Pancakes?" Krista suggested, "Fluffy ones? With real maple syrup?"

Clara turned and nodded without a word, though she did feel perkier when pancakes were mentioned. Krista was looking at her with purpose. She was probably planning to stash snacks around the room. She imagined she *could* be lured out of bed with food for a few more days.

"You know what's really delicious?" Clara said, still staring into nowhere but this time looking a bit more dreamy, "My grandma used to make these Dutch pancakes, really thin and huge; they cover your whole plate and still spill over the sides. Yum. They were as light as air and you could put anything on them."

"What do you mean, anything?" Krista asked doubtfully, "like what?"

"Anything. I just sprinkled powdered sugar if I was feeling lazy, but sometimes I would put bacon and cheese or brown sugar and raisins, or cheese and tomato slices. My Grandma had a real gift for it. She would always tell us her favorite, cherries and ice cream, and then she would tell us her dad's favorite: bacon, apple, and cheese; and her mom's favorite, uh… brie and salami."

Krista grinned at her friend's fascination with pancakes. Clara was actually smiling. Krista nodded along in encouragement.

"She could go on forever," Clara continued, "she could probably tell you her grandma's neighbor's cousin's favorite type of pancake."

"Bacon, apple, cheese? I am trying to imagine it- oh, wait, there it is; my mouth is watering. Yum. Why have you never made these for me?"

"Oh, my Grandma was the only one who could do it properly. My mother could never get them thin enough, so she just gave up. I've never even tried."

"You should really try to find the recipe." Krista had a glint in her eye now, but Clara was too distracted with her pancake daydream to notice.

"Oh, I'm sure we have it. You know us, Dutch to the core; we don't throw away traditions like that."

"Maybe we could make them sometime this week," Krista suggested.

"What?" Clara asked, looking around as if expecting to see a hotplate and frying pan plugged in on the warping composite hotel desk, "but how would we make them?"

"Well, I do have a home, Clare. We could go there. Get you out of this dump," she murmured under her breath.

"Well," Clara thought about it, tipping her head to the side and looking around with a quantity of disgust, "I suppose we could."

Krista grinned, but then put on a straight face.

"You could probably work from home better there, right?" she asked Krista hopefully.

"Yes, definitely," Krista agreed.

"Okay, then." Clara agreed, "Let's do it. Tomorrow you can pick me up on your way home from work. Okay?"

"Great!" Krista cried, possibly a little too enthusiastically.

"I don't know about this recipe, though" Clara said as she popped another crunchy piece of bacon into her mouth, "I might have to go all the way to Holland to get a real copy of it."

Krista smiled.

"Well, maybe you should go," she said, at least a fraction seriously, "Find yourself a good recipe, take a little vacation. How about it?" She smiled widely at this new idea, seeing that it was, truly, a very good idea.

"Ha," Clara shook her head. "I'm sure that would be the best way to keep my job and go back to life as normal, go on an unexpected and extended vacation."

Krista glanced at her when she heard "back to normal."

"I mean..." It appeared that Clara, too, had just realized what she'd said.

"So," Krista began, maneuvering slowly into the difficult conversation. "What exactly... What's, um, what's your plan for next? Have you thought about it at all?"

*The View* was on in the background, and Clara suddenly interested in Taylor Swift, taking interview questions from Whoopi. She picked up her orange juice and took a sip.

"You don't have to know," Krista started again, "I was

just wondering."

Clara slowly dragged her last bite around in the syrup. Krista watched her intently with a look of concern on her face. Clara was listening, and she was sure there would come a time when she would let Krista push her towards life, she just wasn't sure if it was time yet.

"How's the French toast tasting?" Krista redirected the conversation. "Couldn't be nearly as good as this omelette. Delicious! I just can't get enough of these onions, though it could use a wee more salsa," she admitted.

"Good," Clara said, "Thanks." She paused, "But those pankoeken... I really should find that recipe. You'd love them." She wrinkled her nose, "If only I didn't have to visit my mother to look for it. Ugh," she cringed.

"Pankoeken?" Krista asked as she refilled their coffees.

"Yeah, it's the Dutch word for pancakes. I'm sure I'm not saying it right, but it's something like that."

"Oh, gotcha."

Clara sighed, and returned to her window gazing. "Maybe I should take a little vacation."

"Yeah!" Krista practically shrieked.

Clara looked over at her, a little startled. "I mean, I could go to Tahoe for a few days and hike and eat those tiny cherry pies from Sugar Pine Bakery. Yum."

Krista laughed a little, "Yeah, yum for sure, but Clare-make the most of this 'leave of absence.'" She used air quotes to define the unwelcome life gap. "It could be the chance of a lifetime."

"Yeah," Clara sneered, "the chance of a lifetime to run away while my husband brings some hussy in to stay on my side of the bed."

"What!?" Krista gasped.

Clara pretended that she hadn't spoken.

"What?" Krista questioned again, but Clara just shook her head robotically, and after staring for a long moment Krista again turned the conversation from a discussion that would be nothing but heartbreaking for Clara.

"You know, you *could* go to Holland," Krista suggested again, "You could learn how to make those pancakes, and your family's so Dutch, you really ought to experience the real thing sometime in your life. Maybe you should get out of this world for a while. Jump out of this American box we all put ourselves in—it might do you a lot of good."

Since Clara wasn't adding anything to the conversation Krista continued, "Tons of people speak English there... I think." She looked over at Clara to see if she was planning to give any input. "You could even stay for a while, if you wanted. Use your mom's maiden name to fit in or something. Plus, you can smoke pot there! It'd probably help your stress level a lot. It sure helped my mom when she was splitting up with my dad."

Finally Clara grinned. "Okay, a few things. First- wasn't your dad leaving your mom solely because she was a ... a flower child or something like that?"

"Ahhm.. neither here nor there. The weed helped! She told me."

"Yes, yes. I'm sure it did." She shook her head pessimistically. "But still, what would *I* do in *Holland*? It's not like I know anyone. My family was from there, but no one besides my grandmother has even stepped foot in the country. Dutch pancakes, windmills, and tulips are about all I've got."

"But you love tulips!"

"Yes, that's why I love tulips."

"And I thought there was some stubborn aunt that still lived in Holland? The one that came for Christmas that one year and told your grandmother that she'd gotten so fat that she looked like Mrs. Claus?" Even Clara couldn't help but laugh at this tale.

"Yeah," Clara said, "that was my grandma's sister. When their family moved from Holland to the United States, she refused to come with... *'Holland is where my heart lies,'* that's what she said. She was only sixteen, too; and super stubborn from what I've heard. Broke my grandmother's heart; they were best friends." Clara sighed and stood up to move back to the bed, "But still, that doesn't make me any more likely to make it there. My grandmother *did* come."

Krista followed her to the bed and they both flopped down on the pile of lumpy pillows.

"Maybe you should check it out anyway. Find out where exactly she lived. There has to be something about her in one of those crazy Dutch books your parents have lying around."

"What Dutch books? There's no way, Krista, I couldn't seriously move to Holland. Plus, I told you, they practically disowned her."

"Who?"

"My great aunt!" she said in an exasperated voice, but Krista still had a twinkle in her eye. It made Clara wonder if Krista was deliberately trying to get her riled up, just for some sign of emotion. "I only remember meeting her that one time, and it wasn't just her who was mean, my grandparents were also mean to her. I couldn't believe it. Think of how they would treat me, and what would my sister say? Wait! What would my mother say? She would definitely disown me."

"Well," Krista said, "it's at least worth looking into. You don't have to *move* there, you just need to get the hell out of here! You can get some space and a fresh perspective, check out the art galleries, maybe even meet some nice European men," Krista gave her a nice wink along with this comment.

"Krista! I'm not not-married yet!"

"I also heard that they have live sex shows!" Krista exclaimed, but Clara had already turned sadly towards the window.

"I don't know." Clara whispered, hardly getting the words out. She shook her head in defeat. "What do I do?" she asked, looking over at Krista.

Her eyes were red but dry, and so in pain. Krista shivered. *Yes, the look on her face probably was that traumatizing.* Maybe it *was* too soon to consider what was next.

"I don't know either, Clare. I'm sorry, I don't know." They both turned to the television where Aimee Mann was just starting a live rendition of "Wise Up."

The song was too much for Clara, and she sat silently, trying to block it out and wondering what she had meant by a normal life. *Where* was *she going?*

She looked over at Krista out of the corner of her eye. She knew that she would never tell her the truth: that she would go back to her normal life if she could. She hated Jack for what he did, but that didn't mean that she was over him. It didn't mean that if he changed his mind and wanted her back, that she wouldn't gladly accept. The dream of the heartbroken was always there. Maybe he would take her in his arms. They could start over fresh... She looked down at her clasped hands. Her wedding ring was still on her ring finger. She just hadn't been able to take it off. It was a part of her hand, and if she tried to take it off, it would leave her broken. Not whole.

She exhaled sorrowfully at the thought. Not whole; it was safe to say that she wasn't whole now. The last week had ripped her apart so badly that she wasn't sure she would even recognize herself in the mirror anymore.

*Maybe she should leave*, she thought. Maybe what she really needed was to just get the hell out of here, out of Sacramento, out of California, out of this country, out of this life. She would miss things, but she could always come back. Right now, feeling the way she did, she could hardly put her finger on a single thing that was important enough to continue here like this—not living.

She looked over at Krista, who had somehow fallen asleep in the five minutes of silence and was now slumped against the headboard.

She would miss Krista the most. It hurt even to think about not seeing her for an extended period. She was so weird and unorganized and... dominating—but caring and observant at the same time. She could pick up on Clara's intentions in a second and if she felt something wasn't a good idea or wasn't strong enough or *feminist* enough, she would interject, veto, and smoothly implement a better, and usually bitchier, route. Plus, she was so much fun.

Just thinking about the years that they had spent together

made Clara smile. Why couldn't she be just a little bit more like Krista? A little more confident, a little more pointed, direct.

She should get out of here. She shouldn't have come to this hotel in the first place, Krista wouldn't have. Krista wouldn't have even waited for a taxi, she would probably have hitch-hiked and been to Las Vegas or Tijuana or Ass Crack, Wyoming by sundown. Krista would *never* have stood for this. She certainly wouldn't have been waiting around in a hotel downtown, just blocks from her ex-house, waiting and wondering if the man who married her and then cheated on her and then left her... would come back.

Clara looked over at Krista, her light brown hair falling over her eyes.

*Yes, Krista would get out of here, so why shouldn't she? Why couldn't she?*

She had nowhere else, as depressing as that was to admit, and even a week or two ought to spark *something* in her. Heaven knows she could use a little something shocked into her. She snuggled back down under the covers, this time keeping her head out and feeling the tiniest bit optimistic. Maybe, just maybe, she would be going somewhere soon.

six

Krista woke up when the second *Bridget Jones* was finishing on TBS.

"Good morning," Clara said, enjoying that Krista was the one waking up in the middle of the day, rather than the other way around.

"Hey, Clare, what have you been doing?"

"Just thinking," Clara said, biting her lip.

"Yes? About what?" Krista asked.

"What do you think? Do you think I could actually-?"

"Whatever it is, just do it. That's what I would do."

Clara smiled at this command; it was exactly what she

27

had been drilling into her head for the past few hours.

"But Holland?" Clara asked, "Do you think I could really do it?"

"Yes. I do," Krista said simply. "You can do anything you want, that's the way life works, or at least that's the way life *should* work. Do you think I would be able to get paid to judge other people's work all day if it wasn't what I *really* wanted to do?"

"But that's not really me," Clara countered. "I've never been able to just... do whatever I wanted." Krista did project proposal analysis for the state. She truly was paid to just rip apart other people's work—sometimes years of work. As a teacher, Clara had always felt that she lived in a different sort of world. She got paid much less for doing more and more every year. She liked it, but that didn't necessarily mean it couldn't be improved upon.

"Well, why not? Why doesn't everybody just try to do what they *like* doing a little more often? All this hypertension and weight gain would go away, I can tell you that," she grumbled. They were beginning to hit on a few of Krista's sore spots about a stressful society. Plus, she'd just woken up and a freshly awake Krista was always pretty entertaining.

"I don't know." Krista somehow always found a way to live the life that she wanted to live, and prosperously. Clara, however, did not.

Krista looked up at Clara with a suddenly tender look on her face, very unlike Krista. "Clare," she said, "just go. You're done here."

Clara looked hurt at this statement, but Krista went on.

"That's not to say that this won't be the place for you again someday, but it just isn't the place for you now."

They locked eyes and Krista saw that Clara knew exactly what she meant.

"I really don't want to leave you," Clara began.

"Wait! No, no, no, no. Clara, this isn't about leaving *me*, it isn't about leaving anyone! This is about *you*. If you are going to turn this all around, if you are *ever* going to be just—

happy—with your life again, this *has* to be about you."

"I know, I know," Clara responded, "I was going to say that next, really." Krista looked skeptical but didn't interrupt this time. "I was going to say that I don't want to leave you, for my sake, because you're my best friend and I'd miss you so much."

"But," Krista was ready to start in again.

"Wait." Clara commanded, "*But,*" she emphasized, "I feel it too; I feel kind of, not *lost*, but, without direction, without inspiration. I just feel... nothing." She looked towards Krista, sadly, but there was something there. "Well, I feel hurt too. So hurt, in fact, that when I think about what happened I feel like I've been just pummeled. You know what I mean?"

"I know what you mean."

Clara put her arm around her best friend and looked towards the screen. This is what would happen then. She would go, and try again for herself—only for herself. She supposed she had never really done that before.

She tried not to think about leaving Krista. That would be the hardest part. At some point in the past 15 years, they had come to an understanding that life was just more fun when they lived close to each other. Now, that would be changing, and while it hurt to think of leaving her one and only bosom friend, it stung a whole lot more to think about staying here. She cringed and felt a shiver run through her body at the thought. She really had to get out of here. She didn't need to go as far as Holland, but considering the very few places she'd been in her life, when it came down to it, she was really only familiar with Sacramento. Her ties to Holland were about as good, if not better, than to any other place, in the U.S. or otherwise.

She would look for a ticket tonight, she decided, while her resolve was strong. Tomorrow, she would begin packing and she would check out of this crummy hotel. She had already caught herself thinking of it as home once, and for this particular Desert Sands, that was more than enough.

"So, I think I need to go. For me, like you said." She took

a deep breath, a kind of happy breath, and then cocked her head to look at Krista. "But I'll miss you so much," she added, reaching out to hug her again.

Krista hugged her back and smiled, "I'll miss you too, Clare."

Clara smiled, but looked up just in time to see a smirk forming on Krista's face.

"What?" she asked.

"Don't we sound just like fifth graders?" Krista asked, "with this 'best friends' talk? I swear I haven't said that phrase for fifteen years."

It was so like Krista to ruin a nice moment.

Clara tried again, "Well, I think we should say it more." She smiled and squeezed Krista's hand. "I hope we're friends forever." She looked over at Krista.

"Alright, BFF," Krista replied, "but don't call me tonight, best friend," she said as she got up and grabbed her jacket, "because I'm going to be hella busy making friendship bracelets, if you know what I mean." She winked at Clara as she backed out the door and Clara threw an empty tissue box at the back of the closed door before laughing.

*Seriously, though,* she thought, *if she was going to fly across the world—even if just for a week or two—what would she do without Krista?*

She grabbed the television remote after Krista left, flipping through the channels to avoid the unnecessary silence.

There was so much to think about when it came to going abroad. Could she really do it? She had better start packing, that was for sure. She needed to pack; she needed to quit her job. And *ew*, she thought, she needed to tell her mother. That wasn't going to be pleasant. She had always wanted to do something like this, maybe not to Holland, but at least somewhere new. She had *never* come this close to actually doing anything this crazy, this different.

*Wow!* she thought, she was excited! What a change from her old, steady routine. She felt a small flutter in her stomach, not a bad feeling, just weird. *What was this? Excitement?* She had been doing the same thing for so long, she couldn't be sure that it wasn't just indigestion.

She made a quick decision and picked up the phone. She might as well make the most of her present energy and courage. She sat in silence as the phone began to ring; she probably would have been more nervous, but she hadn't let herself think. She found that sometimes she was better off this way—blocking everything out and sitting unemotionally, as if bored, at least then she didn't get too nervous.

Her mother picked up after the fourth ring, just as the answering machine picked up. *You have reached Don and Laura Mason.*

"Oh, shoot!" she heard her mom exclaiming above the monotone drone of her father's voice on the answering machine.

"I hate this thing," she continued, "I can never... HOLD ON!" she yelled far too loudly considering she was probably holding the receiver between her chin and her shoulder.

"Just push the red button, Mom."

"Clara? Clara, is that you!?"

Great, now she was more distracted.

*Beeeeeep...*

"Mom?"

"Clara?"

"Yes, it's Clara, Mom; can you please turn that off?"

"Uh, yes, of course." Clara could hear her fumbling with the buttons, though it sounded more like she had pushed every button on the phone and had yet to figure out where the answering machine was.

"Mom?"

"Uh, yes?"

"Are you at the desk?"

"Yes, I am, I'm, uh- I'm trying."

Clara wondered if she would soon be disconnected because her mother had ripped the cord out of the wall.

"Mom, just push the *red* button on the square black machine to the left of the phone."

"Oh, that's right."

Immediately there was a beep and the machine clicked off. She heard her mother sigh with relief into the phone.

"Oh, Clara, I'm so glad you called. I have been just dying to tell you about my book club event! It was just lovely. I had *nine* people! That's the *entire* club! Can you believe it? The entire club hasn't made it to anything since my Christmas luau of '07. I think it's because they all heard that I was baking a variety of fruit pies to go along with this special Chai tea that I just found. It's really unique, it's like tea, but kind of milky, and has a nice honey, cinnamon scent to it...

It went on like this for a while before Clara even had to respond. This was exactly how she had gotten off so easily last Wednesday. Her mother, when busy with her "events," was quite self-involved.

Eventually there was a pause, either Clara's mother had to take a breath, or she had become distracted by the thought of a new and unique recipe for pumpkin sorbet to serve at her next luncheon. Either way, Clara cleared her throat and took some initiative.

"Mom?"

"Yes?"

"Is Dad there?"

"Uh, yes, he is... Why?"

"Can he get on the other extension please? I would like to talk to you about something... talk to you both."

"O-kay... I guess I'll go get him."

A muffled minute and a holler later, she heard a click and her father's hoarse voice on the line.

"Hello, Clara."

"Hi Dad."

"You have something to tell us?"

"Um, yes, well, obviously some change is in order," she paused, "since my life is such a mess right now." Her voice shook. The nerves were starting to get to her.

"Oh, Honey," her mom began, "things will get back to normal."

"Laura, tschshhh," her father shushed her, "let her say something before you start in with your opinions."

*Hmmm, that was interesting,* Clara thought, *just what were her mother's opinions?*

"Don, that was uncalled for, you could just ask me, rather than shush me."

"Laura!"

"Fine, whatever you say, *Don.*"

*Well, this was nice. Nothing like a quality conversation with your parents...*

"I'm going to take a trip to Holland. I'll be gone for a while."

The silence that ensued was peaceful and yet deafening at the same time. She considered just hanging up, but she didn't want her mother coming down there again.

"That damn aunt of yours!" her mother yelled, "always getting ideas into people's heads."

"What?" Clara asked.

"Not you, Clara. Don! You see what she's done!? That crazy woman!"

"She was your aunt, Laura, not mine. And did you even meet her? She wasn't crazy." Her father was laughing now.

"She was crazy! Never lived a normal day in her life! She used to tell me this story, about cattle and fresh cheese, grass cheese, she called it. Weird, that's what she was. Clara you may *not* go to Holland! That would be highly inappropriate right now."

At this, Clara had to laugh. She expected the outburst, but this, this was a surprise even from her mother.

"Uh, Mom, I don't think I was asking for your permission. I'm more than 30 years old. I was just letting you know." Clara thought she heard her father chuckling silently in the background. She wondered about his thoughts; he basically hadn't said anything at all.

"Clara!" her mother shrieked, "that is no way to treat your parents!"

"She didn't do anything to me," her father added, much to

her mother's dismay. *Ahhh*, there it was, so he *was* on her side. Impressive.

"Clara, you cannot go to Holland right now. What about your house? What about your job? What about Jack?!"

Clara gritted her teeth as she felt a fog coming over her. She could get through this. She couldn't let her mother's words get to her.

"Mother," she said," I have no house; I have no job, I practically quit, and I have no Jack."

She hung up the phone, not knowing whether she was about to scream or cry. Before either could occur, she got up and walked to the table where Krista had left her laptop. She brushed her finger across the touchpad and her screensaver disappeared.

She maximized the internet browser that Krista had been using and smiled. *Expedia, Travelocity, Kayak,* and a bright orange website... *Visit Holland* is all that she saw.

*Oh, Krista*, she thought, *always there when I need you.*

# Part 2

## *Amsterdam*

### één - one

Clara found her seat in the plane, a window seat two rows from the front of the economy section. This surprised her; she had purchased the ticket only a few weeks before. She was a single, though, and just one little person with no husband or family could be plugged in about anywhere. She must be seated by a couple, she decided. She sat down with the sad realization that she had never traveled alone. She had flown a few times before, but never on her own, only with her parents, with Delia to visit some relatives in Southern California, with Krista once, and of course with Jack.

How strange that she was 31, and this was her first time on a plane by herself. She tried to be excited about it rather than nervous and, she had to admit, a little nauseated.

Even after the day in the hotel when she told her parents she was going, she flipped back and forth dozens of times. She talked it over in detail with Krista and with Krista's cat, Quiche, when Krista wasn't around. She didn't really discuss it with her mother or Delia. Getting into it with either of them would have been just too much.

After considering many possible paths, she decided that what she needed most was a change in environment, though maybe she didn't need to go all the way to Europe to get a little space. The most feasible option was San Francisco, so she left Sacramento and took the Amtrak to the Bay Area. She spent most of her time down by the piers, looking out over the bay. She even walked across the Golden Gate Bridge one day.

Over the course of the week, she thought about her family, her job, her friends, and Jack. She felt as if she had run it all through her head a thousand times, and still she seemed to have no options. All she could think of was running away— getting as far from this life as possible.

Finally, she decided to head back home, or at least back to Sacramento, she didn't really have a home there anymore. Once back on the train, she sighed a breath of relief and realized how nice it was to be on a train, the familiar click as the wheels rolled down the track. It was somehow comforting to her and she needed that. She leaned her head back and looked out over the bay. *Good enough*, she thought to herself. Europe had a lot of trains, and she was feeling at home in this one right now. Plus, she loved those Dutch pancakes.

*Just for a visit*, she thought. If she didn't like it, then she would leave. If she did like it, she could prolong her trip. She bought her ticket that night and felt another strange wave of relief. Although the feelings weren't possible to entirely explain, she knew she was leaving the nightmare that had been her life.

She stopped back at Jack's once. It was entirely *Jack's* now, not hers; she knew that well enough. She had called the assistant at his office to make sure that he would be at work and not off taking one of his slightly more than occasional "sick days" when he sat at home, made a mess, and watched baseball. Once she confirmed that she wouldn't be running into him, she headed to the house. When she parked Krista's car in front and looked up at the place that had once been her home, she found it wholly unfamiliar. Instead of feeling nostalgic about her life there, she found that it looked like someone else's house. It was as if nothing special, nothing worth remembering had ever happened there.

She thought that she'd be in and out as quickly as possible, but instead, she examined all the rooms, as if in the house of a stranger, visiting for the first time. She tried to get some perspective, looking from the outside, tried to get a feel for *her*, for who she had been there, but it was next to impossible. There was nothing "her" about it, and it wasn't just because her possessions were gone. It had never been her place, she realized. She couldn't believe she'd lived there for 10 years. Where did she fit in? Had she ever fit?

She had no place, literally and figuratively. There was not one seat in this living room where she liked to sit. There was not one wall that she liked looking at. She snapped her head towards the stairwell, remembering the O'Keeffe that had been there. It was still gone. *Bastard*, she thought. It's not like she would have taken it, it wasn't hers, but still, he couldn't even leave it on the wall? She would never have a chance to see it again, the only thing in the house that she had liked. He had never liked it. *Big, fat, purple flower*, he had always said, *taking up the whooole wall.*

She shook her head roughly, pushing away the thought of the petunia, painted in a purple so rich it was almost black, so brilliant it was almost alive—growing; it had stirred something in her that she didn't want to feel. She needed to move on.

She emerged from the memory and looked around the plane, wondering where the people sitting around her were heading. She herself was flying through Iceland. The ticket was a great deal, about the same as a flight to New York out of Sacramento, so that was nice. Plus, after this, she could say that she'd been to Iceland, and who's gone to Iceland!? It was a one-way ticket, the most outrageous aspect of the whole ordeal. This was Krista's doing. She had argued that it was better both ways—if Clara liked Holland or if she didn't. Either way she would be able to go home whenever she wanted, Krista had argued.

Would these people be staying in Iceland or flying on to other locations? She wasn't exactly sure how big the airport was. Would the flights from Amsterdam mostly fly to other places in Europe? Or would they continue on to more exotic and far-off places around the world?

It was all so exotic for her. She had only been on a plane a few times in her life, and never anywhere too exciting, though she and Jack had gone to Mexico once. She shivered a little in the cold plane. They had now turned down the lights, probably trying to get them all accustomed to a new time zone.

*Like she could sleep.*

Her stomach was churning like never before, and for a second she thought she might actually throw up. She hoped the takeoff would be quick. She couldn't handle much longer without some soothing music in her ears and they had already made the *no electronic devices* announcement.

Just after takeoff, the headrest television flashed on and they announced that passengers could now utilize the in-flight entertainment. Clara could hardly get her headphones in her ears fast enough. She flipped through the screen, her hands so cold that it seemed to be slow at responding to her touch.

The menus froze, of course, so she tried to amuse and distract herself by people watching, but she couldn't see anyone too interesting from her cramped window seat. She glanced between the seats at the woman in front of her. "Are You Helping Your Child's Brain Development?" She thought about taking out a book to read, but even the words on the screen menu were swimming in front of her.

Eventually, the screen responded and she made it to the television section and took a look at the possibilities. Laughter was definitely the best medicine for times like this, so she considered anything that might make her laugh. She settled on *Friends: The One with the Jam.* She loved this one. She liked how Joey could just eat jam with a spoon; she had done the same thing as a kid, not that she had ever let anyone see her do it. This was the ticket to relaxation, some familiar friends. She cranked up the volume so that all she could hear was Monica's piercing voice.

The drink cart arrived quickly and she ordered ginger ale to calm her stomach. Unfortunately, the man next to her decided that tomato juice was the right choice for an 11 a.m.

flight to Amsterdam. As soon as he cracked open the can, she actually jolted upright in a motion that wasn't all that hard to recognize as heaving. She felt as if she could smell the acid emerging from the can.

*Damn middle aged businessmen. People in suits that nice should just go ahead and spring for business class and leave the rest of us alone.*

Joey picked up a spoon and a jar and she smiled, but then felt that same rolling feeling in her stomach. *Yuck, jam, that sounded horrible.* She was sure that if she had a jar of jam sitting in front of her right then she would want to throw it across the plane.

*Ughh! Just go to sleep.* She had never had motion sickness this badly before. In fact, she had never been sick in a vehicle *ever* before. Maybe this was a sign. Was she doing the right thing? Should she go online right now and buy a return ticket? She could probably move right in with Krista.

*What was with her today? So she was flying across the world, did that really make her feel like she was going to vomit!? Possibly.* She stared ahead. The woman in front of her had finished learning about all the things she was doing wrong for her child's brain development and had switched to a new article. "Follow that Folic Acid! How to eat right during your Pregnancy."

*Hmm... I think someone is pregnant,* she chuckled to herself.

She wondered if the woman was happy that she was pregnant. Having to read a patronizing parenting magazine for ten hours didn't seem all that appealing to Clara.

Joey had just realized that there was no more jam. *Yuck, jam,* Clara thought again. She had forgotten about this part of the episode. Monica wanted to have a baby with a sperm donor. She never liked that part. Why would anyone voluntarily have a baby on their own? She was glad when it all blew over and Monica just went back to mothering the others.

She gritted her teeth as she realized that she was right back there. About the time she should be starting a family, she was single again. That last night had been amazing—at the time—but now that she knew what she knew, she wished it had never happened at all. For the slightest of moments that night, when Jack first turned on music and filled two glasses with red wine, she thought that a child was what he wanted. For just a second, she'd thought that was the reason for the perfect evening.

She counted backwards.

*Ew*, she thought, that last night was prime ovulating time. In fact, there were too many days since then.

But it couldn't be… She was feeling hot all of a sudden, despite the frigid temperature in the dark plane. She had hardly thought about birth control in the last year, what with all the not-having-sex and all. She couldn't be pregnant. There was no way, not now, not like this, alone. In spite of her feverish flush, her teeth chattered.

She heard laughter—Rachel's, Ross's, Chandler's.

The agony in her stomach began to intensify. People don't have babies in foreign countries.

*Well,* she supposed that wasn't entirely true, but people certainly don't go to foreign countries to have babies. This was a pretty extreme form of medical tourism. The 10-hour flight suddenly seemed much longer.

*What was she doing? Alone on a plane flying to Amsterdam? Who in their right mind would do this? Worst of all, who would do this…* she couldn't even make herself form the word… *pregnant?*

She closed her eyes and felt the world spinning around her. She couldn't tell if she was about to throw up or if stress and panic had just finally gotten the best of her and she was about to black out. She wondered if there was any way she would make it through.

## twee - two

The sound of the Captain announcing their descent woke Clara from a very unrestful slumber. What a time to be in the window seat. Clara's stomach flipped for the thousandth time. She forced her eyes shut as the plane slooowly made its way to the terminal in Iceland.

She couldn't really be pregnant. Was it really a possibility at all? She hoped this was just a temporary nightmare, just the worst close call of her life, worse than that one slip that was *exactly* nine months before their wedding date, even worse than that time in the school parking lot with Jerry Brawn—her *high school* parking lot—when some things happened that she still couldn't correctly identify as real sex or not.

Her intestines did another twist. There was no use looking out the window. They had been on the ground for fifteen minutes, and as far as she could tell, the pilot didn't have a clue where their gate was.

Finally, the fasten seatbelt sign turned off and a majority of the people on the plane stood up at once. She tried for a second, but felt a sudden rush of dizziness just thinking about what she had to do next. She let out a breath of air as she plopped down on the seat again and groaned to herself.

*Noooooo.* Not this. Not now. She had made it through high school, no high school pregnancy; she had made it to 20, no teen pregnancy; she had even gotten married and breathed the final sigh of relief, no baby before wedlock. Finally, she'd made it through—hadn't gotten pregnant at the wrong time or place. Her mother could be happy. Now, here she was: on a plane to Europe, no husband, no job, no home, and possibly pregnant. Was she really this reckless with her life? Or just unlucky? *Unlucky.*

She sneered too loudly, and a businessman in front of her turned to glance at her.

*She got screwed*, that was the truth of the matter. *Screwed!* She knew what she had to do. She packed up her carry-on and waited.

*Velkomin til Íslands*, the sign greeted her, and she was off, bag in hand and pushing and weaving her way through the Reykjavík airport looking for any place that might carry feminine products. She had no idea where to start, so she looked for anything that wasn't a food stop.

If they have magazines, she thought, they might have hand sanitizer, and if they have hand sanitizer, they might have lotion, and if they have lotion, they might have toothpaste, and if they have toothpaste, they might have deodorant, and if they have deodorant, they might have condoms. And let's face it, if they have condoms, they should sure as hell better have pregnancy tests. *Sexist bastards.*

*Oh, the mood swings.* Maybe she was pregnant. She raced up and down the hallways of the airport—all three of them, looking for the appropriate store and eventually beginning to wonder how inappropriate it would be to start asking everyone around her if they knew where she could find a pregnancy test. She thought it might be a bit too awkward, especially considering the amount of sweat that was now running down her face, and the fact that she had picked up a 15-pound Toblerone at the first store that hadn't had a pregnancy test, just deodorant. She'd felt weird walking out of the store with nothing, especially considering the 99 mini-boxes of tampons that she had knocked off the shelf in her hurry to find out whether or not she would have to buy the damn blue cardboard boxes again for nine months. On the plus side, if she wasn't pregnant, they certainly seemed to have plenty of normal tampons here. She'd heard that wasn't always the case in foreign countries.

Finally, there it was; sitting on a shelf between condoms and dental floss, was a pregnancy test. She grabbed it and headed to the counter, grabbing a bar of dark Swiss chocolate on her way. She didn't want to *only* buy a pregnancy test.

The nice blonde cashier rang up Clara's two items and offered her an opaque white plastic bag, which she accepted gratefully. The woman said the total and Clara's head snapped up to look her in the face. She had no idea what the currency was here or how much it was worth, but she did know that she had none of it. *How had she paid for the Toblerone?* She had paid for it, hadn't she? Most likely she had simply handed over American dollars, but that couldn't be, could it?

"I'm sorry," she said, "I am just passing through, so I don't have any, um, Icelandic money. Could I pay another way? Is there anything else you accept?" It would be so horrible to have to get on *another* plane not knowing whether or not she was pregnant.

Whether the cashier was telling the truth or just observant enough to know that Clara was going to lose her mind if she wasn't able to make her purchase, she responded positively.

"Oh, we accept pretty much everything," the cashier stated with a smile. Clara practically threw up her hands in thanks, *Hallelujah!* Finally, she'd caught a break.

Just twenty-four short minutes later she was sitting on a plane on a runway in Iceland with a pregnancy test from the Iceland airport—still in the box—staring at her, *glaring* at her, from a long thin cardboard rectangle in the pocket of her jeans. All that running around and here she was, just sitting in her seat, putting it off. She plugged her headphones into the hip radio station that Icelandair provided to their passengers. Abba.

Of course, why wouldn't Abba be playing? And "Chiquitita," nonetheless. A bit too chipper of a song for her current situation. *Where was Abba from anyway?* She thought. This could be a great way to distract herself from the nagging pee stick in her pocket. *Where. Was. Abba. From? Think, Clara, think.*

Nope, not going to happen. She might as well just go and do it. She paused to shift her wary mind to her bladder. It was full enough. She could do it. She took one last swig of her crystal clear Icelandic bottled water and excused herself from her seat. The poor woman next to her probably thought she was about to have a mental breakdown what with all the twitching and the many pained facial expressions. *All in all, she would be right.*

Obviously, both restrooms were full, so Clara stretched her legs and did a few calf raises while she was waiting. She shook her head. At a moment like this, she wondered what she had been thinking when she decided to go to Holland. She could be at home with Krista right now, eating Double Stuf Oreos and dipping them in frosting or something else utterly ridiculous. They would order pizza from the same place they had been going for years and laugh and talk and complain and just bitch about the wrongings of the world.

There was *no way* that Krista had made it out of college without taking a pregnancy test. She would know exactly what to do. Now that Clara thought about it, Krista probably would have even showed her how to properly hold the stick, might have even held it for her.

The door snapped open and a very tall blonde man stepped out of the bathroom. He was so tall that he had to dip his head a bit just to stand in the plane. *Poor guy*, she thought as she wondered how many concussions he had gotten from low ceilings throughout his life. She took her turn in line and stepped into the bathroom.

After a few deep breaths, she regained some control and pulled the pink cardboard box out of her pocket.

Pink. Was that a sign? *Unlikely.*

Another deep breath. She didn't know where to start, so she thought back to what she did know.

*Everything you need to know you learned in kindergarten.*

She ripped open the box and pulled out a long, folded piece of paper. She began to read.

*First, open your Magic Now! Easy, 5 Minute pregnancy test with easy-to-read indicator.*

"Magic Now!" *Really?* She definitely wasn't feeling the magic as of yet. *Well, at least there were instructions in English.*

It looked like a circle meant that she'd be going it on her own and a check meant she'd be ruining two lives instead of just one. She turned to the easy-to-read indicator—a long, white, plastic stick. There was a little opening in the apparatus, presumably the spot where she should pee. She prepared herself, examining the shape of the toilet and the tiny airplane bathroom. After a few minutes, she decided on a strategy and positioned her hand so that the indicator would get wet and hopefully nothing else.

Okay, *breathe, relax, and pee*, she thought.

Easier said than done.

No matter how hard she tried, her bladder was now empty. She tried to think of running water: waterfalls, rivers, cold mountain streams, she even pictured herself drinking copious amounts of Diet Coke, but soon her hand was just getting tired of being in such an awkward position. She decided to take a break, and took ten deep breaths, trying to forget why it was that she was in the bathroom. After a few minutes, she gave it another try.

*Breathe, relax, and pee*, she told herself again.

Unfortunately, this was just not in the stars for her.

The turbulence started at just that moment. It was a large plane, so it started as a slow rolling lean. That wasn't the end of it though. Soon the shaking and jerking and leaning had progressed to Richter scale levels.

After an unfortunately large bump, she found herself gripping the "Oh Shit" handle with one hand, and with the other, she was precariously gripping the pregnancy test to the toilet seat in a place where hands should never go in a public restroom.

So much for that strategy. She heard a ding and glanced up to see the fasten seatbelt light glow red. *Shit.*

Next came the announcement.

"Ladies and gentlemen, we are currently experiencing a small amount of turbulence."

A small amount, *right.*

"Please return to your seats and fasten your seatbelts."

She switched her grip to a more sanitary location and tried to ignore the feeling of nausea that was sweeping over her. If she waited just a few minutes, she could make another attempt. She felt the plane level, and the path seemed to smooth out again. Take three. She readied herself in the appropriate position, this time with her free hand still gripping the wall bar. Okay, go.

*Bam, bam, bam, bam.*

This time, the knocking started before the turbulence.

"Excuse me!" the flight attendant called as she rapped on the door. "You need to return to your seat, please."

*Breathe, breathe,* Clara repeated herself as the lady repeated her request in several other languages. *Breathe. She'll go away in a second.*

"Excuse me! We are experiencing some turbulence and we need you to Re-turn To Your Seat." She emphasized each word this time.

"In A Minute!" Clara barked back. There was no way she was going to leave this bathroom with an open and unused pregnancy test in her hand. It was also equally unlikely that she would toss the pregnancy test and have to scramble through yet another airport just to pay another thousand Icelandic dollars for another test.

"Miss!?"

Here she goes again.

"You *must* leave the restroom at once!"

It was going to be really comfortable when she finally did leave the restroom. At least the last 12 rows of passengers were now fully aware that there was an irritable woman refusing to leave the restroom. They probably thought someone was incredibly sick. *Wait—that's it!*

"Sorry, ma'am…" Clara called out, "I'm feeling very ill." She left a long dramatic pause. "I just don't think it's possible for me to go back to my seat at this time."

That should do it. What does she think is going to happen? They're going to get sued when a head goes through the bathroom ceiling? Probably more worried that she'll fall and punch a hole through something and all of them will die. Damn the high-pressure system.

Fortunately, feigning illness seemed to do the trick. The flight attendant had decided that she had done enough tormenting for one flight.

Eventually, after two more bouts of stage fright, one caused by someone talking loudly just outside the bathroom door about a friend's recent mental breakdown, and another near-droppage into the toilet, the job was done.

After five very long minutes and one hitching attempt at a deep, cleansing breath, she closed her eyes, painfully aware that the answer was now there in front of her. Now that it was available, she wasn't sure if she was prepared to know the answer. She was on her way to a foreign country that she had never been to before. What if she was pregnant? Could she handle it? What would she do? Could she raise a little girl on her own?

Her thoughts suddenly strayed from the more serious topics. *Could a pregnancy test expire?* she wondered. The little pink plus or blue minus or circle or whatever—would it just disappear if she waited too long? Would it fade away once her pee dried? That probably wouldn't take very long. She was lucky to get even a few drops on it after the whole turbulence-and-knocking ordeal.

She took a deep breath and looked down; she might as well just know.

Involuntarily, the corners of her mouth turned up when she looked at the tiny symbol on the indicator. It wasn't a minus, but a bright pink check. She could almost hear it click in her mind: *baby girl: Check!* She actually laughed out loud just thinking about it.

She cleaned up her mess in the tiny airplane bathroom, making sure to wipe the basin when she was finished just like the sign instructed. She went back to her seat and settled cozily with her head against the side of the plane and opened the window shade. Maybe people had been staring at her, but if they had been, she hadn't noticed. She just stared out the window down into a thick layer of fluffy white clouds.

*A baby. Huh.* A child to whom she would pass her wisdom, as little of it as there was. Who would have thought that she'd ever experience this moment, flying over the

Atlantic to somewhere, not towards her home—pregnant and alone. Talk about new experiences.

Clara fell into a doze, miraculously and mysteriously relaxed for the time being. She awoke to the sound of a clear voice speaking over the PA system.

"Ladies and Gentlemen, we will now be beginning our approach to Schiphol International Airport. The weather in Amsterdam is currently 14 degrees Celsius, 57 degrees Fahrenheit, and slightly overcast. We are hoping for clear skies later today. We would like to thank you for flying with us this morning. Welcome to Holland."

## drie - three

This morning? Was it only morning? Clara opened her shade and looked out. She couldn't remember how long she had been traveling. It seemed like forever and nothing in the same moment. *Welcome to Holland,* she thought. She looked out the window, thinking of her great aunt, and how much she must have loved this place. Her whole family leaves, primarily due to economic hardship throughout the entire country, and this teenage girl just stays behind, simply refuses to go.

She suddenly felt much closer to Great Aunt Ilse, though they had met just the once.

Then she thought about what could, or rather what would, come next. It was scary—traumatizing, actually.

It wasn't that she hadn't wanted children, she had just ruled it out until they were financially stable. *She* had ruled it out. For the first time ever, she wondered if Jack had actually wanted to have kids. She couldn't imagine that he had; he was still a child himself. They both were, but was it possible that she had pushed him away? Maybe she had been the problem.

Her eyes were suddenly filling with tears. It was all so much to handle. She couldn't handle this bombardment of thoughts. She wasn't ready to face it yet. As her eyes focused on what she was seeing out her window, the tears fell and began running down her face. Stripes of colors, of flowers, painted the flat Dutch landscape with purple and white and yellow and red and orange—more color than she had ever seen from the sky. She couldn't believe a place existed that looked like this. It was unreal. She almost couldn't believe that she'd lived her life without seeing it.

They landed in the middle of miles and miles of colorful flowers, and at that moment, she knew inside that her child had to be a girl. Little boys just weren't born in a place with so many flowers. *Her daughter would love flowers*, she smiled.

Clara stepped off the plane into a friendly airport which was slightly brighter than usual and had large windows and giant photos of the Dutch landscape hanging regularly along the terminal walls. She stopped to watch where the other passengers from her flight headed. Now that she had arrived, she had all the time in the world.

It looked like most of them were hurrying off to other gates, all speaking different languages in rushed voices. She walked past the other gates, their flights leaving for London, New York, Berlin, Johannesburg, Paramaribo.

*Paramaribo? Where is that?* Ah, Suriname, she saw on a travel poster next to the waiting area.

Flight attendants rushed past her pulling compact little suitcases, all dressed in KLM blue, there was no other way to describe that particular color. The sentences flowing out of their mouths were somewhat German, but sounded as if they had a cold growing in the back of their throat. She remembered trying to learn how to roll her r's in the back of her throat during college German and wondered if Dutch was similar. It sounded like they had found a way to perfect the exercise in a slightly more extreme way.

She let the bustling passengers and flight attendants pass her and slowly meandered down to the baggage claim. She found it without a problem and found herself a cart, which she lazily sat upon while waiting for the carousel to begin tossing out luggage. She listened to the announcements, interested in the variety of languages she was hearing, and let her eyes fall closed as she listened to the melody of each one. They made all the announcements in Dutch and in English—at least she assumed that the melodic, German-sounding language was Dutch. Depending on the flight, they sometimes added French and German, plus the language or languages of whatever place that specific flight was headed.

She was so tired.

Next, she would take a train into Amsterdam. She had done some research, so she knew that she could take a train to get there. She could probably also take a bus or taxi, but she loved the trains. She might as well utilize them as frequently as possible.

So tired.

She had always been interested in the idea of train travel... ever since her Grandpa told her stories about his father being a conductor for the rail line. She was still daydreaming of her grandfather in a navy blue striped conductor's cap covered in coal soot when she was awakened from her sleep-deprived trance by the clunk of the conveyer belt starting on the baggage claim.

She moved her cart a little closer to the baggage carousel and sat back down. The metal cart wasn't all that uncomfortable now that she thought about it, perhaps due to her extreme level of tiredness. She squinted through her half-open eyes until she spotted her luggage. She had two suitcases, but luckily they weren't very big and, she thought sadly, they didn't really contain anything of much importance. They both successfully made the trip in one piece, and as she lugged them wearily off the carousel, her mind scanned painfully through the short packing process.

The neighbor's dogwalker, Jordan, she eventually came to find out, had easily grabbed all of the clothes in her dresser and in her closet. He had also done fairly well at handpicking a few things from the kitchen that "looked pretty cool and worth somethin'," he said. That box had included her mixer, a garlic press, some delicate teacups which he described as "pretty gnarly," and surprisingly, a pizza cutter. She really didn't need much of this, since she obviously hadn't filled her suitcase with silverware, knives, or an ice cream scoop, which oddly enough had also made the cut. Still, she appreciated his efforts. Who knew how long she would be in Holland? She may fail abysmally and be back in California in a week, setting up house.

The clank of the luggage carousel startled her again, and she saw that luggage from the next flight was already appearing. She heaved her suitcases on the cart and headed towards customs, where she got a Dutch stamp in her passport and a ninety day countdown until her tourist visa expired. Ninety days to prove herself... or at least prove that she could take care of herself.

One credit card transaction on a ticket machine and the train was pulling away from the station. When it emerged from a tunnel into a field of flowers, she was almost certain that she was a wee bit hopeful.


vier - four


Ten minutes later, she was feeling a pull in her cheeks as she tried not to let her face break into a huge smile and reveal to those around her just how excited she was. She was very nearly bursting with excitement. She was in Amsterdam! She was in The Netherlands! She was so far from what she knew that she couldn't even approximate the number of miles by which she had just expanded her life's travels.

Amsterdam!

Immediately upon entering the city, she began seeing the romantic canals and handsome, stepped brick facades. Nearly every house had a special look, probably there from a hundred years before. It took just over 15 minutes to get to Amsterdam from the airport, and soon she was stepping off the train with several hundred other people, waiting to head down the escalator and out of the train station into the city. The station felt like it was complete chaos and it was only 10:18 in the morning. What was it like during rush hour? She tried to keep her suitcases close, but there were so many people coming and going, many of them with their own suitcases, that she was having a hard time making any progress at all. Already, she loved the feel of the city. It felt so international and it was a glorious mix of busy and motivated businessmen and women, tourists, and old and new-school hippies all making their way out into the city center.

Finally, she made it out of the station, but only after almost biffing it on a bizarrely steep incline that led out the front doors. She followed the mass out of the station and across a row of tram tracks, some picking up passengers, some empty, and one rather aggressive tram that was vigorously ringing its bell at the group of pedestrians she was in. Apparently they were in the way.

Once across the tram tracks, she stepped to the side and took a look around. In front of her was a row of fast food stands. There was a döner stand, a hotdog stand, an ice cream stand, a fry stand; *wow*, they knew how to do it up right here. Behind the little stands was a small body of water, maybe just a wide section of canal, with long, low boats, presumably to be filled with tourists who would stare in amazement up at the buildings around them. She was about to continue around the bend into the city when she glanced to her right and saw a collection of more bicycles than she had ever seen in her life. It may actually have been more bicycles than she had seen in her life cumulatively. It was actually a parking ramp for bicycles, just like they made for cars. She felt a thrill go through her. This place was something else, and she couldn't wait to be a part of it.

She crossed the street and continued past a huge construction site where it appeared that they were either putting in a subway, building a huge open square, or adding on to the already enormous train station, maybe all three. She looked back at the train station, which was glistening historically in the morning sun. *How come they couldn't make stuff like this in the U.S? Was it just impossible to make something both functional and aesthetically pleasing?*

Clara made her way around to a confusing intersection of pedestrians, cars, bicycles, trams, and buses. Thankfully, there was a nice traffic light and she managed to mix herself in with about a hundred other people crossing the street so as not to get hit on her very first day.

Once she crossed the street, she wanted to stop at the corner to take a look around again, but the flow was unstoppable. She was passively pushed down the wide sidewalk with the other pedestrians, a gentle rush of excitement flurrying all around her. She smiled when she noticed the nice bike path to her left where little bicycle taxis were constantly running by, ringing their bell at lost pedestrians—clearly tourists—who couldn't seem to tell the difference between the sidewalk and the quite clearly marked bicycle path.

After passing a shady looking casino, a vodka museum, a cheese shop, two more fry stands and several Argentinean grills, she reached a large square filled with people, pigeons, seagulls, and of course, bicycles. She took advantage of a monument on one side and sat down to rest on the steps. In this state, she would never be able to find her hotel. Her mind was too busy fluttering around in the possibilities this place held.

She couldn't get over her excitement. She was elated to be in this crazy busy Dutch world. The sounds swirled around her and not one of them annoyed her. The bells of the bicycles and trams served as a chorus, reminding her that here, cars were not king. People were chatting and singing and laughing all around her and it was a constant blend of sounds, sometimes in English or Dutch, but more often in a language that she couldn't even place in her limited knowledge of the languages of the world.

Across the square was something grand and stately, either a city hall, or a palace. She grinned despite herself at the thought of it being a palace. She was so American; anything royal or famous practically made her weak in the knees. There was also a huge church, a bank, a fancy department store, and a diamond museum, *wow*. There was also a Madame Tussauds. She was sure she saw Angelina Jolie standing in the window. *Amazing how many people paid to see wax.*

She continued examining the businesses around the edge of the square and was happy to see a pancake house on one corner along with another Argentinean grill. She had better investigate this Argentina phenomenon; apparently there were some Dutch ties with the country, unless the Dutch just really enjoyed their meat.

Just as they had announced on the plane, the sky cleared and the afternoon was beautiful. The sun was shining and the reflection of the rowhouses on the canals was reason enough to have made the leap over the Atlantic.

Clara finally reached her hotel around four in the afternoon. After a chicken sandwich for a late lunch at a small Surinamese cafe, she had hopped a tram. Unfortunately, she had misinterpreted the curve of the tracks and headed in the wrong direction. This wouldn't have been so bad, but it took her nearly 20 minutes before she realized she was heading the wrong way. She was in a tram running along the harbor when she finally took a look at her map and found that she had gone backwards about two miles.

After getting off that tram and on the same number going in the opposite direction, she finally found her hotel. The hotel was small and basic but very affordable, and located in a great place in the city, near Museumplein, which she assumed to be the location of at least one museum. It was also situated quite close to Vondel Park, a big city park where she hoped to sit and have lunch the next day.

After checking in, she completely ignored her suitcases and fell asleep in her plane clothes happy and completely exhausted. She couldn't believe she made it through the day awake, but there was no way she could have sat inside her hotel wasting time taking a nap.

She had far too much Amsterdam to see for naps.

## vijf - five

The next day, Clara woke feeling like she'd never slept harder in her life. She still felt tired, but the excitement of being in a new place made her anxious to get out as soon as possible. She showered quickly and went down to the hotel lobby, wondering if they had breakfast or coffee. She found hot water for tea and coffee right away and then went to the desk to ask about breakfast.

"Is breakfast provided at this hotel?" she asked.

"Yes, Miss. Breakfast is served every day in the restaurant from 7 a.m. until 10:30 a.m."

*Great*, she thought, and wondered if it was still before 10:30. She was about to turn towards the restaurant when she noticed the clock on the wall behind the hotel counter.

"Excuse me," she asked, "is that clock correct?"

"Yes, Miss," he replied, "it's just after 2:30."

*Two-thirty.* She had slept through half the day already, even after going to bed before five o'clock. She tried to wipe the shocked look off of her face and recovered by quickly asking the man about the closest museum.

In just a few minutes, she was headed out with a map and directions to the Van Gogh Museum, which was just a few blocks away. She arrived within minutes and got into a long line filled with tourists talking loudly and taking pictures of absolutely everything. It was horrifying. By the time she reached the front, her head was pounding. *Wow*, she thought, *being jetlagged is a lot like having a hangover.*

When it was finally her turn to pay, she was pleased to see that it cost less to go to the Van Gogh museum for a year than to go to Disneyland for a day. She considered the annual pass, but decided it was far too frivolous for her first day. She bought a day ticket and passed through the metal detectors into the world of Vincent Van Gogh. The museum was only open for two more hours, but since she'd done the wait, she decided the sunk cost was worth it, and simply vowed that the next day she would at least be up by noon.

The moment she stepped into the main room, it felt right. The clean, white air and clear light filled her with a lightness that she couldn't describe. She immediately regretted not purchasing the annual Museum Card. She already knew she would be coming again tomorrow. It wasn't like she had to go to work, she remembered happily. She looked up through the stairwell. Three floors, definitely enough to warrant another visit. *Hurray!* her heart cried. It had been so long.

She walked towards a self-portrait of the man with hair the color and texture of straw. Van Gogh was somewhat of a mystery to her. He wasn't exactly someone she looked up to, but she did admire how he affected impressionism. He used so much color and color was what had drawn her to art in the first place.

She had always liked to paint and draw and play with clay like any other child, but she wasn't any better at it than the normal seven year old. It was the colors that eventually drew her into the field. As she visited art museum after art museum throughout her youth, she noticed color patterns and tendencies of different artists in different eras. She quickly found that she was in love, in love with color. For the same reason she loved Georgia O'Keeffe; she used so many bright, vibrant colors.

The museum was really nice, with detailed, but very readable descriptions of the various periods of Van Gogh's life. She had no idea he'd done so many self-portraits. He looked so uncomfortable in each and every one. It was almost sinister, since he was the one trying to portray himself.

It was said that this was something unique about Van Gogh. Most other painters were less brutal to themselves and their appearance in their self-portraits. He clearly did not think himself handsome—awkward and disgruntled maybe, but not handsome.

There was something about the self-portraits that startled her, as if she had never really looked at herself in the way that he had probed himself. They really displayed the fact that he was constantly examining. He wasn't just practicing his techniques; his self-portraits were not about that. Perhaps he was looking, examining and looking, at who he was and who he could be... who he wanted to be.

Besides the self-portraits, she spent the longest amount of time at *Gauguin's Chair*.

Was it actually his chair? After all these years? Or else, was it just where he would have sat if he had been with Van Gogh?

Clara had a tendency to think about this type of thing, especially in a new place or a new home. She saw a new room or looked at a new sofa or rocker and thought about who would sit there. Would her sister? Maybe Krista would, or her mother. Everyone has a specific type of seat that's really *them*. She liked to think about it, and always tried to have a perfect seat for the people that were most important in her life and were most often around and needing to be comfortable.

Over there, with her hands placed on the back of the couch, is where her mother would stand. The lumpy spot on the brand-new couch, that's where Jack would sit, taking up the whole couch of course, annoying everyone. This is how she thought of a home. She wanted a place for everyone, so that if they were there with her, they would have the perfect place to sit—not the most comfortable or best spot in the house, but the best for them, individually. She spent so much time thinking about other people and where they would sit that she often forgot to plan for herself, in fact.

Maybe in her next home she would not have a place for Jack. After all, in their house together, Jack's house, she hadn't had a place, she ruminated sadly. What a sad marriage. A home furnished with a place for him, but no place for her.

*Maybe that was why she spent so much time wallowing in bed*, she groaned pathetically to herself. She had no place to sit.

Only once, for almost a whole day, she'd had a perfect seat. She thought back to the plush blue chair fondly, wondering where it was now. It should be at her parents' house, in their attic or garage, but in all probability they had already thrown it out. The baby rocker was perfect, velvety blue and smelling like a century of lilac potpourri every time she sat down on it.

She felt a soft tap on her shoulder and realized that the museum was closing. She made her way to the exit resignedly and promised to return the following day. Having missed both breakfast and lunch, she was starving and went looking for a place to eat. In several minutes she'd found the perfect remedy, a grocery store.

The Albert Heijn, as it was called, was a small store and had plenty of food that was ready to eat. The most bizarre aspect was the fact that the store was actually located on Museumplein, or more accurately, *under* Museumplein. The roof was slanted and it was almost as if the grass of the square grew up onto the building. The effect was both off the wall and fantastic at the same time. The store was almost entirely hidden from view if you were in the park near the reflection pool on Museumplein, and the grassy slant actually created a pretty nice amphitheatre.

Clara found the makings of a nice sandwich, some juice, and a few other snacks and headed towards the checkout. At the front of the store, she stepped around the line to peek at the racks near the register to look for some chocolate. She wondered what Dutch chocolate was like. She hoped it was more like Swiss chocolate than German. She definitely preferred dark chocolate over milk.

"There's a queue!" someone shrieked from behind her, "and this is not the end of it."

She turned around, mortified by the accusation and appalled by his nerve. Even if she was cutting, which she wasn't, she wouldn't have been cutting in front of him. He was still at least four people back.

"I'm looking for chocolate," she hissed back at him.

"Then go to the chocolate aisle. You think we're in a Walmart? This isn't America!"

She felt her face getting hot. She had never been reprimanded so publicly and she wasn't even doing anything wrong. She escaped to the back of the store and eventually found the chocolate aisle, but she was so flustered that she didn't even get anything.

A sandwich later and she was back in her hotel room. She spent a few minutes unpacking her suitcase; she might as well get comfortable. She'd been so out of it when Krista helped her pack that it was kind of fun to look at the stuff. It seemed like most of it had been packed by Krista. She found her mp3 player, a few novels, and her favorite "Keep Midtown Janky" t-shirt. She slipped it on and flipped on the tv, wondering what Dutch television was like. She flipped through and found the usual. There was a weather channel; news, which she watched for a bit but couldn't understand; a British kind of HGTV, and *Gilmore Girls*. For the time being, she settled on that. She'd seen it a few times and it was in English, which was kind of a comfort.

As the night went on, jetlag started to set in. She just couldn't imagine falling asleep. To pass the time she tried to stay busy, continuing the unpacking process and watching whatever she could find on tv, but inevitably her uterus kept coming to mind. It was hard to believe she'd gone all day without thinking about it and now that she had, she couldn't get it off her mind. She didn't have a doctor; she didn't have a home. She knew nothing about having or raising a child. What if it got to the point where she was so pregnant that she could no longer fly, but she still had no home and no doctor?

She pictured herself in Vondel Park under the bridge, in labor and still alone. It was really starting to freak her out, and the sting was only worsening with Jack still so prominent in her mind.

The jetlag made the long, dark hours of the night seem much longer still. She went for the only diversion she could think of and turned to her laptop and her favorite live movie site. She found a good channel and was lucky enough to stumble upon the *Back to the Future* trilogy playing one after another. It was a dream come true to step into Doc Brown's world for a few hours.

She enjoyed herself for a while, relishing the fact that MJF just never changes. They could pull Marty McFly out and drop him in *Spin City* and no one would know the difference. Amazing. Unchanging, that kid.

By the time it ended, she was starting to get hungry again, but since it was four-thirty in the morning, she thought it prudent to hold out for daylight. Thoughts of umbilical cords in the park grass started to swim around her, making the next few hours a bit harder to map out. Eventually, she settled on *Crocodile Dundee*, another trilogy, though she wasn't sure if she had ever seen *Crocodile Dundee in Las Vegas*. That one might be a lost cause overall. Funny, she didn't remember Sue wearing a thong swimsuit in that first crocodile attack scene. Maybe she'd watched the edited version. She giggled as the police officer dropped him off back at the hotel on horseback.

Amazingly, she fell asleep sometime during the first Crocodile Dundee, dreaming about what it would be like to have her own *Mick* taking care of her, giant knife tucked in his back belt and all, keeping her safe from anything that came her way: crocodiles, wild tribesmen, drug lords, snakes, even douchebag boyfriends and husbands.


zes - six


Although she'd sat around for twelve hours waiting to fall asleep, Clara still forgot to set an alarm, and woke up at three in the afternoon. Her adjustment to the new time zone was not going well.

She hopped out of bed and headed straight out the door. She couldn't remember the last time she'd properly done her hair, but now was not the time. She needed to get out of the hotel immediately. The night before had been tough... and very lonely. She began walking towards Dam Square, the square where she'd first sat two days before, and wandered into a few stores along the way. Eventually, she continued down the busy main street. After a fry stand, she recognized the vodka museum and then realized she was heading right towards the train station. How strange that she spent nearly an hour on the public transportation system that first day. This wasn't a long walk at all.

On her right she found a tiny plaza, a perfect place to people watch for a few minutes. The building on one side of the square was labeled, *Beurs*. She had no idea what it meant, but decided to venture inside; it looked like it might be a museum. As she walked through the glass doors, she smiled and her eyes practically sighed shut as she exhaled. The ceilings were high, so high that she couldn't even approximate the distance to the ceiling. There was a café and businessmen and women in suits all around, sipping coffee and eating pastries and sandwiches. She couldn't believe her luck.

She took a seat and ordered a cappuccino and a sandwich. While watching the people come and go, she pondered the likes of this new city. It was easy to see that she was quickly falling in love. It was busy and bustling and densely populated in a way that nearly made her nervous, but she loved it. Maybe she could stay a little longer than a vacation. Perhaps she would get an apartment. She sipped a cappuccino and casually munched on a very good ham and cheese croissant before heading back out to stroll around the city.

"Cheerio!" she heard someone call towards a car that had pulled away from the curb and was now driving down the street. *Why would someone British have a car here in this neat little pedestrianized and bike-filled city? Ugh. Like she didn't get enough of that in the U.S.*

For whatever reason, she had come to think of the British as the European equivalent of Americans in Mexico. They were rude, impulsive, oftentimes drunk, and they never knew the language—not that she could talk. It's not like she spoke a word of Dutch. Still, so far the stereotype seemed to be playing out here.

She headed back to the Van Gogh Museum on her way home. Brand new Museum Card in hand, she walked quickly through the paintings she'd seen the day before and continued up to the second floor. Just as it had the day before, the atmosphere of the museum elevated her mood immediately. She was sure that this would never get old.

It was right then, on the top floor, that she found Odilon Redon.

Thank goodness art museums spent a little space on art education. You come to see Van Gogh, but you know you are going to get others as well—Cézanne; Manet; Gauguin, obviously; and Renoir, if you're lucky. At least that was her opinion.

This time the special guest was Redon. Odilon Redon, she decided, worked as if painting a dream sequence. The colors that he used were amazing. She wondered if he really had been painting from his dreams—that or a drug trip, she supposed.

She spent nearly an hour examining the vivid blues of his work. Even though she could come back anytime that she wanted, she just couldn't bring herself to leave. This feeling, the way that beautiful art made her feel alive, was just irresistible after all that she had been through the last few weeks.

Her stomach eventually reminded her of the time, and she left and went walking towards the city center looking for someplace to get a full meal. Today she would not worry about what time she got back to the hotel. The longer she was out on the town walking around, the more likely it was that she would actually sleep.

She found her way to a canal and wandered for some time, curving her way across the city, not knowing whether she was headed away from or towards her hotel. She stopped every once in a while to watch the water move or to stare in awe at a particularly agile bicyclist.

The breeze was becoming chilly, so when she stumbled upon a fun-looking coffee shop, she went in to get something warm to drink and eat. The place she stopped was bizarre and unbelievable. It was called *Dolphins* and the inside was decorated like an underwater world, complete with fish tanks built into the walls and fish swimming in the hanging lights. She went up to the counter to look at the menu and order.

"Hello," she greeted the tiny brown-haired bartender, "Could I have a hot chocolate, please?"

"Whipped cream?" the young woman asked.

"Yes, please."

"Two Euro fifty."

Clara handed her the correct amount and went back to her seat, unsure if she should wait for her hot chocolate or if it would be brought to her. In a few seconds, her question was answered and the woman brought her hot chocolate out to her table.

"Warmechocolademelk," the woman said, "met slagroom."

Clara tried to remain confident, but the nervous smile on her face clearly gave her away.

"Hot chocolate," the woman repeated in English, "with whipped cream."

"Oh, thank you."

To Clara's surprise, along with the hot chocolate was a small cookie, just as she'd received with her cappuccino that afternoon. Maybe this was a normal practice here; she hoped so.

The cup of hot chocolate was both tasty and picturesque. A pile of ornate whipped cream sprinkled with cocoa powder sat atop the little cup. She examined the room around her as she sipped. Somewhat in confusion she examined the four glowing glass containers opposite the counter. In all honesty, the strange apparatus really looked like something she hadn't seen since her college days—a bong! A fancy one, maybe, but a bong all the same. The glass bottom part was filled with water, and a light bulb below each one glowed red, then blue, then yellow. It was really quite pretty.

The sign above them stated a warning, written only in English.

*Hot! Be careful! Please ask for help, we would be happy to provide instruction.*

As she continued to look around, wondering if this was normal for a coffee shop, a few young guys came in and the barista greeted them. They each ordered a juice, except one guy who ordered tea, and they sat down at a table in the opposite corner of the room.

"No tobacco," she said abruptly, "tobacco must be smoked downstairs."

The four guys all nodded and got up to move downstairs. They must have a smoking room here, she thought. That was nice. She hated being surrounded by smoke. Plus, she noted, she had the baby to think about now. Thankfully, it seemed like the society was set up nicely, just another reason why she liked this pleasant Dutch culture.

Clara finished her hot chocolate, thanked the woman behind the counter, and went on her way. Today, she would buy a few groceries before walking back. There was no way she was going to be searching her purse for breathmints and gum like she had been the night before.

Minutes later she was attempting to board a tram to Museumplein when she ran into the irritable Brit from the grocery store.

"Could you please hurry up?!" he barked as he stepped onto the tram behind her. "Just like every other American tourist," he mumbled under his breath, "can't use public transport to save her life."

Her fumbling fingers were struggling to stamp a date on her strip ticket and he wasn't helping. This was seriously denting her hot cocoa buzz.

*What luck. More than half a million people in this city and she ends up on the same tram as this British sleazebag. And how did he know she was American?*

Clara stumbled off the tram ten minutes later and popped into the first food establishment she saw, a small convenience store. She quickly purchased enough food and snacks for a couple of light meals and then slipped into her hotel before she could run into anything or anyone that would be detrimental to her mood.

Just after ten o'clock, after devouring a cheese sandwich and a bag of sea salt potato chips, she settled into her bed and fell asleep without the least amount of effort. Perhaps this was the end of her jetlag.

## zeven - seven

Clara awoke and turned to look at her clock, hoping that it was still before noon.

11:53! *How glorious!* she thought. About two seconds later, she rolled over and out of bed. Something was off. She went to her window, pulled back the curtains and found herself staring out into the dark Amsterdam night. It wasn't noon, it was midnight. She had only slept for two hours and now she was awake, again, and hungry, again.

She got up and made herself another sandwich. She *was* pregnant; it was probably good that she was eating every two hours. This time she grabbed a bottle of apple juice—appelsap, it said on the bottle—to go along with the sandwich. She found the Dutch word for juice quite to her liking. *What was sap anyway, but the juice of a plant? Beautiful.*

Following her midnight lunch Clara looked aimlessly around her room and exhaled loudly in annoyance and frustration. She was having such a hard time getting to sleep at night. It was partially the jetlag and time change, but more than that, she wondered if she just couldn't get over what had happened. She walked over to the vanity mirror and examined her appearance. She let down her hair and brushed it out thoroughly before winding it up again on top of her head. Her eyes looked terrible.

No, she couldn't get over it. Her husband had left her, her Jack—sweet, muscular, tousled brown hair with a crimp of curl. At 31 she had been dumped, and when it came down to it, she wasn't over him. Why would she be, really? She hadn't left him... she'd have stayed with him forever.

As easy as it was to distract herself during the day, at

night all she had were her thoughts. She lay in her bed staring at the ceiling, wishing that she would just fall back asleep. A string of horrific events flashed through her head. The last night with Jack, the note, the hotel in Sacramento, the flight, the Iceland airport... Then Amsterdam. She really was trying to move on, at least she thought so.

*Let go*, she thought, just let go. But let go of what? She no longer knew what to hold on to. She really *had* liked her job. She liked the kids in her classes, she enjoyed teaching, but, in a way, she knew it wasn't everything that she wanted. She wanted to feel alive, to feel inspired and motivated and joyful every single day. Not all day every day, but at least every day. Was that really too much to ask?

She *felt* like she was heading in the right direction. But had she just run away, heedless of the direction? She was so angry at him; she couldn't possibly still love him, could she? Hadn't she felt a longing for him, seconds before? Clearly she would hold him in disdain because of the life that he was leaving for her child, their child. She should. She would...

She could be a good mother, so it was better, really, that her baby wouldn't have to grow up in the house of Jack. It was pretty likely the baby would be better off without him, father or not... right?

Still, at times she thought it would be nice to have the chance to take him back.

There were fleeting moments when a particularly good memory slipped into her mind, and she caught herself imagining what it would be like if he came back.

He would bang on her door with his fist, having found her by tracking her phone calls or calling and begging everyone she knew or paying off the FBI or perhaps Dutch immigration, and he would yell from behind the door, even before she had a chance to open it. *Clara, I love you! Please let me in. I can't live without you another day!*

When she finally got around to opening the door, after taking her sweet old time, he would take her in his arms like it had been years. In whispered words, he would explain how horrible it had been and how he had tried to ignore it and move on, but in the end, found that there was no way he could live without her. She had to come home, he would beg, he would do anything, give her anything, to have her back and in his arms.

Somewhere in the midst of this tangled daydream, she fell asleep. Although it was a peaceful sleep, thinking that someone wanted her, she was definitely worse off when she woke up again at one-thirty in the morning.

How depressing to wake up and realize that the only way for her to sleep was to daydream that her heartbreaking ex-husband had come and begged to have her back.

She spent the next few hours of the night sitting in front of her laptop wallowing. It was an active decision, to stay awake and wallow, which meant she didn't feel quite as bad doing it. Plus, it wasn't as if there was anything else she could be doing. She wasn't about to go out and find a nightclub. She spent the early hours of the morning wrapped up in her European down comforter, eating airport Toblerone and Nutella with a spoon and risking the future of her laptop by watching poor quality movies from questionable pirating internet sites. Bad decisions all around.

She chose only to watch depressing ones, considering her current state. *P.S. I love You*, *The Story of Us*, *Hope Floats*, only the ones that caused her physical pain, the ones that caused her eyes to burn but didn't quite cause tears to come. She just couldn't bring herself to feel that much.

## acht - eight

Clara woke up the next morning thinking it would take quite a jolt to feel alive again. She figured she'd gotten about four and a half good hours of sleep, split up into three, which wasn't exactly enough to keep her going for a full day.

Eventually, she made it out of bed and to the bathroom to brush her teeth and wash her face. She didn't really have any desire to shower, so she headed to the one basic upholstered chair that sat by a small round table near the window. Tomorrow she would shower. It hadn't been *that* long. She soon realized that she had nothing left for breakfast, primarily due to the fact that she had eaten so much during the night.

Since she had no plans for the day, she decided she had better get out of the room before she simply crawled back into bed and hid. She grabbed her bag and walked through the hotel out the front door.

Outside, Clara was greeted by such insanity that she momentarily considered going back in and diving under the covers. Somehow, though, the hundreds of people on the street made her curious enough to tough it out, even if simply to find out what was going on.

What day was it and how had she not noticed this chaos from her room? Where was everyone going? Or coming from? They certainly all seemed to be quite focused on something, although they were clearly not in a hurry, just streaming all in one direction.

She decided to risk it and took a step out into the crowd, letting herself drift slowly away. She looked all around her as the crowd ebbed and flowed down the street. She was surrounded by people of all ages; old men in brown jackets and leather boat shoes; young college frat boys dressed in orange or pink pastel polo shirts, aviators, and a thick amount of hair gel that kept their hair swiped back into the perfect windblown style. There were children on their parents' shoulders, getting an ideal view above the crowd, and tall Dutch women, young and old, wearing scarves and stylish boots, cute tops layered with light pullovers or shawls. Every one of them carried a bag, straw with leather straps, a colorful flowered beachbag or otherwise, and a glint in their eye. She continued to walk but raised up on her toes, looking for a giant sign that said *Best Sale on Earth*. What was all this?

Suddenly, a new discovery caused her eyes to widen substantially. Orange. There was orange everywhere. How she hadn't noticed it the moment she stepped outside, she had no idea, because *everyone* was wearing orange. The little girl on her dad's shoulders had orange-painted pigtails. The old man just to her right was wearing bright orange pants and a knit orange scarf. Astonishingly enough, these orange pants didn't even seem to have come from a Halloween store. They looked like they may have been Ralph Lauren. She began feeling more and more out of place as she searched for *anyone*, just one person, that wasn't wearing orange. It was impossible. Everyone was wearing something orange. She noticed that the frat boys sported the cheesiest and most outrageous pieces of orange attire. Orange loudspeakers, cowboy hats holding small plastic cups of beer, orange belts, ties, and orange plastic covers shaped like wooden shoes that were strapped to their feet. *Okay, really, what day was it?*

She trolled through her head, searching for the date. She arrived in Amsterdam on April 27, she remembered that at least. She had stared at the plane ticket for April 26 for long enough—she certainly should remember it. It must be April 30, or maybe May 1. Her mother had called on Wednesday, like always, but she had ignored that. Was that two days ago or three days ago?

She remembered overhearing something in the café the day before. The woman had said that her brother was visiting on Saturday because... because of the holiday! One thing down. It was Saturday, it was a holiday, and apparently everyone in the entire country had decided to come to her street and walk down it. With her.

Now, why were they all here and *what* were they walking toward? It was going to be a long, possibly very exciting, day.

Clara quickly decided that she was too embarrassed about not wearing orange. She would have to do something about it, and soon—she was nervous about being discovered. She was already foreign enough, she didn't need to be singled out and ridiculed for any other reason. She shimmied her way to the edge of the steadily streaming crowd and, to her surprise, found that randomly along the edge of the street-turned-sidewalk there were people selling things. Some were selling random stuff like cds, old issues of National Geographic, a microwave; and others were more creative and had espresso and cookies. Some tables were run by sweet little Dutch girls, hardly old enough to be able to count, selling cupcakes with orange frosting and glasses of orange juice. And there, just between a cupcake stand and a man in an apron baking up fresh waffles, was someone selling orange.

He had orange boas, orange hats, orange crowns, orange beads, orange belts, orange ties, orange t-shirts and orange hair color in a can. She was so excited she headed right over. She stopped suddenly when she almost ran over one of the little Dutch girls selling cupcakes. There was a look of sadness on the girl's face as she gazed at her older sister, hardly six years old, but still older—who was busy refilling her empty cupcake tray now that she had sold the last one. The little girl turned to look up at Clara as she nearly knocked the single cupcake out of her hand. The girl eyed her in confusion. Perhaps she was wondering where her orange was, or maybe wondering where she was from, she was so obviously not Dutch.

"Would you like a cupcake?" she asked politely, the tiniest British twinge to her Dutch-English accent.

Clara smiled willingly, "Yes, please," she responded happily.

"Wonderful! Here you are!" she said as she politely handed over the orange frosted cupcake. Now that Clara had it in her hand, she could see there were confetti sprinkles on it as well, also orange, and in the shape of tiny crowns. "Fifty cents, please," the girl continued cutely, and in a quite dignified voice.

Clara dug quickly in her pocket for change. She was almost certain that the little girl was Dutch, her voice sounded like it, she looked like it, and the tall, rather stern looking woman standing behind her also looked like it, but wow, if this is the way they taught children to speak English... She knew that most countries spoke more languages, and learned them more quickly, than they did in America, but this—this was unheard of. This little girl couldn't be more than five. *Wow*.

"Here you are," Clara copied as she handed her a shiny, gold fifty Euro cent coin, "Thank you," she smiled at the little girl, and the girl smiled brightly back at her.

"You're welcome. Have a nice Queen's Day!" The look on Clara's face must have looked odd, because the little girl scrunched her nose as she tipped her head to the right and looked up at her.

"Queen's Day?" she asked and quickly replaced the look with a smile.

"Yes," smiled the little girl, "Queen Beatrix."

*Queen's Day*, Clara thought, *fun!* She had forgotten that there was a Queen here.

"It's not *really* her birthday," the girl's sister piped in matter-of-factly, "It's her mother's birthday."

"I *know*, Janne." The little girl was very offended at her sister butting into *her* transaction. "It's her mother's birthday," explained the little girl.

"But Queen Beatrix was born in the winter, when the weather is just terrible," Janne jumped in again, "and we don't want to celebrate in the winter."

Clara smiled, looking from one girl to the other and back again. What a fun little interaction. She should really try to get out more. The girls looked up at her, possibly waiting for a response. "I see," said Clara. "Well, have a nice Queen's day. Thanks for the cupcake!"

"Bye-bye!" said the girls together.

*Fifty cents*, thought Clara as she continued down the street. *What a deal*. And a chocolate cupcake with frosting and sprinkles for breakfast—what a great deal!

Her next stop was the orange stand. She finished eating her cupcake, took one brief look around her and decided to do it up right. She chose a boa, an orange plastic crown (If she *had* to be a Queen for the day...) and a grass skirt that was orange. For whatever reason, this was apparently perfectly appropriate attire for the day. She continued down the street with more spring in her step and a bigger smile on her face. In just a few short minutes, thanks to two little girls and one man dressed all in orange, she had become an informed and costumed party-goer. Clearly, they were headed to a party—despite the number of senior citizens and children—there just weren't really many other options.

The crowd was getting slightly denser now, so she predicted they were nearing their destination, or maybe more people were just joining the parade. She wondered if there was something special about this street, or if the whole city was full of people. She could hardly imagine that the whole city was as packed as it was right there. From where she was standing, she guessed that she could see nearly 5,000 people by looking just in front of her and behind her, and the street wasn't that big.

Then she saw the canal. It was literally packed with boats. Unbelievable. She couldn't believe that this type of a boat traffic jam was possibly safe—or legal. There were huge, long, flat boats with two or more dozen people on them, all drinking beer or champagne or holding handles of vodka. There were tiny fishing boats with hardly a motor at all, packed to the max, the five people aboard risking their lives to be part of this floating party.

Clara watched as two college-aged girls stood up and walked across the boats—one, two, three, four—across five different boats to get to the edge of the canal. They climbed up onto the street with the help of a couple of rowdy middle-aged men and headed off to the portable toilet across the street.

She looked around, trying to peer through the people to figure out where she was. She soon realized that she was near the entrance to the big city park. She hadn't made it there for her picnic lunch yet, but she had known it was fairly close to her hotel. Maybe today was the day for a nice sit in the park. She made her way through the gates and looked down the long, grassy thoroughfare. There were people *everywhere.*

It was a jovial atmosphere with music and laughing and food in every direction. The whole soiree made her just want to sit back in a lawn chair and drink lemonade. This was people watching at its best.

She continued through the park slowly, picking up a soda at one stand and a cookie at another. There were so many people selling things she felt like it was yard sale day in the city. She spent a few minutes at one spot where an older couple had a blanket laid out filled with antiques and trinkets and old books. She found a bracelet that she liked and put it on after handing over two Euros, the silver charms encircling her wrist with a jingle as the old man helped her clasp it. Just after the older couple was a young boy, dressed unmistakably as Michael Jackson, dancing away like he was the King of Pop of Queen's Day.

A good 20 feet later, she came across a young boy who was playing the violin. She stopped with a few others to listen in. Amidst the chaos she leaned in to focus her ear on the smooth melody.

He was playing "Time to Say Goodbye," and her heart wrenched slightly as he dove into the chorus, playing away her past. Here she was, dressed in orange and surrounded by thousands of others dressed in orange, Michael Jackson included, still holding half of the hotdog she had purchased a hundred feet back, watching a middle-schooler play violin. She wondered what was next for her.

She almost couldn't believe her eyes as they wandered involuntarily around the scene, slightly glistening with a tear that had formed, but not fallen. She wouldn't cry today, not yet, but she could feel stunned. Numb. And almost traumatized by the complexity of the events in her recent past, her life right at this moment, and how she had absolutely no idea what was next.

Eventually the song ended, and after depositing several coins in the young man's violin case, she wandered, unfocused and aimless, until she found herself sitting at the edge of a large pond. There weren't too many people there, relatively speaking.

She found that many of the people around her were acting

as if it were a normal day in the park. They had blankets and picnics and they were throwing tennis balls to their friendly dog: brown, furry, unleashed, happy, and—she noticed, often unchanged reproductively. *How odd.*

She let her back roll down onto the grass, propped her head up on her day bag, which was now stuffed with random finds from the day, and closed her eyes and listened to the sounds swirl around her like a blender of happiness. No matter her personal situation, one had no choice but to enjoy this day.

She awoke to the sound of children playing, yelling and running, clearly all a part of some elaborate game. She turned her head towards the noise and opened her eyes, quickly shading them from the surprisingly bright Dutch sun, and found herself staring at the coolest playground she had ever laid eyes on. It was made entirely of wooden logs and almost the entire play area was lofted nearly 30 feet above the ground.

Kids were running across the roped passageways, crawling under and over, and looking out over the entire park. They were literally scampering in the treetops. Instantly, she wanted to run over and climb up the rope ladder, hoping to play a part, whether pirate or sailor, but her age stopped her in her tracks. Her thoughts drifted to Peter Pan and then right to Wendy, the friend who got old. She got too old to go to Neverland, too old to play with Peter and the other lost boys.

Letting her gaze drift back to the sky, Clara dropped her hand from her eyes and let it relax on her stomach. *Hmm.* She had forgotten. Almost a whole day of bright colors and music and laughter and she had almost forgotten that she wasn't exactly alone in this world. It stunned her to think that she hadn't thought about her impending child at all yet that day. She took a moment now, and didn't feel so bad, didn't feel so alone, or so depressed. For whatever reason, this place was good for her. It was refreshing and interesting, the weather was sometimes a bit cool, but look at today, it had been perfect. *Happy Birthday, Queen Beatrix*, she thought. Beatrix, not such a bad name, she would keep that one in mind.

## negen - nine

Clara yawned and stretched and then reached to pick up a leftover orange cupcake. It was the perfect breakfast after the magnificent holiday the day before. She settled into her chair, replaying the orange surprise and her complete enjoyment of Queen's Day. Just think, if she had crawled back into bed, she would have missed it all!

Sacramento was a world of good yard sales and estate sales. Every weekend you could walk around the grid with no plans whatsoever and find sale after sale. Some people planned their entire weekend around getting to the best sales early. But here, on Queen's Day, it was like nothing she had ever experienced. Clara looked at the pile of goodies on her kitchen table. The whole day was like a giant flea market— except bigger. You could sell coffee or tea or create carnival games that included tobogganing hotdogs or throwing frosted cupcakes. You could let your children sell treats or candy or their toys. You could even let them dance and sing for a Euro or two. It was a fabulous concept for a national holiday.

Just in Vondel Park she found a fancy hat and a cool glass, besides her bracelet and a multitude of edible treats. Outside of the park, she found a load of old, ornate frames, and picked one. Her late afternoon impulse was a Tiffany-style lamp. All in all, she spent less than she would on a normal trip to the grocery store.

She got up and walked over to her new lamp. No light bulb; she had forgotten. She walked over to the plain, brown hotel lamp and unscrewed the lightbulb. She'd return it when she left.

Beneath the light of her new lamp she settled into the chair near the window and grabbed her battered copy of *The Sun Also Rises* from the nightstand. Spain. Maybe a trip to Spain was in the offing. She began to read where she'd left off on the plane, wondering if Hemingway had ever been to The Netherlands.

Within a few pages Clara drifted back to sleep. Her

dreams were both happy and sad, colored vividly orange as she wandered amongst sales. She walked through Vondel Park, the sweetly sad line of a child's solo violin performance providing the melody. She stepped out the gate of the park and she was walking on U Street in Sacramento, just about to cross over 23rd, somewhat aware that she and Krista had been to an estate sale in just this area. Poverty Ridge, it was sometimes called. There was a special kind of sale occurring in this particular Victorian. You actually got to enter the house and wander around, examining their treasures.

Up on the second floor, they stumbled into what appeared to be a guest bedroom, or perhaps the wife's bedroom once she and her husband began sleeping in separate beds and bedrooms. Sitting next to the window, there it was, the right arm faded from the sun shining in for the entirety of its life.

Clara had known instantly that it was the chair for her. She called for Krista to come guard it for her and went down to negotiate. Just a crinkled twenty later, she and Krista were hauling the chair down the old wooden staircase and out to the curb. Krista hadn't been able to stop laughing.

"It's blue velvet, Clare!" she had poked. "Don't you have to be over 60 to want velvet furniture?"

"You can't laugh in an estate sale," Clara had hissed back. "They're," she mouthed, "*dead.*"

Krista laughed even harder. "You don't know that for sure. They probably just moved to Malibu."

At the curb she asked Krista, who gladly obliged, to cop a squat on the chair while she went for a vehicle.

She was already picturing it, the chintz chair sitting in her living room, the same arm receiving the morning sun. It was already faded, she didn't want to traumatize the poor thing by completely altering its environment. She couldn't ever remember being so excited about a piece of furniture.

The next day she had come home after work dreaming of sitting in her new old chair, so soft and plush. She locked up her bike, a little sweaty from the ride—nearly three miles— and walked in the front door of her house. Jack was already there with a couple friends watching the Giants game. She stowed her bag on a hook and slipped out of her shoes. She pulled a book off her tiny cherry oak bookshelf; she was reading *HP & the DH* and Snape had just died. Harry had the memories and was heading up to Dumbledore's office. She loved this part; she loved learning about Lily.

She was actually kind of glad that Jack was occupied. She had a nice night planned—eating gnocchi and pesto and finishing the book in her new blue chair. It was just what she needed on a Monday night after a long day of work.

On the way to the fridge she saw that Jack had already ordered Thai. That sounded pretty good, so she grabbed a bowl and scooped in a helping of pad see ew, adding a dose of sriracha to liven it up. Jack didn't like much spice, so she generally had to doctor hers up a bit. She headed back to the living room, preparing her mind to block out the sound of Kruk and Kuip, the Giants' long-time announcers whose voices were practically the soundtrack to their marriage. She entered the room, looking around for her blue baby rocker. She looked to Jack, who hadn't even noticed her entrance.

"Jack," she asked, "where's my chair?"

"Oh, yeah," he glanced up at her but then went right back to the game, "we had to move it to the porch," he said, "there just wasn't room in here. Plus," he added, "it isn't really the right style, you know."

She let her gaze linger for a second on the overworn leather couch that had remained even after he graduated and his college roommates moved out. Said roommates, Kale and James, were sprawled out there, their feet resting on the beautiful oak coffee table that they'd received from her aunt and uncle as a wedding present. Jack himself was sitting on a huge overstuffed armchair, now centered in the space that had once been shared by her baby rocker and his armchair. She thought it looked cute, his and hers, big and little, manly and feminine; apparently he thought otherwise.

"Wanna beer, J?" he asked, "Kale?"

"Yeah, man," they both replied, "sure."

Jack reached to the left of his chair and popped open a cooler, the one item that had been displaced in the effort to make space for her chair. She hadn't known it was still in use, she figured they'd just forgotten to put it away. Judging by the plentiful beer, the ice, and the system of tossing the beers easily across the room to his friends, she had been wrong. The dirty red and white cooler was still in constant use, a fairly important piece in the living room, and more important than other things or other people, it seemed.

"Sorry, Clare," James said, noticing that she hadn't left the room. *Thanks*, she was about to respond, but he continued, "Sorry, could you uh-" he waved his hand and motioned to the right. She was blocking the screen, that's why he noticed that she hadn't left.

She didn't respond, but turned towards the hallway and headed to the back porch. She opened the screen door to the half back porch-half storage space and found her baby blue sitting on the edge near the stairs down to the backyard. It was raining. At least the chair was only getting a little wet, just the rain splattering on the porch rail seemed to be reaching the blue floral patterned velvet.

Clara shook her head, waking herself from this half awake, half asleep reminiscence. She had to leave this hotel room. She couldn't let herself slip into a coma of depression when she had so much fun the day before.

She moved her hand to pinch the bridge of her nose, attempting to push the gloom away. Her cheeks were wet, a surprise. Times like this, the room felt so claustrophobic. She was enjoying being in a new place, but this wasn't a life.

Temporarily lost is what she was—a bit lost, a bit intimidated, and a lot homeless. She no longer had a home in Sacramento, at least not one to her name, and as a semi-proud 31 year old, she couldn't bring herself to move back in with her parents.

She should go in search of a slightly longer term home, her very first Dutch apartment. She needed somewhere where she felt more comfortable and where she could settle herself in. Then, hopefully she would get better at falling asleep at the appropriate time. She just couldn't be stuck in a hotel room for so many hours in the middle of the night.

## tien - ten

A short term apartment was probably the best place to begin, she decided. There would have to be month-to-month rentals in a city like this. She obviously wasn't quite ready to make a long term commitment, but she could do with another few weeks, or even a month or two, in Holland. Starting today, she would devote herself to finding somewhere more suitable.

She started her search by asking around at the two and three star hotels. They all quoted her prices, ridiculous prices that is, and encouraged her to instead search online or use an agency of some kind. The whole experience was actually kind of funny. She thought she would feel more awkward, clearly American, asking about a short term rental, but the Dutch were so straightforward, they answered her questions clearly with no extra fluff, and sent her forth from there.

Once online, she found that renting would be a cinch. She found a couple of sites for long term vacation rentals and short term apartment rentals in no time. She had a feeling there was a market for Dutch people and a market for foreigners. It might not be all that difficult to acquire an apartment, but there was a good chance that she was paying about 25 percent more than the local population. Still, it was going to be much cheaper than what she was paying now.

After calling and emailing a few contacts, she soon had an interview with a Dutch woman named Ellie who was renting out the top floor of her home. Clara showed up exactly on time and was greeted at the front door of a perfectly traditional rowhouse facing the canal. Ellie was tall and thin, but looked sturdily built, to say the least. Clara's first impression was that this late-middle-aged woman could take her in two swift swings. This was only somewhat intimidating. They entered the front door, walked past the entrance to Ellie's apartment and up a long flight of stairs to the third-floor apartment for rent.

The rental apartment was very pleasant. It was comprised of a large main room with a small and basic kitchen off to the side and a simple bedroom through a doorway at the back. In the kitchen, there was an oven and stove and a small refrigerator. Everything was furnished and Clara would receive new towels each week. For an extra fee, Ellie had explained, she would come weekly or biweekly to do the cleaning, though Clara could also choose to do the cleaning on her own, which she decided she would.

Ellie was polite, direct, and even kind of blunt, not at all flowery in her actions and words. During their short interview she asked some basic questions about the purpose of stay, and Clara explained that she was here to get away and learn a little about her heritage. When Ellie inquired as to how she would support herself there in Amsterdam, Clara quietly described her teaching position in Sacramento, afterwards adding that she was a good saver, which pleased Ellie. Thus, their cordial renter-rentee relationship was formed. After seeing the place and having a cup of tea, Clara signed a rental agreement for one month with the possibility of extending it. Ellie made a copy of her passport and that was that.

The price wasn't bad, 900 Euros a month, and she was able to move in right away since the previous tenant had left a week early.

The next day, Clara sprung for a bicycle taxi and made the move from the hotel in just under an hour. She brought everything at once, though incredibly surprised at how much extra she had managed to accumulate in less than a week.

She really liked the apartment, it felt homey, and she spent the next afternoon becoming acquainted with her new surroundings. She found she had a coffeemaker and a presspot, an abundance of utensils, and plates and bowls of all sizes. There were even large tea mugs and tiny coffee cups as well as four wine glasses.

They had a short "orientation" the next afternoon and the tall, stern-shouldered Dutch woman proved to be incredibly helpful. She provided Clara with a map of the neighborhood, the location of the closest grocery store and bicycle shop, and the schedule for local outdoor markets, something Clara had never thought to consider. She knew nothing about the neighborhoods of Amsterdam, but Ellie made it sound like this was a fairly desirable location. Jordaan, it was called.

Clara soon decided that Ellie was an excellent contact to have. She was very direct, which didn't really mesh well with Clara's delicate emotional state, but she was also entirely unconcerned with Clara's situation as long as she could pay her rent. Besides, Clara was starting to think that being direct was just being Dutch.

Clara was also learning that the Dutch were stunningly private. They asked questions when it concerned them or their livelihood, but otherwise, your business was not their business.

That night, happy to be able to settle in and stock up her new place, Clara headed to the store that Ellie had recommended. She got some basics and a frozen pizza for dinner. She was excited to have an oven at her disposable.

Along with a half loaf of freshly baked bread, Clara got peanut butter and something that looked like peanut butter, but had a different name, *Speculoos*. She thought she would give it a try. She also got another jar of Nutella, just because that seemed like something you eat a lot of in Europe.

While in the produce section examining the tomatoes, she watched a woman pick out tomatoes and bananas and then take them over to a small electronic scale. The woman weighed each item in turn, selecting the correct button and then printing a price sticker for each. At first, she assumed the woman was a store employee, but then she saw that a short line was forming behind the woman. Two more people completed the same procedure before heading towards the checkout. *How strange.* It appeared that in Holland you had to weigh your own produce.

She thought about picking up some grapes, but decided to pass. She would check out the outdoor market later this week instead. The self-weighing procedure was a little intimidating.

Next, Clara stumbled into the Aisle of Sweet, as she would forever call it. She remembered the first time she visited this aisle, just her second or third day in Amsterdam. It was also the first time she had been yelled at by the cheeky British guy. Thinking back, she must have been incredibly stressed, she couldn't believe that she'd walked down the aisle without loading up a basket.

The chocolate in itself was amazing. The brands and types that you would find in a gift shop or delicatessen in the United States were sitting casually on basic grocery store shelves. Côte d'Or, Kinder, Lindt, and more types of Milka than she thought humanly possible. They also had their own "fancier" chocolates: chocolate-dipped orange peel, truffles, and chocolate bon-bons. She grabbed a few different kinds, letting her weakness for good chocolate guide her like a bright light from the heavens.

Next, she moved on to the nuts. Clara never used to like nuts, but here in Europe she just couldn't get enough hazelnuts. Hazelnuts came in everything. You could buy them alone, covered in chocolate, covered in toffee, or even sitting in a half chocolate sphere and then dipped in a chewy toffee. There was also hazelnut gelato. It just didn't get any better than that. Furthermore, the plain, milk chocolate covered hazelnuts came in a small, plastic tube-like container that would make a perfect travel case for tampons. Not that she needed them.

She ended up with at least one Swiss dark, some German milk chocolate, Champagne truffles, and a fancy box of Belgian chocolates—the kind where you get to pick each time and hope it's filled with caramel or hazelnut or pistachio and not filled with some strange fruit-flavored foam.

After filling her basket with a month's supply of the finest chocolates, she turned to leave the aisle and spotted the *stroopwafels*. These, she did remember from childhood. Thin

waffle cookies with a layer of caramel sandwiched inside—
they were perfect for dipping in coffee or warming on top of a
toaster. She grabbed several packs of different brands, hoping
to make a study of it while she was in the country.

She also bought coffee, unable to restrain herself. She
could drink a weak cup in the morning, and maybe eventually
she'd be able to wean herself off, but for now, she was going
to push the guilt aside. She might be able to handle moving to
a new country; she might even be able to handle moving to a
new country while pregnant, but there was no way she could
handle moving to a new country, pregnant, and without coffee.
It just wasn't going to happen.

She spent nearly an hour in the small grocery store,
wandering around and staring at the strange words, the strange
items, and the relatively normal looking people.

Overall, she found that she didn't feel that out of place.
Everyone was slightly taller, and some of the younger men
had something weird going on with hair gel, but other than
that, she could just pretend that she was still in the U.S.

The language, on the other hand, was a bit of a shock. She
had heard that it wasn't all that hard to learn, but the sound of
it—it was appalling! All consonants and phlegm and this
horrible guttural back of the throat rumbling that she could not
imagine her own mouth would be able to replicate.

When Clara eventually reached the cashier, she slipped by
fairly easily, reading the amount from the screen and paying
the proper amount of Euros, down to the cent.

"Wilt u de bon?" Clara was caught off guard by a
question from the young cashier, but the word *bon* keyed her
in. She felt quite lucky that she caught it, she knew enough
Spanish and French to know that this meant *good*. She
recovered semi-gracefully and gave the girl a thumbs up.

"Bon!" she smiled.

The young clerk raised her eyebrows skeptically, but then
gave her a tentative smile and handed her the receipt.

Clara breathed a sigh of relief. They were so friendly
here, wishing her a good day, or maybe asking her if

everything was good. Such nice people, the Dutch.

The walk home took only ten or twelve minutes, but she was still envious of the cyclists flying by her. With a bicycle, she could make it home in minutes. This week was the apartment. Next week, she'd consider a bicycle.

When she got home, she turned on the oven and opened her frozen pizza, frozen pesto pizza, to be exact. While she waited for the oven to preheat, she examined the box. The backside had instructions in no less than nine different languages. In addition, she found that the pizza was actually made in Italy. She was sure she had never eaten a frozen pizza from Italy, maybe Illinois or Indiana, but never Italy.

She baked up the real Italian frozen pizza and settled down with her tourist magazine and map, also turning on the tv to *Veronica*, her personal source for Gilmore Girls, Friends, Seinfeld, about any American sitcom possible.

*Damn, the pizza was good.* It had real globs of pesto among the circles of mozzarella and the tomato chunks.

$$C_M$$

The next morning Clara realized that unfortunately, her coffee purchase was far less successful than her stellar pizza purchase. She had purchased some type of a coffee "pad."

How many coffee pads equal one pot? Something told her this was not how it was supposed to work. She made a mental note to ask Ellie about this. Until then, she still needed coffee, so she skipped down her steps and out the door into Jordaan.

Even though she'd only been there a week, Clara already felt right at home in the Dutch café scene. Cafés here were always so calming, and at the same time, they somehow made her feel like a part of the community. In cafés in the U.S. she always felt like she should be working. You could talk, of course, but people could freely give you dirty looks for interrupting their study and work time with your chatter. Here, it was all about socializing. There was always a peaceful hum of chatter, not loud enough to overhear, but not so quiet that she felt awkward sneezing or sliding her chair noisily across the floor.

The café where she now sat was called De Blaffende Vis, or *The Barking Fish*, according to the tiny Dutch-English dictionary she had purchased and was now carrying around with her. It was one of the most inexpensive cafés she had seen so far. She had paid just 1.70 for a nice cappuccino.

Today she was skimming her Benelux guidebook— apparently Belgium, The Netherlands, and Luxembourg were a tight-knit little trio—while enjoying the super-sweetened foam of her cappuccino. According to her guidebook, Jordaan was a well-known part of Amsterdam. It was known for its tiny art galleries and unique storefronts selling old vinyls, vintage clothing, and handmade jewelry, furniture, and children's clothing.

She was sitting up in the small wooden loft of the café peering out the window at the passersby when a father and son walked in together and chose a table just a few feet away. The fathered ordered a *koffie*, and proceeded to ask his son what he wanted. She expected an orange juice or maybe a glass of chocolate milk, but instead, she heard the word, *koffie* mentioned again. A few minutes later the woman came back with two small coffee cups. As Clara watched them, clearly interested in the situation, the waitress stopped by the table to deliver her freshly-made cheese *tosti*. The Dutch grilled cheese sandwich was a staple at nearly every café and thus far, it fit in well with her cravings for comfort food.

"Can I get you anything else?" the waitress asked, watching her look again at the father and son.

"Do the children drink coffee here?" she asked in a whisper. The little boy couldn't have been more than three or four years old.

The waitress laughed and nodded to the father with a wink, "Well, the boy ordered coffee, yes," she explained, "but the father clarified, that it should be more... just warm milk, with a bit of foam on the top." She laughed again, "You must give in to the children a little," she explained as she clopped down the wooden stairs to the lower level.

*Ah, parenthood,* thought Clara, she only hoped she'd be as clever.

## elf - eleven

At Ellie's place, Clara's stovetop had to be lit with a match. At first it made her nervous to let a spigot spout natural gas. *What if she accidentally bumped it and turned it on?* Without that pestering clicking that American stovetops made, she wouldn't know that she was being slowly poisoned. Of course, as soon as she voiced her concern to Ellie, the wise Dutchwoman came up to give her a very clear orientation on when to strike the match, when to turn the knob, and where to place the match to light the burner easily and most efficiently.

After a few days, Clara was surprised to find that it was a comforting sort of practice. Before she made coffee in the morning, before she made dinner, before she heated water for tea; every time, she had to take five seconds to light a match— striking it along the long edge of the box, hard enough to ignite a flame but not so hard that she broke the matchstick in half. She would turn the knob and then watch the flame slowly encircle the element, one flicker at a time, until the perfect glowing circle was complete. This extra step somehow made her morning routine better.

On one particularly rainy morning, she woke to find that she had a single match to light the stove. Having to light the stove with just one match was obviously too much to ask; in reality she kind of sucked at not breaking the fragile, little matches. After breaking the single match into splinters, she then failed to light the stove with the pitiful piece she had left. The whole ordeal caused her to plummet into despair for a minute or two, but that didn't mean she would be going without her warm morning cup. She trekked out into the downpour in her rainjacket with hopes of finding a warm hearth.

Not five minutes later she found herself once again at De Blaffende Vis. It really was the cutest little café. She took a seat in the cozy upper level and ordered a cup of fresh mint tea, a beverage new to her life that she had now made a regular part of her café circuit.

She sat peacefully in the little brown café, wood surrounding her everywhere around, below and under her. When she'd drained her first glass, they offered her a refill of hot water. With her second glass she realized that her stomach was rumbling, so she paid at the bar and headed back home to make lunch, taking a roundabout route that passed by the Brouwersgracht, one of the prettiest canals in the city, in her opinion. At the moment it wasn't raining, so Clara took her time. She wandered slowly home on the bricked streets, making a point to stop at every other bench just to adore the water passing by. So far, Clara was exhilarated by the Dutch spring. Daffodils popped up everywhere, in any open space, almost as if someone had come by in a truck and just thrown handfuls of bulbs out onto random parcels of grass throughout the city. The yellow and white flowers blossomed along the canals, lined the streets, rose sweetly between the train lines, and spotted the fields of grazing cattle—and this didn't even include the actual fields of daffodils. It was amazing.

Next came the irises. It was currently iris season and bunches of the elegant flowers graced the city. There were purple ones, yes, but also yellow ones, which she had never before seen, spontaneously blooming from the edges of the smaller, less traveled canals.

There was something about the water here that just made everything so peaceful. Now that she had spent time in a country with water like this, she couldn't imagine going back. The rainless summers of the Sacramento Valley seemed so harsh compared to the moist freshness of every morning, afternoon, and night here in Holland.

When she first moved to Jordaan, she'd found it so quiet that it was almost unnerving. The bicycles replaced the cars, and besides the clank of a broken kickstand or the ding of a bell, it was just... quiet. There were many, many pedestrians, constantly walking together, sometimes arm in arm, sometimes in groups, but they didn't chatter loudly like she remembered them doing in Sacramento. It was possible that she was just spellbound by this new nation, but she really remembered even the people being louder in the U.S. Added to all this was the constant flow of water, not really making any noise, but comforting and relaxing all the same. There was really no other place like it. She hoped someday she would be able to walk arm in arm with someone down this very street.

Clara soon turned down her street and walked up the stone steps to her home. She noticed Ellie sitting in her apartment on the first floor. The Dutch often left their curtains open, revealing huge windows into their lives. Still, she had a feeling this didn't mean it was permissible to look in the windows. She really *tried* not to look, but she was so intrigued that it was sometimes difficult for her.

She clicked the door open and headed past Ellie's door up the tall, narrow wooden staircase. It creaked with each step, but so did every other Dutch staircase. She liked that; it made her feel like she lived in a place with history, a place with a past.

Just moments after she got home and settled into a chair with a snack and a book, her phone rang.

"Hellllllllooooo!" Krista called and Clara heard her own laughter echo over the Skype airways.

"Krista! It's been so long."

"Yeah it has!" she responded, "What have you been up to? Traveling? Sightseeing? Museums? Swimming in the canals? Are those clean, by the way?"

"Um, well I haven't really been doing much. I went out for tea this morning."

"Wow," she replied dryly, "Aren't you livin' on the edge. Tea? That's all you've got?"

"Well, I don't think that people really swim in the canals."

"What about museums? Cows? Cheese? Are you getting out at all?" Krista's voice was raising and the volume rising. Clara grinned as she felt a lecture coming on. "You're in western Europe! Take a trip! Hop a train and go to Paris!"

"I'm getting out plenty, Krista. Seriously, you have nothing to worry about. Now what have you been up to? Reviewed anything good lately? Broken anyone's heart or shattered their reality?"

"Oh, yeah- well, no, but I saw a *horrific* business plan the other day for an Italian restaurant. It was actually going to be called, 'Oh Spaghetti Oh!' Can you believe that shit?!"

Clara scoffed a laugh. "Who would call their restaurant Oh Spaghetti Oh?"

"Nobody Italian, that's for sure. Ugh, I hate bad Italian," Krista said. "Nothing is worse than spending the night burping marinara and picking rosemary from in between your teeth.

"Yuck. Thanks for that, but oh, I do miss you, Krista," she cried, "I don't know if it's just because, or because of the traumatizingly vivid mental pictures you create in my mind. I practically choked on my sea salt and rosemary crackers."

"You're eating rosemary crackers right now? Really?"

"Yeah. Weird, huh?"

"Definitely. I miss you too, Clare. As happy as I am that you got out of here and began your life of sitting around and doing nothing in Holland, I mean..." Krista trailed off. "It's at least nice that you're there sitting on your ass and not here."

"Hey! I am pregnant, you know."

"Whatever, you can't play that card yet."

"Why not!?"

"You're like a month pregnant."

"Almost two months."

"Whatev- You're probably not even having cravings or mood swings yet. Call me when you start crying in public."

"You are so insensitive!"

"Hardly. I just tell it as it is bee-atch."

At this, Clara couldn't help but laugh again. "Oh, Krista."

"I know. What would you do without me?"

They both sighed.

"It is just a bit lonely here," said Krista. Clara felt a tug in her chest. It would be so nice to have a good friend here with her. Krista continued, "No one doing ridiculously unselfish and wasteful things, no one to lecture about getting some balls."

Clara laughed in spite of the list of criticisms. She could always count on Krista to ruin a potentially special moment by insulting her.

"Well, I'll let you know," she joked. "I'm sure there's something stupid or too passive or mopey that I've been doing or that I'm about to do that you would just love to lecture me about."

"No doubt," Krista laughed.

"Actually, I do have something funny to tell you."

"Yeah? What?"

"I told my parents about the baby."

"Yeah?" Her voice raised and Clara could tell she was dying to know her mother's reaction.

"You're gonna like this. I was in kind of a weird, rebellious mood that day, so I just sent them all—my parents and Delia—a text that said, 'whoopsbaby.'"

After a short pause Krista responded, "Uh...I have no idea what that means."

"It's what Delia and I always said our mother didn't want us to have in high school. I know, it was kind of in poor taste, but I couldn't think of a better way to tell them, so I thought, what the hell."

"No," said Krista, and Clara could practically hear the approval. "That's actually pretty good, especially for you. You're not usually one to joke about serious things. I'm kind of impressed. So what'd they say?"

"Uh, well, I don't know."

"What do you mean?"

"Well, they haven't responded yet."

"They haven't said *anything*!? When did you tell them?"

"Last night."

"Last night!? You crazy, pregnant woman."

She waited for Krista to continue, probably making a list of ways Clara could be more self-confident and ballsier, as Krista liked to say, specifically toward her mother.

"You know," Krista began again, "it's quite amazing how good this change has been for you. You're different there, you're just... a different you, *just* you, maybe." Clara felt strange hearing someone assess her life like this, even Krista. It read like a third party observation. "But not just you. The you of the past, the Clara that is my best friend..." she paused again, "the Clara before Jack."

There was a minute or two and Clara felt her cheeks reddening. Was she blushing? Is that how rare it was for her to be complimented? Was this a compliment?

"Thanks, Krista."

Krista made a noncommittal hmph, "I call it as I see it."

Clara smiled.

"So," said Krista, "get laid yet?"

"Krista!" she howled, "I am pregnant!"

"So? No man's gonna know that and you can't once you're walking around like the Stay Puft Marshmallow Man, so you might as well give it a try now."

"Ah!" Clara gasped. "You are *so* mean!"

Krista laughed. "So when should I come over? You could be my wingwoman."

"You're going to come over!?" Clara shrieked.

"Dear Lord," said Krista, "hormonal pregnant woman," she mumbled under her breath. "Of course I'll come! But I'd like to make it known that I'm not comin' unless I can hand-deliver your divorce papers, so you'd better get on that..."

"Are you *bribing* me to get a divorce?"

"Hell yeah, I am. I don't want to lose this Clara now that I've got her. Screw Jack. He screwed you."

Clara laughed. "True," she said, smiling, "true."

"Shit, is it already 8:12? I've gotta go. I've got a date coming in like 10 minutes, and I'm still in my sweats."

"A date? Who?"

"Tell you later. Bye!"

"Bye!"

Clara smiled and settled back in her chair. She made a mental note to go to the bookstore later. She needed to pick up a few books on Dutch history and modern-day culture. She didn't know much and if there was any chance that she would be having visitors—she smiled at the thought—then she needed to bone up on her Dutch trivia.

She felt happy to have made Krista happy. It made her feel proud in a daughter to mother kind of way. She was sure she would regret it later when her own mother finally understood the message, but for now she felt quite cheerful about it all.

There was one thing nagging at her, and of course it was Jack. She knew she ought to tell him, too, but she couldn't fathom it yet. She was sure that she couldn't make *that* one a text.

She got up and headed for the kitchen to make dinner, but eventually decided she was in need of both groceries and a cup of hot chocolate. After picking up her groceries she retreated to Dolphins for a nice cup of hot chocolate. She found her way there without a problem, and set her bag at her usual table by the door.

She had been practicing, and was hoping to order *warme chocolademelk* in Dutch today. Of course, she would still have to say, *I would like* in English, but she was making progress.

"Hi!" Clara chirped.

"Hello again," the waitress replied. It was the same woman who had been there the first day.

"Could I have a *warme chocolade*?" Clara asked. The waitress smiled politely at her attempt at Dutch.

"Yes, of course," she said, "very nice Dutch."

Clara smiled back at her even though she knew she was lying.

"It's nice to see you again," the woman told her.

"You have very good hot chocolate, I mean- warme chocolade."

The woman laughed. "Thank you. I have been making warmechocolademelk here for a while, I suppose. I'm Jantine."

"I'm Clara. It's nice to meet you."

Jantine went about making the hot chocolate and then presented it to Clara. "Alstublieft. Here you go."

"Thank you... Sorry, how do you say thank you?"

"Dank u," replied Jantine.

"What?" said Clara. Whatever Jantine had just said sounded almost exactly like *thank you*.

"*Dank u*." Jantine repeated, more slowly. "You can also say simply, *dankje*."

"Well, thanks- I mean, donk ya."

"Alsjeblieft, Clara. Anytime."

Clara took her hot chocolate back to her seat and to her people watching.

"Dank u," she said again in a low voice. "Warme chocolademelk." Two down, only a bajilion to go. Still, you had to start somewhere.


twaalf - twelve

The sound of a ringing computer woke Clara up the next morning. She groaned as she realized it was three in the morning,

She sat up and clicked Answer.

"Clara? Clara? Hello? It's your mother."

*Was it Wednesday? Hadn't it been Wednesday yesterday? And why did she pick up at three in the morning? She must be insane.*

"Hi, Mom. What's up?" she asked in an annoyed tone.

"What's- Up?!" her mother howled back at her. "Oh, I don't know, my eldest daughter has decided to desert her family and friends and move to a foreign country... Oh- and she's *pregnant*. What the hell are you thinking!? You're pregnant! I don't care what Jack did or said. You need to go back to your husband and give your child a decent chance at a family. And why didn't you answer my phone call on Wednesday!? You know it's this kind of tradition that keeps a mother and daughter relationship strong."

*Yeah, right,* thought Clara. "No." She shouted at her computer screen. "I'm not going back to him. He's an asshole."

"Don't you swear at me, young lady."

"I wasn't-"

"You just watch your mouth," she continued. "This is your mother. Have you forgotten?"

"This is my life. Have *you* forgotten?" Clara asked.

"It's not just your life anymore, Clara. Your choices are affecting someone else, someone who will depend on you wholly."

"Mom," she said, mostly unpatronizingly, "I know."

"Well, it doesn't seem like it. Now you get on a plane right now and come back home. I'll go over to Jack's this weekend and start setting up the nursery."

"No!"

"What do you mean, no?"

"Did you hear what you just said?! 'Over to Jack's'? It's not even my house! You know that. I know that. He knows that."

"Well, it takes two to make a baby and it takes two to raise a baby, so you're just going to have to-"

"He cheated on me!"

"Oh, Clara, do you even know that for sure?"

"Yes! He wrote me a letter and told me!"

"I'd hardly call that a letter."

"How do you know what it said!?"

"I know that Krista told me it was a note-"

"Well, Krista didn't see it either." Clara hadn't shown the note to anyone and wasn't planning on *ever* showing it to anyone. In fact, for whatever masochistic reason, she kept the note in the inside pocket of her purse, with her at all times and hidden from everyone else.

"Did you know that he cheated on me once in college, too?" Clara asked. This at least made her mother pause, and she let the silence ride out, hoping she could hold off her mother's bossy commentary for at least a minute or two. "Way back at the beginning... I forgave him that time. I hated him for it and it took years before I was able to really let it go, but I guess the love persevered," she stated sarcastically. "At the time, it was worth the risk for me- the hope that he really was the one for me..."

*The one for her*, she reflected, the thing that every girl wanted—every woman, every girlfriend, every wife. "So now it's my turn. And maybe I don't know if it's the right or wrong decision," Clara shouted defensively towards the computer, she should really get a headset, "at least *I* am making the decision. At least I don't feel horrible about myself. Just about him. And I'm fine with that. And you should be too," she added. "I don't think that's really too much to ask. It would be nice if you would accept my decision... And if you can't, then at least stop going against me. Just leave me alone."

"Fine." Her mother's response came quicker than Clara thought it would, but more was coming, as she expected. "I'll leave you alone, but when that baby hates her mother for the stable life she could have had... Well, don't come crying to me."

Clara let her exhale be heard through the phoneline and across the ocean. It's not like she had been expecting anything different.

"Now, while we're at it,"

"At what?" asked Clara.

"Tscsh," her mother shushed her, "Now while we're at it, young lady, there is a right and wrong time to use text messages, and letting your family know that you are pregnant is *not* an appropriate time. I didn't even know what you were talking about! Delia had to call and explain it to me. Thank goodness for your sister!"

*Great*, thought Clara, *she couldn't wait to get into all the reasons why Delia was a better daughter than she was.*

"You know your sister agrees with me about this," her mother yammered on matter-of-factly. "She agrees that you are acting totally illogically."

"Of course she does," Clara shot back, though she was a little hurt by the word *illogically*. She herself thought it quite logical that she should finally choose herself over someone else. "How many times do I have to say it?! Delia loves Jack! She loves him so much *she* should marry him."

"Well, she has good reason. He has always supported you well."

"What!? Like I didn't have a job?"

"Oh, don't be dramatic, Clara. You know what I mean."

"No, actually, I don't. How exactly did he support me…? Financially? Emotionally? *Physically?*" she muttered to herself.

"Well, he let you live in that beautiful house. What about that? I'd say that was quite generous of him."

"It was generous of him to let me—his wife—stay in his house. Uh, okay."

"You used to be so reasonable, Clara. What happened to you? I should send your baby sister over there to straighten you out."

Clara snorted. "Great. Sounds lovely, I'm sure my *baby sister* could fill me in on where I went wrong."

"I think she could," said her mother, the resounding clunk of the hang-up echoing in her computer speakers.

Clara thought about going back to bed, but elected to work on her apartment instead, thinking it more useful. She stood up and pulled at her hair. *Ugh, her mother.*

She looked around the room, her luggage now half unpacked and half spread all over the apartment, and ran her fingers through her hair fitfully, *Ugh.* She badly needed a haircut, too. Her to-do list was getting longer every second. At least she was now showering on a daily basis.

She stretched and tried to push her mother's words out of her head. She considered trying to organize her belongings, but it was too early to be productive or logical, so she gave up for the moment.

After searching through her cluttered suitcase for a few minutes, she found what she was looking for and pulled out an old school hot water bottle. She boiled enough water to fill both it and a cup of tea and snuggled into her chair. Once comfortable and warm, she at last allowed her thoughts to swarm freely around her.

She took a sip. First, Jack.

She hadn't talked to him since the last night, but should she have? She knew it was possible to fully complete the divorce process without speaking, and this was 100 percent her plan. She hadn't yet decided her plan with regards to the baby. She probably should tell him, it was the decent thing to do. Except that he had left her a note telling her to leave their house so he could shack up with some bimbo—that certainly wasn't decent.

*Was she making the right decision?*

*Of course she was.* She nodded to herself, he had told her to leave. Even if she wanted her child to have a real father, she was sure that he didn't want to be the father. She had made the right decision.

Back then, after his first indiscretion, she probably hadn't made the right decision... back then, the first time he'd wronged her. *Or...*

She thought back to that night, the horrible, horrible night after his confession.

*Clarie*, he'd begun, *there's something I need to tell you.*

She shuddered, remembering how she had pulled away from his hand on her forearm, how she had recoiled from his touch but at the same time wanted him to hold her and comfort her like she never had before. The smell of burning butter and pesto singed her thoughts. She had been making him dinner, live pasta with butter and pesto. No special occasion, just a nice dinner for her potential husband. Needless to say, dinner had been ruined. Destroyed.

She shook her head, trying to push the harsh memories away. She reached her hand down and groped under her chair for the pack of stroopwafels she'd stashed there the day before. Nothing like a ridiculous treat to pull you through. She couldn't help but feel better as she pried apart two of the caramel waffle sandwiches. The sun had melted them a little and the caramel had oozed out the edges, cementing them together. Another warm sip. Now back to the pity party.

She had punished Jack for months after that. She'd stopped doing favors for him, ignored him when she got home. She'd shown him what an asshole he'd been.

*Hadn't she?*

She paused to get another half of a stroopwafel, breaking it perfectly in half along the sugary waffle lines.

Now it just seemed like she'd ignored him for a few months before forgiving him. Had she really punished him at all?

Now that she reconsidered it the punishment seemed much less like a punishment at all. It seemed, she shook her head sadly at herself, like she had just given him some space.

*Could she do anything right?* She pulled at her hair again, trying to shove out the insecurities. *No, she was making the right decision now.*

She had left and she had not spoken a word to him, thus preventing her from feeling any remorse. This had to be the right decision. Before she could finish off the package, she twisted shut the crisp plastic wrapping and bent the tiny gold fastener back in place.

*But was her mother right? Was it too much to ask to take the high road for herself when someone else would soon depend on her for everything?*

Maybe she wasn't pregnant after all. Maybe the last two months were just a bad dream.

Perhaps it was time for her to make some decisions. *How long should she stay here? Should she be booking a flight home? What would happen when summer was over and she was not getting a regular paycheck? What would happen when her employment officially ended, and her insurance with it? How long could she last until she was just being ridiculous, acting heedlessly and without logic when she was growing a new person inside her?*

There it was again, logic. But what was logic at all when the heart was involved? ...when her heart hurt so badly, simultaneously for and against Jack?

Both her heart and the pit of her stomach ached and churned on an hourly basis. The decisions and indecision swirled recklessly in her head until she awoke in a sweat, breathing hard and feeling very, very alone. She turned away from the dull morning light and hid her head from the world.


### dertien - thirteen


Ultimately, she must have fallen soundly asleep because she woke up to a beam of sunshine blasting through her window. She was still on her chair, but wrapped in an old Sac State sweatshirt she had grabbed off the floor at some point during the night. She peeled it off, stretched, and inhaled deeply, breathing in the fresh air spilling through the open window.

*What was that?* The scent slipping in her window was... intoxicating. It smelled familiar, like something warm and happy, something relaxing.

The beach! She could smell the ocean. The ocean breeze was pouring in her open window. This was quite unexpected, and a wonderful surprise. Really, this breeze was probably the reason for her deep morning sleep. There was something about salty ocean air that just put her right to sleep, a peaceful and rejuvenating sleep.

She immediately grabbed her guidebook. Yes, she would definitely find the water today, beach or no beach, warm or chilly, she wanted more of this luscious, salty air.

With the help of a tram, a train, and 45 minutes, Clara found herself basking in the sun on a huge beach in a place called Zandvoort. Among families, groups of friends, and a shocking number of topless women, at least by American standards, Clara relaxed the day away. She got lunch at one of the little yellow-painted beach pavilions lining the beach, bought fries at a pink one in the afternoon, and got a sandwich and a juice for the ride home at yet another. It was a perfect day at the beach, particularly by Northern California standards. While it was no Santa Cruz, the sun was warm enough for her to stay out all day in a tank and shorts without a care in the world. Best of all, Clara had managed to pass the day away without stress. There was no doubt about it, the sun had simply evaporated her early morning worries.

When she got home that evening, she found Ellie sitting on a bench outside the front steps of her house.

"Hallo, Ellie! How are you doing?" she called out cheerfully.

"Hallo. I am well, thank you, and you?"

"I'm great! I was just at the beach!"

"Nice," said Ellie with a neat smile. "It was a lovely day for the beach."

"Definitely," replied Clara. Just then, she noticed that Ellie was not alone. On the steps behind her sat a young, brown-haired man listening quietly to their interaction.

"Clara," Ellie began, "my son will be taking a trip to America next month. You are from California, that is correct?"

Clara nodded, "Yes, Sacramento," she confirmed.

"Wonderful." Ellie continued, "Would you mind if Lars asked you a few questions about his upcoming travels?"

Clara looked from Ellie to Lars and back again and smiled. *Could she answer a few questions for this young, handsome Dutchman that was just barely in her age range? I think so.* She tried not to blush as she remembered Krista's final inquiry.

"Of course!" she responded, "Please come in," she beckoned towards her stairs.

She followed him up the narrow wooden staircase. He was well-dressed, wearing brown pants that had a crisp fit. His brown suede coat was handsome in a way that made her want it for herself.

He let her pass when they reached her door at the top of her stairs, guiding her with his hand but not touching her.

She smiled at him timidly and focused on opening her door without fumbling too much. When he followed her into the apartment she realized that he was tall, much taller than she was, and much taller than Jack as well.

He swiftly removed his light scarf—*How was it that Dutch men could pull off wearing a handsome scarf like that when she hardly could?* While he removed his jacket, she stole a look at his face. His cheeks were pink as if maybe he, too, had spent the day at the beach. His eyes were brown like his hair, which was far too long with much too much gel. Nonetheless, somehow she still found him attractive.

Something about the way these Dutch men used hair gel was just backwards. The rules for usage were completely the opposite of what she considered normal. When their hair was short, they kept it natural. It had to reach a certain length before hair gel could be applied. She wasn't sure if she could pinpoint a length exactly; it was more a look. Does the hair look like it's more than just a little shaggy? Okay, now time for the hair gel. They smear pomade or gel into it and then slick it backwards. Come to think of it, it was probably made easier by their constant bicycle riding. The breeze just kept it flowing back.

"How long are you going for?" she asked Lars, pulling herself back to her guest.

"Not too long, just four weeks."

*Four weeks?* Clara thought, that sure sounded like a long vacation to her. "Nice," she commented politely. "And do you have any idea where you would like to go? I mean, do you have your plane ticket yet?" She was a little worried that she had been recruited to plan a trip across the U.S.

"Yes," he said. "I fly in and out of San Francisco."

"Oh." She could work with this. "Great! I love San Francisco. Where else are you hoping to go?"

"Well, we would like to visit some of the National Parks.

101

Yosemite looks very beautiful and also Death Valley National Park. Next we would drive through Las Vegas and then drive up to Colorado and then visit Yellowstone National Park. If there is still time, we would like to visit Portland and possibly Seattle."

Clara stared at him in awe. He certainly didn't need *her.*

"What do you think, Claartje? Does this seem like a reasonable trip for four weeks?"

"What?" *Clartcha? What had he called her?* "Um, uh." She tried to run through the places in her head again. She had been to most of them, not Colorado, but everywhere else, but she had no idea how much time it would take to visit this string of places. Furthermore, she had no idea what a four-week vacation would be like.

"Are you going alone?" she changed the subject to get a little more thinking time.

"No, I am going with three friends."

"Oh, wow. Fun!" She took a deep breath. "Okay, let's see. Are you camping or staying in hotels?"

"We are camping."

Forty-five minutes, two cups of coffee and a laughably interesting map drawn on a steno pad and Lars was picking up his jacket to go.

"Clara, Claartje, thank you very much for your help. I am even more excited to go now. You know a lot about California—especially Northern California."

"Well, I lived there my whole life." *It's all she knew, actually.* "I am very happy to help."

"Well, you were very helpful! And thank you very much for the coffee."

"You're welcome." She stood up and walked with the charming young Dutchman to the door. He was reaching for the door handle when she suddenly realized what was happening.

"Wait, Lars?"

"Yes?"

"Do you, um, have any recommendations for me? In

Amsterdam or in Holland in general?"

"Oh! Yes, of course. I have lived here my whole life, too!" They chuckled together and Lars returned to the chair he had left not fifteen seconds before. "What do you like to do? Where have you been?"

"Well, I, I," she stumbled over her words. She hadn't been anywhere. "I only know Amsterdam so far."

Lars gave her an understanding nod, "Yes, this is not all that unusual. Many visitors see only Amsterdam. But now," he said with more spirit, "I will give you some general recommendations." Lars picked up the pad of paper and started to write. "Delft is very nice. You know the typical Dutch blue and white dishes?"

Clara nodded.

"They come from Delft. Leiden is a nice town, a university town." He continued to write notes as he explained." In Den Haag, The Hague, there is a very nice beach. Maastricht is also a very nice city, but that's not actually in Holland.

"Not in Holland? What country is it in?"

Lars laughed, "Oh, it's in this country. It's in The Netherlands, but *Holland* is different from the Netherlands. Holland refers to the provinces of North and South Holland. Right now, we are in North Holland, but the city of Leiden, for example, is in South Holland."

"Really?" Clara had no idea where Leiden was, but she knew she had thus far lived her whole life thinking that the two names were interchangeable. "Wow."

"Yes, it is a common misconception."

"Oh, Lars? Is there any place I can go to tour the flower fields?"

"You like the flowers?"

"Yes, of course."

"Well, the best place to go is to the Keukenhof."

"The what?"

"The Keukenhof. It's a very large flower garden near Lisse. You can go by train to Leiden and then by bus to the park. I will write down the instructions. You should go soon, because the season is almost over and the garden will close."

"Okay."

"And I will tell my mother she must keep you informed in the future."

"Oh, she doesn't have to…"

"Also, if you haven't, you should visit the AnneFrankhuis. It is a very interesting and informative museum and is very close. You can walk there in ten minutes."

"It's that close?"

"Yes, just down the street. There is now an additional section as well as the original house. It is well done. I recommend it."

"Okay. Thank you."

Lars stood to go, and Clara rose to walk him to the door for a second time.

"It's Remembrance Day this week. I believe it would be very interesting for you to go to the AnneFrankhuis before Remembrance Day. Did my mother give you a list of the national holidays?"

"No, but don't worry. You don't have to talk to your mother…" Clara didn't want Ellie thinking that she was complaining about her.

"Of course I will," Lars said frankly. "It is always nice to have information, and she can provide it to you."

With that he leaned forward and kissed her on alternating cheeks three times to say goodbye. She blushed and shut the door quickly behind him, praying that he hadn't noticed. She turned back to her apartment and felt a girly smile spread involuntarily across her face. Lars couldn't possibly imagine how long it had been since a man's lips had touched her cheek.

## viertien - fourteen

*First things first,* Clara thought as she considered her day over Speculoos and Nutella toast the next morning. She must see this flower garden before it closed for the season. It wasn't exactly tulip season anymore. What if all she saw were dying plants and the wilting blossoms of what had been a beautifully designed flower garden? A flower deathbed wasn't going to help her often fragile state of loneliness and despair. Lars had assured her that it looked nice throughout the whole season, but she was still nervous that she'd missed it.

Clara followed Lars' instructions, which she had read over religiously the night before. It was funny how it had happened. She had filled him in on what to do in California and the western United States, and then suddenly, when he was on his way out the door, he was telling her all about this beautiful flower garden and chastising his mother for not having given her directions to the Anne Frank house.

She took the train from Amsterdam to Leiden, which appeared to be a small, likeable town, but continued on toward the buses. There was no time to look around today. Just outside the train station she spotted a giant poster of flowers marking a busstop. *Keukenhof,* the bus said. She paid for her ticket and hopped on the bus, which was already nearly full.

The bus soon drove away from the station down bikepath-flanked streets outlined by traditional brick facades. In minutes they were in the country and traveling quickly across the starkly flat, green landscape. The parking lot they pulled into 20 minutes later was practically full. Tour buses lined the edges while cars, trucks, bicycles, and motorcycles constantly cycled in and out, staying or sometimes dropping people off.

There were half a dozen lines, each with a few people. There were families and children, but also a mass of elderly visitors, often in wheelchairs, at times moving together in intimidating numbers. It was the sheer quantity of people that surprised her most.

Just inside the front gate a fountain projected a perfect

sphere of water. She quickly walked past it but came to an abrupt halt just ten steps later. She was surrounded. To her left, to her right, in front of her—in all directions there were flowers—and not just tulips. The magnificent colors around her almost made her head spin. She walked forward quickly; every path was perfect. There was a path of blue on her left, a flowing stream made entirely of periwinkle blue hyacinths. Around the winding stream, the river banks were patterned with orange and yellow and pink and red and purple. She continued along the path to find herself surrounded by a garden of waist high tulips—red, orange and red, yellow and red, white and red. Now there was an actual stream. The banks of the calm brook were again decorated in hundreds, thousands of flowers.

There were many tulips, thousands really, but there were also daffodils, hyacinths, and lilies of all varieties and colors, plus others that she couldn't identify and would likely never be able to identify.

Everywhere she looked the garden was perfect. The vibrant colors were coordinated as if following a color scheme of the week. This week it was based on a dignified shade of maroon. The heights were perfect, tiny annuals and perennials bordering a grand centerpiece of colorful, bobbing blossoms.

Some areas had four foot high irises or monstrous tulips, or even strange yellow and white flowers that somehow reminded her of pineapples. She was about to hyperventilate she was walking so fast, trying desperately to take it all in. She found herself a bench and sat down, catching her breath and trying to get a hold of her emotions. She hadn't expected this, hadn't expected to be so overwhelmed.

Following ten deep breaths, she raised her head. There in front of her were gold stars marking tiny patches of colorful tulips. Donald Duck, these were called, and those, Marilyn Monroe. Princess Diana, she smiled, they did somehow remind her of Princess Diana.

Clara turned again and saw she was near a pavilion of some kind where visitors were sipping cappuccinos and eating apple pie and chocolate cake. She turned back and walked towards a railing across from her bench, and found herself looking at a mural made entirely of flowers. The theme for the year was Russia. The colorful minarets of Saint Petersburg were made of dozens of types of flowers, the colors twisting upwards to create the smooth and even lines of the spires.

All she could see was perfection. The grass was lushly green and the trees were in blossom; how could they possibly keep this up? She examined the flower bed, looking closely. There were empty stems, she could see, but they were perfectly trimmed. The leaves remained, although the blossoms were long gone.

In many cases the crisp, green tulip leaves still played a role, acting as foliage or background for some new splashes of color. Still below these were more buds. There were hundreds of buds, she now saw. Flowers upon flowers were waiting below in the wings, just days away from their turn to be a star.

Lars was right, there was nothing to worry about; it was perfect. How could she even have doubted?

Some areas had just one color that seemed to go on for miles; others had five or six types of flowers, creating a rainbow of color. If she focused on just one type of flower, she found them to be perfectly spaced throughout the enormous flower patch. Sometimes the flower beds themselves created shapes or pictures.

Other areas were all one color, yellow perhaps, but all shades of yellow, all heights of flower, all shapes of blossoms and petals. The effect was astounding. When she thought she might not be able to take anymore—emotionally, at least—she found herself standing in front of an ice cream cart. Handmade vanilla ice cream, it said. She purchased a cone and sat down on a bench to enjoy the rich and creamy vanilla taste.

As she licked, she watched the people walk by. She didn't feel self-conscious at all; it seemed that many, if not most, people were in this trancelike state.

Beyond her quaint wooden ice cream cart she was soon distracted by a long ribbon of flowers. The path of three types of flowers was like a prism, spanning from yellow to red to purple and back to a pale yellow, almost white.

Whoever did this was an artist.

The four foot wide stripe continued down the edge of the property as far as she could see. She took another delicious vanilla lick and turned. What was outside the property?

She should have known.

Fields of flowers surrounded the property. It was then that Clara actually began to cry. As she stumbled blubbering towards the old-fashioned windmill, she let the impressiveness of her surroundings overcome and wash over her.

She followed the flow of visitors, young and old, into the windmill and up the stairs. There were informational signs adorning the walls, but she didn't care. She had no desire to learn about windmills right then, not when she knew what was coming, not when she knew what she would see when she reached the upper level of the old wooden structure.

The blades of the windmill were moving. Its white painted slats turned swiftly with the constant breeze rolling in from the ocean across the perfectly flat Dutch landscape. Past that, for miles and miles, she saw fields of flowers. They were purple and yellow and red. In the distance, she saw white and pink as well and perhaps a light blue on the horizon. She was momentarily distracted by movement in the field and realized that the flower fields were surrounded by waterways. She looked down to see a dozen people loading onto a long flat boat. They were going on a boat ride through the tulip fields.

Clara stood there for as long as she could handle it, the random tear still running down her cheek. This was worth it, she thought. This sight, these fields, were worth the plane trip over. They were worth the struggle of being alone and worth the weekly Wednesday night scolding from her mother. In fact, this garden—the Keukenhof—might just be worth a divorce. That's how beautiful it was.

## vijftien - fifteen

That night Clara dreamed of colors and shapes and a fresh breeze carrying the scent of tulips. She awoke the next morning feeling at ease. She might be a little lost and a little pregnant, but since high school she had wanted to travel, and now she had done it; she was here in Holland. That dream above all others was one that she had filed away in the "Not gonna happen" category. She had accomplished something big, and now she had nowhere to go but up.

Happily gathering her bag and a book, she headed out into the sunny morning for a long walk around the city, still relishing her one accomplished goal as she pondered the adorable Dutch rooflines and watched families strolling hand in hand up and down the cobblestone shopping street. The plaza, or plein, she supposed, was dotted with artists and performers as usual.

*What else had she wanted?*

She wandered across Leidseplein and looked for a certain dark-haired girl, a young woman about her age whose paintings Clara adored. In watercolor, the girl painted canal scenes and Dutch rowhouses, bicycles and cloudy Dutch skies—nearly always Amsterdam street scenes. Whenever Clara found the girl, she stayed to watch her for a few minutes, and she did the same today.

Watching the young artist vend her wares was invigorating for Clara. The bright colors the girl used, the precise, black outlining; it made Clara crave painting.

On her first visit she bought a small painting for her apartment, and each time she passed through the square she found herself coming back for more.

The woman herself was intriguing as well. Her facial expressions shifted as she painted. Sometimes she scrunched her forehead, other times she bit her lip in critical self-examination. Clara could tell she was working hard. When she was selling she looked blissfully happy, as if all her dreams had come true standing here alone on this Amsterdam square, making a living twenty Euros at a time.

It was at this moment that Clara first played with an idea, remembering that once upon a time, it wasn't just looking at beautiful artwork that gave her a thrill. She had loved sketching, painting, and creating her own artwork as well. She had never really done anything spectacular, but as an art teacher, she did have a solid background in most mediums. But she hadn't painted for herself in so long.

A half hour later, rain began to fall and she made a sharp turn back towards her favorite hot chocolate café. Two minutes later she was hopping the steps to Dolphins. She was really making this quite a tradition.

"Hi!" she called to Jantine as she stepped in the door.

"Hello, Claartje," Jantine welcomed her. "You're looking rather energetic today."

"Well, yes, I am thinking about becoming an artist." She smiled with pride, feeling that it was rather ballsy of her to just outright make this statement.

"Nice. Have you been to the *fawn hoke* museum?"

"Uh-" A terrible sound had just come from Jantine's mouth and Clara had no idea what to make of it.

Jantine looked at her with a puzzled look on her face. "*Van hoch?*" she repeated, "the Dutch artist. He is actually very famous."

"Uh-" Clara felt like an idiot. This was her reward for a moment of confidence. *An artist? Doubtful.*

"He painted 'Starry Night,'" said Jantine.

Before Clara could stop herself, she spoke, "Van Gogh?" The light bulb went on. *Van Gogh!* And then the feeling of idiocy really settled in.

Someone had asked her a similar question the other day at the Rijksmuseum and she had been similarly confused. Now that she thought about it, Lars might have asked her the same thing. Their expression was always surprised when she said no, she wasn't familiar with this artist, as if they just assumed it was her first stop.

*What an idiot*, she thought to herself. Of course they

didn't pronounce it the same in Dutch and English. She tried to recover and at least make it into a learning experience.

"How do you say it?"

Jantine smiled at her indulgently, "*fawn... hoke.*"

Now that she knew what she was listening for, she could see that it was similar. The h in *hoke* and the k at the end were a bit throatier than any English speaker could ever make them, and *wow, they really bastardized the pronunciation in English*, but least now she noticed some resemblance.

Five minutes later she could produce a fairly reasonable Dutch pronunciation for Van Gogh, and she was happily sipping her hot chocolate. She could still be an artist, she just couldn't be a linguist.

Since it was still raining when she exited the café, she wandered for only a few minutes before taking refuge in another warm spot. She entered a cute Dutch eatery for a late lunch. After a few minutes browsing the menu, she found what she wanted. She decided to go all out and order a pancake, a pannekoek, like the ones her grandmother made.

"With powdered sugar," she requested, "and butter."

"Well, butter- of course," the old waiter smiled at her. "Coming right up."

The pannekoek was like nothing she'd ever tasted. Her grandmother's had been delicious, but this- this was buttery heaven on a plate.

When she got home that evening, Clara examined her luggage and found that as a former art teacher, she had very little art or art supplies to speak of. In total, she had a sketchpad that she had been using to jot down numbers, names and businesses—like a journal of sorts, and a pencil.

She found she also had a pin that said, "World's Best Artist." She'd received it from one of her fifth graders a few years before and had stashed it in her purse. She'd thought it sweet at the time. Well, she certainly was not an artist yet.

The next morning Clara decided that she would and could begin again. She wasn't expecting anything spectacular. Just an occupied mind would be a nice start. She made a quick and healthy decision and decided to spend the morning out on the town shopping for some art supplies. She was an art teacher. She had a strong enough background, she should use it. She would take another shot, make another run at a grand dream. There was no better time than now, when her life was already so drastically changed.

Clara started with a little art supply store she had walked by numerous times in the last several weeks. She walked down the narrow, cobbled street that would soon widen into the busy pedestrian shopping street. The store carried plenty to easily make a small kit.

When evening fell she began gradually with only a sketchbook and charcoals. She sketched the canal from her window, too timid, intimidated, and self-conscious to even go outside and sit at the edge of the canal with her sketchbook. She glanced down shyly at her work even in her own home. She wasn't confident enough to sit outside, knowing that a passerby might assume she was a real artist. She certainly couldn't work with strangers constantly looking over her shoulder.

She continued cautiously, and as if reverting to childhood, she found herself recreating some of her favorite art projects from her time teaching in Sacramento. In contrast to her days of teaching, she had fun making the projects herself rather than thinking about how to best help her students create them. She made coffee filter butterflies and used tissue paper pasted delicately into intricately cut black construction paper to create makeshift stained glass windows. Instead of the basic elementary school projects that she had guided her students in making for years, she found herself expanding them into huge endeavors. She soon started in on a hanging mural, a huge and colorful piece that would cover the wall all the way up to the high, Dutch ceiling.

She had never had so much fun in her life.

## zestien - sixteen

Clara awoke feeling refreshed, although she had been playing artist until nearly two o'clock in the morning.

After a cup of tea, she pulled out her sketchpad once again and began to play with her charcoals—her book, a coffee cup, and a pack of stroopwafels serving as a simple still life.

Her mind was astoundingly free of worry when she was working. She thought calmly through her week as she sketched the form and crosshatched patches of shadow.

Since Remembrance Day was the following day, Clara had booked a ticket for the Anne Frank house for later that afternoon. She also hoped to get a bicycle this week. Her hair was looking sadly raggedy, so that was on her list, too. Maybe she'd just cut it on her own. She could probably do that. There were many things to do, but at least she had all the time in the world to do them.

For whatever reason, this change—pretending to be an artist—was like emerging from a haze. Things were becoming clearer.

Half an hour before her appointed entrance time at the Anne Frank House, Clara set down her pencil and headed out the door.

She spent almost two hours at the museum wandering through the house and then reading and examining the artifacts in the newer portion of the museum.

First was the actual house, and as she stood in the closet of a room that had been Anne's, she felt a lump forming in her throat. Staring at Anne's pictures still pasted on the wall, now covered by a protective layer of glass, the heaviness of the emotional climate weighed down on her. So many of Anne's dreams were there in front of her, pasted magazine and newspaper cutouts of famous stars for everyone to see. It hit Clara hard when she realized what exactly it was that everyone was seeing. A thousand people probably witnessed this a day, all the young girl's dreams that hadn't come true.

They had one of Anne's many diaries there, too. Again it was seeing Anne's possessions that brought the story to life.

There they were, page after page of her words, spilling out as she tried and failed to be a normal girl and to live a normal girl's life. She had a dream that many other young girls had, to be an actress. But that would never come to be.

The young dreamer had been trapped in this house for how long? The bell of the nearby church the only reminder that the outside world lived on without her.

At the very end there were video recordings to watch—accounts told by those who knew Anne. One video was Anne's father; this one was the most painful of all. Otto Frank seemed like such a good man, but he had lost everything and everyone. Life seemed so unfair.

Clara paused to look at the church, The Westerkerk, as she stepped outside into the fresh outdoors. Just then, the bell rang. Anne had listened to these very same bells. Clara walked somberly home along the canals after the museum. She felt both physically and emotionally drained after the afternoon at the Frank house. It just made her life seem so easy.

Despite everything that she'd been through recently, it was truly nothing compared to what the family and those who worked to help them had lived through; it was nothing compared to what so many people went through. She vowed to enjoy her life more. Krista was right. She was currently living a dream life here in Holland. She might as well stop worrying and feeling sorry for herself and enjoy it.

As soon as she got home, she went back to her art, hoping that the rhythm of sketching, cutting, and pasting could clear the horrible pains from her mind and bring her back the peace she'd found the day before.

Eventually, she allowed herself to lose touch and get lost painting on square pieces of glass using her newly purchased colors. She used Georgia O'Keeffe and the Keukenhof as her inspiration, and created blossoms of hope.

The next day it was geometric drawings, straight lines intersecting and shades of colors blending and meshing. She painted on glass, on construction paper, and on the back of a roll of old wallpaper she discovered at a little home improvement store nearby.

She had now filled an eight-foot stripe which hung floor to ceiling on her wall. A painted square of glass was displayed in her bathroom window so that the soft Dutch light would glow through it each morning as she showered. It was her own personal stained glass window. She'd framed the watercolor of her artistic young Leidseplein muse, and it now hung prominently above her tiny dining room table.

It felt satisfying to decorate her new Amsterdam home. She really hadn't been able to do so since her college dorm room, and even then, Krista's various James Dean posters had taken up most of the space. With Jack, the place was already established as well. He had been living there for years, so there was an eclectic mix of pennants and posters, and a few old pictures from when Mrs. Sanden lived there, her beloved O'Keeffe petunia among them. She sighed, pushing thoughts of Jack away and returning to her new life.

Considering the lovely streak that she was on, the next morning Clara decided it was time to make the leap. It was bicycle day. Clara would spend the day searching for her very own Dutch cruiser. She really should ride a bike in Amsterdam before she got too pregnant. She could always resell it later.

Before she even left her building, she followed Lars' instructions and knocked on Ellie's door to ask for some practical advice, hoping Ellie would be able to direct her straightaway. Unfortunately Ellie was out, so Clara was forced to go it on her own.

She spent the next two days walking through the winding city streets, taking trams and buses to the far reaches of Amsterdam proper.

The first bike shop she found had a huge lineup of beautiful bicycles, shiny and new. She admired the bicycles, but left quickly before anyone could ask her if she needed help. There was no need for an unnecessary and awkward interaction and €800 was just not in her price range. After a stop at a bicycle repair shop that didn't really sell bicycles, she stopped at a nice, typical Dutch café.

She was now quite adept at selecting a café and deciding what she would order at said café. It was sort of a multi-level system of café appraisal.

Was the café brown, in other words, a typical Dutch brown café adorned in handsome smoke-stained wood? If it was, she would order a typical coffee drink. Coffee, a cappuccino, or a koffie verkeerd, a drink she had come to find was essentially a latte.

If the establishment wasn't a typical brown café, then she would continue the evaluation of its genre. Was it an Indian or Moroccan café? Was it hippie or new age? At the end of day two, still bicycle-less, Clara found herself in one such café. It had started to rain, and the colorfully painted Moroccan decor seemed to be the perfect opportunity to avoid a soaking. They served pots of mint tea on giant sequined pillows of red and green.

Sites like this one were excellent for people watching. Amsterdam had better people watching than any place she'd been in her life, San Francisco included. Besides the tourists from all over the world, there were immigrants from all over the world and people of all ages seemed to be out and about doing strange, or possibly normal, things every second of the day.

Brown cafés were good for watching the typical Dutch, old men chatting over newspapers and coffee, maybe a snifter of liquor if it was late enough in the day; old couples meeting their young daughter and her partner for a koffie verkeerd, new baby in tow. It was all so very interesting to Clara.

For day three of bike hunting, Clara decided she had better go the old-fashioned route. She headed back up to her apartment and wrote down every place in her Dutch phonebook that had to do with a *fiets*, a bicycle. She compiled a long list of bike shops and *tweede-hand* shops, or second-hand bike shops—at least that is what she assumed they were.

*Twee* meant two and, well, a hand is surely a hand, even in The Netherlands, so she figured that she was on the right track.

The first shop she came to was indeed a second-hand bike store. Overall, prices were better and there was a better variety of styles and sizes. Clara also saw something else worth noticing. There was a couple in the bicycle shop speaking with the owner, and the woman was pregnant—very pregnant. Clara watched as they talked with the store owner. The woman periodically rubbed her belly affectionately as they discussed, presumably, her new baby.

Eventually, there was a pause and the three of them headed over to another corner of the shop. There in the corner was a style of bicycle that Clara had not noticed until now. It was a family bicycle transport option she never could have imagined. She saw it as the Dutch equivalent of the wood-paneled station wagon. This option looked to be perfect for a bigger family. While the frame of the vehicle was still a bicycle, instead of the front wheel there was a giant wooden box with a wheel on either side. The tiny seatbelts showed that it could hold up to four children, an impressive bicycle taxi for children. There was a clear plastic cover that could be snapped onto the box to protect the children on rainy days, like a convertible, or perhaps more like a riding lawn mower converted to a snow blower.

The couple nodded along happily as the man explained the elaborate bike. Next the bicycle expert directed them to a small cart that could be pulled behind a bicycle. Now this, Clara had seen before. It was more or less the same as a typical U.S. child carrier, except in California it seemed to be used more frequently for small and useless dogs than for children. The Dutch couple didn't appear to appreciate it. They frowned at the little pull carrier and motioned the man forward.

The last and simplest option was to continue on as usual with a regular adult bicycle. By bolting a baby bike seat behind the front handle bars, infants could easily be accommodated. Apparently, once a baby was able to hold its head upright, it was ready for bicycle travel. Due to the rainy climate, the seat was equipped with a small plastic windshield and waterproof leg flaps to shelter the tiny passenger from rain. It all made sense. Why wouldn't you want the little one in front of you rather than behind you?

The whole experience was mind-boggling for Clara. She was learning so much—more than she thought she'd learn on a day out hopping from bike shop to bike shop.

After a few minutes, Clara realized that she had been outright staring at the couple the whole time she'd been there. She quickly busied herself with some of the more feminine-looking bicycle bags in her area when she saw the woman glance in her direction. The men now appeared to be discussing the parts and assembly of the newly purchased front baby seat. The wife wandered over toward the bike bag section of the shop, clearly uninterested in this segment of the discussion.

Clara glanced up at the woman again, intrigued by her situation.

"Hallo," said the woman.

"Hallo," said Clara.

"Nice," said the woman as she approached and noticed the colorful bicycle bag in Clara's hand.

*How did they do that?* Wondered Clara again. *Was her pronunciation of* hallo *really that bad?*

"I think I'll need the big size," joked the woman as she picked up a larger version of the bag Clara was holding.

"Yes," said Clara nervously, "Babies have a lot of stuff."

"Right," replied the woman with a knowing nod.

"Is this your first child?" asked Clara shyly.

"Yes," said the woman proudly. "The first."

"Excuse me," asked Clara, leaning forward shyly, "do you still ride a bicycle? I mean, do pregnant women ride a bicycle here, too?"

The woman laughed so loudly at Clara's timid question that the two men across the shop turned to look at them.

"Why, naturally!" said the woman. "We are people, too!"

"Yes," Clara responded seriously. She was all for women's rights—especially now. "But is it difficult?" she asked with interest. "It seems very hard. I'm... I'm pregnant too, you see."

The woman laughed again, but more kindly this time. "Well, yes, it is more difficult, but I have been biking for a very long time, so it is not a problem. And you? Do you cycle?"

"I'm looking for a bike right now, actually."

"I see. Well, good luck," said the woman as her husband waved at her from across the room and called out something in Dutch.

"Thanks," responded Clara. She left the store quietly and stepped out into the rain, disappointed that still, she had no bike. Surprisingly, it was much harder to find a decent bicycle than an apartment. She decided to return to Ellie for help. Ellie made a call, and instructed Clara to go to a bike shop just down the street early the next morning. There, a young man named Jens and a nice, blue and yellow women's bicycle would be awaiting her arrival.

*Oh, to be Dutch.*


## zeventien - seventeen

"So," Jens said when she arrived, nodding in greeting, "Claartje."

He said it like a sentence, and she wondered what was next.

"Jens, um. Mr. Jens, uh," *Why was she so damn awkward all the time? Had she always been like this?*

Jens had to laugh at her discomfiture, "Jens is fine. Actually, I'm a friend of Lars.' You know Lars, I presume?"

"Oh! Yes, I know Lars. He's very nice."

"Yes, he is. Lars is a very good friend of mine from secondary."

"Oh, really?"

"Yes. Lars and I go way back. But now-" his stern face reappeared, "Claartje." *Oh, dear, here we go again,* "Biking in Holland."

*Ahh, now she understood. The rules. This young man was going to teach her the rules.*

"First," he began officially, "remember that cycling in Holland is not the same as cycling in America. Please forget your previous assumptions," he requested politely and assertively. "It is different here, and it's best if you just do what we do and bike how we bike. You will be much better off."

"Okay," Clara nodded back at him.

"Basically, this means that you think of yourself as one among many. I think in America cyclists are special—very athletic and tough." Jens chuckled as he said this. "Here this is not true. If you don't bike, you are quite strange. Nearly everyone has a cruiser, a typical Dutch bicycle, and many people have another bicycle or two as well. If you want to ride fast, you can get a racing bike and go out in the country to ride. Racing bikes are not for the city," he laughed again, "Plus, you would have so many flat tires. Think of the cobblestone!" Clara laughed with him this time.

"A cruiser is nice because you sit straight up when you are biking. You use your legs and abdomen to propel yourself. Although it may seem slower at first than your American biking, you will find that it is much more relaxing and much safer, as well. When you are sitting up, you can see all around you."

He stood up straight with his arms out as if he were riding a bicycle and clearly demonstrated the turning radius of his neck.

"This will help you to see cars, pedestrians, other bikers, children, dogs, trains, and so forth. When you ride a racing bike, you must lean forward. You have poor visibility on a racing bike. They are not meant for the city."

"Oh," said Clara, "wow. That's amazing."

"Cyclists generally have the right of way," Jens continued, "There are many rules for cars, and many rules for pedestrians that help cyclists, but still, you should be careful of both. In pedestrian zones like the shopping street, you *must* walk your bicycle, otherwise, you will be cited. Signs are usually posted in these areas. Another important symbol is the sharks teeth painted on the path. When they are pointing towards you, this means yield. Next, your bicycle." He gestured towards a beautiful new used bicycle.

"€70," he said, "and it is all ready—front and back lights, bell, and a new chain. Bicycles sold in a shop in The Netherlands must have a front and back light and bell. Yours already has them." Jens gave the bell a little ding. "But remember that the police can ticket you if your bike does not have these three things."

"Um, excuse me, Jens?"

"Yes."

"I don't mean to be rude, but isn't this one a little tall for me? Isn't that one more my size?" She pointed towards a bright pink bicycle leaning against the wall of the shop. He must have had high aspirations for her height.

"That?! Why that's a children's bicycle, Claartje. It is much too small for you!" He laughed heartily and went back to his detailed explanation of the world of Dutch biking.

"Now when you park your bicycle, you should try to park in a designated parking area. If you leave it in a place that is not meant for bicycle parking, it may be taken away by the police. Most Dutch people use an integrated lock." He pointed towards a sort of half handcuff around the back wheel. "With this lock," he slid the lock shut around the wheel, "your bicycle cannot be rolled away. This is most common, but if you are worried about your bicycle being thrown into the canal, I can also show you the other types of locks I have."

*What?*

"Regarding bicycle repair, you can of course come back to my shop and I will help you. I am knowledgeable and I have fair prices. Also, you should remember to grease your chain and lock regularly. We have quite a lot of rain here in The Netherlands and the parts can easily become stiff. Now, you know how to turn on the light?"

"Um...push the button?" Clara guessed, wondering if the question was a joke or a rhetorical question of some kind. She'd been such an idiot about the children's bike that she now felt very unsure of herself.

"Not exactly," he replied matter-of-factly, "you have to push, slide and click. You try."

*So it* was *harder than it looked.* Clara looked at the small black, plastic contraption that sat just beside her wheel. When Jens pushed, slid and clicked the handy device, the tiny roller on one end of it was placed in direct contact with the edge of the tire. To demonstrate, he lifted the front of the bicycle and spun the wheel. A soft whirring announced the glow of the light. It shined more brightly as he gave the wheel another robust spin and then slowly dimmed to off as the wheel came to a stop. He set the bike down and popped the lighting apparatus to the off position.

"It generates power for the back light as well. Did you notice?" Clara could only stare up into his clear blue eyes and shaggy brown locks as if seeing light for the first time—which she was, really. She might have seen Jens smile as he turned back to the bicycle.

After practicing with her light Jens made her try riding the bike in the small shop. She felt like she was sitting atop a unicycle it was so high. The seat wasn't all that much higher than the one on her mountain bike back home, but the handlebars were practically straight out in front of her. She could see that it would be safer and more comfortable to ride sitting so upright, but for the moment she could only think of a clown riding an oversized bicycle at the circus.

"You need the seat a little higher."

"Higher?" she said incredulously. She hardly thought it could go any higher.

"Yes, just three centimeters higher."

Clara silently reminded herself to start using the metric

system as she eyed what she thought to be three centimeters. She would hardly be able to get on the bike if he raised it that much.

Fortunately, three centimeters was about half as much as she thought.

"There you go," he said, "nice," he nodded in a gratified manner.

After another ten minutes of Jens watching Clara click on and off the wheel-powered light and practice locking the wheel lock, she was released. She paid Jens and thanked him profusely for the help. Feeling a little self-conscious, she didn't ride her bike away but began walking it down the street. Much to her embarrassment, after a minute she heard her name being called.

"Claartje!" Jens shouted after her, "in The Netherlands we ride our bicycles!" He laughed and waved as she finally got on the bike and wobbled away down the street.

## achttien - eighteen

Somehow, even after their horrendous phonefight and hangup, Clara still spoke with her mother every Wednesday.

Their conversations weren't any worse than normal; not better, but not worse. Every Wednesday her mother insulted her way of life, insulted and put down her decision making abilities, and affirmed that she was getting crazier every day.

Clara personally did not think there was any basis for her mother's negative comments and incessant insults, but so goes the mother-daughter interface. She laughed to herself as she rounded the corner into Jordaan, remembering their last conversation.

"If you don't stop ignoring your responsibilities, you're going to be a homeless hippie like that lady with the suitcase who always stole your aluminum cans!"

"You're reaching, Mom," she'd said. "I am simply experiencing a new life. It's something I've never done before.

I was always on a path, heading in the right direction. But what was at the end?!" she had shouted. "Nothing for me!"

*Crazy suitcase lady...* Clara rounded the corner, still chuckling, and found herself walking right into a stream of bikers. She sucked in and turned, zigging and zagging to get out of the crowd, the chiming of bike bells reprimanding her at every turn. The bells turned to harsh rolling cusswords, or at least that was the way it sounded. She finally made it out and pulled her scarf up over her head, making a beeline towards her apartment door a mere 150 meters away. She prayed that no one had witnessed her near-death experience. She could only imagine what her hardhearted landlady would have to say to her ignorant, pregnant American tenant.

"Claartje!"

*Oh, no.* Her name- a deep, Dutch voice was calling her name. She tried to ignore it. *Retreat! Retreat!* She wasn't sure if she could handle a scolding right now, and she was sure that's what was coming. Just as she reached the door, she heard them calling out again, more sternly this time.

"Clara!"

She turned, and striding toward her with those long Dutch legs was Lars.

"Lars!" she smiled; it was always nice to see Lars.

"Clara!" he called out again, "What on Earth were you doing! That was very dangerous!"

*Dear God, he'd seen her almost cause the 10-person bicycle pileup. How humiliating.* Now she wished it had been Ellie. At least Ellie wasn't one of her sure hopes for a friend, but Lars—he was a potential friend.

Clara could do nothing but give him a pathetic puppy dog look. She was ready to admit it was dangerous. There was no doubting that.

"Oh, dear. I thought that I was very clear with Jens about teaching you about cycling."

"Oh, but he did!" defended Clara, "He taught me all about parking and biking and turning and shark's teeth..."

"Yes, that's fine, but he clearly did not teach you how to

walk among cyclists."

*What?* she thought to herself, *Wasn't that the mistake in the first place? Walking through a group of cyclists?*

He walked right up to her, put his arm around her shoulder and physically took her by the hand. She wasn't sure whether it was sweet or mortifying.

"Now," he began calmly, sitting her cautiously down on the stone front steps, "when you walk through a group of cyclists," he began, "you must walk straight. Simply use predictable movements and the cyclists will go around you. Do you understand?"

She stared at him, stumped.

"Really? Shouldn't I just not walk through a large group of cyclists?"

Lars chuckled, clearly relaxing now that his lesson of the day had been given.

"This is a civilized place, Clara; you can certainly walk across the street. We are very able cyclists on the whole, but it is dangerous for you to make quick and erratic movements."


negentien - nineteen


*No,* Clara thought firmly to herself as she saw her reflection in the bathroom mirror. She was holding a pair of semi-sharp scissors, poised and ready to snip off the bottom inch of her hair.

*What was she doing?*

Even in college when she didn't have *any* money, she paid for haircuts. Wasn't she here to be a part of the culture? To actually meet people and talk to them, even just in English? She should go out, find herself a friendly Dutch stylist, get a nice Dutch haircut, and be a part of the Dutch world. She set the scissors down and slipped on her shoes to go.

She counseled herself on the way there. She didn't really know any Dutch, but she would at least say, "Hoi!" when she walked in. She heard many people use this greeting and it seemed simple enough. She wondered if the hair places here worked the same way as they did in the U.S. Was it normal to go to the same person for your entire life? Probably. That just plain made sense. Was it normal to spend the entire wash, cut, and dry gossiping about anything and everyone? Maybe. She figured she would find out soon.

She picked a random street, in a slightly more populated direction, and started scanning the street for a hairdresser. It was raining lightly now, but soon enough, she found one, a *Knapper*, she saw it was called. She examined the normal looking glass window and the people working inside, two older men, it appeared, one balding and one with the strangest graying red curls. The prices were surprisingly good at €12 for a cut. They also appeared to do beard trims and shaves. How quaint, she thought. She hadn't ever been to an old school barber shop.

The bell jingled as she stepped inside the door.

"Hoi!" she smiled and greeted when the tall balding man looked up at her.

"Hallo," he responded calmly, stopping there. She stared at him and he stared at her.

"Can I..." she began, "Could I...Do you think..." Her breathing speed increased. How had she not considered what she would say after hello?

"Can I help you, Madam?" The curly haired man had noticed her and come to her aid. She now saw that he wore a bowtie the precise color that his hair used to be. How cute.

"I was hoping to get a haircut," she responded timidly.

"Ahh, yes, but you see Madam, this is only a barber for men. Try the unisex hair coiffure down the street. They cut ladies' hair very nicely and they have good prices also."

"Oh, uh, thanks." Clara thanked him and left the little barber shop.

She scolded herself silently on the street. *Would she go to a barber shop in the U.S.? Of course not.* A traditional barber shop was just that—a barber shop for men! They didn't serve women. *A barber shop quartet didn't include women.* Such poor logic. *Had she been this dim-witted in Sacramento?*

It was raining harder now outside. She pulled her scarf up over her head and looked left, then right.

*Which way had he said to go? Damn it!*

She stared across the canal as the raindrops bounced and splattered off the water. Should she go back in and ask, or just go home and put the first 30 minutes of *Hope Floats* on repeat?

She turned ever so slightly back towards the tall glass windows of the barber shop. The kind, curly haired man was looking out at her. He raised his hand and pointed left, down the street. Involuntarily, she smiled at him and he smiled back. She gave a tiny wave and headed left down the street, more appreciative than he could ever imagine. Too bad there weren't more men like that in her age bracket.

She found the hairdresser in no time and stepped out of the rain into the warm shop. A tall blonde man walked up as the door flung open. It was lighter than she thought.

"Hallo," he called. Her heart fluttered a little bit. This tall, fit man was definitely in her age bracket. His hair was buzzed short in a way that was terribly attractive considering it was likely meant to disguise a receding hairline.

"Hoi," she responded politely with a nervous smile.

With one blink, he spoke to her again, "Can I help you?"

*How did they* do *that?*

"I'd like a haircut."

"Okay," he said cheerfully. "I am free now if you'll follow me." She took a deep breath as he led her to a chair halfway back the little shop, "So how do you like The Netherlands?"

"It's very nice here."

"You're from America?"

"Yup, I mean, Yes."

"Ahh, nice. And what do you think of the Dutch?"

It was soothing to sit and chat with this nice Dutch stylist. They talked about the big differences—the bikes, the language, the flat land—and joked about each one in turn.

Thirty minutes later she walked home with a bounce in her step and a cute, new cut with a few fresh layers. The rain had slowed to a gentle mist, making her walk along the Prinsengracht feel more peaceful than ever. She reached up and touched the cleanly cut ends of her new do and felt quite satisfied with her day. On a bad day, the accidental stop at the barber shop could have pushed her over the edge and sent her running back to her kitchen shears, but more and more often she was now able to work to find it entertaining, rather than stressful or embarrassing.

Today's experience was so nice that she already felt she had a new friend, Kees, her striking and amiable hairdresser.

By the time she arrived home, Clara felt quite content. After a quick lunch she would make some more elementary school art projects. While it was a bit simplistic, she couldn't help but feel soothed by the familiar repetition of the projects, concomitantly pleased and inspired by the creative outlet she now had in her life.

She turned down her street and smiled as she saw her rowhouse, her home. Five steps later, she stopped, staring at the five stone steps up to the front door.

There, on her front steps, sat her sister Delia.


## twintig - twenty

Clara stared at the front steps where her sister was sitting. Had her mother mentioned a possible Delia visit? She may have, but Clara certainly hadn't believed it would actually happen.

She took a deep breath as her eyes connected with her sister's. Delia waved happily. Clara avoided returning the disgustingly cheerful wave by looking in her purse for her keys.

"Hi!" Delia called out to her, very Americanly loud, "What's up, Sis!?"

"Hel-lo." She said the word slowly and in overly separated syllables. "What's, uh…What are ya' doin' here?"

"I came to see you! It's been so long!" Delia put one arm around Clara's shoulder and gave her a squeeze.

Funny Delia hadn't thought it was all that long when Clara still lived in Sacramento a mere 20 minutes away. She wondered if her parents had covered the ticket. They were probably sending Delia to London for a week afterwards, a bribe to get her to track Clara down and lean on her.

*Bring her home and* we'll *pay…* Clara could hear her mother's ringing taunt in her head.

They walked up the stairs to Clara's apartment in silence. Apart from the clunk of Delia's suitcase banging up the stairs, she could only hear the disturbed rhythm of her own breathing. She wondered warily about the length of Delia's stay.

Clara unlocked the door and led the way inside. Delia looked around, clearly taken aback by her surroundings.

"Wow…" She looked around in awe. "Clara," she shook her head, "This place looks like an art studio." She turned to look at her sister, "I didn't know you could do stuff like this."

*Stuff.* Clara didn't respond but continued into the kitchen to put on some water for tea, hanging up her scarf, coat, and umbrella on the way.

When she returned, Delia was settled into a wood-framed chair with lumpy peach-colored cushions. Clara couldn't help but grimace. When Ellie had first shown her the apartment Clara had thought of Delia when she'd sat in that chair… it was almost as if it had summoned her here. *Damn it.*

"I yelled at him for you," Delia gloated.

"What?" Clara asked. Of course they would be talking about Jack first thing.

"I told him he was a jerk for writing you a note, and that he should have *manned up* and at least spoken to you in person."

"Uh…" Clara wasn't really sure how to react to this.

"I mean, Jack was always such a guy-guy, you know?"

Clara just stared.

"At least have the balls to tell someone *in person* that you don't want them anymore."

"Uh, ouch, am I just the 'someone' in this?" Clara responded, but Delia ignored her and went on.

"And he's a bit dense, at times, but he's usually not intentionally *cruel.*"

Clara stared, silently contradicting with her eyes.

"Actually, he's *more* than a bit dense." At this point Delia actually giggled. "But he's not cruel," she continued, "he's just a little self-involved."

"What!?" Clara finally choked out. "He's a bit more than self-involved. He's also self-centered, uncaring, ignorant, arrogant, insensitive..." Clara stopped, closed her eyes and shook her head. "I'm sure he was too worried about whether or not the Giants would win that day to take a moment to consider my feelings."

She couldn't believe that *how* he had told her was the part that bothered Delia. Though in a way, it was still surprising- surprising that Delia cared at all.

Clara continued, "Besides, I can't imagine how I would have acted if he had decided to tell me in person. Do you remember what it's like to have someone break up with you? At least this way, I got to deal with it myself, in my own way, on my own time."

"Didn't you wallow in a hotel for a week before even Krista could find you?" Delia asked.

"I think I was more concerned with the cheating and leaving in general," said Clara. "Most of the pain and humiliation was centered upon that, I'd say."

"What do you mean humiliation?" Delia asked, a little too nonchalantly for Clara's taste. "So he hung out with somebody else. He probably hardly slept with her. He'll forget her and ask you back and then it will all be okay again. Don't worry." Delia turned towards her. "He'll be back for you, Clara. You won't be alone for long."

Clara stared at her sister. She had been there no more than

15 minutes and already Clara felt humiliated, stupid, and worthless. She felt like she had during that hellish week in Sacramento, in fact. Had her sister always been such a blind, man-loving bitch?

"How can you *hardly* sleep with someone?" Clara demanded. "You either sleep with them or you don't. You either have an affair or you don't. You're either honest and loyal, or dishonest and disloyal. It's very simple."

Delia ignored all of this, "He's in denial anyway," she smirked, "there's no way that he doesn't already want you back." She settled back into her chair, clearly content with her assessment of the situation.

"How long are you staying?" Clara asked through clenched teeth, not even attempting to be casual.

"Tuesday morning," Delia responded lightly.

Clara got up to find a calendar. She might have to stay in a hotel until then.

één en twintig - twenty-one

The next morning Clara stayed in bed as long as possible. The night before had been quickly filled with Indonesian takeout and spicy Italian red wine for Delia. Clara did everything she could to keep her younger sister's mouth full so as not to allow excessive talking. Luckily, that wasn't too hard.

Tonight, Clara planned to bring Delia to the movie theater, hoping to quickly use up some of the time left in Delia's stay, a fairly reasonable four days, she had come to find out. She checked out the possibilities ahead of time and decided to see the new Woody Allen movie.

"So this is going to be in Dutch, right? With English subtitles?" Delia confirmed.

"No, it will be in English, with Dutch subtitles."

"You mean *Dutch* with *English* subtitles?"

"*No*," Clara emphasized, "I mean in English with Dutch

subtitles."

"Are you sure?" Delia asked, "Because when I went to Rome it was dubbed into Italian, and it was like that *everywhere*, no matter what city I went to."

"Well, Delia, this is not a city in Italy at all. It is an entirely different country, so they just might do things differently. Plus, I live here, and I have gone to the movies here. I would think that you might give me the benefit of the doubt."

"Fine," she responded, "I guess we'll see when we get there."

Clara rolled her eyes and they walked in silence for the last five minutes.

After the movie, Clara took Delia to a café, hoping to make amends. She had spent the first 45 minutes of the film steaming, but eventually realized that she had missed the first half altogether. There was a high road, and she could take it. She was supposedly the older, wiser sister.

"So," Clara began, "I was thinking we'd go to the Keukenhof tomorrow. It's a huge garden outside of the city and it's tulip season, so it should be really beautiful.

"Sounds cool," replied Delia. "Want some coffee?"

"Tea. I try not to drink so much caffeine now that I'm growing someone and all," she tried to joke lightly. It wasn't entirely true, she still liked her coffee, but she did try to keep it under a cup a day, and her sister certainly didn't need another reason to tell her what to do with her life.

"Oh, yeah! I heard."

*I* bet *she heard*, Clara thought to herself.

"Baby Clarita or Jackie Jr.," Delia sang teasingly.

*Dear. God*, thought Clara. This relationship was out of this world. Conversing with her sister was like trying to communicate with someone from another planet.

When they got home, Clara sent Delia upstairs with the key, explaining that she needed a walk before she went to bed. She wandered around the city. Just like the movie theater, she fumed for the first half hour before recognizing the error of her ways and turning to instead watch the summer sun set over the tall Amsterdam rowhouses. She spent the walk home admiring the magical evening light.

She returned home more at peace but vividly remembered Delia's jabs the instant she put her key in the lock and heard the noise of someone else inside her home. She entered her apartment to find Delia sitting on her sofa covered in a soft green throw, Clara's laptop on her lap. Clara had been hoping that she would have already fallen asleep so she could get some peace, but alas, life really wasn't fair.

"Hi," said Clara flatly.

"Clara," Delia said softly, "I'm sorry about our first convo. It's just that it's really hard when two people you love so much are ending it. It's almost—well, actually more than almost—it's painful for me."

Clara looked at her with daggers.

"I know, I know. I'm sure it's nothing like it is for you, but still, it's painful. I can hardly remember you alone."

Again with this about her alone. Clara's eyes fell closed, out of pain or maybe from the indignity of it all. She could *be* alone. She was alone now.

"You've been with Jack for so long that even if he was a jerk, I just have this instinct to want you back together. Because that's the way it's been and I feel like, well, like that's the way it should be."

Clara watched her with a blank and un-understanding stare. How is it that a sister, her sister, could be speaking these words?

"*How* are you even my sister?"

"Clara, I'm not being mean, I'm just being honest. You've never been able to be on your own."

"I'm fine on my own," she countered.

"Even in college, you always had Krista to take care of things."

"I took care of myself just fine," she huffed back. "I graduated, I got a job."

"Yeah, an elementary school teacher—who can't do

that?"

"Ahhh!" Clara was about to lose it.

"I mean look at these pictures, they're like you- they're guided projects. You can never just step out on your own. You have to be led- guided."

"I came up with some of these projects!"

"Yeah, some," she scoffed.

Clara took a deep breath. This was enough. This was *her* home, whether she was here alone or temporarily or sometimes lost, it was still her home.

"Stop!" she yelled, "You are such a bitch. This is my home and if you plan to be in it, you are going to have a little respect for me and my situation—my situation as *I* see it, not how you see it." She stepped to the wall, pulling on the cord that held her wall hanging roll tied tightly to the ceiling. She usually kept it rolled up when she wasn't working on it. "Here. Here are some non-projects," she spat at her sister. "And this is my second roll, so clearly I can handle more than planned projects," she sneered.

"Clara..." she began, standing up and taking her hand to lead her to the couch like she was talking down a child having a temper tantrum. "It's nice," Delia smiled condescendingly, "I really like them. They're nice."

Clara didn't allow herself to be led to the couch, but did prop herself on the arm on the opposite end.

Delia scooted closer to her on the couch and squeezed her shoulder. "Don't worry Clara, you'll get him back... someday. He'll be back to take care of you." Delia was nodding in a sycophant, Stepford kind of way.

"What if," she threw Delia's arm off of her, "I don't want him back!?"

"Oh, come on. You don't want him? Yeah, right, Clara. You love him. You need him. You're nothing without him."

Clara was nearly choking. "Nothing?" she sputtered.

"I don't mean *nothing*, I just meant that you need him. You're not *you* without him. Jerry Maguire and all that jazz. And soon he's gonna realize that he needs you too."

"I!" Clara yelled, "do *not* need him!"

"Clara, please," Delia begged, "just sit down. This stress isn't good for you."

For some reason, Clara took a deep breath and sat down, probably because the anger was, truly, making her see spots.

"Clare, please…"

"Why did you come here?!"

"Just listen and let me finish."

Clara glowered at her but decided to give her one last minute.

"Whether you hate each other or not, whether he hurt you or not, whether you are miserable or not, I wish for it, like a child whose parents are getting divorced. I remember you together, so I just… that's the way I prefer it. I'm sorry, Sis. I just can't really remember you, who you are, or who you were, without him."

The words tore at her. There was a childlike honesty to her words, yet it was so, so traumatizing. When in a situation like this, you know what you *should* do—as a woman, and as an independent, confident, and proud human being. At the same time, you also know that there is at least a part of you, sometimes that part is bigger than the rest, that just wants him back no matter what he did. Clara had been working so hard to keep these thoughts out of her head, to never allow them to cross her mind, and here Delia was, throwing them at her. She hated it, hated Delia for it. She didn't want to be that woman. She didn't want to be that *kind* of woman, the kind of woman that Krista would be ashamed of, the kind of woman that she should be ashamed of.

But she also knew that there was a part of her—that there was a part of any woman—that didn't care in the slightest what he did or who he did and when he did it and how many times. That part doesn't care, and never will. That part of you, that part of her, just wanted to be back in Jack's arms, no matter the price of her self-respect or her pride… or her heart.

Delia's words interrupted her agonizing deliberation, "So he slipped up once. Does it really matter?" she asked.

And there it was, the end question: self-respect or self-disrespect, husband or no husband. Clara was shocked to hear the question aloud. She couldn't have spit out an answer if she'd wanted to. She was choking. She was choking on her words.

"Yes!" she finally yelled, "of course it matters!" It came more easily than she expected. *Of course it mattered.* That's why she was here. He had cheated on her. He had kicked her out. He had broken promises. He had stopped caring for her. She shook her head roughly, trying to get it out of her head.

"I am not going to be that woman, the woman that took him back after he- he..." she felt a hitch in her breathing—*he slaughtered her*. He had left her behind, and left her with nothing, left her alone to fend for herself in such a huge world.

And there it was—alone. She had known it all along and hated it every second that she had known it was there but pretended it was not, the worst part about the marriage ending. She was now alone.

twee en twintig - twenty-two

After that fight, Clara didn't see or speak to Delia for almost twenty-four hours. She snuck out when she was still sleeping in the morning and spent the entire day someplace else—the café, the library, the grocery store, the Van Gogh Museum, the café again.

Unfortunately, although she'd left to escape her sister, Delia's words swam in her head all day long. *You've never been able to be on your own.*

She couldn't stop the whirlwind of thoughts in her head.

The rain transitioned from spitting on her to real rain, which was both worse and better. She was really getting wet now, but she couldn't deny that the thousands of drops looked beautiful as they splattered on the still waters of the two intersecting canals where she stood.

On this particular corner nearly every structure looked the

same. Dark brown brickwork, each building the width of a room, but still connected with every other, standing side by side, four floors tall and each window on each floor of each building flanked with painted red shutters. Everything seemed to fit. For several hundred years they'd been standing, tall and alike, and here she stood, so out of place. She was alone and wet, alienated by even her own sister, without husband, and apparently not whole. She stood in wet pieces in front of the canal and wondered sorrowfully if Delia was right.

*Was it really better to go back to him, just so she wasn't alone?* She shuddered to think what Krista would think of her. And next, more evil thoughts, all courtesy of Delia. *Did she really need Krista to approve of her actions?*

The walk back that evening was much longer. She had to go home, whether her home was occupied by the enemy or not. When she got there, she felt more exhausted than ever. She had been dreaming that her day-long efforts would be worth it and her sister would already be asleep, but when she got home all the lights were on in her apartment.

She turned and sank down on the steps of the building. Maybe she could wait it out. She felt a change inside her and realized that from the front steps she could hear the tinkling of piano keys. *Did Ellie play?*

Chopin. It was nice, a quick rhythm that was familiar and interesting. She followed the melody up and down until it wound into a finale. The line mellowed out and transitioned into a new song. Ellie was quite good—or maybe it was Lars—she couldn't help but smile at the thought of the handsome Dutchman at the keys, his long fingers running up and down the ivories.

Instead of another lively tune, it was a soft, quiet, and sad song. It was the theme from *Terms of Endearment.* Clara's peaceful mood went sour. This was not Ellie playing, nor was it Lars. It was Delia.

Clara turned and stormed up the stairs to her apartment. *How was it that everyone liked Delia?* Even *she* had only been in Ellie's apartment twice, and here Delia was, playing her piano, probably sipping tea and eating her Dutch cookies. Clara ripped her door open, Delia had left it unlocked, and burst into her apartment, roughly throwing down her bag, pulling off her scarf and throwing her sweater onto the floor with her umbrella.

Sure, she was kind of having a temper tantrum, but really, how long was it going to be this way!? Nobody *dis*liked Clara, but she had never been able to draw people in like Delia could. "Delia just has an understated, confident air about her," her mother had once explained.

Well, Clara didn't care. As soon as Delia was done hobnobbing with *her* neighbor and landlord, Clara was kicking her out. She would be gone—out—back on a plane to the States.

She stalked through to her bedroom, slamming the bedroom door behind her, and flung herself on her bed, tears running down her cheeks. She was pregnant, maybe that was why she was taking this so badly, or maybe she just couldn't believe that Delia was getting on in Holland better than she was... after just two days.

The tears came harder when she pictured Delia on the piano bench with Lars next to her, laughing and playing a chirpy duet of "Heart and Soul."

*Damn you, Delia.*

Clara didn't bother to try pulling herself together. It would probably be hours before the vivacious chatter was finished. She had time to cry.

Unfortunately, before Clara could fall asleep she heard the door open.

"Hey Sis-" Delia called out as she snapped the deadbolt behind her. She walked into Clara's room, knocking softly on the doorframe as she entered. "Sorry about before."

Clara didn't move but gave her pillow a good grimace. She wasn't ready to face her yet.

It was too bad, after her sister had come almost 10,000 miles to see her, that they couldn't get along for a few days.

"G'night," said Delia when Clara failed to roll over.

*Go home*, thought Clara to her pillow.

Delia shut the door quietly and Clara was left in darkness. She shivered. The door was so thin that she could still hear Delia tapping the keys of the keyboard, but at least there was something in between them, a buffer between Clara and someone who wanted her to be the type of person she never wanted to be.

## drie en twintig - twenty-three

"So," said Delia as she flopped down on Clara's bed and propped herself up on her elbow, "What are we doing today?!"

At first Clara didn't speak. Delia really shouldn't be this chipper after the day she'd just put Clara through. Still, as much as she despised her sister at the moment, Clara had decided that she should still take her to the Keukenhof. No one deserved to be denied the opportunity.

"Mom says you do a whole lot of nothing-but-moping-and-mourning around here."

"What!?" Clara snipped back, sitting up with a start.

"Don't shoot the messenger!" said Delia, her hands in the air to signal surrender.

"Can you ever just keep your mouth shut?" Clara gritted her teeth, "and that wasn't a message," Clara growled, "it was just mean... And not true," she added defensively. "Are we really going to start this again?"

"Oh," said Delia, indifferent to her defensiveness, "well, it was supposed to be a message."

"What?" The morning was not starting off well.

"Mom says that you don't do anything and you need to wise up, get a job, and either go back to your husband or start dating and find a decent father for your unborn child. I prefer the former," she noted with an air of wisdom. "She's disappointed in how you're letting yourself go and thinks that this is no way for a proper mother to act." She took a deep breath. "There." She paused and asked, "Did that sound more like a message?" and flopped back on the bed. "Oh," she propped herself up on her elbows again, "actually she said," Delia grimaced, "that you should find a decent *American* father for your unborn child."

Clara just glared, half furious with her nerve to actually relay such a message and half wondering how long she rehearsed it on the plane.

"Well," Clara huffed, looking to maintain even the slightest amount of dignity, "at least I," she sneered, "was able to pay for my own plane ticket over here. I'm sure Mom and Dad bought yours." She felt like her financial independence was about the last thing she had left. She was a planner and a saver. Delia was not.

"Nah," Delia responded, not bothering to even glance over at her sister, "Actually my work paid for it. I'm supposed to check out the operations here and report back." She grinned like a fool at Clara, whose head fell back to her pillow, face first.

$$C\mskip-3mu\mathcal{W}$$

Somehow, Clara managed to pack a quick picnic lunch and get out the door without killing Delia. The fresh air helped, and they were soon stepping through the Keukenhof entrance. To Clara's surprise, they spent the morning wandering around in relative silence. Delia must have been impressed.

The garden, without a doubt, looked just as amazing as it had the first time. Even the trees were still flowering, sweetly sprinkling white and pink blossoms down on the sidewalk below. Clara found delight in watching people walk under the pastel canopy. Most often they looked up, enchanted, and held out their hands to catch a few of the gently falling petals. Clara heard a bell chime and turned to see a handsome bell tower that she hadn't noticed before. She turned back just in time to see a soft breeze run through the flowering tree beside them, showering her and Delia with delicately pink blossoms.

"Lovely," said Delia softly, and Clara nodded silently in agreement.

By lunchtime they were almost treating each other civilly, so Clara consented to sit next to her sister on a bench during the meal.

They were at the entrance of the park by the front fountain, a ball of water that looked like a fourth of July sparkler. Behind it, a colorful crank organ was blasting out a tune for the crowds.

Clara turned to people watching after she ate her lunch, mostly examining the people that lingered around the bizarre-looking musical apparatus. Delia, she noticed, was doing the same.

"What type of person would really buy those cds?" Delia asked, staring at the chipper old man in charge of the crank organ.

"I- don't know," said Clara, eyeing a woman in a yellow t-shirt with a rainbow across the front that was now handing over money for a cd.

"Judging by the people that have been lingering around it," she turned to look at Clara, "weird people."

"Is it just me," asked Clara, "or is it like the soundtrack to a weird, B horror movie…?"

"It feels like a nightmare," Delia said, "and I'm outdoors in the middle of the most beautiful garden in the world. Think what it would be like in your own home. Makes me think about kittens, creeping up on me in the night, gouging my eyes out," she shuddered and Clara laughed.

"Sounds about right." Clara stood up. "Let's get going before one of these lovingly chirping birds dive bombs me in the eye."

"You want the rest of my cookie?" Delia asked.

Clara looked down to see half of a stroopwafel sitting in Delia's extended hand. "Yes, thanks." And together they walked off across the grounds, quickly weaving through an army of wheelchairs to get to the tiny path that was about to be taken over. It looked like a tour from the local nursing home was about to begin.

Post-lunch the day only got better. They spent time in the children's maze, walked through the petting zoo, and had tea and chocolate cake in the Queen's pavilion as they watched a young Dutch family devour a picnic of cheese sandwiches.

To Clara's surprise, she was actually enjoying her sister's company. They talked about their childhood and reminisced about family vacations as they examined a giant photograph of the snow-capped Carpathians which served as the backdrop for a sea of red tulips.

Delia liked the tulips best, bright yellow ones that had pointed and frayed petals. Some spanned three inches in diameter while others were barely an inch across.

When Delia complimented the strange variety of black flowers, Clara made fun of her goth tendencies, unseen since her ninth grade year. They laughed together and joked and talked like they hadn't in years.

"This really is the bloomiest place," said Delia.

They were walking across the pond in peaceful silence— literally walking across the pond—on wooden lily pads that were flush with the water. As the swans swam around them, they appeared to walk on water.

Delia admitted that she never imagined such a place existed, and Clara took this as the highest of compliments.

While they shared a paper plate of little Dutch pancakes dripping in butter and dusted with powdered sugar, Delia spotted some traditionally dressed visitors across the park.

"Oh my God, Clara. That woman is wearing clothes identical to the old Dutch costume that Grandma used to have! Look!" she screeched, pointing at a woman wearing a long black dress and white Dutch bonnet.

"Don't point!"

"Do you think she works here?"

Clara examined the woman. She was walking arm in arm with a younger woman. Two small children danced around them.

"No," said Clara, "I think that's the way she dresses."

"No way. Nobody actually dresses that way anymore."

"How do you know? It's not like you live here."

"Well, how do you know?"

"I *do* live here."

"Hardly," Delia retorted.

Clara heaved a sigh and rolled her eyes. *Were they really going to start this again?* Clara let the moment pass, and they covertly watched until the woman rounded the corner.

"Who knows," said Clara.

"No way," responded Delia. Clara just rolled her eyes.

Just before they left for home, they crossed paths with the ice cream cart and Clara forced an ice cream cone on Delia.

"But I don't like vanilla ice cream," Delia whined.

"Take it."

"But-"

"*Take it!*" Clara almost screamed. "I got it for you!"

"You're getting so pushy. Lucky Mom's not here. I bet you two would really butt heads now."

"I'm not pushy," Clara defended herself. "I'm just sick of being pushed around."

"Krista pushes you around."

"Not anymore."

"I doubt it."

"Shut up and eat your ice cream. You know I can tell you're enjoying it even if you don't say anything. You're practically gobbling it up."

"Well, I don't usually like vanilla ice cream."

Clara turned away, a smirk on her face. At least she won every once in a while.

They headed back on the second to last bus of the day, and Clara felt the air thicken as they stepped off the train in Amsterdam. She sighed. *You couldn't always be wandering around in a flower garden, but wouldn't it be great if you could?*

On the walk home from the station they stopped by a small eatery filled with teens and ordered a gyro.

"Do you want to walk around a little more?" asked Clara.

"Sure. Sounds good."

They ate their dinner out of the foil and continued their walk around the city.

Clara showed Delia the main square and Leidseplein before heading back towards Jordaan.

"By the way," said Delia on the way home, "does it *ever* get dark here?"

"Yeah, it's pretty crazy, isn't it? I think at the peak it won't get dark until like 11."

"What time is it now?"

"Quarter to ten."

"Are you sure?"

"Of course I'm sure! I know how to read a clock, so yes, I'm sure," Clara snapped back.

The next day was Delia's last day in Holland, something that had not and would not escape Clara's attention. Clara had decided that they would spend it at the two biggest museums on the Museumplein. She never minded a museum visit. They would spend the morning at the Van Gogh Museum, have lunch at a Pannekoeken house, and pass the afternoon at the Rijksmuseum, the royal museum, which had great artifacts—some rather impressive ones from their days as a colonizing empire—and Rembrandt's *Nightwatch*.


vier en twintig - twenty-four


"Bye Sis." Delia called as she headed through the sliding glass doors at the airport, pulling her fancy rolling suitcase towards a seat in business class that had apparently been comped.

"Bye Delia."

She waved through the glass to her younger sister, still shaking her head at the bizarre few days that had passed since the surprise arrival. They'd managed to enjoy the day of museums, but Clara was sure that was only because it was a quiet place. Loud, pestering commentary simply wasn't allowed; even Delia knew that. Clara had tried to host a nice breakfast that morning, but Delia had of course criticized her coffee, her coffee cups, and her coffee consumption altogether, so they had still parted on mediocre terms, Clara felt.

"And don't worry," Delia's voice suddenly called. Clara looked up to see Delia sticking her head back through the doorway.

"He'll be back for you!"

*Less than mediocre, actually....*

Back home, Clara inarguably felt better now that she was on her own again. Spending just a few days with Delia had been utterly painful. It actually felt good to be back on her own, independent and with so much space in her head and home. Here, she had time and space to think and cry, and when you're in a funk, that's really all you need—time, space, and to not be pregnant so you could drink heavily without worry.

*At least she had two out of three.*

Thinking back, the school had been surprisingly cooperative when she'd taken her leave, not that she'd been in any fit state to discuss it. Mr. Rivera, the principal, had been the one to hire her eight years before and she'd hardly taken a sick day since then. He probably sensed that something devastating had happened. Or perhaps maybe he thought a mental breakdown was long overdue; she'd smelled a lot of Elmer's glue in the last decade.

Whatever their understanding of the situation, it was summer now and she had one more month before she had to tell them for sure if she was coming back or not. Just the thought made her feel more relaxed.

*See? She could be on her own.* She turned to get her rainjacket, hoping a walk on the canal could help her muster renewed hope. At the door she reached for her umbrella only to realize that Delia had misplaced it. After a thorough search, she eventually found the umbrella sitting under the kitchen table.

*So Delia.*

She picked up the still-wet umbrella, giving it a shake and turned briskly towards the door, ready to leave at last. Like a doof, she fell flat on her back on the wet kitchen tile. *Thanks, Delia.* How funny that, although she was no longer there, her presence was so strongly, and painfully, felt.

Clara rolled over with a groan, at the moment thankful that at least she hadn't cracked her head open on the kitchen sink. Her neck gave a distressing crack.

*Ouch,* she thought to herself, *could she even get up?* She rolled back onto her back with another groan and the realization hit her.

*What if she couldn't get up?* She had no cell phone, and if she did, she still wouldn't have anyone to call. She had no Skype credit, so the only people she could call were her mother and Krista. 911? She doubted that was the emergency number here. She could be dying on her kitchen floor and nobody would even know until she rotted up the floor boards and Ellie smelled the stench seeping down from above.

*Plus, even if she could get up now, when she was pregnant and moody and fat how was she going to take care of herself?*

A horrible, terrible, awful thought crossed her mind.

*Maybe Delia and her mother were right.*

Tears burst from her eyes. Before long she was howling and cursing, half at herself and half at Delia for moving the damn umbrella in the first place. How easy it had been to destroy her good mood. In next to no time at all, her confidence had been shattered and now the truth was shining right in her face—right in her eyes. When lying on the floor on your back howling with pain, no one there to help you up, it all looked pretty clear.

And her pants were wet, which made her cry even harder. What a mistake it was to get out of bed this morning. She closed her eyes and let the tears run swiftly down her face and into her disheveled hair.

She hadn't cried this much since... the day before she left for Holland. That was the day the tears had come. Only once had she ventured into the outside world between the day she was kicked out by Jack and the day she flew out. On her last day in the U.S. she decided to make a trip out to buy some staples for her new life, Yogi tea, double Stuf Oreos, the usual monthly comforts.

It happened in an odd way. She had momentarily locked eyes with a man in the dairy section at the grocery store. He was kind of cute, her age, and wearing a tie, making it one of those moments that you might tell your girlfriends about—the chance encounter with an available businessman at the grocery store. But at that moment, she had realized that she was alone. She realized that she was back to that stage again, the stage when she was on her own and searching for someone. She wasn't even out the door when the tears began. Her groceries remained sitting in a basket next to the organic milk, next to the cute guy.

She sat on the curb behind the store, the smell of orange chicken wafting from the Chinese restaurant next door, and gazed at the spring buds sprouting from the trees through a swirling sheet of tears, a swirling mess of broken memories and lost dreams and fantasies.

*Dreams*, she now considered despondently. So many times they just got forgotten or judged to be nothing more than the hope of a pretty good job, an okay place to live, and a man. It was hard to believe that somewhere, deep inside, there were big, exciting dreams... goals to work towards.

*Ha.*

Maybe they used to be attainable goals. They weren't even dreams anymore. She tried to think back.

*What were her goals? What were her dreams? Did she really believe she would accomplish them? What had she wanted to be when she grew up?*

Clara rolled over, and on her hands and knees, made her way back to her bed, trying to remember what her dreams had been.

*Ugh. Was this her life?*

Clara crawled in the bed and pulled the covers up over her head. She couldn't remember. After a while she fell asleep, a dreamless sleep for her dreamless life.

*Damn it, Delia.*

## vijf en twintig - twenty-five

Fading light surrounded her when she next opened her eyes. She swung her legs off her bed and sat up, her back cracking something like forty times in the process. In an attempt to keep her mind quiet, she went to the stove to put on some hot water for tea.

The water came to a boil, and she put in a teabag. The minutes passed quickly as the tea steeped and the water darkened in color, but she was hardly concerned that the minutes had passed, only glad that they had.

*Was this her life?*

She shook her head sadly and took her cup of tea to the living room, where there was slightly more light despite the rain pouring down outside.

As she sat in Delia's lumpy chair at her window crying into the rain, the memories came back. It seemed her mind was being cleansed by the heavy sheets of Dutch rain, and her dreams came back, one by one.

She couldn't remember exact plans, places, or people, but flashes of her future success, her once imagined future successes. Clara remembered a colorful painting of a bridge, the dull gray of concrete turned vibrantly three dimensional. She received an award. She sat at her easel, staring out at the bay.

In high school she had wanted to get out of Sacramento. There were too many state workers, too many freeways, too many chickens, too many unfulfilled dreams. She had wanted to go someplace different, either for college or an exchange trip—maybe even just for a month.

Again, she saw a flash of the painting of the bridge. This time it was on display on her parents' living room wall.

The thought caused her to laugh out loud, and she awoke from her trance. Her tea was half gone and cold. Her neck hurt.

*How long had she been staring out into the rain, trying to remember her dreams?*

*This wasn't a life at all. How had it gone downhill so quickly? Wasn't she happy just days ago?*

She wasn't making it. She had walked around and enjoyed the change of scenery, but so far she hadn't done a thing to show that she was different than the woman that she had been. If she wanted a new life, she needed to get moving and start living it. So far, she hadn't.

Wondering just who she was, she stared at her reflection in the double-paned glass, now backed in darkness. *What a week. Thanks a lot, Delia.*

Her heart nearly jumped from her chest when her computer rang. Krista.

"Hello?" she answered weakly.

"Hi!" Krista responded cheerfully, "It's me!"

"Yeah, hey. How's it going?" Clara tried to force some emotion into her words, but she just couldn't. The last five days had beaten it out of her.

"Geez, what's up? Wake up on the wrong side of the bed?" Of course Krista noticed something was wrong right away.

"Well, kind of. Delia was just here... Came to tell me how much I need Jack."

"Whooooa. Bitch. What was she doing there?"

"She said that I don't know how to be alone!" Clara was crying now, not a weeping cry, though, a pity-me cry.

"And that I have never been alone and won't ever be able to." The horrible thoughts that had been suffocating her were rolling out. Now was her moment to let them go, "She said if I was smart I would get him back, which apparently she thinks I'll be able to do... especially now that I'm pregnant with his child."

Krista actually growled, and as if an involuntary reaction, Clara began to laugh. For at least two minutes straight she laughed a hearty belly laugh. She was rising from the dead. *Sanity.* She breathed a deep sigh of relief. It was what she needed.

"Are you okay?" Krista asked. "I'm not sure if you're weeping or cackling or choking." Clara continued undeterred. Her stomach and ribs were genuinely starting to hurt.

"All," she choked, "three."

"Okay, well you seem at least slightly more coherent now, so I'm going to begin. You can *obviously* be on your own, since you up and moved to a foreign country without so much as a hotel reservation."

"I had a hotel reservation."

"Tsssh. Did you have a return ticket?"

"No."

"Do you have a return ticket now?"

"No."

"Then you're about as independent as humanly possible considering that you had never left the Central Valley in your entire life."

"I've been to-"

"If you say Reno, I will strangle you so help me God. I am trying to defend your self-worth and you are interrupting me. Now I know what being around Delia does to you. For some reason you have always let that little, haughty, self-centered, arrogant bitch sister of yours continue to play a role in your life even though she has done nothing but think of herself and make your life worse, but I will no longer stand for it and neither should you!"

Clara had stopped breathing, despite the fact that she was only being championed, as far as she could tell.

"Clara. You are doing great. You are living a life that is yours and you are doing it entirely on your own."

There was silence, which Krista was satisfied with. Clara could almost see her nodding to herself in approval.

"Anything to say, dearie dear?" After any lecture Krista switched back to jokes as soon as possible.

"Thanks."

"And don't you forget it. Now, let's get down to business. So I have an idea. Does your great aunt live in Holland still? Because I was thinking that you should look her up."

"Well, yeah, maybe. I guess I could."

"Great! I'm sure you could use an in, someone who knows what it's really like to be Dutch. Do you know anyone else who lived there? Or do you know where your grandmother's family used to live? Maybe you could go visit the house, meet the neighbors."

Clara was silent as she considered it. As far as she was aware, her aunt Ilse didn't have any family. The rest of the family had moved to the U.S., so she didn't know anyone else in Holland, but she did have her great aunt's address. She could at least go and visit the place.

"Well, I don't know, I do have her old address. Possibly a telephone number, too."

"At least look her up, Clara. What if she's awesome!?"

"I guess it's possible." Her voice was wavering erratically between skepticism and anxiety. "We haven't exactly kept in touch over the years." She pondered the possibilities. "What if she hates me, hates my grandmother, hates all of us?"

"Why would she hate you?"

"You know, the whole disownment thing."

"What's that about again?"

"Well, my grandmother's family decided to immigrate to the United States. There were three daughters and their parents decided to move to the U.S."

"Why?"

"Mmm... because of a job or something."

"Okay."

"But my grandma's younger sister, Ilse, just said no. She wouldn't go."

"How old was she? Couldn't they just make her go?"

"I don't think it was like that. I think that would be very, let me see, *un*Dutch, you could say. They wanted her to make her own decision."

"But weren't they pissed at her? Isn't that the whole point of this story?"

"Well, yeah, but they still let her make the choice on her own. They were just mad because she didn't make the right choice, according to them at least."

"Which brings us to the fact that, dut duh da! This great aunt is there, just a short flight away."

"Well, actually it would be kind of ridiculous to fly anywhere here. Practically the whole country is a two hour train ride away."

"Shut up, Claire," she interrupted. "This great aunt lives in the country in which you are currently living, correct?"

"Correct."

"Then call her up! Stop by! Bring some biscuits with jam."

"They don't really eat biscuits here."

"Okay, what do they eat?"

"Actually, they mostly eat stroopwafels."

"What? Waffles? I though those were Belgian."

"Not really a waffle, more like a cookie sandwich, a waffle cookie sandwich, with caramel in the middle."

"Yum. Sounds pretty good actually."

"They are."

"You should really bring some back when you come."

"Oh, I will."

"Great."

"Or maybe you should come here to get them," said Clara.

"Oh, I will."

"Great!" Clara laughed.

"Well, whatever they eat, just bring something. Don't go empty-handed just asking for love, it's rude."

"Yeah, I suppose so. You make me sound pretty desperate!"

"Aren't you?"

"Hey! What happened to standing up for me?"

"Okay. Never mind."

"Okay."

"Just don't forget to bring something."

"I won't."

"And call me when you meet her."

"I will."

"Bye!"

"Bye. Thanks for calling."

*Ha,* thought Clara proudly. *Krista was right, she was independent. More importantly, Delia was completely wrong—just wrong.*

She could live on her own, and hell, she might even have family in the country, something she hadn't considered since she'd arrived, though she should have. She should at least try to visit her aunt. Even if she was a busy woman with family and a career and no time for socializing with her long lost American grand-niece, it would still be nice to meet her. Maybe Clara could get some advice from her about living in The Netherlands. Maybe.

As if conforming to her indecision, the week was plagued with intermittent downpours of heavy rain and bouts of sunshine. Clara frequently thought about giving her aunt a call, but these thoughts were often mixed with more pessimistic thoughts of Delia and her recent brutal vocalizations.

Unfortunately, when it was rainy it was much easier for Clara to feel that she had little to nothing to do to occupy her time. Since Delia's visit she found that she painted much less frequently. She just didn't have the heart, and her head was still too full of all the things that had been said.

While she pondered the idea of a familial visit to her great aunt, she munched on stroopwafels more than ever and otherwise occupied her time with typical Dutch rainy day activities. She made split pea soup at home and read by candlelight in cozy Dutch cafés. She generally avoided biking in the rain, preferring to walk with her black umbrella rather than endure a thorough soaking each time she went out. She noticed the Dutch could both ride and hold an umbrella, but this was unquestionably beyond her.

Early the next week, after a morning of supreme dreariness, the sun suddenly popped out from behind a cloud. Clara quickly rerouted her path—she had been on her way to the grocery store—and headed to an outdoor café on the Rembrandtplein.

She found a lone chair sitting empty at the last available sunny table on the entire plaza, ordered a cup of tea and leaned back, trying to soak up as much sun as she could. After a while she took out a book, but she didn't get much reading done. The flurry of happiness all around her was contagious and a little distracting. There were groups of friends overflowing the tables all around, chatting and laughing, drinking tiny glasses of Amstel in the midday sun. She wondered if they were students or if it was permissible to have a drink during the middle of the day. Perhaps anything was possible here. A taste of the sun just breathed optimism into her.

After a few minutes, she spotted a large group of tourists congregating around the statue of Rembrandt in the center of the square. They were crowded around a tour guide who looked to be describing Rembrandt's life in The Netherlands. Shortly thereafter they were herded away from the statue and over to her half of the plein. She couldn't help but laugh at the way they moved, bumping into one another and repeatedly tripping on the cobblestones.

"As you can see," spoke the tour guide, "on a sunny day the squares fill up rather quickly. Many are having their lunch break from work and have chosen to sit outside to enjoy the sun. We have to take advantage of it when we can, here in Holland."

The guide laughed at his own joke as he gestured towards the café where Clara was sitting. She looked down at her book but continued to listen.

"I love how the Dutch dress!" she heard one woman

exclaim. She reminded Clara of her own mother, loud and a little clueless. "Look at that woman with the bright green and blue scarf. I just love the scarves here."

*Were they talking about her?* She was wearing a green and blue scarf. She couldn't believe it. And now they were taking photos, taking photos of her, thinking she was a local! She knew that they were really just oblivious tourists and not locals thinking she was a local, but still, at least she knew she didn't look like one of them.

As she was sitting there, basking in the glory of appearing to be a local, she remembered her now oversteeped tea, added a little milk, and picked up her cup to take a sip. Just then, something slammed the back of her chair. She let out a yelp as tea sloshed out of her cup and spilled all over her hands and down her front.

She turned around and found herself staring at the same obnoxious British man. She couldn't believe it. What were the chances, really? Just when she had been feeling happy about appearing to be Dutch and *he* shows up at the same café.

"Sorry about that."

*Ugh, that British accent just grated on her nerves.*

"So sorry. Let me buy another. Was it a coffee?"

"What?"

He stared at her strangely as she stumbled over what was happening.

"Your coffee, I'll replace it." He was pointing at her tea.

*Oh,* well that would be nice. Polite, too, actually. She paused. "Earl Grey." He looked startled and peered over at her cup.

"Really? Earl Grey? That looks awfully dark to be Earl Grey."

*Okay, not polite.*

"It's Earl Grey," she retorted, starting to get worked up again.

"Earl Grey?" he asked again, "But aren't you American? Why would you drink that?"

"Yeah. So?"

"Yeah," he mimicked, laughing, "Well, why do you like English tea? Isn't that a little British for you?"

*Who* was *this guy?!*

"I can drink Earl Grey if I want," she responded, feeling more irritated by the second. He was just *ruining* her day! "Besides, aren't those, those..." She looked him up and down. There had to be something—Nikes, an iPod, a polo shirt with a Ralph Lauren logo. *Shit.* She hated this guy. Clearly she was going to be running into him for the rest of her life. "That's about enough out of you!" she declared simply.

"Can I get you something?" said the waiter, responding to the Brit's wave from earlier. The man looked at the waiter.

"One cup of Earl Grey, please."

"Of course. Would you like a pot?" asked the waiter, observing the empty cup in the Brit's hand and the overturned mug in front of Clara on the table which her British nemesis was now picking up.

"Are you sure this was Earl Grey?" he asked, "How long did you allow it to steep?"

At this, Clara began to cry.

"Oh, Lord," said the Brit.

"Miss," said the waiter, "are you all right?"

"I'm fine," she blubbered to the waiter.

"You!" she pointed at the Brit, "are the meanest man in Amsterdam!"

"I beg your pardon, but we have never met!" he cried, looking at the waiter with an exasperated expression.

"Ha!" she cried, "I've been in Holland for a month and you've yelled at me three times!"

"I most certainly have not," he contested.

"On the tram, in the grocery store, and here."

"I, I... I don't think I have."

"Yeah, that's right, stutter. Sounds like something you would do, isn't it!? Well, you have, and I would appreciate it if you would just leave me alone from now on!"

"Miss," asked the waiter, clearly trying to do his best to diffuse the situation, "can I offer you a nice slice of warm appeltartje?" he asked, "On the house?"

Clara began to weep even harder. "That would be wonderful," she cried, "Thank you."

"With whipped cream?"

"Yes. I love slagroom."

"Oh, and very nice Dutch, miss," said the waiter. Now he was definitely trying to placate her.

"Thanks," she responded, trying to wipe the gushing of tears from her face with her hands. "Sorry. I'm not always like this," she told him. "It's just that trying to start a life in a foreign country with no job, friends, family or acquaintances, and getting criticized by this jerk all the time," she said, thumbing towards the British guy, "and there's just so much rain. I was just trying to soak up some sun and get some vitamin D after my sister came and- and... she is just so mean! And then he had to go and spill my tea..." She gulped, trying to get control of herself but not really able to manage it, "It's just really hard."

She looked up into two bewildered male faces.

"And I'm pregnant!" she threw on at the last minute, flinging her hands in the air.

"Pregnant!?" cried the British man. "You shouldn't be having tea!"

"Oh, shove it up your arsehole," she responded.

"You can't say arsehole."

"And why not?"

"It's not a proper term."

"Whatever." Clara looked up to see the waiter turn and scamper off towards the inside of the café. He looked quite relieved to have escaped.

"*Ja, buitenlanders*," she heard him explain to another waiter as they walked towards the kitchen. How nice that he was getting her apple tart and whipped cream.

"Look, I'm really very sorry about your tea- and the tram... and the store, if that was me."

"It was!"

"Okay, fine, fine. I'm sorry about all of it."

*How are you in my life?!* She wanted to scream at him, but instead her loneliness got the better of her. "Well, don't yell at me anymore... and, and... I'm Clara."

"Oh, right, well, nice to meet you, I suppose. I'm Ian."

"It's nice that you're not yelling at me at the moment."

"Now, wait just a minute. I am trying to be cordial."

"Fine," said Clara. "Sorry."

"Should..."

"What?"

"Should I sit here, if you don't mind—there is truly so little sun and it would be quite nice to sit and enjoy it over a cup of tea."

"Yeah," she answered, "that's fine."

"Yyyeaaaah," he mocked her again, but stopped when she gave him a look of pure evil.

"Now," she said once he sat down next to her at the small table, "What's your last name anyway? Something odd and British? Paddington? Hempstead? Picadilly?" There had to be something British she could get a chuckle out of. *Or a chortle*, she laughed to herself. She really read too much Harry Potter altogether.

"Those are all tube stations. Don't you know any other British names?"

"Why should I? Plus, isn't Picadilly a circus?"

"That's simply the name of the junction," he rolled his eyes back at her. "And a tube station as well," he murmured to himself, "it's an entire line, in fact."

"What's that you're blundering on about?" Clara asked in her best British accent. She was actually kind of enjoying herself.

"Your British accent is awful, by the way."

"Oh, *horrific,* is it? You find it *quite shoddy*, do you?"

"We don't say that."

"Yes, you do, I heard you say it already once this month!"

"I- did- not!" he said adamantly.

"Yes! You did! I heard you muttering about the *bloody* tram queue and you said that besides that, the tram itself was quite shoddy. That was no more than a week or two ago!"

Ian glared at her, giving her one long, slow, accusing blink.

"You were on that tram?"

"Yes."

"Oh," he paused, "I didn't see you." He looked down, "bloody awful trams here," he muttered under his breath.

After she finished her cup of tea, they parted ways. He paid, as promised, and muttered something under his breath about trying not to yell at her anymore. While they hadn't exactly enjoyed each other's company, they both definitely enjoyed the sun.

On the walk home, Clara stopped to sit on a bench near the canal. As long as there was still sun shining down on her, she was going to remain outside.

She took a deep breath of warm air. What a treat it was to witness the silence. Sometimes she couldn't even believe this was a city. Often it felt like a small town or village. She could only hear the soothing lullaby created by the Amsterdam canals—the sound of the water and the feel of the breeze pulling lightly at her colorful scarf—it felt like the environment itself was somehow accepting her.

She thought back to Ian. Somehow he just looked British, which made her giggle and picture him next to Mr. Bean. He'd had that funny, floppy British hair and nobby chin, too.

The sun fully emerged from behind the clouds and the light touched her chilled cheeks. *Perfect*, she thought.

She sat for a long time like that. Several times over, the clouds rolled away and exposed the sun at the exact moment she started to feel too cold. The sound of the water nearly lulled her to sleep and she hoped she would never again live in a place without water nearby. Mountains were beautiful and the sun was of course a welcome feeling now and then, but the way the constant flow of water calmed her, chilled her out in every way; it was priceless.

That evening, instead of making dinner at home, she went out for a pannekoek. Her first taste of real Dutch pannekoeken had begun a love affair that would surely last her lifetime.

This restaurant had the feel of a cozy log cabin. Brown wooden walls surrounded her, each displaying a blue and white painted plate. While waiting for a glass of mint tea, she eyed the table next to her. It looked delicious. When the waitress returned, she promptly asked her what they were having.

Bacon, apple, and cheese—perfect. She ordered the same.

## zes en twintig - twenty-six

The next day the rain returned and with it came Clara's desire to have a nice cup of hot chocolate at her beloved Dolphins café. She withstood the pouring rain for a mid-morning *warme chocolademelk*; it was worth it for the cozy underwater world inside.

She sat in her usual spot by the large picture window at the front of the café and opened her book to read. She felt very content; unemployed rainy days were perfect for taking time to read, stare around at the extraordinarily decorated café, and chat with Jantine.

The barista started right in on her warme chocolademelk with slagroom the moment Clara stepped in through the sliding door. On Clara's last visit, in fact, Jantine had found out she was both pregnant and loved stroopwafels. The thoughtful young woman now threw on an extra stroopwafel with Clara's hot chocolate.

As Clara sat looking around and watching people come in and out, she started to think, as she had on other occasions, that there was something both special and odd about this place. It was truly a work of art. The sponges protruding from the wall just behind her were amazingly realistic considering they were made out of foam. The giant dolphin painted on the ceiling was certainly something as well, but it wasn't the décor that made it feel different. The fancy, water-filled glassware that glowed from the counter next to her may have been part of it. Big curvy letters spelled out *coffeeshop* on the front window, nevertheless she wondered if it really was a coffee shop.

A young man in a black hoodie walked in then. He looked like a skateboarder, but carried no skateboard. At the counter, he ordered a juice and took it directly downstairs, where Clara had never been. The people coming in and out sometimes did seem a little weird. What was really stunning was how much juice they sold. Jantine sold five times more juice than she did hot chocolate, which was shocking. There was never anyone middle aged in the café either, not even anyone her age. Brown cafés were typically filled with old Dutch men. They read the paper, chatted, and drank Amstel, more often than not. But this strange underwater café was for the younger population, she now realized.

They didn't serve beer here, she suddenly recognized. Perhaps that was the difference. There was only juice and coffee beverages for sale, which was probably why they called it a coffee shop rather than a café.

Just then, Jantine brought over her hot chocolate, complete with a stroopwafel on the saucer beside the cup.

"Here you are," Jantine said, "Alsjeblieft."

"Thank you. Dank je."

"Claartje," she said as she set it down, "can I ask you something?"

"Yes, of course," Clara replied. When it came down to it, Jantine was her oldest and possibly only friend in the country.

"I enjoy having you here. It's nice to have another older woman here."

Clara did not take offense from the word *old*. Jantine couldn't have been more than 30 herself.

"But, Claartje, you know this is a coffee shop, right?"

"Yes, of course," she replied, "I really like it here. It's warm and cozy."

"Yes, it's *gezellig*."

"What?"

"*Gezellig*. It's a typical Dutch word. It means... cozy,

small—and warm, of course."

"Ahh," she nodded in agreement, "Yes, so it is hasellick," she gave the foreign word a shot. By the cringe on Jantine's face, her pronunciation was way off, but it couldn't hurt to try, she felt. "And you make excellent warme chocolademelk." Clara could at least do alright with that one, "and you're very friendly."

"Thank you."

"Thank *you*." Clara repeated. Jantine eyed her, sort of sizing her up. It was hard for Clara to imagine what she was thinking.

"You know that a coffee shop is somewhat different than a regular café?" she asked Clara.

"Yes," Clara responded with hesitance. *Did she?*

"Okay then, Claartje. I just wanted to make sure."

Clara stared back at here, the mystery still wholly unsolved. Jantine had confirmed it. It *was*, indeed, a coffee shop. *But what did that mean?*

As Jantine nodded, smiled, and turned to walk away, Clara scolded herself. Jantine had clearly been trying to make sure that Clara understood her environment; she shouldn't have pretended she'd known what she was talking about. Now she'd missed her chance to understand.

Right then, a woman their age stepped into the coffee shop and walked up to the counter. Once at the counter, she ordered and Jantine went to work right away. Under a minute later, Jantine handed the woman several tiny bags. The woman opened one up, smelled it, and nodded.

Clara couldn't be sure what was going on, but it looked... Well, it looked *very questionable*. The woman walked out the door with the tiny paper bags in her hands, and Clara again turned to look at the glowing, clear glass bulbs on the counter. She'd thought it once, but now they really looked like bongs.

*Did they* sell *marijuana here? All these visits and she'd never noticed? The city* was *kind of known for hippies.*

"Jantine," she said abruptly and probably too loudly, "Is that..." and then she couldn't think of any word besides reefer, which was *clearly* not the right word to use. Honestly, *doobie* came to mind as well, but she was not going to voice that aloud. She realized that she knew absolutely nothing about marijuana on the whole—what it looked like, how to consume it, or should she say *use* it? Nothing. How she'd managed to remain so ignorant growing up in California, she had no idea, but it had happened.

She attempted to recover from the extremely long pause. "Could I have another warm chocolade with whipped, uh, cream?" *Phew. What a recovery.*

"But Claartje, you still have one. Your slagroom has not yet even melted."

*Damn. Apparently she wasn't out of the dark yet.*

"Claartje," Jantine spoke again, looking at her suspiciously, "you know that a *coffeeshop* is where people come to buy weed?"

"What?"

"You know, marijuana? Cannabis?"

*Well, that certainly explained it. Was this what Krista meant when she said she could smoke weed here? She had long forgotten that comment back in the Desert Sands. No wonder Amsterdam was known for hippies.*

"Um, should I leave?" she asked.

"No," Jantine laughed. "You don't have to leave. You're perfectly safe. They can only smoke tobacco downstairs."

*Again with the tobacco!* Clara turned back to her hot chocolate. She still had so much to learn.

"What do you mean?" Clara asked, "tobacco downstairs?"

"The smoke from tobacco is considered very harmful to those around you, so it can only be smoked in designated areas."

"Yes, this is the way it is in the U.S., as well. So you can smoke marijuana anywhere?"

"Not exactly everywhere, but you *can* smoke pure weed here—upstairs or downstairs. You may only smoke tobacco downstairs."

"Oh." Clara paused. "But I've never seen anyone smoke

up here."

"Yes, that's true. You usually come in the morning. And," Jantine added, "the seating downstairs is more comfortable."

"Hmm." Clara nodded and thought for a moment. "Do *you* smoke weed?" she tried to ask as politely as possible.

"No."

"But you work here? In a..." she wanted to get the terminology right, "coffee shop?"

"Yes."

Clara nodded and turned back to her picture window. She finished her cup and her stroopwafel in peace as she pondered, digesting her new knowledge of Amsterdam and her favorite café, and wondered if she'd return now that she knew what she knew.

That afternoon, Clara dropped in at the Rijksmuseum to get some use out of her museum card. The museum was thoroughly enjoyable without Delia hovering beside her, and halfway through she discovered a new favorite piece. The painting was by Hendrick Avercamp, a Dutch artist from the late 1500s. The piece was a magical portrayal of a winter scene during that time—an entire community out enjoying the frozen canals, almost like a Dutch *Where's Waldo* on ice. Clara could almost hear "The Skater's Waltz" in her head as she examined the painting. It wasn't just a skating scene, but a mural—a depiction of a town or a society—perhaps what it was like to be Dutch.

It made her unpredictably curious about the Dutch winter. She didn't normally like the cold, but if this was the background, maybe she should stick around to check it out.

When she left the museum to go home that evening it was pouring again. She was beginning to wonder if she would ever use her bicycle again. On her walk home she pondered the fact that she had been visiting a coffee shop, essentially a marijuana dealership, on a weekly basis since her arrival. It was outrageous that she hadn't realized, and possibly crazier still that, at least according to Jantine, it didn't really matter. She'd hardly noticed something was atypical, after all.

Dolphins was always quiet—upstairs at least, it sounded like downstairs was just one big cloud of tobacco smoke—and Jantine was always nice to her, so why ruin one of the good things she had here in Amsterdam? Maybe she would go back; she just wouldn't mention it to her mother, though it did make her smile to imagine what her mother would have to say about it.

As if to solidify how uncivilized she was, she spent the night reading about the Red Light District in her guidebook. She would walk over tomorrow, she decided, just to see what all the talk was about. It was time for this elementary school teacher to open her eyes to the world and live.

Clara hadn't really known what to expect, so the next day when she found herself enjoying just another unique Amsterdam neighborhood, she was impressed. There were more bars and plenty of coffee shops, which she now proudly understood didn't sell much actual coffee. The abundance of museums and venues related to sex was genuinely the most interesting thing about the district. There were posters and advertisements for sex shows and shops selling x-rated videos and sex paraphernalia of all kinds. Tallying the actual number of *doors*, on the other hand, was admittedly more startling, but at least they were all closed and covered with heavy red curtains during the daytime hours. She assumed the heavy red curtains had something to do with the name, Red Light District, though she would have to wait for another day to actually verify. This week had already been eye-opening enough.

At one sex show *venue* that was closed for the moment, she took a minute to examine the show schedule and prices. Apparently people were quite willing to pay good money to watch others have sex.

"Well, this is *quite* inappropriate," she suddenly heard from behind her.

It was Ian, looking scandalized, his jaw literally hanging open.

"What? Why? I'm not doing anything wrong."

"You shouldn't be having sex."

"What are you talking about—having sex? Am I knocking on windows?"

"Well, you shouldn't be here at all."

"Why shouldn't I?"

"Well, you're pregnant."

"So." She looked at him crossly. "And besides," out of nowhere she began outwardly defending herself. "You think I'm not going to think about sex for nine months?"

"I should think not!" he shot back.

"Oh, yeah? And you, *man*," she sneered, "Could you make it even nine *minutes* without thinking about sex?"

"How inappropriate!" It sounded like he was choking and his eyes were so wide it looked like they were going to pop out of their sockets. He took a breath through his locked jaw. "I am becoming quite uncomfortable with this conversation."

Clara sniffed and turned her nose up at him. She had been having such a nice afternoon in the RLD, and now here she was, fighting with Ian—again. "I can have sex if I want." She straightened herself up, going so far as to throw her chin in the air.

"Come on!" he howled. "No one is going to have sex with you. I certainly wouldn't and I would hope that no one would do you that disfavor. Have you no shame?"

The color drained from her face, and a pained, half-crazed expression replaced her confident demeanor.

"Am I," she started, her throat gripping the words as they came out, "does no one want me?" she asked. "No one loves me?" Her voice strengthened with the increased pain and she was very nearly shouting in the street now, drawing the attention of the many tourists also enjoying a taste of the risqué Amsterdam neighborhood. "No one wants me!?"

"No, No, Madam, it's just-"

"Madam! I am *not* a madam!"

"No, you're not, I'm sorry, I- I couldn't remember your name for just that one second."

"I'm unmemorable!" she shrieked. "Unmemorable and

unlovable."

He took a step back, knowing that no words could improve the situation, and frantically looked around for someone who would know what to do. Eventually his face brightened and it was clear he knew what he had to do. There was really no other way to cheer up an emotional, distressed, pregnant, American woman.

"Fine," he sighed heavily in a resigned manner, "My family name is... Kensington."

Clara stopped crying immediately and looked at him with surprised, wide eyes.

"Ian Kensington!" she said in a horribly fake British accent. She let out a loud peal of laughter. "Mr. Kensington!" she laughed, "Care for a spot of tea?" Ian rolled his eyes, and turned away. "We could meet Harry there, Harry Potter."

"That is about enough now, miss."

"Miss- you still don't remember my name, do you!?" she demanded.

He turned away from her with a guilty look on his face.

"I have trouble with names! And these American names are all so fantastically ridiculous. How am I supposed to remember every American name."

"*Every* American name? Is that really what's being asked of you? And it's Clara—you know, from Peter Pan—which I believe is English by the way, Sir Kensington."

"I am not *Sir* Kensington. You can't just give someone a title. It actually means something here. And J.M. Barrie is Scottish."

"Here?" Clara raised her eyebrows, "In Holland?"

"Well, not here, but in Britain-"

"That's what I thought," she snapped.

"I will not continue to stand here in the street arguing with you," said Ian, "especially not in this deplorable neighborhood," he muttered, "don't know what you were doing here..."

"You were here, too," she responded loudly. "In the sex neighborhood."

"Shhh," he hushed her with embarrassment. "I was on my way over to the Nieuwemarkt for tea, so I hardly think I need to be defending my actions."

"Sure you were," said Clara.

"Just walking *through* a neighborhood," he muttered.

"Fine, let's go," said Clara.

Again, Ian's jaw dropped. She got the feeling this was because he hadn't *exactly* invited her for tea. She strode down the street ahead of him. Served him right for forgetting her name.

Again Clara and Ian had tea together, this time at a cozy, gezellig café on the other side of the Red Light District. Clara had never been this far from the center, or her house for that matter, and found that they were right in the heart of a little Chinatown.

"Where are we?" asked Clara, "I've never been over here before."

"That street there," he pointed, "curves all the way to the train station."

"Really?"

"Yes, it's rather convenient in the end. Well, I'm going to stop in the Albert Heijn," he added as they crossed the square on their way back to the center, "I need to pick up a few quick things."

"Great," said Clara, "I could use a couple croissants."

He looked surprised for a second, but then let it go. "A couple," he repeated with a shake of his head. She was pretty sure she also heard the words *American gluttony*.

They entered the store and gathered their items before meeting up again at the register. As always, they asked Clara if everything was *bon* and she gave them a thumbs up. The Dutch were just so friendly.

"What are you doing!?" Ian shout-whispered, "They're asking you if you want the receipt. A thumbs up?! Ridiculous. You are so sadly and hopelessly American!" He grabbed his purchases without bothering to pack them in his bag, his face red with embarrassment.

"Ohhh... I see." Clara nodded, "I did think that was kind of strange."

"Good Lord," Ian muttered.

They parted ways, Ian muttering to himself, and Clara wondering how many cashiers she'd given a thumbs up to in the last month.


zeven en twintig - twenty-seven

The next day Clara again found herself standing in the middle of an Amsterdam square. This time, she was on the Leidseplein, standing alone with her daybag and sketchpad. It was a moderately cloudy, moderately warm, and moderately breezy Dutch day.

It seemed quieter than usual, and she realized that after the busy weekend traffic, she was virtually alone on the quiet square on a Monday morning—out even before the weekday tourists hit Leidseplein for brunch.

When she left her house that morning, she'd felt like drawing for the first time in a while. She had set out for a nice brown café but instead found herself here.

All at once she was reminded of the young girl whose work she had so admired. Since it was still early, the usual Amsterdam artists—both performing and her style—were not yet out on the square peddling their talents and wares.

Inspired by the thought of the woman's beautiful watercolors of the Amsterdam canals, Clara found a spot at a small table there on the plein and took out her sketchpad, visualizing the young woman's style, which used bright colors flowing into each other in exaggerated, psychedelic swirls. Clara used pastels, she obviously didn't bring watercolors out on the town, and tried to document the square using a similar style. She outlined each shape with charcoal, which worked nicely with the oily pastels. The girl used a black felt-tip pen, she remembered. It was interesting and unique, and Clara liked it. After her experimental work on rolls of wallpaper, she now better appreciated the use of a variety of mediums.

She finished one portrayal of the Amsterdam street scene and looked around for another angle. The Amsterdam American Hotel and the handsome, art-deco Café Americain would be the centerpiece of her next work of art, she decided. Every time she saw it she was reminded of JFK, though she wasn't sure why. She was fairly certain that if John and Jackie visited Amsterdam, this grand old building was where they stayed.

Clara moved to a bench at the edge of the canal, continuing to imagine Jackie O waving to her from the top balcony drawn lightly on her sketchpad. Eventually she returned to the relentlessly varying scene surrounding the hotel and café. There was a canal just behind the hotel and a bridge crossing the canal where pedestrians, cyclists and trams all crossed in a maze of organized chaos. She toyed with the water, trying to capture the slow, fluid movement of the canal in an authentic way, but was continually interrupted by the flashing faces and emotions passing by on the tram, intercepting her focus while at the same time steadying her devotion to the representation in front of her.

Her gaze moved from the water to the patch of grass on the other side of the canal where a bench sat opposite her. This bench was occupied as well. Unlike her situation, a long wooden bench where she sat alone, there a family sat together. Clara was momentarily distracted by the couple who sat on the bench observably relishing the minutes spent with their little boy.

She stared for a moment but then looked away. Boy or girl, whatever she was growing she would be handling alone. There would only be two on the bench. She closed her eyes and rolled her shoulders, tipping her head back and exhaling as if trying to make the worries roll right out of her head and down her back.

Instead, there was a picture in her head. She was on the bench with a little girl with soft brown hair on her lap. To their left, to her surprise, sat an old Dutch man, reading the paper.

She had such an imagination. Maybe this meant she wanted to stay in Holland forever...

She actually jerked her eyes open when she realized that on her right was Jack—diaper bag in hand, trying to find a container of Cheerios. She shook her head; that could *not* be what she wanted.

She eyed the family. Maybe someday she'd be one of three, but for now she was just one, and she had a lot of work to do on the one before even number two showed up. Clara looked down at her sketchpad to see a lovely Dutch canal scene. There was color, although she had used only charcoal, and that color brought life to a simple, blank piece of paper. She did that.

She did that...

*She* did that.

In a second, she was up and off the bench, not quite running, but definitely walking quickly back to her house. She would do it, she would definitely call her great aunt today. She liked it here, and she liked who she was here. Krista was right. She was independent here. In Holland, Clara was an artist, and she would continue on this path and fight for this life for as long as she possibly could. She couldn't go back. She just couldn't, so there had to be another way.

Back at her apartment, she got out her address book and opened it to I.

Under "Great Aunt Ilse —> Holland," she found a long string of numbers. She started up her laptop, turned on Skype, and typed in the number. After her previous week's panic she had been sure to buy Skype credit and look up both the Dutch country code and the emergency number.

Her call worked correctly the first time and started ringing, amazing since she hadn't even typed in the country code. Skype just knows, she supposed.

"Met Ilse van der Wilt, Goedemiddag."

"Hello," said Clara clearly and loudly, hoping to quickly reveal her American background—and language. "This is Clara Jean Mason. I am Inge's granddaughter."

"Ah, really? Well, Clara Jean, I am Ilse, Inge's younger suster."

"It's nice to meet you, Ilse. I'm calling because I am currently in Holland, and I was wondering if it would be possible to meet someday, I mean, sometime."

"Why, yes of course, I can surely meet wit you. Would you like to come to Harderwijk?"

Clara had no idea where Harderwijk was, but she might as well go for it—you could get anywhere in this country in a few hours, isn't that what she'd said? "Yes, of course! That would be wonderful."

"Nice. How about de day after tomorrow? Could you come in de morning?"

"Yes, Yes, definitely. Um… Do you know how long it takes to get from Amsterdam to Harda- Hardavike?"

"Why, yes. You will be traveling by train?"

"Yes."

"From Amsterdam you will need about one hour and a halluf. You know how to manage de Dutch rail system?"

"Yes, I should be fine."

"Yes, good. You will have to switch trains. You can ask in de Amsterdam station if you need instructions."

"Great. Okay. And… What time should I come?"

"Perhaps we should say 10:30. Then you will have plenty of time for de train."

"Okay. See you soon."

"Do you need directions to my house, Clara Jean?"

*Why, oh why had she begun with Clara Jean?*

"Oh, yes, sorry. How can I get there?"

Ilse gave her an address and explained how to walk there from the Harderwijk train station. Clara was happy that it seemed like it would be a quick and easy walk. *Thank God for the unbelievable language skills.* Even Ilse, who was probably almost 80 years old, spoke impeccable English.

When Clara hung up the phone, she exhaled a huge sigh and smiled. She couldn't believe how easy it had been. Krista had been right again. Ilse sounded like a normal and very likeable woman, and just the person to help her get her bearings in this country.

Clara spent the next few hours creating a detailed itinerary of her rail schedule. She would have to switch trains, twice actually, but she didn't mind. She hadn't had a train day for a while. When she was done with the NS Rail site, she moved on to examining the Nederland map in her guidebook and found that there was a surprising amount of Holland still north of Harderwijk.

An idea entered her mind, and she went to her room to start packing. Maybe she should head out tomorrow morning, or better yet—right now. She would have the whole day tomorrow and there was plenty of Holland to explore. She wasn't sure about accommodation, but she was sure she could find something. She quickly packed a bag and her laptop with a feeling of excitement building in her chest that was refreshing after so much of the same old nothing special with Jack.

## acht en twintig - twenty-eight

In the end, Clara decided to wait until the next morning to take off, but by 9 a.m. the following day she was on a train from Amsterdam to Utrecht, where she would switch to a train and turn north. She'd spent the whole night reading her Netherlands guidebook and found that the city of Utrecht was criss-crossed with picturesque canals as well. She planned her train times so that she had about an hour to explore Utrecht before getting on the next train.

In Utrecht, she found herself in a surprisingly vast train station. There were something like 20 tracks, and trains heading all over the country and out of the country to places like Dusseldorf, Luxembourg, and Moskva, which she could only assume was Moscow, though she couldn't imagine how long that train ride would take.

It took Clara nearly 20 minutes to find her way out of the

train station, and at the door, looked out into a gloomy downpour of rain. It hadn't been raining this hard in Amsterdam. Facing this kind of a greeting, she turned right back around and headed back into the maze of a mall that she had just come through.

She spent her remaining 40 minutes wandering around picking out treats for her long upcoming ride. She ended up with an array of snacks that included sushi, croissants, and fried croquettes. The best part of her stopover by far was a strange snack stop that had rows of tiny ovens that held individual servings of treats. In amazement she watched nearly two dozen people come and go in just under two minutes, emptying the tiny ovens of their sausages, croquettes, and chicken nuggets. Each customer inserted coins and then handily flipped the oven door open. After pulling out their hot, fresh snack they went on their way, the tiny door snapping shut behind them.

In the end, Clara decided on something called *bitterballen* and something that was supposedly stuffed with rice and curry.

As soon as her snacks were in order, Clara found a bench and a cup of tea and watched the peculiar departures and arrivals board that stood proudly in the center of the huge station. Like every other train station, the board posted the time, cities, and track number for each train coming and going. What was special was that it was old-fashioned. It displayed the news on one flap of a many-flapped spool and when the information changed, the spools spun around and around until the flap with the correct information displayed.

Every few minutes the whole board began to spin, moving every departure and arrival up on the list. She had never seen such a board in real life and when it came time for everything on the board to move up she found she had to bite her lip to prevent a delighted smile from taking over her face.

She ate her hot snacks first and was happy to find that *bitterballen* were more or less mashed potato balls flavored with the most warm and comforting blend of spices she could imagine. On a rainy day like this she couldn't imagine anything better. The fried pocket of curry and rice, on the other hand, was quite disgusting. She threw it away after a few bites.    Her bench was starting to get uncomfortable, so she decided a bathroom stop might be a good idea before getting on the train. She gathered her things and stood up to look for a WC sign, taking one last look at the fancy flipping board.

The top line now read Groningen/Leeuwarden, 10:21, +10, followed by a sentence in Dutch. She wondered what the plus 10 meant. Since it was in red, she thought it might not be a good thing.

*And Leeuwarden? Wasn't that where she was going?*

She turned towards the sign for track 12, where the train was supposedly departing. Was this her train? The time was different, and so was the track number. Had she missed her train? Where was Groningen? *What* was Groningen? She turned and walked quickly towards the first uniformed person she saw.

"Excuse me," she asked, "I'm very sorry, but I'm trying to get to Leeuwarden and I'm a little confused."

"Sorry, where?" the woman asked, obviously perplexed by her pronunciation of the city's name.

"Lee-you-warden," she repeated, turning toward the flipping board, "the top one."

"Ahh, yes. Well, you are in luck. The train is delayed a few minutes. You will have just enough time to get down to the track. Now, be sure to read the signs on the door of the train. Only half of the train will go to Leeuwarden. The other half will go to Groningen."

Unfortunately, the pronunciation of place names was also lost on Clara.

*Only half the train? What did that mean?*

Clearly the rail employee recognized her furrowed eyebrows and gaping mouth as complete and utter confusion because she quickly pulled a small folded map out of a pouch on her belt, simultaneously steering Clara in the opposite direction and toward the correct track.

"Look here," she explained as they took the escalator down to the tracks, "Leeuwarden and Groningen are both in the north. For efficiency, we use one train to go to Zwolle. See here?" She pointed out Zwolle on the map of the country's rail lines. "In Zwolle, the train splits. One half continues to Leeuwarden and one half continues to Groningen."

"Oh... I see. Wow. Thanks!" she told the woman, "I'm not sure I ever would have figured that out on my own." They walked down the platform a bit to the correct end of the track.

"From where did you come this morning?" the woman asked.

"From Amsterdam."

"Amsterdam South?"

"No, just the central station."

"Oh, my. You didn't need to come to Utrecht. You could have taken a train directly to Hilversum."

"Oh, really? Shoot." Clara paused, "Um, do you think I could have that map?" She pointed to the map still dangling in the woman's hand.

"Yes, of course."

"Thanks. I'd like to get to know the system a little better."

"Of course," she responded with a kind smile, "Now you had better get on your train before it leaves without you."

"Yes, definitely. Thanks again!" Clara gave her a quick wave and hopped on the train.

The train was rather different than the trains Clara had taken so far in Holland. Usually they were sleek, two stories, and had seats with clean, modern, textured vinyl coverings. This train was just one story and had long cars with cushy seats covered in a soft, dark fabric. She found herself an empty set of two—the train was pretty full—and settled in next to the window. Her stomach still felt heavy from her fried mashed potato balls, so she put the rest of her snacks away in her bag and instead pulled out a book, her water, and her mp3 player for the two-hour ride. As an afterthought, she unfolded the map of the Dutch rail system and decided that studying it would probably be much more helpful than finding out how

David Sedaris and Hugh were settling into their new Paris apartment.

At the first stop, even more people entered the train car. It was so full, in fact, that she found a young twenty-something staring down at the seat next to her, occupied only by her bag.

"Do you mind?" the girl asked.

*How* did they do that? How foreign was she?

Clara picked up her bag, and nodded. "Of course."

"Do you want me to put it up here?" the girl asked as Clara struggled to shove her overstuffed backpack under her seat.

"Uh, sure. Thanks." Clara handed her the bag.

"Sorry to be nosy, but I just love David Sedaris. Have you read his new one?"

*Ahh, this girl was American. That's how she knew Clara was a foreigner.*

"Yeah, I think so. I've read pretty much all of them."

"Me too. I usually don't read them on the train because I tend to laugh out loud." She smiled as she glanced around the full car, "Then everyone keeps looking at me trying to figure out what book I'm reading."

"Yeah, I suppose that is a risk with Sedaris," laughed Clara.

"So," asked the girl, "are you here visiting or do you live in The Netherlands?"

"Uh, something in between, I guess. I've been here about a month and I'm hoping to stay longer—if I can find a way," Clara explained.

"Cool."

"And you? Are you a student?" The girl had a rather heavy looking bag that Clara assumed was filled with textbooks.

"Yeah, I'm working on my PhD at the University in Groningen."

"Doing your PhD in Groningen, cool. Wait! You're on the wrong end of the train! I learned all about it from the rail lady in Utrecht. Or... Wait. Am I on the wrong end? Did I still get on the wrong end?"

The girl laughed. "Don't worry, it's me. I'm actually getting off in Zwolle to meet up with a colleague. There's a museum we want to check out there. I'll get on the right train later today."

Clara ran her hands through her hair feeling both anxiety and relief, "Phew, good."

The girl laughed again. Just then, someone came by to check tickets.

"*Alstublieft*," the girl said as she gave the man her ticket.

"Dank je," he replied.

"Dank u," she said as he handed back her punched ticket.

Clara did the same, but with fewer words.

"Dank je," she thanked him, and then turned to the girl. "What did you say to him? Al-something?"

"Oh, alstublieft. It means something like... 'here you are.'"

"Oh, nice."

The girl laughed. "Wow, you're already sounding kind of Dutch. 'Nice.'" She repeated, "They always say that."

"Really? Hmm... I'll watch for that in the future."

"Yeah, it's because they have this word, *leuk*, that is like saying, 'nice.' They use it allll the time. It's a great word for the Dutch. They acknowledge the situation, but God forbid they feel strongly about it. It's just: 'nice...' 'leuk.'"

They laughed together. It was really interesting to hear the girl's observations. Clara had noticed some things, but she surely had less contact than this girl did.

"The Dutch only feel *really* strongly about a few things," the girl continued on, lowering her voice, "soccer, the color orange, and tiny beverages—you know, tiny coffees, tiny beers."

"They do drink from rather small glasses," mused Clara.

"Oh, and maybe also the Febo. Have you been to the Febo?" asked the girl excitedly.

"Um, I'm not sure. It doesn't sound all that familiar."

"Well, it's a snack place that's open basically all the time.

They sell all these," she paused and lowered her voice even more, "bizarre deep fried snacks and you pay with only coins and then you have to open this little, tiny oven door."

"Oh!" Clara practically shouted, "I went there today!"

"Shhhhhh!" came a voice from two seats back.

Clara declined saying sorry in hopes that she wouldn't make the "loud Americans" stereotype even worse.

"I just had those today!" Clara whispered, and the young girl laughed. "Bitter balls!"

"Oh, the potato-filled ones! Those are good. And the *best* drunk food ever. Can you imagine?"

"Yeah, I suppose they would be."

"You haven't tried it yet? You should. It's well worth the experience."

"I will sometime, I mean—I'm pregnant now, but hopefully I'll be able to try it sometime." They had been bonding so nicely.

"You're pregnant?" the girl asked, a little shocked but openly interested in a little gossip. "So is your husband here with you?"

"No," said Clara, "he's… he's out of the picture." She felt wise using this phrase, *out of the picture*.

"I see. A jerk, huh?"

"Yeah," confirmed Clara, "pretty much." It felt weird for her to be saying these things out loud—and to a stranger— even if she agreed with them.

"Wow, so what are you doing here? Why did you come?"

*What a question*, thought Clara. "To, you know, get away, to get a little break from life in the U.S."

"Wow," said the girl, "that's brave. I don't think I could ever do that if I was pregnant. What does your ex-husband, or," she paused, contemplating the situation, "the father, what does the father think of you being here?"

"Well, the father was my husband, and he- well, he doesn't know about the baby yet."

"Wha-o." She said it in two syllables with wide eyes.

It was then that Clara realized that this was the first time she'd had this conversation. In California, she had escaped it, and in Holland it hadn't yet happened. So why was she having it now? Was it because she was finally talking to someone? Or because she was finally talking to another American?

As her breathing began to accelerate, she quickly decided to change the subject away from her impending motherhood.

"So, how do you like living and studying here?" If this girl was a true American, shifting the conversation to her life shouldn't be a problem.

"I like it a lot," said the girl. "It's different and interesting but not all that hard to adjust to—*I* think."

The girl took control of the conversation, and Clara spent the rest of the ride to Zwolle hearing about her experiences in Groningen and commenting here and there, all the while simply trying to keep her thoughts away from her own life.

When the girl stepped off the train, they bid farewell and wished each other luck. Clara pulled her bag down from the top rack and got out a croissant, wondering if there was a beverage car on this train. She left her bag on the empty seat once again, hoping that it would deter any other American passengers from joining her. She'd had about enough conversation for one day. She sat back down in her seat, and for the first time in her life, she felt less American than she once had.

Two or three stops later Clara decided to start paying attention again. The train had emptied out substantially since the split from the other half of the train. She glanced around at the people in the seats nearest her. Across the aisle and up two rows a group of three people was sitting around a table chatting animatedly.

Clara tried to listen in, but of course she couldn't understand a word. She thought she noticed something funky about their Dutch. It sounded kind of different than it usually did, but what did she know?

After another half hour, she felt convinced. She didn't really know Dutch, but she was starting to think that this was not Dutch. She eventually pulled out her guidebook and moved to the section on Friesland, the province where she was going.

She smiled as she read the short intro about the province. She was right, she had actually entered another language zone. Here they spoke Frisian. At first this made Clara more nervous, but she hardly spoke a word of Dutch anyway, so it didn't make much of a difference whether they spoke Frisian or Dutch. They probably spoke excellent English here as well. She would have to see.

Leeuwarden proved to be a small but nice Dutch city. She had a latte and then spent half an hour walking around the town. Just before two, she found herself back at the train station. She had unknowingly made a loop. Feeling a little restless and a little nervous about her appointment for the next morning, she found a seat in the afternoon sun and took out her tiny rail map to examine her new perspective.

Leeuwarden was about as far north as you could get in Holland. To the east was Groningen, which wasn't all that far away from Germany, or even Denmark. She wondered how many hours it took to get to Denmark from Leeuwarden—certainly too many for her day's schedule, so she next looked at Harderwijk. She let out a little laugh. It looked like she had actually gone through Harderwijk this morning on her way north. She was pretty sure they hadn't stopped there, but they had at least passed by it. Funny she hadn't noticed that earlier.

She decided to visit the tourist office at the train station and get some advice on where to go for the afternoon and where to stay that night.

Twenty minutes later, she emerged from the station office in a delighted state. Then, she turned back around and headed through the station and out the other side to the tracks.

*Whoops, wrong side.* She needed to go out the back to the tracks; she was just so excited.

She would be going west to the coast to the North Sea, where she would stay the evening in a little B&B in a small Dutch fishing village called Harlingen Haven.

This time, she got on a small train they called a stop train.

It was basically light rail. Less than thirty minutes later, Clara stepped out into the amazingly fresh seaside air.

She found her accommodation without a problem and spent the rest of the day wandering around the tiny village among Frisian families and fisherman. What a life.

The next morning, she awoke completely refreshed. She took a brisk walk around the village looking for breakfast and quickly found a place that was selling half and full loaves of the freshest and best-smelling *suikerbrood* she had ever laid eyes upon. The aroma of the warm, yeasty sugar bread was intoxicating, and the taste was even better.

After eating her fill, she collected her belongings and left for the stop train, openly devastated about leaving this romantic little fishing village. She swore she would be back. Maybe she would even learn Frisian, if just for the bakeries.

On the train, she poised herself for the switch. She needed to transfer quickly to the southbound train in order to make it to Ilse's on time. Despite having to rush, she couldn't have been happier about her little overnight trip. Twenty-four hours like this made her wonder what she'd been doing all her life. There was so much out there to see and do that sitting around in one place seemed outright ludicrous.

Clara made her connection just fine and settled in for the ride to Zwolle, where she would change again. Rail staff had told her the day before that she had indeed passed through Harderwijk on her way north, and that she would have to switch to a stop train in order to actually get off the train there.

She leaned her head back on the soft seat and fell asleep dreaming of old fishermen with worn hands skillfully maneuvering their sailboats through the tiny bridges of a coastal fishing village.

## negen en twintig - twenty-nine

"Zwolle!" the voice rang out over the speakers. "Volgende halte, Zwolle." Clara woke to the thick, rollicking

Dutch voice and grabbed her bag before her eyes were fully open. She couldn't miss an appointment with the only person she was related to in the country. She was off the train and standing on the platform before she was able to focus her eyes.

*What a magnificent nap*, all dreams of Dutch North Sea views and salt coated wooden fishing boats. She sighed and then hastily walked towards the station building. She had better figure out which platform the next stop train left from before she fell back into another seaside trance.

The platforms were well-labeled and once she found the correct one, she settled down on a bench to await the next train.

In no time, Clara was walking down the street in Harderwijk. Her eyes were glued to the half sheet of notebook paper with the directions from Ilse. It now took great focus to ignore the nagging nervousness in the back of her mind.

Soon enough she was walking up the sidewalk towards a deep red front door, and then she was there. The address on the heavy wooden door matched the one on the neatly lined piece of paper in her hand.

She pushed the small buzzer and heard a bell ring just inside the door. A few seconds later a tall Dutch woman came to the door. The woman looked so much like her own grandmother that Clara felt pressure on her tear ducts. She immediately wanted to hug the woman but resisted, guessing that a hug would be quite unDutch.

"Hallo," she greeted Clara, extending her hand properly. "You must be Clara Jean. I'm Ilse van der Wilt. Please come in."

"Hello, Ilse. It's very nice to meet you."

Ilse examined her briefly and a look of restrained satisfaction appeared on her face. "It's a pleasure to meet you as well. You look a little similar to your grandmother, in fact."

"Inge," Clara stated, still enthralled by the woman's own similarity to her grandmother. "You look very much like her as well."

"Do I?" she asked politely. Clara wondered when Ilse last

saw her eldest sister before her death.

"Yes," responded Clara. The heartfelt voice that emerged from her mouth made her realize just how much she missed her grandmother, "very much like her."

"Oh, nice," said Ilse with a nod. "Would you like a cup of tea or coffee?" she asked. She seemed to be steering the conversation elsewhere.

"Yes, please," said Clara, "a cup of coffee would be lovely."

Once they were situated in Ilse's front room with a cup of coffee each, the conversation resumed.

"So, how long have you been in Holland?" asked Ilse.

"Oh, just over a month."

"And what do you think of our country so far?"

"Oh, it's very nice. Very quiet, peaceful... It's a very nice place to live."

"Yes," Ilse nodded, "it is peaceful. And you live in your grandmother's house?"

"My grandmother's house?" *Huh?* "Uh, no. I live in a small apartment in Amsterdam. I rent it from the woman who owns the rowhouse."

"Ah," she said shortly, "I see. I thought it quite strange. I think I may have the only key."

"My... my grandmother had a house here?" Clara stumbled over the words of the perplexing sentence.

"Yes. Would you like to live there?"

*Whoa. What was happening right now? Was she being offered a home? A house in Holland?!?* Because Clara hadn't responded and likely had a stunned expression on her face, Ilse continued.

"It's in Breda. That is in the south of the country, though not nearly as far south as Maastricht. It's in Brabant. It was your grandmother's house and no one is living there now, so you are welcome to it."

"Wow. I, I haven't been to Breda, but I," she nearly blushed at this unbelievable turn of events, "I love Holland, I'd love to stay here."

"Oh. I see." Clara was surprised by her aunt's sudden sullenness. "Yes, Holland is quite nice. I just thought you might be interested in your Grandmother's house, if not so it isn't sitting empty. I lived there for many years, she said I could live there as long as I liked when she moved to America, but it is technically de property of your family—Laura Mason—your mother, I believe, since she was de eldest. I must visit it every few months anyway, to check it and prevent it from being taken over by squatters, you know. No one has lived there permanently since my daughter, who occupied it for de years before she was married. But if you prefer to stay in Holland, that's fine.

*Wait! What was happening!? The dream was slipping away as quickly as it had come. And Laura Mason! She was going to kill her mother.* "No, no, I would- I would *love* to live there. I would love to live in my grandmother's house. Breda sounds lovely, just wonderful."

"Oh!" Ilse's chipper demeanor instantly returned. "Then if you don't mind leaving Holland..." she nodded, "Okay. Nice."

Clara stared at her. *Leave Holland?* "Where is the house?" she asked to confirm, trying to continue to appear both pleased and enthusiastic, despite her confusion.

"In Brabant. Actually, Breda is one of the largest cities in the province of North Brabant."

"Ohhh..." *That damn Holland versus The Netherlands thing had gotten the best of her again,* "Brabant," she repeated, "and now I live in Holland, but I will move *out* of Holland."

"Yes. Well, you live in North Holland now, and you will move to North Brabant."

Finally Ilse understood her hesitation—caused by confusion and nothing else—and soon they were looking at a map of the country. Eventually she got it all figured out. She really should have invested in a nice map of the country as soon as she arrived. Clearly her guidebook just wasn't cutting it.

As she and Ilse chatted, Clara felt a nagging need to confess that she was pregnant, if only to clear her conscience. She probably didn't *have* to, but some underlying guilt was clearly creating an urge to do so—in the name of full disclosure. She was being offered a house, after all.

When they finished their cup of coffee Ilse suggested that the two of them go for a walk around Harderwijk. Clara agreed and decided that her news could wait a few more minutes. They walked down the simple main street out towards a body of water.

When they reached the edge of the water, Clara found herself confused and once again a little entranced.

The body of water she was staring at was… strange.

She could see land on the other side, but just barely. It extended as far left and right as she could see, but it was not a river because all around the edge there were rocks and boulders upon which the waves were crashing; there was a tide and also fairly substantial white caps. All around the bank cattails grew into the water, framing the rough waters. She was simply unable to identify what sort of body of water this was.

"What is this?" she asked Ilse. "Where does this water come from?"

"It was the ocean," Ilse said.

Clara said nothing in response. *Was it possible that something* used to be *the ocean?*

"But there was too much flooding," Ilse continued, "so it was filled in with land."

"It was filled in?" Clara asked the question in a reverent whisper. *They filled in the ocean?* That explained the unfamiliar look of the rugged coast. It wasn't the bank of a river or the edge of a lake. It wasn't the coast, but it had been.

"Yes." Ilse stared off into the distance, and Clara followed her gaze, wondering when they had completed this project. *Had Ilse lived here when it was still coast? Was that a happier time? Or was it better now, away from the ocean, but safe?* Something caused Clara to keep her questions inside.

"You know," Ilse chuckled, "some say, not usually us, but some say that God created the world, but the Dutch... the Dutch created de Netherlands. We know how to work with the water, you understand?"

"Yes," Clara smiled, "I understand." She could understand about anything here in this place. With each passing day she was becoming more intrigued by this small, peculiar and extraordinary country.

"This place is beautiful, Ilse. I can see why you live here. It's so peaceful."

"Yes," she said, "it is peaceful." This time, her tone seemed to disagree, but again, Clara refrained from responding.

"Ilse," Clara began, "I just thought you should know that I am going to have a baby..." Clara glanced at her great aunt out of the corner of her eye. "I mean to say... I'm pregnant."

"Ah, nice. *Gefeliciteerd.* There will be plenty of space in the house in Breda." Ilse shook her hand and then turned back to the water.

"I, I..." Clara felt as if she ought to say more; it was utterly alarming that Ilse didn't have any questions for her. "I was married, but I..." Clara just didn't know how to continue. She had assumed she would be flooded with questions, but that clearly wasn't the case. With nothing to go on, she didn't even know where or how to start her explanation.

Ilse turned to look at her once again and chuckled at the bewildered expression on Clara's face. "It's quite alright. This is not America, Claartje. The Dutch are typically quite private. I'm sure you will handle your life simply fine. You are free to do as you wish." Ilse turned back to the water, this time with a tiny grin on her face, perhaps proud to live in a country with such principles.

Again, Clara saw a gap between American and Dutch culture, and again she was pleased to be on this side of the divide. She smiled to herself and turned back to the ex-ocean.

Neither of them said much on the way back to Ilse's house until they were entering her front door.

"Have you done much traveling?" asked Ilse as they reentered her home through the sturdy front door.

"Well, a little. I went to the Keukenhof a couple of times."

"Ah. Nice. A typical Dutch attraction."

"And I went to Leeuwarden and Harlingen Haven yesterday."

"Yesterday? You didn't come from Amsterdam?"

"No, I decided to make a trip out of it."

"Well," she whistled at the idea, "that is quite a trip."

"Is there anywhere else you suggest?" asked Clara, happy for an opportunity to receive advice from a real Dutchwoman.

"There are many interesting places to visit. It depends very much on what you would like to do."

"Do you have any favorites?"

"Why, yes, I very much enjoy Friesland, and de islands, so I'm glad you went there."

"The islands?"

"Yes, there is a string of islands in the North Sea. In low tide, you can walk there." Ilse smiled. Clearly she understood that this was an intriguing notion. "We call it *wadlopen*," she continued, "walking in de mud." She grinned and gave Clara a nod. It seemed like she had done a fair amount of wadloping in her day. "Now when you leave Amsterdam, make sure you inform de town hall. You will then need to register with de town hall in Breda. So many people forget to do this properly when they move house."

*Register with the town hall?* Clara had no idea what she was talking about, but she was sure that if she entered the Amsterdam town hall, they would have no idea who she was or what she was doing there.

"Do you have a lot of belongings?" asked Ilse.

"No, not really. Two trips," pondered Clara aloud, "and a bicycle."

"Is your bicycle foldable?" Ilse asked.

Clara stared back at her. *A foldable bicycle? Was this a normal question?*

"Apparently not," said Ilse, who went on to explain. She seemed to be enjoying her day of entertaining a foreigner. "Most Dutch people have three bicycles; one bicycle for everyday use; a faster cycle, for between cities; and a foldable bicycle to take on the train. Then you don't have to pay," she explained.

Clara nodded in understanding. Interesting.

"Would the first of the month be too early for you to move?"

Clara gulped. "Um, no. That should be perfect." The first was less than a week away, but what else could she say? "I'll just need a few days to pack and, you know, say goodbye to Amsterdam." Ilse shot her a strange look out of the corner of her eye. Clara assumed this meant she had again made some strange cultural *faux pas*.

"Right. Then I will pick you up with my car at 11:00 on the first of June? Will that do?"

"Oh, no, you don't have to-"

"Don't be ridiculous. I will pick you up and bring you. You may reimburse me for petrol."

"Of course," Clara responded, still startled by her Aunt's kind offer. "Of course."


dertig - thirty


In the upstairs apartment of Ellie's rowhouse Clara awoke and immediately entered a state of shock. She had been in Amsterdam for more than a month, and now that was all ending. She had gone down to explain the situation to Ellie, who had been understanding and possibly a little excited for Clara. It was hard to tell. While it was unfortunate to see Clara go, she had explained, she was glad to hear she would be staying in the country. She even told Clara to be sure to leave her forwarding address. Somehow over the last month, Clara had earned Ellie's approval as a resident of The Netherlands.

She spent her morning cup of tea making a list of all the

things she had to do, one of which was to explore the possibility of staying in the country for more than 90 days. Her tourist visa would eventually expire, and now that she had a place to live indefinitely, she couldn't help but dream of the possibilities. Perhaps she *would* be around to see frozen canals.

What a difference a new place could make. She was certain that she was changed forever from this experience, and she now had high hopes that there was more to come.

Over toast spread thick with swirls of Nutella and Speculoos, she passed a few minutes wondering if she was crazy to be making this move. She was pregnant, so she should probably start thinking about her plans for the more distant feature—distant meaning six and half months. What was the word Lars used to describe her?

*Erratic? Is that what she was?*

While her grandmother's house emerged in her mind as an excellent opportunity to put down roots and stand still for a while, she wondered if the carousel of life would allow it. She would eventually run out of visa, she would eventually run out of money, and she was going to be a mother.

She stepped lightly out her door and began to make her way over to and down the Prinsengracht, curving around the city center past the Anne Frank House and past the Westerkerk. Suddenly Breda seemed a very scary place. Sure, she had gotten used to this pleasantly adorable city, but there was something more than just familiarity.

She was feeling afraid, of course. Her apartment and her little Amsterdam life had become comfortable and homey, and now she was starting all over again. She was suddenly unsure if she could do it. After an invigorating hour-long walk, Clara found herself unexpectedly buying a cell phone. After about a dozen stores, all almost identical in their products, she picked the nicest salesperson and the best combination of deals. The world of prepaid phones was a bit new to her, so it took some research—she'd actually had to spread out her questions among the many stores so she didn't feel completely ignorant—but by the end, she had her very own Dutch telephone number, country code 31.

She decided to take a break to satisfy a slowly intensifying craving for apple pie and found a small café with outdoor seating. She chose the sunnier of the two available tables and closed her eyes, leaned her head back on the brick café wall, and listened to the chatter all around her, relishing her place in the Dutch phone directory.

"Hello," she heard a voice next to her, "do you mind if I sit here? All the other places are in the bloody shade and Lord knows what it's like to have some sun around here."

She looked up and squinted into the sun, half blocked by Ian's face.

"Hey," she responded, "sure."

"Thank you," he responded as he sat down on the chair next to her.

"I'm going to order a cappuccino. Fancy a Fosters old chap?"

Ian gave her a scandalized look. "That's Australian! ...and an awful beer."

"Oh, sorry. Fancy a Guinness?"

"That's Irish," he scoffed, "and bloody overrated at that..."

"Okay, fine then. Get your own bloody beer." Clara stood up and glared down at him.

"Fine, fine. Could you just get me a- a- oh, just bring me an Amstel."

Clara smiled at him meaningfully. "You do love Holland, after all, don't you..."

"I don't *love* Holland." He sighed enormously and looked around, "but, they do say you need your 10 minutes of sun a day," he conceded, "and it's at least easier here than in Britain."

Clara looked over at him and then looked up into the mild Dutch sun. "Wait. It's better *here*?"

When he gave her an affirmative nod, she laughed loudly. "You're kidding!"

"Well, you can almost always get a nice ten minutes of vitamin D a day—often more, in the summer at least."

Now Clara sat back down and let out a roar of laughter. "Ten minutes a day? That's your standard?"

"Well, do I look like a Spaniard to you? A ruddy Italian or a *Sicilian* for heaven's sake?!"

"In Sacramento in July it's sunny like 98 percent of the time, and I mean full sun. It doesn't rain from May until the end of September. Okay, okay, last year it rained once in June, I admit, but it was like a drop, and everyone thought the apocalypse was approaching."

"Really? What's the temperature like? Does it reach 90?"

Clara's laugh was shaking the table. "Does it ever not reach 90?! I *pray* for an even 90. 90 degrees is a blessed day in the valley."

"You *must* be kidding."

"No, I'm not. This is probably the least I've ever exaggerated."

"So... you're from hell." He smiled as she laughed.

"Maybe," she pondered.

The waiter came just then, and Clara ordered a cappuccino and Ian got an Amstel, though not without muttering under his breath how cold Dutch beer was compared to British beer. This relationship was so strange. He was crabby and mean and never satisfied, but amusing because of it. As a matter of fact, he actually reminded her a bit of her mother. The thought made her laugh out loud.

"What?" he asked with a look of suspicion on his face.

"Nothing."

They sat in peace at the sunny café table, Clara sipping foam and regularly adding sugar to her tiny cappuccino and Ian making a foul face each time he took a sip of beer.

"By the way," he began, "I will be going to Leiden tomorrow, and if you would like, you could go as well."

Clara tried to hide the look of surprise on her face by pretending she was just stunned by the bright sun.

"It's a lovely city," he continued, "a student town. It's

actually the site of the oldest Dutch University."

"The oldest? How old?" *Was he inviting her on a day trip? Or... a date?*

"I don't know the exact age. Do I look like a Dutch tour guide?"

*No*, she decided. *Definitely not a date.*

"It's plenty old. It's where the Queen went to University."

"The Queen?"

"Yes, and the prince too, I believe."

"I've never seen the Queen."

"Well, she's not there now," he responded with a roll of his British grey eyes. He huffed for a bit before going on. She grinned. His constant moodiness was so amusing. "You Americans," he mumbled under his breath, "so interested in famous people."

"Well," she huffed back, "you British, so disrespectful towards royalty."

"Why should I care about the Dutch Queen? She's not my Queen."

"Well, you're living here. And I bet she's friends with your Queen."

"I don't care who's bloody friends with my Queen. Like I haven't had enough of that rubbish... Elton John, knighted, for Pete's sake."

"So we're going tomorrow?"

"Yes, tomorrow. I'll meet you outside the front of the Leiden train station at 11:00."

"In Leiden? You don't want to ride the train together?"

"Do you need a babysitter?"

"No, but I just thought..."

"I will not be arriving from Amsterdam," he interrupted, "so you'll have to manage it on your own."

"O-kay," she responded unabashedly, "You know you invited me, right?"

"Yes, fine, I'll be coming from Rotterdam. Just stop prying already!"

She snorted a laugh, but the look on his face kind of

perplexed her, so she chose to let it lie.

"Hey, I've got a question. Who's Elaine Paige, anyway?"

"Geroff," he scowled. "Blasted Susan Boyle, nothing else to do with her life."

Clara let him rant for another few minutes before inciting him again. This was fun.

Once at home and alone Clara pondered this most recent encounter with Ian. *Would she ever think of him as more than a friend?* She turned the thought over in her mind. *Were they even friends, really?*

She brought a book and pulled her chair a little closer to the window overlooking the canal. As the Prinsengracht flowed by, she found it quite difficult to concentrate. She felt fidgety. She pulled her sketchbook out from underneath a stack of books on the windowsill and grabbed a piece of charcoal from the tub of fragments she had stashed under her chair. It relaxed her. In seconds she felt at home again. Some days she felt like it was almost an addiction for her, but it wasn't really; it was somehow different—as if it were a part of her without which she couldn't possibly be whole.

A smile spread across her face as she watched a cyclist with a startlingly orange t-shirt pass by on the opposite side of the canal. She shook her head in amazement and turned to her sketchpad. She doubted she would ever have a window to the world quite like this ever again.

één en dertig - thirty-one

Clara woke up riding a wave of excitement the next morning. Besides the fabulous sun that was shining outside, it was almost like she had a daytrip with a friend.

She prepared a bag for the day, popping in a book, an umbrella, a sketchpad, and a colorful purple and blue scarf. Just after nine, she headed towards the train station. She purchased her ticket and headed to the screen to figure out which platform would be hers.

After alternating between her pocket-NS Rail map and the incoming train screen four or five times, she decided that the train on platform one would do the trick. It seemed there was more than one way to get to Leiden from Amsterdam. The train was already there when she arrived at the platform, and she quickly found a foursome of seats facing each other where there was just one other person, a girl who looked to be in her twenties. Clara asked politely if she could sit opposite her and the girl nodded happily.

"Where are you going?" she asked as Clara pulled out her Lonely Planet.

"I'm going to Leiden for the day," said Clara cheerfully.

"Leiden? I woke up there once," replied the young woman.

"You stayed there once?" Clara responded, correcting the error in the girl's English.

"No, but I woke up there," the girl smiled back cheerfully. "I was coming back from Rotterdam. I had been at a discotheque—the best are in Rotterdam—and was taking the night train home, but I fell asleep." She laughed at herself, "The night train is a loop, you see, so I went around and around, and then the conductor woke me up in Leiden in the morning. The train had ended and I had to change trains to get home."

Clara laughed now too. She should have known that the Dutch girl knew what she was saying.

"In a circle?" Clara asked.

"Yes, but just the night train."

"I'll remember that," smiled Clara.

"You should."

When the train pulled into Haarlem a few minutes later, the girl hopped out of her seat.

"Dooi!"

"Dooi," Clara called back.

Not a half hour later, Clara got off the train in Leiden. The moment she stepped out of the station she felt something different in the air. Partially she remembered the excitement of going to the Keukenhof. At the right time of year the bus for the heavenly garden left from just outside this station. She walked down the street away from the station and felt comforted just thinking of it.

Leiden was peaceful, somehow even more peaceful than her own Jordaan, a place she considered one of the most tranquil spots in the world.

She wandered around the station for a few minutes, and then popped into the tourist office, the VVV, as they are called in The Netherlands. At 10:45 she started to pay attention, watching for Ian's dusty brown hair and lanky stature. She passed the time by examining her new Leiden map. It appeared that Leiden was, or at least used to be, a walled city with a moat.

At 11:10, she entered the train station to check the schedule. There should have been a train from Rotterdam just before 11, and there would be another in just a few minutes. This time she waited inside the train station, meandering in and out of shops while still watching out the glass windows for Ian.

11:30 came and went, and after spending 15 minutes in a small Target-like store, she decided she may as well just enjoy herself. So much for a daytrip with a friend.

She left the train station and set out to enjoy Leiden, an old Dutch city with a very homey, small town feel. She set out down the main street towards the town center, feeling astoundingly well-oriented after an hour staring at her map. Soon enough she found the Museum Volkenkunde. She wasn't sure what type of museum it was, but since she had no plans, she figured she might as well give it a try.

She entered the gates to look for the entrance when suddenly a door swung open and two dozen children burst out, talking and laughing loudly all around her. Her first thought was fear. She hadn't been around this many children since her last day of work. She also hadn't been around children *at all* since she found out she was pregnant.

Her heart sped and panic set in. She wasn't ready for this;

she couldn't handle it yet. It just reminded her too much of the life she'd had, and also of the life that she would soon have—alone.

But then, as she looked around helplessly, she realized that each of the smiling children was holding a colorful pinwheel. Some were blowing on them, some were waving them above their heads, and still some were spinning in circles with the pinwheel held straight out from their side.

She loved pinwheels.

Such happiness was addicting. Wouldn't the world be a better place if no one lost their childlike tendencies? As she looked around at the Dutch children streaming all around her, she realized that maybe this was the key—enjoying life. *Could it be that simple?*

She felt a warming glow within her that had previously been absent. It took an entire pack of children swarming around her and 25 spinning and dazzling, shimmering, glimmering pinwheels to channel towards her the joy that had been missing, the energy that she had been lacking. This had been her favorite part about teaching art. The creativity that children had inside them was something that couldn't be replicated. They were just bursting with life, there was no way around it.

She smiled and felt the tension release from her neck and shoulders, the tightness and stress that she had been letting build for so long was now melting away. Even her scalp seemed to be relaxing. The oxygen and the fresh air filled her lungs as she let her nose take in the scent of mud and cherry Kool-aid.

She felt almost giddy surrounded by all of this energy, all of this fun.

"Ian?" she said. Ian was standing right next to her. Oddly, he seemed just as surprised to see her standing next to him.

"Hello?" he greeted her.

"Was that a question or a greeting?" she asked.

"Do you know someone here?"

"No, why?" She was stunned by his question, "Do you?"

Ian looked surprised, but then smiled proudly. "As a matter of fact I do. The girl with the brown hair and the red shoes," he pointed out, "that's my oldest daughter."

*Daughter? Oldest daughter?* Clara looked over at the children. She was actually speechless. Ian had more than one child? How had she not known about this?

Clara recovered from her shock and turned back to him. "What happened? Where have you been?"

"I, I had some personal business to attend to."

"Oh." Clara was confused, but relieved that he'd at least shown up. She hadn't really felt like wandering around by herself. "How did you find me?"

"I didn't have your number," Ian responded numbly.

"What?" She paused and examined his profile. He seemed weird or... tired—off in some way. "What do you want to do now?" she asked. He looked towards her and gave a noncommittal nod, and then turned and gazed in the direction the children had run off. "Do you want to get some coffee, or tea?" she added as an afterthought. Maybe he hadn't had any caffeine yet today. This was kind of how she acted when she was lacking caffeine—half aloof, half out of it.

"Okay," he responded and turned to follow her passively. She saw him glance back at the museum. The children had now gathered in small groups, each with a leader or instructor now talking animatedly. "Okay," he mumbled again.

*Strange*, thought Clara.

They wandered in Leiden's town center for a while, Clara in the lead. Ian still hadn't said so much as a word. She stayed along the canal, finding it to be the most pleasant path, until she eventually found a café to her liking. The small two-story café was situated at the top of an interesting and intricate canal overpass. The large canal they had been following split into two and in the fork, or more accurately, on the fork, sat this café, along with several pleasant umbrella-covered tables.

They ordered and drank their caffeinated beverages, and still, Ian didn't speak.

Clara was enjoying the view, yes, but this was weird.

Generally Ian wasn't soft-spoken or withdrawn in any way. On the contrary, usually they bickered their afternoons away. When they weren't bickering, she had trouble reining him in. He seemed constantly at odds with everyone around him.

She could only imagine what he'd say if she stuck her nose in his business, so she tried a relatively neutral conversation starter. "So what do you do?"

He turned to look at her, the corners of his mouth turned down.

"Why do you want to know?"

She squeezed her lips together, trying to fight the smile that was itching her cheeks. "Just wondering."

"Yes, I'm sure you were."

She had to laugh now. "How is it that you can't just give me a normal response!? It's not like I asked you how many times you use the bathroom every day, I asked you what you do!"

"Well, I expect the loo question is next, knowing you." He turned away. "Bloody nosy American," he mumbled under his breath.

"You are ridiculous. *You* invited me to meet you here and you haven't said a word all day! Wait, no. First, you don't show up. Then you refuse to speak for nearly an hour."

"Well maybe you shouldn't ask so many bloody questions," he shot back at her.

"Do you know any adjective besides bloody?"

"Yes- nosy." He stood up, and walked into the café.

Clara watched him pay, and then he turned around and left without looking at her at all. Her jaw dropped. How was this even possible? The British were worse than she'd ever imagined. She hurried into the café to pay her bill only to find that he had paid for her coffee as well.

This stumped her further.

*Who was this guy? Was it possible to have a 100 percent entirely dysfunctional personality?*

She began speed-walking down the street in the direction he'd gone. She would *not* tolerate this. Here she was, a pregnant woman in a foreign country, and he was treating her like this. Maybe this was a self-serving perspective, but *come on!*

She caught up to him just two or three minutes later. He was on the busy shopping street, but he was the only person moping along slowly, so he was easy enough to find.

"Come back here you British chippy!"

Ian spun around in surprise, a horrified look on his face. "I am not a chippy!" he hissed.

All around, people were turning to glance at the ruckus. Several had amused expressions on their faces.

"Hey-" she began aggressively, "you cannot just leave me at a café, alone and pregnant."

"Oh, bugger, I forgot you were pregnant."

"You forgot I was pregnant! How could you forget? It's practically my only quality!" she screeched, "I'm alone, and I'm pregnant! And you left me alone and pregnant!"

A few tall Dutch women were looking at him with disapproving looks on their faces. She could almost hear them cracking their knuckles.

"Alone and pregnant?" he repeated skeptically, "Those certainly aren't your only qualities. You're also nosy and loud and American and..."

"That's not helping!" she shouted back at him.

Ian took her arm and led her off to a side street.

"I'm sorry," he conceded, "I apologize for leaving you there alone, but you were just asking too many questions!"

"I wasn't-"

"Yes, you were," he interrupted.

"I asked one!"

"Fine, one, but you were still asking questions I didn't want to answer. I hardly know you! Why should I tell you my life story?"

The corners of Clara's eyes were starting to burn. Soon the tears would come.

"But, you're practically the only person I know. If I, if I..." The first tear slipped out, and she could no longer hold back. They came one after another. "I have no friends, none at all. I will probably be alone and pregnant forever."

"Oh, come on. You certainly won't be pregnant forever... That's hardly possible." He spun on his heel and started off down the street. Clara's jaw dropped and she stared at him in disbelief.

"Have you ever met a woman in your life?" she shouted at his back as she puffed along after him up an old stone staircase. "You are the most insensitive person I have *ever* met. And keep in mind that I was married to a complete douchebag, so you have quite a lot to live up to. Where are we going? Isn't this about enough stairs for the day? I am pregnant, or have you forgotten already?"

"Bloody 'ell!" he yelped, "*We* are not going anywhere."

Clara could only sob in response.

Finally at the top and out of breath, she turned and looked out at the view. It was nice, even through the tears Clara could see that. They were looking out over the city from the top of some sort of circular stone fortress. For the minute she was distracted and took another set of stairs up to the top edge of the wall.

From the walkway on which she stood she could see all the way across the city. She glanced over at Ian only to find that he had already walked halfway around the top to the other side. She sighed heavily as she pondered his tight, hunched shoulders through a blurry veil of tears. If only she had a friend. With a shorter, more resigned sigh, she pulled her cellphone out of her coat pocket.

"I'm in the fortress! Come save me!" Clara texted to Krista. Simply the thought of her friend slowed the tears.

After just a few minutes Clara received a text back.

"There are fortresses there!?"

"Yes. Please come," Clara texted back. "I need a friend."

For half an hour Clara stood unmoving, dreaming about someone standing next to her. Eventually she turned her back to the view and without a glance in his direction, made her way back down the steps. He hadn't so much as turned and looked at her the whole time, so she felt no need to inform him of her departure. If he didn't need her, then she didn't need him. She was done with one-sided relationships.

She walked down the small street a ways, trying to shake the feeling that her stance, hunched and defensive, now looked a lot like his. She gazed around, generally disheartened, trying to force herself to be interested in examining the fine-looking church she had seen from the top that now stood in front of her.

When she came across a charming little café with a group of people chatting merrily outside its doors, she felt a pull of happiness. The Bonte Koe, whatever that meant, had an idyllic location on the curving cobblestone street. It was almost invisible behind the church, in a sweet spot tucked away on a path taken by few. It had a wooden, windowed patio that extended out onto the pedestrian street, and there were people enjoying themselves—just what she needed.

As she first slid the heavy wooden door open, the smell of lilacs surrounded her. With an inhale, she felt her tense shoulders fall for the second time that day, and in an instant she saw she had discovered a hidden gem of a café. It was exactly what she was looking for after the day she'd had. The ups and downs practically made her laugh aloud, only it wasn't funny. *Was her life always so much like a hypoglycemic attack?*

She selected what she decided was the finest of the tables and settled onto the wooden bench. A flowerpot sat on every table, and out of each one, three or four lilacs grew. This wasn't how lilacs normally grew, these seemed to be growing from bulbs, but they sure smelled like lilacs. The Dutch could do amazing things with flowers. Behind the counter, a giant cow was painted onto the ceramic tiles. How perfect. She wondered if it had a name.

Suddenly Ian was there in the café right in front of her. She glared at him, but he only joined her at the table, looking about and observing his surroundings.

Clara gave a little hrmph, but could think of nothing to

say; she was stunned that he had followed her. She decided to ignore him and turned her attention to the menu. The café had been around since 1890. The quaint menu was put together in a plastic photo album like you used to get when you had pictures developed. There was a section telling all about the first owner and photographs of Leiden University students from generations past.

It appeared that the Bonte Koe served more than a few beers, wines, and warm coffee drinks. Old school cafés like this were hard to find, but when you found them—what a heart-softening treat. The cozy setting was interrupted by Clara's phone humming the arrival of a new text.

"Ok." Krista texted back. Two letters, but two nice letters. Clara's heart soared as she wondered if Krista really meant it.

"I really was coming to Leiden, and I wasn't using you or anything of the sort. I simply knew the girls would be here on a field trip, so I thought I would stop by. I figured you wouldn't mind, you are going to having a child soon too, so..."

"So," Clara questioned, "you weren't actually coming from Rotterdam?"

"Well, no. I wasn't."

"So you made a huge fuss about my prying and then still lied to me? Am I that untrustworthy?" she asked. Her tone was not accusing, she was just very confused.

"No, it's not about trust. I would simply rather not discuss my personal life with such a... a new acquaintance."

"Wow," Clara said dryly, "what lukewarm sentiment."

"You must recognize the brevity of-"

"Anyway," Clara interrupted, "to return to your previous question, of course I don't mind that you were going to see you daughters-"

"Well, I don't need to ask your permission."

"For Pete's sake! Can I not say a single word!?"

"Fine." He nodded and rolled his eyes under closed lids, she was sure of it. "Go on."

Clara tried to ignore the denigrating tone he used and continued, "I was just going to say that it's interesting to know you have kids. And I'm not really worried about you uh, *using* me, or whatever because I'm pregnant, and it would be kind of ridiculous for you to prove a point with your ex by showing up with a pregnant woman. It would just make you look like an asshole."

"Yes, that would be a bit daft." The corners of his mouth pulled a little, but he couldn't manage a real laugh. "And, um, she's not my ex."

"Oh..." Clara readjusted in her seat so she had time for her thoughts to catch up with her.

Thanks to Ian's inquiries, in no time they had a platter of handmade bitterballen and local sausages in front of them. They dipped both in delicious, rich Dutch mustard. Fried balls of seasoned and herbed mashed potatoes were an ingenious bar snack and definitely right up Clara's alley when it came to unhealthy cravings. As warm as they were, they also went nicely with the rigid atmosphere. On a cold winter day she imagined they would be just about heaven, in fact.

After a long pause, still somewhat hoping for an explanation from Ian, Clara decided to pry. She couldn't not.

"So, do your daughters live with your um, wife?"

"Yes. They do."

"And you?" she continued, a little patronizingly, "Do *you* live with your wife?"

"No," he said immediately, but weakly. "No," he said again. Clara did not understand what was going on, but did the best she could.

"Why did you never tell me?" she asked.

"What do you mean?"

"Well, even if we aren't *friends*, per se..." She paused there, looking for some type of confirmation or denial, but of course none came. "At any rate, we have spent several reasonable periods of time together. Isn't this kind of a noteworthy piece of information to leave out?"

"No." He halted, looking at her pointedly. "I'm not American. I don't feel the need to tell everyone everything."

"Oh don't give me that *you're American* bullshit. You

Brits are always gossiping and blabbing on about one thing or another."

"We are not!"

"Oh, yeah, well last week a British woman on the tram told me all about her husband's recent lower back surgery. I didn't ask for that!"

"You might have… Stupid, nosy Americans," he muttered under his breath.

"I can hear you muttering over there!"

"Surprising, by the volume you Americans think you need to talk."

"Go to hell."

"So what then?!" he demanded, "You want to hear my whole story? You want to hear about my living alone, in a studio apartment? You want to hear how my lovely wife left me because she thought I was crowding her? How my daughters can hardly remember my first name, despite the fact that I up and left my home and job to follow them here, they so infrequently spend time with me?"

The tears welled up in Clara's eyes as he went on, ranting in his unique BritoHolland idiolect. It was the first time that Clara heard the British rhythm without laughing. For the first time, there was sadness and there was emotion. She couldn't believe she was hearing all this from Ian. She couldn't believe she was hearing all this from a man…

This is what *she* wished she could do… let it all out.

*Poor Ian.*

"The way my wife ignores my words and actions and the fact that I openly admit that I'd do anything to have them back? Anything at all!" he trailed off, but Clara picked up where he left off.

"Yes," she said plainly. "Yes, I do want to hear about it."

Ian looked up at her with angry, hurt, and wet eyes.

"Now," she commanded, "start from the beginning. Where'd you meet this British chippy?"

Ian blinked, but amazingly, responded to her question.

"She's not British. She's Swiss."

"Fine. Where'd you meet this Swiss broad?"

A smile pulled slowly across his haggard face as he finally let Clara in. They settled in for a chat, Clara with a cup of fresh mint tea and Ian with a beer that cost him just 1 Euro 60.

She could tell he wasn't completely sure of his actions, but it appeared that he was somehow stubbornly relieved to finally be able to tell his sad tale to someone—even his new, loud, gossiping American friend.

## twee en dertig - thirty-two

By the time she got home that evening, Clara was downright exhausted. She felt almost too tired to take out her sketchbook, but couldn't stand the thought of a whole day without a creative release. She grabbed a spare piece of paper from the windowsill next to her and a piece of charcoal from the tub under her chair.

It was a strange day, not necessarily a whole lot of fun, but worthwhile. She felt good knowing more about Ian. She hadn't realized that she had known so little. Her situation was so thorny that she never stopped to imagine that he was struggling too.

The words from Ian's mouth were like nothing Clara had ever heard him speak. It took more than a few minutes for her to recognize what she was hearing. When she stripped away his forever irritated exterior, his arrogance, and his British accent, she realized what it was and at that moment she had been very glad she was looking down and not into his wet, grey eyes.

Ian was in love, in love with someone who did not love him back. When she saw it for the first time she felt a wave of pain roll over her like a dark cloud. All these times that he had yelled at her or been angry at her, he had been hurting.

*Sure, he had probably been taking it out on her, but who didn't deserve that every once in a while—who didn't deserve a well-earned punching bag?*

That day they had talked for the first time. Clara did most of the listening, but she was there, and that's what friends were for.

There was a lump in her throat, though she couldn't figure out exactly why.

Ian had been chasing someone. He had been chasing *his* someone. *Was this the cause of the lump? Her someone? Jack.*

Clara didn't miss the fact that this was the first time she had thought his name without it dripping in anger and resentment.

*Jack.*

*Did she still feel for him?* She was carrying his child. *Shouldn't she at least tell him that? What kind of a person would be pregnant and not even tell her husband, the father of her child?* It was slightly horrifying that this was the kind of woman she was now.

Her cell phone beeped. Krista—as if she could hear Clara thinking these thoughts.

"I'm coming," it read, and under that, "15 July, 11:10 a.m. arrival, Lufthansa, 4550."

Her heart did a little flip.

Krista was coming for a visit. Krista was coming, tomorrow was Clara's last day in Amsterdam, she was moving to a new house in Breda, and she was pretty sure she had at least one friend whom she might even tell about her upcoming move—not that he was apt to display any evidence that he cared.


drie en dertig - thirty-three

The next thing she knew, it was time. As Clara packed her things and brought her bags down to the entry, she relived her last morning in Amsterdam. She already missed the vivacious international city.

That morning she had gone to the market with the idea

that it would be a nice quick trip. Instead, the sun, the people, and the cruising boats had taken her captive and she instead wandered amongst the crowds for an hour, eating freshly baked stroopwafels, cubes of young Gouda and freshly fried calamari, and admiring the bustling market activity. She bought flowers for Ilse and strawberries for the drive.

The crowds of people at the market were amazing. Absent was the usual rush to be first in the cheese line; instead there was an almost sedated form of happiness that can only be induced by wandering with a melting ice cream cone or sitting on the canal drinking wine or cappuccino and watching the boats drift by.

Some boats were tied up to the edge of the canal, located as conveniently as possible to the market. In one handsome, honey-colored wooden boat, an old man was still there, shirt off and working on the start of what—by the end of the summer—would be a large, dark brown belly. There were wine glasses next to him, half full of a nice summer Riesling from a few hundred kilometers away across the German border. His wife was missing, probably picking up sandwiches or herring.

As Clara continued down the stretch past the fish men, regretting her decision to buy a bouquet of roses first thing, she passed a cellist, an acoustic guitarist, and later, a violin-playing puppet. On days like this, it was all so much like a dream that it was hard to believe that she actually lived here.

She sometimes wondered about these memories she was collecting. Years from now, would she remember that she actually lived like this? Or would she forget just how vivid and colorful life could be?

Back at her perfect canalside apartment, Clara sat at her window one last time to watch the water of the canal float by, the very same water that the handsome wooden boat spent its life in.

Just a few months before, she'd had a plain, typical American life. She hadn't known there was a change coming, but here it was. And although the baby was certainly unexpected as well, the change in her had very little to do with the baby. It was just about her.

She was regressing. Regressing in age, regressing in experience, she was slowly but surely working her way back to who she once was. All the lines that had come in the last ten years, all the stress that had plagued her, the uninspired drone that she had become—something about this Dutch life was letting her release it, helping her to just let it all go.

She was glad. Despite the confusion and the pain, Clara was beginning to see. The many things that had been camouflaged by life—regular life—were being set free. She now understood that the life that she was due would someday arrive. She was on a path that was wide open and with it an infinite number of other paths had appeared.

From her chair, gazing wistfully out at the canal, she sighed in relief at the hope that she had never before possessed within.

## Part 3

## *Breda*

### één

"When you get settled in, you should schedule a Dutch class. If you are going to live in The Netherlands it is only proper that you speak Dutch. You should look at the University and also at the community centers and libraries. I believe the BplusC normally has quite reasonable courses. You should have at least three hours of courses per week, as well as work for you to continue at home." Ilse smiled with a tiny self-assured nod at the road ahead. "You'll be speaking in no time."

So far the trip down to Breda with Ilse had been quiet, with little more than a greeting and a few instructions explained. It was hard to get used to this Dutch manner of minimalist communication. If there is something to be said, you say it—and directly. If there's nothing to say, you don't really bother with it. That's not to say that you *don't* exchange pleasantries and make the applicable introductions, it's just that it doesn't get too in-depth, at least not quickly. Your personal information is just that—personal. There's no need to share too much. In addition, there's no need to be overly gratuitous or abundant with your praise or thanks, as Clara found out quickly at the start of the car ride.

She was so thankful for Ilse's moving help that she had been lavishing thanks upon her for the first four minutes when Ilse simply turned to her.

"Stop, Claartje. I understand that you are grateful; I am perfectly fine with helping, now let us move the conversation elsewhere."

*Whoa,* she had thought. Had she been chastised for being *too* thankful?

Clara chose her words more carefully from then on, mentioning the flat Dutch landscape, the crops in the smoothly passing fields, and the weather.

They drove for just more than an hour across the lush, green Dutch countryside. There was farmland, fields for grazing, and more farmland. Each field was enclosed by small waterways so that the water level of each and every piece of land could be perfectly controlled. The Dutch really did create The Netherlands.

Slowly the brick houses got closer and closer together until the streets were lined with rowhouses. Their facades matched, yet they were unique. Brick and white paint were the two main requirements, bringing together the square angles and on occasion, curved molding over the front door. Everything was symmetrical.

The sidewalks were brick also. Perfectly laid with square openings for knobby trees which emerged regularly, street by street, Clara watched them go by as they approached the center of the city.

Ilse pulled the car to the side of a quiet street, parked the car, and cut the ignition. "Here we are," she stepped out of the car and looked around.

Clara stared up at the precise brick and white-painted architecture of the street. It was quiet and cute, not that she'd been worried. It seemed perfect.

Ilse showed her into the house, helped her bring in her things, and handed over the keys. Clara gave her an appreciative thanks and tried not to gush, which her great aunt seemed to appreciate. Ilse recommended that she give her a call the following week to let her know how things were going, and of course, to give her a call if she had any questions on life in The Netherlands in general. After asking if Clara needed anything else, she was gone, and Clara found herself standing in the entry of a large, sparsely decorated, typical

Dutch rowhouse. *However had this happened?*

She was alone now, living in a town called Breda. She realized then, as she swallowed a lump in her throat, how accustomed she had grown to Amsterdam and the many casual acquaintances, both human and structural, she'd made there. Refusing to cry on a day that should be filled purely with excitement, she turned on her heel, stepped outside, and locked the door behind her, devoted to exploring her new city.

Breda's biggest asset was a wonderful city park. It was situated halfway between the train station and the city center, approximately 15 minutes from her house on foot. It had a small sculpture garden, a pond with a nice fountain, and the most beautiful plump rabbits. They looked like someone had purchased them from a pet shop and then released them to run free in the park.

The town square was where the market was held. The large plein was where she spent the first afternoon people watching. A cup of Dutch onion soup was all she needed to make her first day in Breda cozy rather than frightening. She stayed on the square almost the whole afternoon, admittedly a little nervous about returning to her rowhouse.

*Her* rowhouse. She shivered absurdly.

At dusk there was nothing left to do but go home, and she was soon at her door, about to step inside. She stood in the doorway and stared in. The light shone duskily in behind her, casting her shadow right in through the doorway and across the dark hardwood floors, her only friend.

Like a child, she tried to put on a brave face. She stepped inside and turned to carefully latch and deadbolt the door behind her, finally forcing herself to turn towards her supposedly happy future, but she could not. She sat down on her suitcase and burst into tears. Maybe one fresh start was all she'd had in her.

Clara slept on her suitcase that night. It was horribly uncomfortable, but the morning's light brought perspective and she was able to pick herself up off the ground. Still, nearly twenty-four hours after Ilse's departure, Clara was simply walking around, finally getting acquainted with the house. Her stuff stood silently in a pile in the center of the room downstairs. She hadn't touched a thing.

Upstairs there were two rooms, one of which faced the street and had two large windows looking down on the pedestrians and compact cars passing below. She peered out the left window, where she could see the wide canal running along the main street that connected with her smaller street. Yes, she liked Breda, and given the chance, she might come to love it. She shook her head in disbelief. She couldn't believe that this house had been here the whole time empty and waiting for her. Now that she thought about it, this house may have been the cause of her mother's panic when Clara had declared she was going to Holland in the first place.

A mother on a bicycle rode down the street below, and just behind her rode two children on smaller bicycles that were painted bright orange. She turned to face the room. On the left hand side there was a chest of drawers painted a pale blue. Clara walked over and examined them, but found nothing inside. On the far wall was a small closet with some hanging space. To her surprise, a small, but delicate lamp sat on the closet floor. The wrought-iron stem was only about eight inches tall, but wrapped with scrolls of elegant branches. The shade was made of glass and was reminiscent of Tiffany lamps, though the pattern was made of geometric patterns of pastels rather than flowers and leaves of vivid kelly green.

*Yes.* With time this would be her room.

She picked up the lamp and placed it on top of her dresser, but then realized that the plug would not reach if she placed it there. She glanced around the space, taking the time to really visualize her belongings here, something that she had not yet felt inclined to do.

Every part of this was surprising, so why wasn't she more excited?

She decided that she would need some sort of a bedside table for the lamp. She would also need a bed, obviously. She couldn't sleep on her suitcase forever, or even one night more.

It was surprising that Ilse hadn't given her more instruction on where to find a bed and furniture. On her quick tour, she had noted that there were some things they preferred to store in the attic while no one was living there. Clara quickly headed out of the front room, past the purple wooden door of the back bedroom and up the smaller and steeper staircase to the attic.

It was warm and dusty in the attic, but otherwise surprisingly uncluttered for an attic. Clara and Ilse hadn't come up here on their mini-tour. Clara wondered if Ilse's knees preferred to stay on the bottom two floors.

She looked around at the random assortment of things placed neatly in the attic. On her right was a handsome wooden bedframe. It was old, for sure, but well-crafted, not the type of frame that would sway each time she got in and out. There was no mattress, but Clara supposed that a mattress was the type of thing you wouldn't want to keep in an attic indefinitely. There were several small tables stacked curiously on top of each other as if a modern art exhibit. Most things in the attic were made of wood and looked rather old, but in a very good way. Clara picked one small, round table to bring back down to her bedroom. It would be about perfect for her new bedroom.

Rather than tackling her suitcase, she chose the more scenic of the two upstairs windows and took a seat cross-legged on the floor in front of it. The clear skies from their drive the day before had disappeared and the blue was now shut out by a thick layer of clouds hanging so low in the sky she could scarcely believe they were real.

There was a strong wind blowing in, and just the sound of it made her shiver. She pulled her knees into her chest and wrapped her arms around them. For the first time since her freshman year in college, all she wanted to do was see her mother and father and sit on the living room floor in front of them, a thought more terrifying than being alone in just about any foreign country.

Again that afternoon, she left the house without having unpacked a thing. She was in a new city, and she felt that in order to feel at home, she needed to get to know it and understand it.

*But how could one come to understand a city?*

She wandered around the *singel*, the canal that encircled the city just outside the old city wall. There were a number of bulwarks which Clara assumed were watchtowers in the past. At each one she stopped for a few minutes and gazed around at the surrounding city. Compared to Amsterdam, Breda was utterly silent. There were people, but it wasn't nearly as densely populated as Amsterdam was.

It was the way in which they were communicating that was most significant in Clara's eyes. The people that were wandering in and out of the city center were cheerfully socializing. They walked arm in arm sharing tales, however, these people were not co-workers or acquaintances or new friends, but clearly the closest of friends. They were friends that had been there for each other for decades—sisters and brothers even. They were not out enjoying the city life, they were simply living their lives.

The playful chatter and jokes somewhat soothed her loneliness and cleared out a few of the worries from the cracks of her mind, distracting her with the hope of having friends and a family here in Breda. Her fears soon began to dissipate, and she became so intrigued by the potential that she followed one jovial group of chatterers into *Café de Huiskamer*.

She ordered a hot chocolate and sat at a table across the room, still feeling the warmth of their gezellig interaction. It was comforting, despite the fact that she was not a part of it, like happiness by osmosis.

When she later emerged, she discovered that she was just a few hundred feet away from her house. She had walked the entire path around the city. She headed towards home, but in an effort to continue her Breda-warming activities, stopped the moment that it came into view. She stood there silently for ten minutes, examining the place where she could potentially be living for as long as she liked.

Her lassoing stroll around the city helped her to see

another important difference between Breda and Amsterdam. Amsterdam was temporary. It had been an extended vacation from her problems filled with pannekoeken and warme chocolademelk and afternoons at the Van Gogh Museum.

Breda, in contrast, was a typical Dutch town filled with typical Dutch people with jobs and families. Unfortunately, she was not Dutch. Clara was a wandering American— without home and without purpose, growing something inside her that she was skeptical she could even take care of. Nonetheless, Clara had a beautiful rowhouse standing in front of her empty, waiting for her to enter and make her own.

*What was she so afraid of?*

The afternoon sun shifted just then and the fantasy of color that reflected off of her first floor windows was purely inspiring. She suddenly surrendered all of her focus to the tall, wide first floor windows that looked out at the wide sidewalk. They would be the perfect place to showcase her art. If only she could actually have a studio to display and vend her pieces, she thought dreamily. She promised herself that she would soon set up her own makeshift art studio on the first floor. *Why not tempt destiny a bit?*

With a restorative breath, she went inside to get to work on her suitcase. Letting a touch of positive energy carry her on for a few more hours could lead to nothing but good.

The evening was spent munching on loempias from the food cart set up just down the street. The sweet and spicy sauce she dipped them in was a great spice fix, and warmed her up for hours of organization and set up.

First was her easel and work area. She arranged it just like in her apartment at Ellie's, but now she had a whole floor rather than a measly 20 square feet. Obviously she didn't have the table where she'd put in so many hours at Ellie's, but she did find a small, square wooden worktable hidden away in the attic. She placed it in front of the window so it looked out at the pleasant Breda street scene. She spread out her pastels and set up her paints. Tomorrow she would use the deposit returned promptly by Ellie to replenish her supply of sketchpads, paper and blank canvases.

She sat down at the table very happy. The caramel finish on the table was worn away in a comforting way. She imagined her own grandmother diligently working there. Perhaps in the end she would find that she was, in fact, a typical Dutch woman. So what if she didn't have a single piece of clothing in her dresser. At least she had her workspace set up.

Two hours of unpacking and organizing eventually led her to the bookshelves, which were covered with a layer of dust. This sent Clara on a trip to the Target-like Hema where she bought some basic cleaning supplies. By midnight Clara's belongings were unpacked and the house had been cleaned from top to bottom.

She walked around the house the next morning buzzing with a sense of accomplishment. The downstairs was still practically empty, but the tall windows were sparkling after Clara's hard work the night before. The light that entered there left absolutely nothing to be desired. It had an angelic quality to it that gave everything in its path a frost-like shimmer.

She had to make a mattress her first priority this morning. Despite her earlier pronouncement, Clara had spent the night on a mattress of sweatshirts, jeans, and scarves. As much as she adored her hardwood floors, they weren't the most comfortable platform for sleeping.

A few hours out on the town and Clara had successfully found a mattress store and a slim and firm mattress would be delivered to her house later that afternoon. The whole process was seamless, so seamless in fact that Clara couldn't help but think of her day back at the barber shop.

The next day Clara continued forth and followed her aunt Ilse's instructions. She went to work finding a Dutch class, and she figured she was about due for a doctor's appointment as well.

It was a warm day and she wandered around the city center in search of the VVV, the tourist office. She walked all the way through the main square and north out toward the train station looking for tourist information but found nothing. It wasn't until she was on her way back from the station that she spotted the VVV on the street she had walked only five minutes before. She wondered how she had possibly missed it until she examined the other side of the street. This was the spot where she had first noticed the Prince-themed coffee shop. Complete with neon lights, Prince memorabilia, and "Purple Rain" playing in the background, it was no wonder she'd missed the entrance to the tourist office on the opposite side of the street. She wondered if Prince knew such a high homage to him existed in this far out Dutch town.

The people in the Breda VVV were simply delightful. They had tourist magazines and a newspaper; several maps, both current and historic; and Dutch goods of all kinds. Clara was quickly filled in on local holidays, fairs, and celebrations and was given a comically detailed description of the history of the people of the area.

She went home with more information than she could read in a month. She would soon probably be more well-educated on the history of Breda than she was on the history of her own hometown of Sacramento.

At the last minute she remembered to ask about Dutch classes, and as a result was detained for at least 20 minutes more for a fairly inconcise lecture on the best way to go about learning the Dutch language.

Clara stepped out the door and immediately stripped off the extra layer she was wearing atop her t-shirt. It felt good to bare her arms and feel the sun on her shoulders, but felt even better to peel off the weight of 90 minutes of new information.

After a quick peek in the Prince coffee shop—she could hardly abscond when such an interesting establishment was so close by—she followed her map to the BplusC, apparently the best option for Dutch classes. As a matter of fact, she had been told that the BplusC offered community education classes of all sorts; she had the complete list of this season's classes to prove it.

At the library, at least that's what the BplusC appeared to

be, Clara quickly found a simple and useful textbook of Dutch grammar, *Essential Dutch Grammar*. Unfortunately, she quickly became confused about how exactly to check out the book. There was some kind of membership fee that had to be paid via bank transfer. She looked over at the librarians, who looked friendly and willing to help, but couldn't fathom another minute of carefully listening; she had expanded her horizons too much for the day. She returned the book to its shelf and swiftly exited. This is what the internet was for.

To her relief, the search for a general practitioner took no time at all. She found a nice guide for expatriates in the information the VVV had provided and began by calling a few of the female names listed. It wasn't that she didn't like male doctors, and it had very little to do with the recent betrayal by her husband, she just thought she might be more comfortable with a female doctor. She asked if they were accepting patients, which is what the expat guides had instructed her to do.

The scariest part was her own worry about how to explain her situation, but she learned soon enough that it didn't matter whatsoever. They either had openings or they didn't. Beyond that, a patient was a patient. They didn't care why or how she ended up pregnant and needing a new general practitioner in The Netherlands; they simply got down to business.

Clara soon had an appointment scheduled with one Dr. Booij, and although Clara had only spoken with her assistant on the phone, she already felt optimistic about the doctor-patient relationship. The assistant had assured her that the timing was appropriate for a first visit and told her that they not only spoke English, but were looking forward to meeting her. It was a warm and genial interaction. Neither "pre-existing condition" nor "COBRA" was mentioned at all. Once again Clara was left thinking that perhaps she had been born on the wrong side of the Atlantic.

Early the next morning Clara meandered into the town center for a cup of tea. She had now reduced her caffeine consumption to one cup every third day, which she was very proud of, though the transition was mostly caused by the lack of a coffeemaker in her new home. She knew that a little caffeine was okay, at least in the U.S. that was what they said, but she was worried that they would be stricter here in The Netherlands and she'd get a lecture on her first appointment.

She got a cup of tea and then found herself on the long, cobblestone shopping street. Halfway down the unusually quiet street, she realized that all of the stores were still closed. She checked her phone, and saw that it wasn't Sunday, but Monday morning, so it was strange that nothing was open yet. She continued down the empty street until the turn toward her house, feeling more than a little befuddled. She should really start making a list of everything about Dutch culture that confused her.

*Why do men use so much hair gel? What was so bitter about bitterballen?*

twee

On the day of her first doctor's appointment, the weather was beautiful when Clara stepped outside. She thought about this moment and how far she'd come. She felt kind of proud of herself as she shut the door of her home, a nice, traditional Dutch home in a pleasant Dutch city. She seemed almost normal.

After a fifteen minute walk in the direction opposite the center, Clara spotted the address she was looking for. The building was slightly modern—perhaps built in the 60s— square, and medium-sized. She wondered how this could possibly be a hospital, or even a clinic.

The sign on the door listed three names, two besides her own Dr. Booij, so she let herself in and walked up to a small desk where a friendly looking young woman was working at a computer.

"Hallo!" the woman greeted her cheerfully.

"Hallo," said Clara, "I'm Clara Mason. I'm not sure if I'm

in the right place. I have a 10:15 appointment with Dr. Booij."

"Yes, excellent. Here you are, Clara." She handed Clara a clipboard with several generic looking forms. "Please fill these out and then bring them back to me."

Clara filled out the forms, all of which were in English, and returned them a few minutes later.

"Thank you. Dr. Booij will be right out."

Indeed, just two or three minutes later a woman emerged from a door just down the hall and, looking at Clara curiously, spoke her name.

The woman wore brown slacks, a blue blouse with buttons down the front and a brown and dark blue patterned sweater. She looked nothing like a nurse, which of course she wasn't.

"Ms. Mason?" she asked with a polite smile, "I'm Dr. Booij. It's nice to meet you."

Clara shook her hand and followed her back down the hall into a small office and examination room. Never, in all of her life, had Clara been met in the waiting room by the doctor. All the fears she'd had about the overly small clinic, being lectured by her GP, and about possibly having a baby in The Netherlands in general, all flew out the window.

She spent ten minutes talking with her doctor about her pregnancy, how she was feeling, and her eating and exercise habits. After a short examination, Clara was sent on her way with an appointment for a few weeks later and instructions to call if she had any concerns or questions.

On her way out the door, she nearly ran headlong into the next patient, a tall, friendly-looking woman with long, glossy brown hair.

"Oy! Sorry!" the woman said, stepping back to allow Clara to exit the building.

"Sorry!" Clara repeated, though in straight English rather than the melodic Dutch *sore-y.* The woman smiled as Clara thanked her for holding the door and they both went on their way.

Clara pondered her first experience as she walked down

the street back to her house. Compared to what she was used to, this place was just... something. She couldn't even put a label on it.

The street on which she was walking was bordered on either side with the strangest trees. They were the knobby trees she noticed when she first entered Breda, only now they had grown a little more and she could tell that they were molded very specifically. They only grew flat, as if they had been trimmed carefully and strictly each year of their life. They provided shade and gave the street a fresh green look while at the same time staying strictly in the space of the sidewalk. She could hardly imagine these trees ever causing a problem.

*Was this a metaphor for the way the Dutch society functioned? Cleanly, attractively, efficiently, and within proper guidelines and regulations?* She laughed to herself as she continued down the tree-lined street. The happiness bubbling from her lips felt euphoric. Out of nowhere, she skipped. It felt so good that she skipped again.

*Whoa.* Perhaps the pregnancy was emotionally flailing her far more than she'd thought. *Oh, no!* She had forgotten her colorful purple and silver scarf at the doctor's office, so she turned around and skipped back in the other direction.

At the doctor's office, she quickly retrieved her scarf from the waiting area and wished the young woman a good day on the way out. The timing was such that the brown-haired woman from before followed her right out.

Clara gave her a smile, and waved to her as well, wishing her a nice day.

"A nice mood for you?" the woman asked with a smile.

"Yes," Clara laughed, "definitely. I have been feeling so blah all week, and now somehow it has just gone away."

"Oh," she nodded. "Yes, that's pregnancy."

"You think?" asked Clara.

"Oh, yes. No doubt about it. Is this your first?"

"Yes," replied Clara, pondering the woman's explanation of her emotional nothingness. "I guess... I guess I'm not even sure what I should or shouldn't expect. It's all so new."

"Yes, it can be quite surprising. Even from one child to the next."

"How many children do you have?" Clara asked.

"This is my third," explained the woman, "and I've had some unique experiences with each."

"I see," said Clara. "Are you going this way?" She pointed in the direction of her house and the bizarrely shaped trees.

"I am," she confirmed. "Shall we walk together?"

"I'd love to!" said Clara, probably a little too enthusiastically, "I'm Clara, by the way."

"I'm Karin. It's a pleasure to meet you. Are you very new to the country?" Karin asked.

"Yes, fairly new," Clara explained, "I've been here about six weeks."

"Wow, yes, you are new to town. And why did you choose to come to Breda?"

"Well, my grandmother was from Breda."

"I see. Well, I have to turn here," Karin gestured to a street just up to the right, "By the way, I am part of a yoga class for expecting mothers. If you like, you are welcome to join us."

"I'd love to," said Clara.

"Terrific." They exchanged phone numbers and Karin gave her the address of the yoga studio. Afterwards, Karin explained, they often went to a café to chat, and Clara was welcome to come along to that as well. Many of the women in the class already had children, so she would be able to learn a lot about giving birth and raising children in The Netherlands.

*How exciting.* Her week's mood had been reversed and she had a friend date for the following week. She never imagined that her day would be this successful.

To add to it, when she got home, under her mail slot sat her very own copy of *Essential Dutch Grammar*. Its prompt arrival was startling. Somehow, Clara had already been living in Breda for two weeks.

More and more with each sunrise, she was feeling a pull

that made her want to spring out of bed. Every morning she went straight to the window, always wondering if it was all a dream, if she would look out and there would be no canal, no swans, no scarves waving in the wind, and no bicycles.

One afternoon she came to the realization that a house owned by her mother in a foreign country was already far more hers than anything else she had ever had. Jack's house had been far less so, even after 10 years.

Almost immediately she began work on tracing a mural on her new studio wall. For a second she considered calling Ilse to ask if it was okay, but she just as quickly decided that it would be far too ridiculous of a call to ever make.

*Can I draw a huge picture on the wall?* There was no way she was going to call Ilse for that interaction. If she moved out, she could always paint over it.

Clara planned carefully, marking it out and noting the colors to be used—bright areas full of color contrasted paths of nothing but clear and abstract outlines in black and white, rigid outlines with abrupt shapes and lines.


drie


That night, Clara decided to go out on the town. She'd learned in one of her Welcome to Breda books that the city had something called a *koopavond*. Every Thursday the stores in Breda were open late so that citizens could run errands, go shopping, or spend time socializing with friends.

Around six she left her house, having decided to do some window-shopping on the bustling shopping street before going to an interesting Indonesian eatery she'd seen advertised in the Breda city magazine. That trip to the Breda VVV had been life changing.

Clara popped in and out of stores for nearly an hour. She watched families pick out sausages from the meat shop, teenagers try on dozens of pairs of sunglasses, and middle-aged women pick out scarves and earrings for each other.

At the end of the street she was about to pull out her map to figure out how to get to the Indonesian restaurant when she saw a store that she hadn't previously noticed.

*Prenatal* was a store for mothers.

She would soon be a mother... She willed herself to be strong enough to handle it and turned sharply to walk in.

She was momentarily enchanted by the pale colors, toys, and stuffed animals as she walked through the menagerie of childhood. She wandered around the store for a while, examining much but touching nothing.

A saleswoman noticed her and began to walk toward her after a few minutes, presumably to ask if she needed any help, but then turned and walked away at the last minute. Maybe she noticed that Clara was a foreigner, or perhaps she saw how deep in thought Clara was and sensed that she just wanted to be alone.

An old-fashioned crib was set up in a darling way in the corner. Clara walked up to it and couldn't help but reach out her hand and run her fingers on the smooth, carved wooden rungs that spiraled upwards, just the type of sensory item that could somehow improve a child's development. The sheets in it were pink satin, which was slightly comical. She could only imagine what spit-up would look like on pink satin. *Yuck.* Though she supposed she would have to get used to that.

Atop the pink satin sheets was a baby quilt covered with giraffes in every pastel color known to man, and edged with cream eyelet lace. A friendly giraffe sat perched in the corner of the crib on the blanket. It had a smile on its face and a string poking out of its foot. Clara assumed it would play a lullaby when pulled, perhaps "Rock-a-bye Baby" or a jaunty, "Baby Elephant Walk."

She turned away from the crib before the display of pallid giraffes brought tears to her eyes. She turned to face rows upon rows of baby bottles and sippy cups, these in bright primary colors and patterns of all kinds.

There were lullabies playing in the background, she realized, probably a cd mixed with soothing music of all kinds. It *was* soothing, and kind of made her feel drowsy at the same time. The comfy purple rocker in the middle of the book area looked just about perfect for drifting off for an afternoon doze.

She strolled over to it, noticing books, pacifiers, baby dishes, and tiny socks, shoes, and hats. At home alone each of these was entirely intimidating, but here looking around, who could be frightened by such tiny gear?

Confidently, she sat down in the rocker and looked up at the colors covering the walls floor to ceiling. As she stared at them, they seemed to come closer and the amount of merchandise around her seemed to multiply. She would need to acquire all these things. If not all, many, and more importantly, *when* and *where?*

She was living here now, but where would she be in a month and a half when her visa expired? She closed her eyes as the room began to spin and the tears filled her eyes. They were running down her cheeks when she felt a soft hand on hers. She opened her eyes to see an older woman staring down at her.

"Ma'am," the silver-haired woman spoke softly, "It's alright. It will be alright." The woman handed her a tiny cup of tea and a book, an English version of *Harold and the Purple Crayon*.

Clara opened to the first page and read in silence and sipped her tea, altogether unable to comprehend the understanding in the older woman's eyes. Perhaps she owned the store; perhaps she was a grandmother with a hundred grandchildren; perhaps she had lived the panic that Clara was feeling right then. For whatever reason, she had shared a piece of wisdom with Clara that she would never forget. This journey that Clara was on stirred her in so many ways. Maybe the stress, the confusion, and the loneliness were just stepping stones on the path that would, with hope, lead her in the right direction.

## vier

Without thinking, Clara answered the phone call that was ringing in.

"That is not your house, Clara."

Clara actually groaned.

"Clara!" her mother reprimanded her. "Don't *groan* at me. Now you get on a plane right now and come home before it's too late."

"What do you mean, 'too late'?"

Her mother huffed at her and went on, "If I wasn't so scared to go over there…"

"Scared!?" Clara yelped, "Why would you be scared to come here? It's all flowers and fluffy bunnies. I wouldn't be surprised if Rainbow Brite was actually born here. How could you not tell me that you *owned a house* here? Don't you think that's something I might have wanted to know?"

"Oh, I don't think so young lady. I know the way you think. You are just getting yourself in deeper and deeper. You do not need any *motivation* to stay over there. Now you come home right now. I made a doctor's appointment for you on Monday. It's with Dr. Bromsun. You remember him, right?"

"Yeah, Mom, I'd love to go have a doctor's appointment with Jack's great uncle, who is both a gerontologist and 150 years old."

"He is a nice man and *very* experienced."

Clara laughed loudly. *True. He was experienced.*

"No, no, no, and no. I'm sorry, Mother, but I will not be making it to my appointment with Dr. Bromsun next week because I will be out of the country and living my life. I will not be coming home, but instead will be living in a house that you own in a country that you have never been to—and that you would love, by the way. I can hardly believe you've never been here. It's frickin' idyllic."

"Do *not* swear at me, young lady."

"It's not a swear word, Mom," she argued, though she did regret bringing up the idea of a motherly visit. After the Delia fiasco, she wasn't sure if she could take anyone but Krista. "How's Dad, anyway? I haven't talked to him in ages."

"He's fine. He's working. He doesn't have time to lecture you on your poor life choices." She tsk, tsked a few times before going on. "Apparently he's left me to do that on my own."

She let her mother go on for at least five more minutes, focusing her attention on her new Dutch language book during the lecture.

"Well, I've gotta go, Mom," she spoke eventually.

"Fine, but let me tell you, you had better take a good, long, hard look at the life you're building and see if it makes any sense at all. Do you understand me?"

"Yes, Mother." She tried to keep the sarcasm out of her voice, which was difficult, though apparently she did it well enough to keep her mother's chastisements at bay. They hung up and Clara sucked in a breath of clean, independent air. *How had her mother found out about the move to Breda?* That one kind of stumped her.

She turned her attention back to her textbook and worked her way through the first chapter. When she finished, she moved to her guidebook. Krista would arrive in just under a month, and Clara wanted to have a whole week of fun planned out. If things worked out badly on the visa front, she would be about to leave the country. *Ouch.*

She used the book to map out a plan for showing Krista around the country. They would definitely hit up Amsterdam, and probably Leiden, and then maybe The Hague, or *Den Haag*, as it was called here. Many of the international courts were located in Den Haag and she thought Krista might be interested in a tour of the facilities. She would take Krista to the beach, and then back to Breda to relax for a few days.

Once she'd drawn out her map, she went online for more ideas. The bright orange national tourism website was filled with ideas, and Clara noted a few of the more prominent locations and museums.

Next, since she was on a roll, she moved to the

immigration website. There, she was able to find a couple more possibilities for Dutch courses. There were beginner courses all the way up to the last course, which was just before taking some official test. Apparently, the test was one of the steps on the path to citizenship, as were the discounted Dutch classes. Since you kind of had to be on the path to becoming a citizen in order to be eligible for the reduced fee, she wasn't sure if she qualified. She liked it a lot, but she wasn't sure if becoming a full citizen was something she was ready to commit to. Plus, her mother would probably disown her.

At that moment, her cell phone vibrated. It was a new message from Karin, her new pregnant yoga friend. Class was canceled.

*Shoot*, she thought, there goes her chance at finding pregnant Dutch friends. A second later, another new message displayed. Although class was canceled, they would not be canceling coffee. She should meet them at *Café de Bommel* at 1 p.m.

## vijf

The café was only about half full when she walked inside. She took a moment to let her eyes adjust. It's too bad they hadn't picked an outdoor café. It was such a nice day, and it was a shame to waste it. Before her previous thought had slipped in and out of the current of her mind, she spotted two pregnant women—two tall, Dutch, pregnant women—and she found herself wordlessly following them through the café and out the back door to an outdoor patio just off the canal.

*Perfect, what a lovely find.* She would surely be coming back. She looked for Karin and found her on the left side of the table, happily chatting in Dutch with the woman next to her.

Clara felt a swell of nervousness and shame come over her. She did not speak Dutch, and as much as she wanted to make some new Dutch friends, the guilt was nearly overwhelming her already. She almost wanted to turn around and leave rather than have to make the women switch over to English just for her.

At precisely that moment, Karin turned her head to the side as she laughed and caught sight of Clara.

"Claartje!" she cried. "Wonderful. I'm glad you came. We're about to order. Ah! Here's the waitress now."

Clara turned to see a teenage girl in all black poised and ready to begin taking their order. She looked to be about 19 and her dirty blond hair was pulled back in a feathered ponytail.

"Goedemiddag. Hoe kan ik jullie helpen?" Clara eased herself into a chair on the same side of the table as Karin, close enough to chat even though the seats directly on either side of her were taken. She nodded politely to the women around her, acknowledging their names as each woman introduced herself. There was a Janneke, an Annemarie, and possibly a Mary, though that didn't seem very Dutch at all.

She quickly noticed that one other woman spoke English as well. After watching her out of the corner of her eye, she found that the other woman wasn't all that good at Dutch either, which was a relief for Clara.

The waitress continued around the large jumble of tables taking orders, most asking for pannekoeken, omelettes, pastries, or appelgebak, a warm and cinnamon-filled dessert somewhere in between apple pie and apple tart.

The center of the table was already cluttered with tiny glasses of fresh squeezed orange juice and cups of tea, coffee, and hot chocolate. Clara ordered a Spanish omelette and a cup of decaf, needing the burst of energy but not wanting them to think she was a bad mother because she occasionally had caffeine. Today she'd have to settle for getting it placebo-style.

A few minutes later there was a tiny shuffle when one woman stepped away to make a phone call, and Clara found herself sitting next to the other English speaking woman.

"Hi," the woman smiled, "I'm Beth. I'm from Boston."

"Hi! I'm Clara."

"Yeah, I got that. Clara-Claartje, it's nice you already have a Dutch name," she laughed.

"Yeah," Clara responded with a self-conscious chuckle, "a Dutch name—when everything about me screams 'American!'"

"No," said Beth, "not screams. Maybe... quietly states." She gave Clara a reassuring smile, "You just look so nervous. Did you just arrive?"

"Um, well, kind of. I've been here almost two months," Clara exaggerated slightly. *Did she really look that nervous?*

"Well, you are fresh off the boat. And your husband is Dutch?"

"What? No. I don't have a husband. I mean, I do, but he's no longer with me."

"Ahhhm..." she hummed in response, "I see," and with an understanding nod that was that. No questions, no pitying looks.

*How strange*, especially from an American.

"Karin told me all about the woman from California who would be coming. Claartje, Claartje, Claartje. It's funny, they always assume we will be just thrilled to meet another expat." She shook her head, "though it is a relief to be able to speak English for a while—my Dutch is terrible. So where are you from in California?"

They chatted about California and New England until the food arrived, when Clara finally had an opportunity to talk to Karin. They chatted about her job and her kids, and then Clara was passed on to the woman on her left, Annemarie, who asked her about her yoga practice and her plans for learning Dutch. Clara felt kind of awkward telling Annemarie that she had never actually *been* to a yoga class before, but Annemarie didn't find this problematic at all.

"Look at us!" she laughed, "We are all pregnant and eating enormous plates of food. I think it's safe to say that we're all here for the social aspects as much as we are for the health benefits."

This comment made Clara very happy. She liked Annemarie. She reminded her just a little bit of Krista. Once again, Clara was stunned by their English skills. It was like she was in a country of native speakers with just the slightest twinge of an accent. As a matter of fact, she was fairly certain she could understand a Dutch person speaking English better than she could understand someone from Georgia or anyplace else with a similarly byzantine drawl.

After they made plans for the following week and dealt with the check, everyone stood to exchange goodbyes. Listening to the chorus of Dutch salutations, she turned to Beth once more.

"Don't you feel so guilty? Making them speak English just for you, for us?" Clara didn't really mean it as a question, just a statement—a mutual understanding—so Beth's answer surprised her.

"Not really. Maybe I used to, but I have been studying Dutch for a while. I try very hard, but to be perfectly honest, I suck at it. My three years of Spanish basically amounted to being able to say a fairly confident, 'Feliz Navidad.' Still, I try," she stated emphatically, "but they always, always switch. No matter how hard I try and no matter how many times I respond in my pitiful Dutch. Eventually, I just let them win. I always start in Dutch and in a group like this, I can hold out pretty long, though inevitably if I am in a one-on-one conversation, we end up switching to English. Their English is just inarguably better than my Dutch will ever be. And I've been here for three years," she added.

"O-kay," said Clara, her jaw hanging slack, "Good to know."


zes


That evening Clara wandered to the park for a nice long sit. She spent the time reading peacefully and slipping in and out of daydreams. The weather had been absolutely perfect over the last few days. She hoped it would be the same in July when Krista was there. At dusk she closed her book and stood to leave when a movement nearby caught her attention. She turned just in time to see a fuzzy brown creature scamper across the park grass. She tightened up, hoping it was just a squirrel or a rabbit and not a dirty rodent.

*Yuck.*

Now that she thought about it, she couldn't remember ever seeing a squirrel in Breda—or in The Netherlands. She peered through the shadows in search of the animal. This strange scuttling creature looked a little small to be one of the fat, plush, show rabbits she regularly saw here in the park.

*What was in a park if not squirrels and rabbits?* She shuddered involuntarily and then shrieked as the creature suddenly reappeared and zig-zagged across the grass towards her, stopping and starting with each of her shrieks. As it came closer, her shrieks grew louder, and it stopped, turned and made a beeline across the path away from her.

She exhaled, but tensed again as she saw it stop just 20 feet away. In the dark, it looked to be pausing to nibble on a little something on the ground. She heard a noise behind her and turned to find herself looking down at the highly amused faces of an older Dutch couple. It was then that she realized she had jumped up onto the park bench when the strange little thing began running towards her.

"Kunnen we je helpen?" they asked her.

"Uh…" Clara looked from the gray-haired couple to the shadowed parkland where the creature had last been spotted in the dark. The older woman followed her gaze and let out an understanding chuckle before saying something unintelligible to her husband and pointing into the darkness.

"Wh-What is it?" stammered Clara, not even bothering to ask if they spoke English. She was too thrown off for any formalities. Rodents and strange creatures scurrying around in the dark did not bring out her best characteristics.

The man chuckled now as well and turned to her, "It's an egel."

"A what? An eagle?"

"It's an egel. What is that in English, Margot?" His wife ho-hummed and tilted her head.

"Well, I don't know as a matter of fact." She chuckled warmly again, "I can't seem to recall the English name at the moment."

"Don't worry," her husband continued, "it won't hurt you," he smiled.

"But is it a... a rodent?" Clara asked timidly.

"Mmm, yes," he nodded, "I believe so."

Clara shuddered again, causing them both to laugh.

"It's not a rodent," his wife disagreed. "It's just nocturnal."

The man stepped forward and extended his hand, "Can I help you down?"

"Yes, thank you." Clara took his hand, and let him help her down off the bench.

"Which way to your home?" he asked.

"Um, this way," she explained, pointing in the same direction that they were heading."

"Ahh, nice." the woman replied, "We can walk together if you like."

"Yes, thank you," said Clara. "Have you always lived in Breda?" she asked after a minute.

"Yes, we raised our family here," said the woman. "You have a family as well?" the woman asked.

"Not quite yet," Clara smiled. When they parted ways and wished one another a good evening, Clara quickly stopped to pull out her dictionary. *What on Earth was an egel?* She paged through, but found nothing. Apparently knowing the English name of this little being wasn't a priority for the makers of her little *woordenboek*.

On the walk home, Clara paused by a glowing window, lingering secretly behind the sheer cream curtain while one of the house's inhabitants played a beautiful piece of music on the piano. She felt like she was looking in on a magazine scene or watching a movie. The room had a high ceiling, paintings hung elegantly on the walls, and a sparkling chandelier which created a glow that somehow complemented the melody flowing from the perfect grand piano. In the U.S. houses were so much further apart and so much further from the sidewalk. Here she felt like she could secretly peer into people's lives. She wondered if they did the same to her.

$$C_M$$

Clara began attending the yoga class and social hour every week. By leaving her scarf in the doctor's office just once, Clara had become part of an active social group of pregnant mothers. The confidence that having friends brought to life was pleasing beyond all belief. Annemarie had now visited her twice, and Clara had even accompanied her to the park to meet her sister and mother-in-law once. She otherwise spent her time reading, sketching, studying Dutch, and attempting to make her house a home while slowly counting the days until Krista arrived.

At the last post-yoga social gathering she'd found out that the mothers in the group were almost exclusively homebirth advocates. Between the group and Dr. Booij, Clara found she was actually considering the possibility. According to the good doctor, since she was considered low risk, it was a perfectly normal choice, at least in this country. She could not think of a single person that had chosen a homebirth back in the U.S., though she did know one cousin who'd had one kind of by accident. She'd wanted to finish watching the final episode of *Friends*. Seemed normal enough to Clara.

She had plans to meet with a local midwife who had been recommended to her by Annemarie. Marieke, who had delivered a load of babies over the years, had worked with another international mother that the ladies at the pregnant yoga class knew. Sure, Clara might be deported before then, but why worry until it actually happened? Sometimes she couldn't believe how Krista-like she had become—*flying by the seat of her pants with a baby on the way? Who would have thought it possible?*

"It takes a great deal of focus to constantly live by the seat of your pants," Krista had once told her. Now that Clara was living that life, she wouldn't exactly describe it in that manner. She believed it took more ambivalence than focus, but she had to admit it wasn't a bad way to live.

zeven

And then one day, it was July 15. Krista would be arriving today. Clara literally jumped out of bed. She pulled on her jeans and a green t-shirt and grabbed a long-sleeved shirt as an extra layer, assuming that it would be cool that evening in Amsterdam. At the last minute, she wrapped her turquoise pashmina around her neck. She bought it at the market the past week and couldn't help but feel a little extra European when she had a long, silky scarf wrapped several times around her neck. She was heading towards her new Dutch boots, short, black and slightly heeled, when she glanced at the clock—7:37.

Even if she went to a café for breakfast, stopped at the market, and then took a stop train—the slowest option—to the airport, she would still be early. She thought about making breakfast or maybe doing some dusting, but decided against it. This was a special day: her best friend was coming to visit.

She grabbed her bag, a book, and a bottle of water. She primed her mp3 player for her stroll to the station, scrolling straight to Feist, just because she was feeling a little feisty. Krista was arriving!

The process of getting to the airport felt like it took forever. After Clara got to the station, she caught the first train to Amsterdam, a fast intercity train with just one switch. She stepped off the train below Schiphol International Airport just before 10 a.m., more than an hour before Krista's plane was set to arrive. She could have stayed on and gone all the way to

Amsterdam to pass the time, but she decided she couldn't risk missing the moment of arrival when Krista came bursting through the tulip doors. Clara took the escalators up to the main floor and first stepped outside. Perhaps there was a town outside of Schiphol, she considered, but no, there didn't look to be much of anything outside of the small entrance plaza. Clara turned around and went back inside. There were plenty of shops in which she could attempt to pass the time.

If only she felt like shopping.

After some forced window shopping and a ham and cheese croissant from the *AH to go*, she stationed herself directly in front of the international arrivals door. Just as when she'd arrived some 75 days before, they were patterned with cheesily festive tulip cling. She loved it.

The next few minutes passed quickly as she observed the people around her. Airports were always such interesting places what with all the people coming and going and the greetings and goodbyes. She was glad that today she was here for a happy greeting and not a weepy one like some of the others around her were clearly suffering through.

She heard a forceful snap in front of her face and came back to reality.

"Hel-lo!" Her best friend was standing right in front of her, not 18 inches from her face. "Welcome back from fantasyland. Did you bring me a souvenir?"

"Krista!" Clara hooted, "Yay!" Clara wrapped her arms around her and squeezed with all her might.

"Uf-" said Krista. "Glad I turned down that weird breakfast burrito. Might've lost it there. What's up, darlin'? Geez, you don't even look all that preggers. What's up with that?"

"Nghuh." Clara shrugged. "I guess I'm only getting started?" She answered with a question, though it's not like Krista could give her an answer. Krista was probably the only person less informed on pregnancy than she was.

"I guess," Krista nodded in agreement, "so what are we doing? Gotta plan?"

"I just might have."

"Huh?"

"What?"

"You talked funny."

"Shut the hell up." They both laughed giddily. At least the real communication wasn't a problem.

"Now, I'm starving," Krista stated. "Food, first. What do ya got here?"

"Everything. What do you feel like?"

"Everything. Hmmm..." she pondered, "something with meat."

"Meat? For breakfast?"

"It's not breakfast my time!"

"No, it's two in the morning your time."

Krista belly laughed. "Like I said, meat."

Clara eyed her but then gave one firm nod and grinned. "Okay. Meat." Finally the abundance of Argentinean steakhouses was going to pay off. She hadn't been to one yet. With that they hopped on a train into Amsterdam.

After a nice, square meal centered around a huge slab of beef, Krista pounded a few espressos and was ready to go.

"Should we go to the beach? I remember you said you went once and that sounds nice. It's been hot as shit in the valley and today," she held her hand out and felt the perfect, 80-degree air, "would be a sweet day for lounging in the sand."

"I guess," Clara laughed, "It's actually not far from here and we have all day. We just have to make it home by, I dunno, 3 a.m. maybe?"

"Let's do it. I'm ready."

Clara smiled and turned to lead the way. On the way back she took Krista past Dam Square, pointing out the National Monument and explaining the history of the square.

"...It's actually built on top of a dam, you see. Because it's all about controlling water."

"So," Krista interrupted, "is this whole trip going to be a Dutch history lesson? Should I expect this every day?"

"I just thought it was interesting. I thought you might, too."

"Yeah, not really. Are there palm trees on this beach?"

Clara began laughing. It's not that she was all that experienced or wizened, but Krista's ignorance was comedic. "Krista did you look at a globe at all before you got on the plane?"

"Hey, I'm not a history major. I make my money by judging people that I don't know anything about, and I do it well. Why would I start educating myself now?"

"It's not like I'm asking you to tell me the capital of Uzbekistan, Krista. I'm talking about the distance between The Netherlands and the equator."

"We're near the equator?"

"No, that's the point, we're not even close to the equator. I'm not even sure where the closest palm trees are, maybe Spain?"

"Spain? How close are we to Spain?"

"Not close."

"Shoot. I've always wanted to go to Spain. Hey, I thought that the whole benefit of going to Europe is that everything is so close that Americans are stunned by it. You can go everywhere in six weeks."

"Uh, not exactly. It is pretty compact, but it still takes... I don't know, like 20 hours by train to get from here to say, Budapest. That's not exactly a quick ride."

"Where's Budapest again? Turkey?"

"Hungary!"

Krista laughed. "I knew it was something delicious."

"Oh, my-"

"I was kidding, Clare." Krista interrupted. "Now if you would like to inform me exactly what latitudinal conditions are reasonable for palm trees, go ahead, I would love to hear about it."

Clara punched her in the arm. "Never mind, forget I said anything."

"So, just to sum up: we're not going to Spain?"

"No."

"and we're not going to see any palm trees today?"

"No."

"Son of a- Alright, but we'll eat some cheese right? You're always talking about cheese."

"Yes," Clara replied with a large smile, "we will eat cheese."


## acht


"Don't we have to buy tickets for all these train rides we're taking?" Krista asked on the short train ride on the way to the beach. "Or is this some kind of glorified socialist perk— free train travel?"

"Ha, ha… I wish," said Clara dryly. "It's nice, but not that nice. I got us a day pass for today, just so we wouldn't have to worry about buying tickets left and right." Clara smiled broadly. "I wanted my friend to be able to go wherever she wanted on her first day in Holland."

"Cool. Grazie. What are we going to do with my stuff? These wheels won't do well on sand."

Clara pondered for a moment. She hadn't really considered the bag. Krista was always such a light packer— the size of her rollaboard was even surprising. "I guess it depends on where we go."

"I'm up for anything, really. Where were *you* thinking?"

Clara smiled and patted her friend's hand significantly. "Well, I was actually hoping that you would say something like that. Like I said, we have a day pass, so I was thinking that if you were up for it, we could have a little Holland crawl. The beach in The Hague, maybe a stop in Leiden or Rotterdam, then some sort of pub stop, probably in Amsterdam, and then we can head home on the loopy night train. It'd be a long day, for sure, but you would really get a feel for the country and this area in particular, which is where most of the population lives."

"Loopy?"

"Is that all you took from that?"

"You can't use a word like loopy unless you're going to explain it. Is it like a tourist train? Like a tequila train or the Skunk Train or that wild-ass one that goes from Sacramento to Reno on Friday nights and has a cigar car and karaoke and stuff?"

"I have absolutely no idea what you're talking about."

"Why's it loopy?"

"Oh, it runs in a circle."

"That isn't loopy!" Krista wailed.

"Shhh..." Clara hushed her. "We have to use inside voices on the train."

A look of outrage passed across Krista's face, but then she just stared at Clara, pondering the expression.

"You shushed me."

"Yeah, sorry, I didn't want you to get in trouble. You have to kind of watch yourself. It's easy to get carried away and they just really don't like it when you talk loudly."

Krista simply stared at Clara. "Hmm... Well, I guess Brian was right."

"About what?" asked Clara with interest, but Krista didn't respond, she was eyeing Clara with a look of utter... glee. "What did Brian say? And are you still with him? Wow. I'm a little shocked to hear his name. It's been months."

"Yeah, four months. Crazy, eh? Who'd a thunk?"

"Focus, please." Clara waved her hand in front of Krista's blinking eyes. "Now what was he right about?"

Again Krista was distracted by something. This time she smiled, gave her head a little shake and continued. "Okay. Dirt, dirt, dirt." She inhaled through her nostrils and went on, "When Delia got back she had a lot of things to say about you, or so I heard."

"Wait, from who?"

"I'm getting to that."

"Okay. Then hurry up."

Krista chuckled but resumed her story. "Delia was full of

stories about all the crazy things you did—supposedly—fantasy ice cream and tulips and crank organs, subtitles, whatever. A lot of them I had already heard from you, so it was just confirmed. But one day Brian was at Café Bernardo for the champagne brunch. I wasn't there, he was with some buddies, but there was a group of girls there, and they were talking about traveling and studying abroad and how it was their one chance to have, like, a life-changing experience."

Clara nodded along. "Certainly."

"And then one girl cited a certain piece of evidence. She said that one of her old UOP roommates said that her sister had just moved to Europe. Well, they actually said that she moved to Sweden, or Belgium or something, but whatever, that's not the point. They said that—now, I'm really sorry about this—that she had always been kind of a pushover and that she'd always let her family and her loudmouth best friend-" here Krista paused to point at herself proudly from above as if she had been paid the highest of compliments, "pushed her around, but that *now*, she had become... well, kind of a bitch."

Krista sat back in her seat and exhaled loudly. Clara didn't respond, she just stared at Krista, blank-faced and blinking. Finally, she spoke.

"So," Clara started, "you're telling me that you heard from somebody you've been dating for a trivially small number of months-"

"Hey!"

"that they sat next to a group of girls that were gossiping loudly—oh, wait, over a *champagne brunch*—that one of their friends that went to a university that my sister happened to go to—along with 2,000 other privileged females," she added as an aside, "said that her sister changed a lot after she moved to Swe-den." Clara said the last word slowly to point out the utter absurdity of it all, but Krista was ready with a rebuttal and defense.

"First of all, ouch! Trivial? WTF bitch?" Krista gave her a mock-scandalized look, but still looked quite content overall.

"Now I'll give you the UOP thing. There's a pretty fair chance that a fair number of female UOP grads eventually move to Sac and regularly frequent Café Bernardo. *But,*" she emphasized, "your sister is certainly one of them. Plus, now no offense, but you were kind of pushed around at times in the past."

Clara scoffed. "Whatever," she said fiercely. "Why would I care about all of this? Did you think I would actually be bothered by this 25-person tale of hearsay?"

Krista was glowing. She shook her head in amazement at Clara, "Like a duck in water," she whispered under her breath, "amazing."

"Like a duck to water? What are you muttering about over there?" glared Clara.

Krista let out a loud laugh, but then quickly gained control, pursing her lips to hide yet another huge smile. Clara could see that she was liking something, but as of yet, she couldn't figure out what.

## negen

The train pulled into the outskirts of The Hague and they shuffled off to find a place to store Krista's luggage before hopping on the tram to go to the beach. They were going to Scheveningen, one of the larger, longer, and more developed beaches in the country.

"Why do you care about palm trees anyway?" she asked Krista after they'd stowed her luggage in a storage locker and were on the tram to the beach. "There are palm trees all over in Sacramento."

"Yeah, but it's not the same."

"Why isn't it the same? They're trees."

"Yeah, but we don't have a beach. I like palm trees on the beach. It's like… a praying mantis. They are beautiful and exotic and interesting when they're lounging in the flower bed or on your pepper plants, but then they're on your patio, and you're like, *yuck, get off my patio, praying mantis.*"

"That didn't make sense at all. Have you always been this crazy?" Clara asked.

"Uh, have you always been so blunt?" Krista asked. Again, she gave Clara the oddest look, as if trying to size her up, her forehead creased skeptically and all. Then she winked.

"Are you hitting on me?" Clara accused playfully, "because I'm pregnant."

"I might be," Krista responded, making a kiss noise in her direction.

"Our conversations are totally ridiculous."

"Yeah, I know," said Krista. "I love it."

"Yeah. Me, too."

They spent an hour wandering down the beach. It was wide and lined with cafés selling fries, drinks, and oftentimes more. Although the weather was nice, it was still a little windy, so Clara suggested that they stop for a snack. Krista declined at first. It seemed she was still struggling to get her legs stretched out after the long plane ride, but after another half a mile of walking in the sand, she suggested a purple cabana-like café.

They sat in relative silence as they sipped their drinks, both examining the rough waves coming in and the bravery of the little boys who were jumping in and out of them despite the frigid temperature. Krista had thus far refused to even touch the water.

"I know what warm water looks like," she had claimed, "and that's not it."

Of course, Clara agreed, but she still thought that Krista should make the most of the opportunity and touch the North Sea. It wasn't every day that you got to walk in a notable body of water. Presently, she was very into making the most of new opportunities. She wondered if that was a new thing or an old thing, but couldn't remember. The thought also reminded her of Krista's behavior so far that day. She kept looking at her so strangely with a look that Clara wasn't familiar with. She spent a minute hoping that their friendship wouldn't be too negatively affected by her move across the world, but decided to let it go. Krista had to be seriously jetlagged. She was probably just tired.

After one more espresso they hopped a tram back to the station. Unfortunately, as soon as they arrived, they were confused.

"Where are we?" Clara asked.

"Uh, shouldn't I be the one asking that?"

"Yeah, I suppose. This isn't the station where we came in, is it?"

"I have no idea. My ignorance at this point would appall you. I am 100 percent entirely unsure of my current location."

Clara spent ten minutes walking around the train station, in and out of exits and up and down from the platforms before she turned to the NS Rail staff to ask for help.

"Well," she began as she emerged from the station and approached Krista, "We're in The Hague still, but apparently we're at a different station."

"Apparently." It was becoming clear that Krista was slipping into a flight-day coma.

"Fortunately, we can still get to basically wherever we want from here, so we just need to decide where we want to go next."

Krista's face was expressionless. Clara wondered if she was actually asleep.

"How about some dinner? Would you like that?" Clara asked.

"Yeah, sure. Dinner's good."

The two of them got on the next train and decided that Leiden would be the site of their dinner. They wandered out of the station and right into a small café, the Grand Café La Gare, where they settled in with a cappuccino. It was a perfect place for a late afternoon bite. It was a grand room with stone floors and a fireplace that was just being lit. Each table had a tall, white candle in a grey stone candleholder, making them feel like they were dining in an ancient castle.

They followed it up with the most delicious tomato basil

soup Clara had ever tasted. After the soup, they spent just a few minutes walking around. Overall, Leiden was a sweet town. While most cities in Holland were constantly bustling with people and activity, Leiden seemed to preserve a special peacefulness that allowed its citizens: families, students, and businessmen alike, to slow down and stroll through the city streets.

"How are you feeling?" asked Clara. Although the meal seemed to help, Krista was beginning to look a little pale.

"I'm alright," she responded, but didn't add anything else to the conversation.

On the train, they sank back into their seats. Clara, too, was happy to sit for a few minutes. They were headed back to Amsterdam, presumably for a nightcap, though she was starting to think the whole plan had been a little insane. Krista was out in seconds, and Clara decided to let her sleep. They had a half hour, and Krista might be able to soak up enough Zs to perk her up for a few more hours of her grand tour.

Clara shook her shoulder when they pulled into Amsterdam. It took a minute to even get her to open her eyes. By the time Krista was standing, or more like swaying, most everyone had already exited the train.

Krista groaned the whole way out of the train, but once they reached the central corridor of the Amsterdam train station she started to perk up, just as Clara hoped she would.

"Wow, look at all these people. Going out!" she cried, "And hey, I can be loud now! Nobody even notices."

They headed out from the station, but turned left instead of crossing the tram tracks towards the main square. Clara had decided that a nice stroll through the Red Light District would be the perfect way to wake Krista up. They meandered through the small streets, noting the smell of marijuana on many a corner. They saw red windows with women available and red windows glowing from behind heavy red curtains. Krista was enthralled by the variety of activities going on all around her. They walked arm in arm for more than an hour, sometimes observing silently, sometimes discussing the pros and cons of their surroundings academically, and sometimes nearly collapsing from laughter. As they reached the main square at last, Clara leading the way, Krista called out from behind her.

"I need a drink. There's still gin here, right?" Clara laughed. Like she could forget how much Krista loved gin.

Krista repeated herself, her voice raising a bit, "There's still gin here, right? Even with all the reef?"

Clara laughed and nodded confidently. "Well, yes of course, but-" she raised her eyebrow, "there's also something better." Krista seemed both intrigued and skeptical. "To Wynand Fockink!" Clara cried, pointing towards the sky in a very Buzz Lightyear way.

"To gin!" Krista cried.

"No." Clara strongly reprimanded, "to jenever." She grabbed Krista by the arm and swung her around quickly in the opposite direction. She led Krista down a thin alleyway to where a number of people were already congregated. "Hey, wait," Krista stopped halfway down the short stretch. "But you don't drink, do you? What with the... being growing inside of you?"

"What exactly do you mean by *being*? And no, I don't drink, but I *do* eat cheese, something you can do *everywhere* in The Netherlands."

"Ooh, yum!" Krista looked very interested in more cheese as well, "Can I have some, too?"

"Jahoor!" Clara responded, and with Krista's very confused look, added, "of course."

"Oh," Krista stated in awe as she entered a tiny wood-floored room and found herself staring at rows of bowed wooden shelves, all housing several dozen bottles of warm-colored liquor. She turned to Clara with a gleeful grin, "I like this place."

"Goedeavond!" A slight but wiry bald man greeted them as they entered. Krista understood from his cheer that he *also* enjoyed the jenever. "Kan ik u helpen?" he began, "How can I help you?" Krista smiled at her familiarity with at least one of the two sentences, and took a step forward towards the worn wooden bar, practically dropping her purse into the wooden sink holding a number of delicate, tulip-shaped glasses that sat soaking, just waiting for her to order.

"I like this place," she repeated again, "and I looove gin." Clara frowned at the word gin, as did the barman.

"Yes and no," he said, "yes, of course you like this place, who wouldn't!? And no, this is not gin, this is jenever. Gin," he said, "is what happened when the English tried to make jenever!"

Krista gave him a pensive look, although her pouty lips and squinted eyes made her look more drunk than anything else.

"What's kaneel?" she chirped. "Ooh- *vanilla*, that sounds good too."

"Kaneel is cinnamon," answered the bartender, "and both are quite delicious, although if I may, cinnamon is an excellent jenever to start with."

Krista met his suggestion with a nod. "Yes," she said, "let's go with the cinnamon."

"And for you, miss?" he asked, turning to Clara.

"Kaas blokjes, alstublieft," she replied in response.

"Ahhh, kaas blokjes, cheese blocks," he repeated, "coming right up." He pulled a bottle off the shelf. It was filled with a flawless honey-colored liquid. He pulled out one of the tulip glasses, shook it off and set it firmly on the counter before filling it up, not just to the rim, but bubbling up in a smooth, trembling dome. He smiled and bowed into the back room, likely heading to start on her cheese plate.

Clara had heard about this place, so she had known what to expect, but she was sure that Krista hadn't.

"Are you ready, Krista? For your first jenever?" Clara asked.

"Yes!" she smiled, "but..." her smile faltered and she leaned over to Clara, "he filled it a little full." They both looked down at the glass, which would have been a perfect science lesson on surface tension.

After just a minute, the barman was back with a platter of cheese blocks next to a pile of rich-looking Dutch mustard.

"Ah, that's right," the barman noticed their hesitation, "this is your first time."

Krista nodded eagerly.

"With our jenever," he explained, "you must sip here first, and then you can pick up your glass and take it outside to relax and sip. Watch here," he beckoned to the couple next to them who had both just received a deep red jenever, probably cherry or fruits of the forest. They both leaned forward, almost in sync, and took a long sip off the top of the glass, still sitting on the bar.

"Mmm," the woman said, "lekker!" She nodded to the bartender, and the couple headed out to the wide windowsill across the alley where they took a seat.

"She thinks it's tasty!" the barmen explained to Krista, "Now, it's your turn," he gestured to her glass.

Krista looked around to make sure that it wasn't all a joke, and then leaned forward to take a sip. She made a slurping sound, and nearly choked as she began laughing at herself. Once upright, her eyebrows raised in surprise.

"Yummm..." she hummed, and Clara smiled, knowing in an instant that she would be bringing back jenever for Christmas for the rest of her life.

"So... cinnamony! That's great! And a bit of an edge, but not too much. How is this made?" she turned back to the bartender. Clara took the plate of young Gouda and headed outside to reserve a bit of ledge, hoping that Krista would be out eventually.

An extended period of time later Krista emerged, this time carrying a glass with a deep blackish-purple liquid.

"And what kind is this?" Clara asked with a grin.

"Blackberry!" Krista shouted excitedly, "and oooh, it's even more delicious than the cinnamon or the vanilla."

Clara laughed, wondering if those were the only three she had gotten, or if there were more. "I think I'll try the almond next," Krista pondered as she examined her surroundings in the small alley. "Why does it smell like pizza?"

Clara sniffed the air and looked around, "I think there's a pizza place just down the street." She nodded her head toward the end of the alley, "and what's in the bag?" She had just noticed the tall, thin, brown paper bag that Krista was carrying.

"Ahhh, you noticed," Krista beamed. "It's for you! It's a post-baby present!"

"No! You didn't!" She smiled in surprise and pleasure, "That's so sweet! What kind is it!?"

"Well," Krista turned to her, "it's a special kind, just for babies—well, not just for babies, but *because* of babies," she explained. "There were actually two kinds, one that announced the baby and one in celebration of the baby being born. That's the one I got you, in celebration of your little creature just shooting out! Painlesslessly!"

Clara stared at her; she wasn't sure if she could possibly tackle all the things about that sentence that were weird, so she just laughed.

"Thanks! Now come sit by me. I've been out here alone forever." She looked down sheepishly at the empty platter. "And I accidentally ate all of the cheese. Sorry."

"No worries, there's plenty of time for cheese."

"So, what's your favorite kind so far?"

"Hmm, I dunno…" Krista trailed off. "I think I really liked the first one."

"The cinnamon?" Clara asked.

"Yeah, the cimminnon. But I also *really* liked the last one."

"What kind was that?" Clara asked.

"Uh, I think it was blackberry, but it might have been black cherry. I can't remember which one I ordered first."

*Okay,* thought Clara. *That was four now.* She didn't think they were too strong, maybe 20 percent, but Krista had to be at the end of her rope what with the combination of jetlag and inebriation.

"So, are you getting hungry again? It's gotta be…" she

thought for a second, but Krista beat her to it.

"It's time for a jenever brunch in CA!" she cried out and high-fived the guy standing next to her, who seemed entirely unsurprised by the interaction. Clara was astounded by the speed with which Krista had calculated the time difference and wondered exactly what she'd missed inside.

"Dinner, Krista?" Krista hardly noticed her question; she was just finishing her glass, smacking and licking her lips. It looked as if she was ready to lick out the tiny glass. "Krista!"

"What?" she responded innocently, startled.

"We'll be back," she smiled and turned to the tiny wooden window to pay their bill.

"Already done," Krista chimed. "I couldn't let you pay for your own baby gift."

Krista returned the petite glass to the tiny window before slipping her arm through Clara's. Together they headed arm in arm down the alley towards the square.

"Yes," confirmed Krista, "food would be fine with me," she nodded, "considering my state," she smiled mock-angelically at Clara.

"Oh, have I got something to share with you." Clara stopped walking and grabbed Krista's shoulders, turning her to face toward her. "How hungry are you? You need something substantial or just a bite of spice and deliciousness?"

Krista pondered for a second, and then decided. "I'd love a little spice and deliciousness. Actually, little to medium, little to medium."

"Great!" said Clara, and they turned to continue walking toward the train station.

"Just to be clear," Krista rambled, "I meant little to medium food amount—not spice. I like spice."

"Yup, got it."

"Actually, why don't you say medium to lots. I mean, I'm fine with lots. You only have *one* first night in Amsterdam, and I am kind of hungry."

As they neared the train station, Clara turned to Krista again, "Alright, just wait here and when I get back, you're gonna wish you lived here." Clara rushed into the nearest stand to order a Turkish pizza, a shawarma-like wrap baked with a coating of spicy beef and filled with chicken, lettuce, tomato, cucumbers, yogurt and sambal.

Once Clara had ordered, she stepped outside the small stand to watch her friend revel in her surroundings. Krista had walked a few steps over to the edge of the bridge and was looking out over the canal. It was wide there and filled with long tourist boats. Krista alternated between staring out at the canals—one of Clara's favorite pastimes—and staring around in awe at the number of people streaming in and out of the train station every second. It was now almost ten, and the city was chock-full of fellow revelers. At that moment, Clara wondered if her friend didn't already wish that she lived right there in Holland. Clara could only hope. The man behind the counter waved a hot, foil-wrapped Turkish pizza at Clara and she thanked him as she went out to join her friend.

"This," said Clara as she handed the steaming wrap to Krista, "is a *Turkse* pizza. A Turkish pizza."

"This isn't a pizza," began Krista, but the commentary halted there as she took her first, rather enormous, bite.

"Fuuuuu..." Krista cut herself off with another bite. "Heaven in lavash bread," she groaned once she'd swallowed.

Clara had her own, but mostly just enjoyed watching Krista eat. She had to imagine that after a few sippers of jenever, a Turkse pizza would pretty much hit the spot.

Once Krista regained control of her senses, Clara led her to the train station to head home to Breda at last. Just outside the door of the station Krista froze.

"Shit," she said loudly, and blinked twice, looking at Clara, "my luggage." They stared at each other, both very obviously considering the location of the luggage in relation to their current location.

"It's okay," said Clara thoughtfully, "we'll find it. We'll just retrace our steps and figure out where we left it. We know that it's here in Holland somewhere."

"In Holland!?" Krista shouted. "That's what you're going

to give me?! Granted," she lowered her voice, "I don't remember where I left it either, but Holland!?" Her voice raised to a screech once again. "You're narrowing it down to a country? Why yes, Clara, I agree. It's in the country. I didn't forget to bring it on the plane."

Clara laughed, but remained calm. "It's better than that. The Netherlands is the country, Holland is just two of the provinces."

"Uh, although I don't know what the hell you're talking about, I didn't hear the words, 'I know where your suitcase is,' so I'm going to ignore it. The locker—what city was the locker in?"

"The locker was definitely in the first city we went to."

"Which was?"

"The Hague. Definitely The Hague."

"Is that also the city where we ended up at two different train stations?"

"Hmmm... Yeah, I guess that's why we forgot it. Okay," Clara regrouped and started again confidently, "Let's go talk to the train people and make sure we can get on the right train."

"What do you mean *make sure we can get on*? Why wouldn't we be able to get on it?"

"Loopy."

"Not this again," Krista mumbled.

"The route isn't the same as it is during the day. At a certain time it changes to a night loop or something. People can still get home and get around but you just do it in a different way," she hesitated, "and you can't necessarily," she enunciated slowly, "get everywhere that you can during the day." She gave Krista a wary look but then turned to lead the way into the station. Krista followed blindly, "Don't worry, we'll find it," Clara called, and she was right. She stepped away from the information desk very optimistic.

"Apparently the loopy train hasn't started yet," Clara declared, and, although Clara could hardly believe it because it was so completely out of character, Krista let Clara take her hand and lead her through the station. They got the next train, which stopped at the NS station in The Hague, whatever that meant. Clara could only hope that when they got off the train, they would recognize the station as the one with the lockers.

Krista didn't sleep on this ride, but stared out the window in a trance. She seemed a little on edge about her suitcase, but also just very, very tired. Clara was now getting worried that she'd run her a bit ragged for the first day.

They got off in The Hague, and Clara sighed in relief. It was the right station. They collected Krista's suitcase from the locker and paid the fee for the insane number of hours it had spent there. They then immediately headed back up to the platform where they got on a new intercity train that took them directly to Breda. Krista fell asleep the moment that they got on the second train, though her right hand actively gripped the handle of her suitcase the entire ride.


tien


Clara walked into the kitchen the next morning to find Krista already showered and there, sitting at the kitchen table. A pot of coffee sat in front of her, as well as a few croissants on a plate in the center of the table.

The bakeries in Europe were amazing. Not only were there plenty of tiny mom and pop bakeries, but the supermarkets also had pretty legitimate bakeries. One in particular made the croissants extra buttery and just the tiniest bit underdone. Clara had picked up a few the day before and Krista had clearly found them and warmed them in the oven.

"Croissant?" Krista offered as Clara entered the tiny kitchen. It made Clara's heart skip a little just to see that her friend was there in her kitchen, happily awaiting her.

"Sure," Clara replied as Krista got up to pour her a cup of coffee. Krista handed her a steaming cup and sat back down at the table. Clara joined her at the table, but eyed her friend suspiciously.

After taking a small sip of hot coffee, Clara helped herself to a croissant.

"Can I get you any milk or sugar?" asked Krista. "No, just black. You know that." She looked up from the croissant, flaky bite in hand, "Do you need something Krista?" Clara knew that she was *not* a morning person, so all this preparedness and chivalry, not to mention the general alertness, was out of the ordinary. *Something* must be up. Clara continued to stare at Krista, but the latter only browsed the paper nonchalantly.

"Isn't that in Dutch, Krista? You can't read a word of it."

"Yeah, I know, I'm just checking things out." She turned to the back page, "And I can read weather maps, by the way."

Krista hadn't bothered with a croissant, but instead alternated between spoonfuls of Nutella and Speculoos.

"Nice breakfast," Clara said when she noticed.

"I know. I found the Nutella in the cupboard and then I found *this* stuff," she held up the jar of Lotus Speculoos spread, "and it is amaaazing. Oh, my God."

"I know, right!? It's made of this type of gingerbread-like cookie that they always serve with coffee. And I guess somebody sometime thought, 'Hey, let's crush up these cookies and make a paste so I can literally spread cookies on cookies.'"

"Awesome," replied Krista, taking another spoonful and wiping it onto a croissant she had just ripped open, "You're only in Holland once," she stated.

Clara looked up at her, startled. "I hope not."

"Well," Krista replied in return, "you know what I mean."

The second that Clara had the last bite of croissant in her mouth, Krista began her efforts at full force.

"So," she began, "what are we up to today?" She sounded breezy, but Clara suspected deeper intentions were in store. "Did you have something, um, in mind, I mean, already planned for us to do today?" An excited smile was now growing on her face.

Clara laughed, "Did *you* have something in mind,

Krista?"

Krista bit her lip and then just burst. "Let's go back to Amsterdam today! What do you think? Should we go? I already packed a daybag and everything." She sighed, "I really want to go back. I just loooooved Amsterdam."

Clara laughed and spoke as soon as she finished swallowing, "And Amsterdam?" she smiled, "this wouldn't have anything to do with jenever, would it?" she laughed out loud. Leave it to Krista to have an international fling with a liquor.

"To Wynand Fockink!" Krista yelled.

"To Wynand Fockink," Clara agreed. They grabbed their coats and Krista's prepacked daybag and headed out the door.

Two hours or so later, just outside the Amsterdam central train station, they—somewhat accidentally at least—bumped into Ian. After the awkward hellos and a look of suspect glee on Krista's face, they invited him to come along for the ride for the rest of the day's adventures.

They stopped at a café first to fuel up and plan out their grand day in Amsterdam. At the café, Krista immediately excused herself to use the restroom and then eyed Clara meaningfully. Clara obediently followed.

"Excuse me," Krista said when they were safely squished inside the absolutely tiny Dutch bathroom.

"Do we have to be in here?" Clara interrupted. "Dutch bathrooms are a one-person ordeal."

"Excuse me-" Krista began again, more sharply. "You know that guy," she quickly accused Clara. "You know a cute British guy that is also an out-of-place expatriate in The Netherlands."

This was not a question at all. "Yes," Clara replied blandly, "We've met before..." she paused, "on several occasions."

"How did you not tell me this!?" Krista yelled.

Clara laughed. She wondered if this had ever happened in a Dutch bathroom before. "It's not a big deal. We're not dating. Most of the time we're not even on speaking terms."

"But you have a man-friend!" Krista was delighted to be able to say this, "and a British man-friend at that!"

After some firm prodding, it came out that Clara had texted him to ask about the name of a café that they had visited together when she was living in Amsterdam, so he knew Clara would be in Amsterdam that day. That they both happened to be in the train station at that time, she supposed, was destiny. They emerged from the bathroom four minutes later, with both Ian and Krista smiling devilishly. The latter, because she had just learned a half-secret of Clara's life; the former, because he had learned that American women truly did go to the bathroom together, even in Holland.

Their first stop in Amsterdam was a small meat and cheese store. They bought some pepper salami and old Gouda, young Gouda, and some nice French port salut for their forthcoming picnic at Vondel Park. The next stop was a bakery where they purchased fresh bread and croissants. Ian swung into a *wijnhandel* for a bottle of wine and surprised them at the park by pulling out a glass bottle of pear juice for Clara as well.

Several hours later Krista let out a groan from the patch of grass where she was sprawled. "Ugh... I don't think I've eaten this much cheese in my life. I think I might die, but I don't care... It just tasted so good," she paused and Clara looked over to see her eyes closing. "I just feel so sleepy," she trailed off.

Clara laughed at her and laid down on her back as well. "It's called a choma."

"A what?" Krista asked.

"A bloody what?" Ian asked. Instead of answering his question they both burst into laughter at his verbiage.

Once they'd settled down again, Clara explained.

"It's a choma, a cheese coma. It's basically when you are

intoxicated by eating too much cheese, usually during an outdoor picnic on a perfect day with bread and wine and cheese—specifically really old, salty cheese or really fatty, stinky, yummy, buttery-"

"Yeah, we got it, Clare." They had been forced to listen to her complain about being unable to eat stinky cheese for a greater part of the first hour of their ridiculously rich picnic. She did manage to eat her fill of the aged Gouda, despite her constant mourning for soft, stinky cheese.

Eventually they packed up and soon they were making their way back towards Dam Square and down the familiar alley for another drawn out evening at Wynand Fockink.

Ian had been there before, so he and Krista went right in to order while Clara stayed to reserve a nice spot on the ledge. After a few minutes, the lone bench opened up and she quickly claimed it, hoping her two comrades wouldn't mind that it would be a tight fit for the three of them.

Krista and Ian emerged a few minutes later, each with a tulip shaped glass. Ian's was a dark gold and Krista's almost black.

"Look at you, sitting so pleasantly there on your own. You look so comfortable." Krista smiled proudly at her. "Isn't it nice how independent she is, Ian?"

"Why, hm, yes, I suppose so." He let out a short but hearty laugh. "In fact, she's always seemed quite independent to me—yelled at me twice."

"Really?" asked Krista with interest.

"Yes. In a café and then in the street."

"*In* a café *and* on the street!?"

Clara interrupted. "It was in an outdoor café on a busy square, so hardly anyone even noticed, and the street was in the Red Light District, so there's no way anyone noticed there." She spoke defensively, and Krista was just eating it up. "It's not like I was having sex in the street," she mumbled.

Krista laughed and Ian looked scandalized.

"By the way," Krista changed the topic to another subject that was surely uncomfortable for Ian, "how are you funding this operation, Clara? Are you still on your summer paychecks?"

Ian inhaled sharply and turned away quickly, but both Clara and Krista caught his reaction first.

"What is it Ian?" Krista taunted, shooting a smirk in his direction. "Do you have loads of *quid* or something?"

"Yeah, Ian." Clara felt like she was 12, but it was still fun. Krista just had so much more balls than she did.

"You are so *American*," he sneered, "Can you talk of nothing else but money?"

"Hey!" Clara snapped, "I have never once discussed money with you!"

"Yes, well, you are now and it is *quite* inappropriate," he continued. "Besides, the amount of money hardly matters, it's still worth loads more than that blasted Euro. And the dollar? Pitiful." All of this was spoken rather quickly and rather smugly under his breath, just loudly enough for them to hear.

"Hasn't the Pound been dropping like a rock for months now?" Krista countered loudly, pointedly interrupting his mumbling.

"Well! It most certainly has not! Now if you would excuse me, I am in need of a refill."

"That's fine, go on," Krista replied in her best fake British accent, which was pretty atrocious overall.

"Fine," Clara repeated in the same accent.

"Sloppy American accent..." he rolled his eyes.

"Stupid British dialect..." Krista countered.

"Stupid!" he exploded, "Dialect!? This attack is *quite* uncalled for!"

"Um, Excuse me, sir," Clara said, glancing around at the surrounding patrons, all the while fluttering her eyelashes, "This is a public place. That was *quite*," she enunciated, "loud, and *quite* rude," she reprimanded.

"Bitch," he muttered and stood to go inside.

Both Clara and Krista laughed darkly. "Bitch," Krista laughed, "We're American!" she cried after him, "That's hardly even an insult."

"You know," said Krista once Ian was inside, "I like him."

Clara smiled at her, proud of her British find.

"What can I say? When people yell at me repeatedly, I eventually shape up and yell back."

"Yeah," Krista said, just as Ian's head peeped around the door frame, "if only you'd done the same to the complete asshole you married."

Ian, apparently having forgotten his reason for returning, stepped out, looking surprised, "You married a complete asshole?" he asked Clara, "Are you still married to a complete asshole?" He was clearly intrigued by the topic, which made Clara unexpectedly uncomfortable. They hadn't really gotten into the topic of her love life.

"No." Clara responded quietly.

"Thank God!" Krista practically shouted, and then shot a wink at the tall blonde Dutchman who had turned to check out the source of the exclamation.

*Man, she had nerve*, Clara thought to herself. Perhaps someday she'd try a wink.

It took Clara a moment to realize that Ian was still staring at her. She opened her mouth to respond, but nothing came out, so she settled on closing it again and shifting uncomfortably in her seat.

Ian turned to Krista instead and gave her an interested nod, "So," he began, "about this, ahem, arse...?"

The moment the word came out of his mouth, Krista let out a roar of laughter.

"I'm so sorry," she choked, motioning apologetically to everyone around them, all of whom were now staring at the commotion. "It's just so funny-" she laughed, "to hear someone actually use the word *arse*."

"What do you mean *actually* use the word?" asked Ian, "you mean," he paused, "at present?"

"What?" asked Krista, still laughing inappropriately loud. "Let's just get back to the ass." Now she shot *him* a wink and turned to Clara with an evil smile. "Tell us, Clare. Tell us about Jack." She threw out the name like a live coal.

"Oh," Clara said, unsure of how much he really wanted to know and equally unsure of how much she wanted to share. "I dunno, he was my husband for... a, a little less than ten years."

"Cla-ra!" Krista snapped disapprovingly. Clara turned and looked into her best friend's raging eyes. "He kicked you out," she said through gritted teeth.

"I, uh.. I'm."

"Oh, geez." Krista turned to Ian, obviously getting ready to begin a nice long rant on the subject. "Well, his name was Jack—that's short for Jackass. Obviously." She grinned at Ian, guessing that he would appreciate this crude American humor, which he did. "Clara married him during college, or was it just after college, Clare?" She turned to look at Clara, who was staring blankly. "Anyway," Krista continued, "this guy was *typical American*, if you know what I mean. There was no hope from the start."

"Wait," Clara interposed weakly, "There was no hope from the start?"

"From the start," Krista said firmly. She was clearly not going to be interrupted during this scairytale of bad marriage. She always loved a captive audience.

"This guy couldn't remember her birthday for the first *two years* they were married. As far as I can tell, he never got their anniversary figured out. I mean, he was such an idiot. He could hardly remember *my* name."

Ian's eyes widened and Clara's rolled. She was making it out to be quite a tale.

As she listened, Clara felt herself looking back over the decade that they had been together. Truth be told, Krista was right. He did often forget her birthday, unless reminded. But he also forgot pretty much everything else, too. He made all the usual bad boyfriend mistakes, sometimes worse. He had been hopeless.

She shuddered, thinking of the wedding envelope, but then pushed it out of her mind.

Maybe his hopelessness was what had attracted Clara to him in the first place. He was so cute, and available, and funny... And he'd had that great house. He had seemed like a great catch at the time.

When he'd proposed, he had written in to The Sports Guy at ESPN—Bill Simmons, was his name—and told him how he always read the columns aloud and how they always laughed together, and now he was thinking about proposing. Somehow, the question was included in a mailbag and The Sports Guy had included a response of his own and a response from The Sports Gal, his wife. It was awfully cute.

To her horror, she found herself smiling at the memory. She shut it down quickly before anyone noticed. *So what if his proposal was good?* Had anything else in the marriage been good? Were any of their memories even worth the space in her brain?

It wasn't just birthdays and anniversaries; he'd ignored his college thesis for six months, too. She'd all but signed his name on the final document. Job applications had fallen to the wayside as well, and she'd finished those too. He had always been great at interviews, though. She just helped him get there.

At the end of the night they walked back to the train in relative silence. Clara was pondering. There were things running through her head tonight, what with all these memories stirred up. Thinking about Jack, what it was like and what he was like, it stung.

This time it was Clara who fell asleep on the train ride back to Breda, but after the nap and the walk home through the city park Clara reawakened.

"There was no hope from the start?" Clara inquired the moment they entered the door, "Since when?"

"Not worth a discussion," Krista yawned, "you know it, I know it—no use defending him..." Krista continued to the upstairs bedroom. Clara flopped down on the couch and pressed her fingertips to her temples. She felt a headache coming on.

A few minutes later Krista reemerged at the bottom of

the stairs in her pajamas.

"Speculoos," she sang, turning to the kitchen.

Clara sat up and smiled. Perhaps she shouldn't write off the night quite yet. She turned on her laptop to put on some music, and in a few seconds Krista was back. Clara noticed she was using a stroopwafel to scoop Speculoos from the jar. Something bulky was in the pocket of her hooded sweatshirt. Clara wondered if it was the Nutella.

"So, Clare," said Krista, settling in on the couch next to her and looking down at Clara's belly, "you're pregnant."

"Yes," she said assertively, "I am."

"How are you doing with that? Are you feeling okay?"

"Yeah," she replied casually, taking the stroopwafel out of Krista's hand and taking a bite. "I'm fine... now, at least." She stuck a sugary bite in her mouth before going on. "It was pretty rough for a while, especially considering that I made the discovery on the plane on the way to live in a foreign country."

"Really?" Krista asked, "That's when you found out?"

"Yup," she said, "during some turbulence."

Krista began laughing so hard that Clara had to think back to what she had said. *Was she funny in Holland?*

"Clara!" she choked out between laughs, "that's hilarious!" she said, "and the best part is that you were never hilarious like this before. You were fun and we always had a blast, but you were never funny like this—on your own, unprovoked. The sense of humor that you have developed is so impressive. I'm so happy for you!"

Clara stared at her and she smiled back.

"What? You want an acceptance speech or something?"

Krista screeched another laugh and flipped her hair happily. "Oh, man... So go on, what was it like? To realize that you were suddenly growing a creature inside you?"

"A creature?" Clara repeated, but laughed. "Well, the thing is, I wasn't exactly *ready*. But I was ready for a change, for something new in life, something... just for me, I guess. So, I think that it will work out. I don't know what I'm doing—at all—but really, what first time mother does? Besides those supermoms, anyway. I at least babysat when I was in high school, and I never lost one or killed one or anything."

"Killed one?" Krista asked, "Lost one?"

"Yeah, a kid," she clarified, "I never lost one, I always did alright. I fed them, bathed them, put them to bed, so I should be able to that for Pally."

"Who's Polly?" Krista asked.

"Oh, it's a name I'm trying out. I thought it would be cute for a daughter. Except that it's spelled with an *a*, P-A-L-L-Y, but pronounced Polly, like Polly Pocket." She grinned when she noticed Krista's confused stare. "I am going to spell it that way so the Dutchers know how to pronounce it and don't say pole-ee or anything."

Krista now wore a look of disbelief. "Uh, whatever. I was mainly stunned that you already knew it was a girl and had a name picked out but hadn't told me yet. Horrible name, by the way."

"No, it's not."

"It is when it's spelled with an *a*."

"But then people here will know how to pronounce it."

"But people in the U.S. won't."

"So? They'll get it."

"Yeah, right, 'cause they're so open-minded. Your mother and all of her reading group friends are definitely going to see the name, learn that it's pronounced like *Polly* and understand why you would spell it with an *a* instead of an *o*. I'm sure that they'll be sure to tell all of their friends and that all of their friends will understand and pronounce it correctly as well. I'm sure your daughter won't be known as Pally—your Pal, Pally—in the good 'ole U.S. of A."

"Shut up."

"Hey! There's Pally! She's your pal! My good 'ole Pal-ly. Get it?"

"Yeah, I get it."

"No, I mean do you get that this name sucks?"

"Uh!" Clara wore a hurt and slightly angered expression. "You are mean!"

"Whatever. I'm not sorry. Your daughter, whose name isn't Pally or Polly or whatever, will thank me one day."

Clara rolled her eyes. "Anyway, I don't really know that it's a girl. I'm just assuming."

"Yeah, I wondered about that. I don't know much, but it seems a little early. How are you assuming, by the way?"

"I dunno, I figured that after all the shit I've been through it's only fair that I'd get a girl."

Krista stared at her. "I don't know if that's how it works. Gender isn't usually determined by karma."

Clara shrugged. "It might be."

"What are you even talking about? You're talking like a drunk, but I've only seen you eat cheese so far tonight," she looked at Clara warily.

Clara stuck her finger in the jar for a swipe and then stuck it in her mouth. "And Speculoos."

"Hey! No dirty fingers in the jar! Give that to me!" She grabbed the jar out of Clara's hand and muttered to herself, "What is *in* this stuff? Is it an intoxicant?" and got up to go to the kitchen.

"Where are you going?" Clara asked, "Don't put it away yet." She heard a cackle from the kitchen.

"Just getting a spoon!" Krista called. She walked back into the room and handed Clara an open package of stroopwafels.

"Anyway," said Krista, "Back to the baby talk."

"Yeah, okay. But just for the record, this is a new subject for me. I haven't talked about it much." She smiled and aimed her index finger at the center of her belly, "Nobody here is much for gossip, so I've had some time to come to terms with it."

"No gossip? Really?" Krista tilted her head to the side in interest. "But, wow!" she swung the subject again. "A kid! Look at you all grown up!" Krista stared at Clara with an almost adoring look.

"You're freakin' me out, Krista. You never look at me like that."

"Sorry."

"Uh, you don't often apologize either. What's going on?"

"Well, I dunno, I just can't believe how different you are."

"Different?" Clara asked, "What do you mean? Like, free?" she joked.

"See? Even that. You would have gotten all insecure if I had said that before, but you've changed. You are free. It's all you there, but almost..." She puckered her lips in thought, "it's like your essence is stronger now. Your Clara being is clearer and tougher."

"Weeelll," said Clara skeptically, "*That* clears it all up. It's so nice to have weird friends, don't you think? You never have a boring life. You never really know what they're talking about..." She eyed Krista meaningfully, "but it's all in good fun."

"See!?"

"See what?"

"You're different! You're a changed man."

"I'm a changed *man*?"

"Well, Whoa-man," Krista laughed.

Even Clara knew there was no denying that she had changed over the past few months. She might not be confident enough to say it out loud, but she knew what her friend was talking about. She was a changed Clara—and not just because she was growing a *creature* inside. She laughed lightly to herself and then turned her attention back to Krista.

"Um, may I?" Krista asked as she pointed to Clara's infinitesimally rounding belly.

"Sure, but it's only stroopwafels so far."

Krista gave her belly a light poke."

"I, uh, couldn't even feel that."

"Hey, I like the shirt," she said, appreciating the silky, fuzzy red sweater Clara had pulled off the back of the couch and thrown on.

"Yeah, I know. It's super comfy."

"So I can poke it?"

"The sweater or the baby?" Clara asked dryly, and poked the side of her own belly. She had noticed this week that she was starting to be shaped differently, though hardly.

"The belly," stated Krista, holding her finger in ready position. Clara nodded and Krista gave her belly a prod. "Hmm," Krista nodded. "Kind of feels like mine. Oh-Godmother!" she yelled as her left arm shot up in the air. Clara jumped.

"Man, that scared me. Geez, Krista." She took a deep breath. "And it's not like calling shotgun. You can't just call Godmother."

"Whatev- Suck it, Delia," she said, pointing to the window.

"Where are you pointing?"

"The U.S."

"Like you know which direction the U.S. is."

"Do you?" challenged Krista.

"Whatev," Clara laughed, "but the point is, you would have responsibilities as Godmother. You would have to provide guidance for her, you would have to give her good presents, and most important of all, if I lose my mind or get hit by a train, then she would be your responsibility."

"Hit by a train?" Krista asked.

"Well, this is The Netherlands. We're a train country. I'm not going to get in a car accident."

"Yeah, but hit by a train? You're more likely to get hit by a bike. There are bikes everywhere and the speed at which they ride here is pure insanity!"

"Well, don't worry about that, the bike is like an extension of your body here. Just walk straight and they'll maneuver around you."

"Extension of the body," she repeated as a grin pulled at one corner of her mouth, "Interesting... Wait- are you avoiding the topic?"

"No," Clara replied frankly, "of course you're going to be

the Godmother." She smiled. "I mean, you're right. It's either you or Delia, and I just kicked Delia out of my house because she said she couldn't picture me or my life without Jack, so she's definitely not getting Godmother."

"Whoa-ah-ah. More please."

Clara spent the next hour filling Krista in on all details of the drama centered around Delia's visit. By the time they were done, Krista was in a fit of laughter. It seems that for their entire friendship, Krista had been under the impression that Delia would be Clara's ultimate demise. It was only now that Clara was starting to see the truth in it, and this without a doubt made Krista very cheerful.

"I mean, how could she *love* Jack?!" Clara shouted at one point. "Once, I found a bra in the laundry that wasn't mine. I tried so hard to think of anyone who could have possibly left it there—a friend of mine, a girlfriend of one of his friends, and I came up with a few options, none of them at all realistic."

"What?" Krista said seriously. There was no joking in Krista's voice now. "Are you kidding?"

"No." The nonchalance in her voice was startling even to her. "Plus, I had just been out of town at a funeral for a few days, which made it even more difficult for my imagination."

"What do you mean, imagination? That's some hard crackin' evidence. Did you ever confront him?"

"No."

"Why not?"

"I don't know."

"You don't *know*?"

"I was afraid to accuse him, as his wife."

Krista gasped, "Yeah, and he's your husband. Shit, man. Why didn't you tell me? I would've put it to him, I can tell you that."

"Yeah, I know..." She looked away, thinking. "At the time, I thought you'd stick it to him a little too hard, I think."

"Oh, Clara. You should have said *something*. To me, to him, to *someone*. Yes, you were his wife and he was, is, was, whatever—your husband, but don't you think that means that

269

there should be some accountability? I mean you don't need to keep an eye on him twenty-four-seven, but shouldn't there be at least enough answerability that every bra is claimed and accounted for? Clara!" she spoke angrily, "you don't deserve this! You never deserved this!"

To Clara's surprise, Krista's eyes were wet. It was Clara that leaned over to hug her friend, despite the fact that they were tears over her failed marriage.

"It's done, Krista. I'm out of it now."

Clara had seen Krista cry, but she had never seen Krista cry when she hadn't been crying as well.

She lifted her head and looked at Clara with red eyes.

"Well," she huffed, "if you're definitely done with it... I guess I have a story," she paused, "if you want to hear it."

"Why not?" asked Clara. She might as well get all the dirt out in the open now, even if only to ensure that she would never, ever think positively of him again. "Bring on the Jack bashing."

"Okay. You asked for it." Krista paused, as if to consider just how to start the waterfall of awful truth that was about to spill. "Well, I went over one day to talk to you. I figured you were on the back porch, so I just went on back around the side of the house."

"When was this?"

"I don't know, hardly matters really," she continued, but Clara got the distinct feeling that the timing would be more scarring than she could take. It was Krista's way of protecting her, at least a little.

"And he was there talking to some friend," Krista continued. "I didn't actually know this one. I heard Jack say something about how he just loved Vegas. It sounded like he was about to go again. And he asked the friend about the little cards they hand out on the street and if he knew, you know, what they were for... which of course he did."

"Yeah," Clara commented. She could feel what was coming.

"And he was laughing his ass off. He said that he didn't

figure out what exactly they were until his bachelor party."

Clara's heart, already so crumbled, sank a little more. Krista had been under the impression—as they all had—that Jack had gone to Aspen to ski for his bachelor party, though that wasn't exactly what had gone down. Clara remained silent, so Krista went on.

"So the guy said to him, 'I thought you went to Aspen to hit the slopes. Didn't you rent a huge chalet and everything?' and he—Jack—just laughed and said that he did rent a chalet, but then he decided that there were a few more things he wanted to hit before getting married." She paused and opened her mouth to add something more, but didn't speak.

"Something else?" Clara asked drearily, but Krista didn't respond.

"Just remembering his exact wording," she mumbled and Clara watched a shiver run up her arm to her shoulder.

Clara was silent. She wouldn't ask for the exact wording. She could spare herself that.

They locked eyes, and Clara immediately looked down. She knew that he'd gone to Vegas. She'd seen it on the credit card bills. He wasn't the keenest fish in the school.

She took one long deep breath and then looked over at Krista feeling surprisingly clear-headed.

"Geez, Jack."

"I heard something else."

"Yes?" Clara asked slowly, "What else?"

"I heard that this Jane was shooting her mouth off."

Clara squeezed her eyes shut. She hadn't told Krista about Jane and she hadn't ever intended to, yet Krista knew—had known... for a while.

"And something about nuzzling."

Clara groaned and opened her eyes. Out of nowhere, a smile was stretching across her face. "Nuzzling?" She was actually smiling now—and then laughing. "Nuzzling." She leaned her head back, and in the most unDutch and immature way ever, screamed. It was something between a yell and a howl and a shriek and it said everything that she had been wanting to say for the last three months.

"I hate him."

"I know."

Krista poured Clara a glass of sparkling water and then raised her own. "Bottoms up," she stated, and then forced a grim smile. "To you."

"Thank you."

"You know who I do like?" Clara said. "The Sports Guy." She nodded arrogantly. "Hell, I'd've jumped over the monogamy fence if Bill Simmons would have come to town, though that wouldn't have been fair to the Sports Gal," she conceded sweetly. "And what about you, Krista? How's your lov-er?"

"Man, you've changed!" Krista stood up. "I just can't get over it! No offense, but you were always a bit of a pleaser. Not a pushover, but you were *only* concerned with making everyone else around you happy. You were a great friend, by the way—not that you aren't now—but sometimes, I just wondered if you had any idea what *you* really liked, who *you* were."

Clara said nothing. She had known that Krista felt this way, though maybe not fully. Over the past few solitary months she'd realized just how little she'd known about herself. It was beginning to become clearer.

Krista shook her head in amazement. "You were always saying sorry. You apologized for everything and to everyone, and for doing nothing wrong!" her voice raised, and then sunk, "Hell, most of the time it was probably my fault. You probably saved my ass a thousand times over in the past 15, 20 years. Thanks, by the way." She smiled at Clara, but it wasn't the smile that made Clara feel warm inside, it was the feeling of respect that was resonating. Suddenly, she wasn't sure if she'd ever felt it outside of an elementary school classroom.

"I am glad to see your walls," Krista added, motioning towards the pieces hanging on the walls. "At least there's something that you *clearly* love. You did good," she commended her. "Of all the confused and lost people, you managed to pick the right major, so I guess that's a testament to you knowing yourself."

Krista swiveled on her heel, and much to Clara's pleasure, began to walk around the room and examine the artwork on the walls as if in a museum.

"It rocks in here, just so you know. I love it. I love it so much I'm freakin' jealous you didn't rock this out back in Sac. My house is desperately in need of a redo and it seems," she looked around in approval, "that you could do it up right."

"Hey, thanks."

The song changed and The Flaming Lips were on next. Clara felt there'd been just about enough analysis for the night, so she shamelessly began to sing along.

Krista rolled her eyes and laughed, but eventually joined in. About two-thirds of the way through Clara started in on her own topic.

"You know, just like art, music has always been able to bring me to life. You can forget, but then, the moment you hear a song that just makes your heart breathe... it's so nice. Sometimes it's just pure joy. Like when I hear 'Dancing in the Moonlight.' The first time I heard the Toploader version I thought, 'This- this is what I want every second of my life to be like.' You can't imagine forgetting that it has such an effect, but of course you do... Maybe it's the revival of the feeling that's so great, the return of sensation in an otherwise boring life, but music can just be so, so- orgasmic."

"Ahhh!" Krista roared. "You have *changed*!" she shouted the last word either for emphasis or to vent and release her evidently unending amazement at Clara's new persona.

Clara just shook her head and ignored it. *Enough about her already.*

"You're like a walking billboard for the humanities. Wait- what is this crap?" The song had changed and clearly Krista didn't appreciate it.

"What!?" Clara screeched, "This is 'Independent Love Song...'" She looked at Krista for understanding.

"Scarlet..? Nothing? Really?"

"Nope."

"Ooh, the other one that's great is this new one I found on YouTube."

After a minute at the computer, upbeat lyrics emerged from the tiny speakers on Clara's laptop.

"Who says!?" Clara yelled and jumped up and stepped from the floor to the kitchen chair. From the chair she spread her arms and danced like a teenage girl at her first slumber party.

"Oh. My. God, Clara. This is Selena Gomez."

"I know!" she called out over the tinny sound of the speakers. "I love it! It's just so optimistic!"

"That's because she's like 12! She has no reason *not* to be optimistic."

"So!?"

"Who are you and what did you do with my best friend?!"

"Damn you, Jack! Damn you to hell!"

"She first made it big on the Disney Channel!" yelled Krista.

"To an American hell!"

"Hey!" yelled Krista.

"Where there are no flowers!" In a clean swoop, Clara pulled the flowers from the vase on the kitchen table. As she swung them around, the water showered the room, the floor, everything, Krista included.

Krista began to laugh despite herself. "Who *are* you?!"

"Don't wanna be with Jack anymore!" Clara began to sing along in her own words until Krista had no choice but to join in.

"YouTube suggested it to me when I was listening to music that day the first week when I was looking for tickets home."

Krista frowned and froze, "You were looking for a ticket home?"

"Yeah, I wasn't doing so well back then…"

"Well," Krista sighed, "At least you're doing fabulous now."

Clara shrugged. "It's not me, it's the kid," she claimed. Ilse's stern criticism of her excessive thanking popped into her head, but Clara decided to refrain from relaying it to Krista. As she danced, she didn't worry about whether or not she had changed as much for the better as Krista claimed, she just danced. In her very own hall of art in her rowhouse in The Netherlands, it was lovely just to dance.

elf

Another two songs and Krista collapsed on the couch to rest.

"So, why have you been so secretive, anyway? It seems like all your ups and downs are just now coming out. Is there a reason for that?"

"What do you mean?" Clara kind of knew what she meant, but she wasn't sure that she actually wanted to reveal. She was already a little worried that the amount of keeping to herself she'd done was unnatural, but it was easier than explaining what she did every day. She felt like the last two and a half months had been a constant exploration of herself and who she wanted to be, and that was something that she had a hard time imagining anyone else wanting to be a part of. Plus, when it came down to it, other people probably shouldn't be a part. *Wasn't that what soul searching was about? Being alone?*

She looked up from her swaying dance and Krista was watching her intently. She wondered if she'd said something or if she was simply watching.

"What?" Clara asked.

"Nothing. I just wondered... I just want you to know that you can always tell me—if you want—no matter what it is. If it's about your lame-o husband," at this she made a vomiting gesture, "or that you had a really awesome day and," she turned toward the wall, "you painted a lovely flowing river on your wall in deep blues and greens."

"It's a canal."

Krista laughed and Clara thought she heard her mutter something else under her breath. *Change* was the only word she caught.

"Plus, you know," Clara claimed haughtily, again in an attempt to shift the subject away from her, "I just really didn't want my mother to find out my secrets."

Krista gasped, "You thought *I* would tell your mother! I am your best friend!" she defended herself. "Wait! You don't have a new Dutch best friend do you?"

"*Best* friend?" she taunted, but then laughed. "I know like five people in the country and the one I'm closest to is the waitress at my favorite café. I have no chance of a best friend here."

"Well, with the way you're spelling Pally," Krista tsked, "it seems like you're planning to be here a while."

"Who knows?" Clara replied light-heartedly, "I *do* like it here. It's so pleasant; everything's so well-planned."

"Yeah, I'm not sure what to make of that. I do see that it has a certain pleasantness, but I'm not sure what you mean by 'well-planned.'"

"You know, trains, planes, no automobiles. Lots of walking and canals and fat, fluffy bunnies."

"Bunnies? What?"

"I'll show you tomorrow."

"So, how would that work?" Krista asked, "staying?"

"Yeah, I don't know quite yet. Maybe all you need is a KLM frequent flyer number. I think I've got that." Clara laughed and Krista laughed along politely for a second before prodding again.

"Really, though. You've got a pretty sweet deal right now, what with the paychecks still rolling in, but what about after that? Do you... Do you have any thoughts? What's the visa situation here in Europe?"

"To be perfectly honest, I've been avoiding thinking about it. I love it here, I seriously do, but that doesn't mean that I feel confident enough to stay here or to have my child here or work here or…"

"Okay. Cool."

"And I guess there is probably some kind of a visa I would have to apply for. I'm on a tourist visa right now."

"Oh, yeah, I totally forgot to ask you about that. Did I need to get one of those? Because I totally didn't."

Clara laughed. "No, no, you're fine. Basically everyone gets a 90-day tourist visa upon entering the country. I have that, too. I just have to figure out what I want to do for day 91."

"Hmmm…" Krista hummed and Clara looked at the ceiling. It was good to start thinking these things out. She needed to do so eventually, and it was nice to do when Krista was around. She was usually a good person to bounce things off of—especially strange things.

"So when is day 91?" Krista asked, interrupting her internal mental processes.

Clara stood up and walked over to her purse. She pulled out a small planner with a picture of wooden shoes on the cover. Calmly, she opened it and paged through.

"July 25."

"Hmm," Krista mused. "Can I see that?" She pointed to the pocket calendar.

Clara looked at her suspiciously but handed it over nonetheless.

"Wow," she laughed as she examined the month. "You're pretty wide open." She laughed again, but louder. And then she let out a full-on cackle. "This is awesome! Every woman's dream! You don't have to work while you're pregnant. You can create art—you know, work out your libido rushes through art—go to yoga classes, eat stroopwafels and spoon Speculoos into your mouth from a bowl on your belly. Plus, you've got to have some alimony coming? Child support payments from Jack? Man!" She flipped to the next page and then back a few pages. "This is just awesome. You *have* to stay! Are you paying rent for this crib? Ha-" she laughed, *crib*."

"No, I just take care of the utilities and I suppose the tax and stuff. Actually," she tipped her head back and laughed. "I think my mom might already do that." She let out a hoot. "My mom! Paying my way to live in The Netherlands."

"Sweet ass deal," Krista agreed. She stood up from the couch and turned to go upstairs.

"Hey, wait. What's a libido rush?" Clara yelled after her. "Come back! Pregnant women don't know these things! We need guidance."

Krista was only gone for a minute or two, but when she came back she miraculously had a bottle of vanilla jenever in one hand, and in the other, a tulip shaped Wynand Fockink glass.

"How?" asked Clara.

"The bartender and I, we're," Krista intertwined two fingers, "like this."

Clara's jaw dropped open.

"Plus, I paid for it," Krista added. "I could have gotten a sixth one free if I bought five."

Clara burst into laughter. "You're a nut!"

"Whatever," said Krista. "I don't know about you, but when I'm on vacation, I drink, and while I'm here, this is what I'm drinking."

They spent the next few minutes laughing over Krista's new addiction to jenever and the many ways to solve a libido rush, both in Clara's case and Krista's.

"Hey-" Krista said suddenly, "Just cross the border! That's what people do in Mexico. You leave for a few days and get a new tourist visa. Bam, 90 days more."

"Nah, it doesn't exactly work that way here. It's not just a Dutch visa, well, it is, but it's for Schengen."

"Where's Schengen? Man, these new countries just come out of nowhere." She shook her head, "Wait, no, I know. It's that one by Spain, right? The one that's hardly a country? But wait, why would the Schengens bother you?"

"Wow." Clara said seriously. "We had better get you a globe, stat." She smiled indulgently.

"Speaking of which, do you think I could get some wooden shoes while I'm here?"

"How is that a speaking of which? And yes, I'm sure you could."

"Great! I'd like it if they were painted blue and white with little tulips and my name on them, too." Clara couldn't quite tell if she was being sarcastic or not. She could just imagine her maniacal smile thinking of painted tulips and the swirling letters of her name, probably surrounded in tiny yellow daffodils.

"Uh, okay."

"Great! I just really want to *feel* Dutch."

Clara laughed loudly. "Yeah, because walking around in wooden shoes with your name written on them in tulips will really make you seem Dutch. Should we pick up a bonnet for you as well?"

"Huh?"

"Never mind," Clara responded. Krista was now examining the pair of wooden shoes on the front of her calendar.

"Uh, whoa. You know that July 25 is like a week away?"

"Kind of."

"What exactly does that mean? 'Kind of.'"

"Well, maybe you can help me figure something out. If I *don't* get it figured out, you won't have a Holland connection anymore anyway."

"I thought we decided that. Just go to Schengen."

"No, Krista, I am already in Schengen."

"Wait, what? If this is another piece of that Holland versus The Netherlands puzzle, then I'm out, I just don't understand why they make the *name* of their *country* such a difficult and confusing affair."

"No, Schengen's like… a secret European society."

"Oh!" gasped Krista, "That's awesome. How'd you get to be part of a secret European society?"

"Okay, it's not really secret. It's just a European society."

"So you're a society girl?"

"Krista!"

"Well, be more specific. Your explanations are terrible. Sometimes I wonder how you get around at all! Leaving my luggage in some train station locker," she muttered with a smile.

"It was your luggage!" cried Clara.

"Nice host," Krista mumbled.

"Fine, I will try to explain more clearly."

"Good."

"There are many countries that are considered part of Europe," Clara said in a dry, monotone voice. "Depending on where you live, sometimes you can cross a country border only 30 minutes from your house."

"Isn't that true everywhere?" Krista interrupted. "Isn't that the way it is for people in Buffalo, New York, for example?"

"Do you want an explanation or not?" Clara inquired sharply, and Krista gave a pompous nod for her to go on.

"This can be very difficult," said Clara, switching back to her Ben Stein voice, "carrying your passport every day and waiting for border officials," Krista began to laugh at the ridiculous tone, "so they decided to come up with an agreement and form a union so that people could travel freely and even work in neighboring countries."

"Wait, is this the E.U?"

Clara shot her a look and Krista shut her mouth with a restrained smile. "Thus, Schengen was born."

There was a long pause, and then Krista erupted.

"That was the end of your explanation!? That was shit! You didn't answer any of my questions and I still have no idea what a Schengen is."

"Geez! Listen!" yelled Clara, half laughing. "It's basically the E.U. countries, plus Switzerland, minus, like, I dunno, Romania."

"Why?"

"What do you mean, 'why?'?"

"Why not Romania? Doesn't that just make them feel

bad? Why can't people travel to Romania. Oh! Is it because of Transylvania and the vampires?"

Instead of responding, Clara picked up the bottle of vanilla jenever, slowly unscrewed the cap, refilled Krista's glass—excessive surface tension included, replaced the cap, and gave her an instructive nod. Krista leaned forward and took the top sip and smiled, smacking her lips together in satisfaction.

"Nice."

Clara sighed. "Phew…"

"Nice explanation, by the way. Much better. I almost understood."

Clara nodded thanks.

"If you ever get a dog, you should totally name it Schengen."

They spent the rest of the night laughing at the innumerable *Schengen the dog* jokes they came up with.

twaalf

The next day Clara finally got Krista out and walking around Breda. At one point that morning they had been dangerously close to getting on a train, but Clara eventually got Krista to admit that she was tired and could use a day to chill at home. Tomorrow they could take another daytrip—though possibly somewhere in the south rather than back to Amsterdam.

Clara was now leading a walking tour around town in the direction of a café.

"Wait…" Krista began laughing as they crossed over into the Breda city park. "Did I just see an entire family biking by, chatting happily?"

"You haven't seen nothin' yet. This place is like no land you've ever seen. I swear, children actually bike from the womb. Oh, and then as soon as they learn how to bike, which is around six months of age, they just start speaking fluent

English. I bet they check themselves out of the hospital in five languages. It's crazy."

"Yeah, I, uh, don't really believe you, but I did just see another happy family bike by, and I think they had a newborn in the front seat."

"Told you."

"It was wearing sunglasses, and it could hardly hold its head up."

"I know! I'm telling you, it's crazy. They do things differently here."

Krista shook her head as if shaking off shock, and followed Clara into the park.

"Maybe I'll cook you something tonight." Clara said as they strolled through the park towards the little sculpture garden framed in hedges. "We could just stay in and hang out."

"That sounds nice." Krista approved. "What kind of food? Dutch food?"

"Well, maybe... but people don't really seem to like Dutch food."

"Why not?"

"Well, I hear it's a bit... dull."

"What's in it?"

"Meat, potatoes, kale."

"Which one is kale, again?"

"It's green, leafy, looks like parsley, tastes like nothing-"

"Again, like parsley."

"Supposedly it's different."

"Hmm..." she paused for quite a while, "sounds pretty gross, actually; worse than dull."

"It's not that bad."

"What else do they eat? Fish? They're surrounded by the sea, right?"

"Yeah, that's true." Clara was pleased at the sound of this addition. "We could make fish. That'd be fun."

"Whoa."

"What?" asked Clara.

"Nothing, I just heard the 'we' and it caught me off guard."

"What, you're not going to help?"

"I'll help. I'll pour the jenever and prepare spoonfuls of Speculoos—one hell of an amuse-bouche if you ask me."

Clara laughed, "That's definitely true. Maybe I'll make hutspot or stamppot."

"Hmm," Krista deliberated, "Sounds, uh, okay." She made a face, probably imagining what a stamppot was. "What else could we make?" she asked, "Dutch apple pie? Something with Dutch cocoa? Something in a Dutch oven?"

"I'm not sure how related any of those things are to Dutch culture nowadays."

"Oh."

"What *is* a Dutch oven anyway? Do you know?" she asked Krista.

"I dunno."

"Dutch cocoa, I don't know what that's all about, either. It's actually kind of a pain to find baking cocoa here, period, let alone some special Dutch kind. Should we go to the café right there?" She pointed to the café that sat right on the park grounds. "I think we might be able to get apple pie there. And it's Dutch."

"Let's."

A few minutes later, Krista was looking at her glass, which was filled with a thick, vibrant orange liquid. She was laughing intermittently with the look of a slightly sillied sailor, or maybe a clown. It suddenly occurred to Clara that people became rather strange in foreign countries.

"What's a wortel?" Krista giggled. "It's what I ordered." She laughed again. "And this is what I got."

"I don't know," Clara responded. "I know *some* Dutch words, not all of them."

"Actually I ordered a wortel *smoothie*. They actually said the word smoothie. That's not Dutch, right?"

"I think it's probably borrowed from English."

"Wowww, look at you, 'borrowed from English,'" Krista

repeated in a mocking and slightly British voice. "You are getting so grown up, Clare," she said as she pinched Clara's cheek, simultaneously spilling a little wortel juice down the front of her polka dot blouse. "Shoot!"

"Just drink it," Clara commanded.

"What do you think it is?" Krista asked, "Juice of warts?"

"Look at the color, it's probably tangerine juice or something."

"No, it's not tangerine juice. It's too thick."

"Well, what do you think it looks like?"

"I don't know," Krista lifted up the glass and examined it from all angles through the glass. "Thick," she noted scientifically, "consistent, freak orange... It looks like liquid rubbish," she finally declared.

"Rubbish?" she asked, "What's this about Krista? You're not British and you never will be, so don't even try."

"Ian says it, so why can't I?"

"He *is* British. He's allowed to say it. Seriously, use your eyes. What kind of juice does it *look* like?" Clara had a pretty good guess as to what type of juice it was.

"I don't know! Um, cheese?"

"Cheese juice? You think that it's cheese juice?"

"Well, you told me to look at it. It's the color of cheese."

"No, it's not."

"Yes it is, think of cheddar cheese."

"Okay, but they don't make *cheese* juice. That's just milk. Come on! Just get on with it and drink your warts!"

Krista took a deep breath. "Okay..." She closed her eyes dramatically and took a sip.

"Hmmmm...."

"Good?" asked Clara. "Bad?" She watched Krista, eyes still closed, waiting for a reaction. Krista squeezed her eyes shut tightly, tipped her head back and chugged the glass before slamming it down on the café table.

"Great!?" confirmed Clara.

"Nope. Carrot juice, yuck. I hate carrots."

Clara laughed, "Then why did you chug it?"

"Nyeah, it's good for me—whether I like it or not."

"You are such a lunatic in Europe. Crazier than ever," Clara nodded happily, "and you would never make it here, no sense of intuition and no sense of self-preservation," she muttered.

"Oh, and you *are* making it? You're just so good at adapting," she taunted.

"Yes! I am." Clara said, as surely as she could muster. She *thought* she was doing okay, and up until this conversation she'd believed that Krista thought so, too.

Krista paused, eyeing her. "Are you?" she smiled at her best friend.

"Yes," she repeated, though it was starting to sound more like a question.

"I think so too," said Krista with a smile.

"Really?" Clara asked in a delighted voice. "I mean I think I am too, but you never know. In Sac, I never seemed to know whether I was being a fool or not. So it seems like I'm doing okay?"

Krista turned her head to look over at Clara, and to her surprise, kissed her smack on the top of the head. "Actually, it seems like you're doing great. You have a home, you have a hobby that could become a career, you have friends and activities—you actually have a life, Clare. It's great. I'm really proud. And kind of impressed." She lowered her voice and continued, "It's kind of weird to live life not knowing what the hell's going on around you," she chuckled.

"Thanks," Clara responded simply.

"About bloody time you got around to doing something for yourself."

Clara shook her head and then frowned at Krista, "Americans," she sneered, "always want to be bloody British."

Krista laughed. "Yum," she declared as she finished her last bite of appelgebak. "Good apple pie. Basically just the same as our apple pie, but drier somehow, and tons of cinnamon. I like that." She appeared to be thinking deeply all of a sudden, and then a twinkle appeared in her eye.

"You know what would go fabulously with Dutch apple pie?"

"Let me guess, cinnamon jenever?"

"Hells, yes! You guessed it!"

Clara laughed and went back to finishing her own piece. "It's pretty good with the cappuccino, too," she commented.

"Yeah, whatever. Tell it to Wynand Fockink."

$$C_M$$

That night, Clara and Krista made hutspot together. At the least, Clara made hutspot, narrating throughout, and Krista made fun of her.

"Hutspot is basically a huge pot of mashed potatoes and winter vegetables," Clara explained, "meaning that onions and carrots will do. There is a spice packet you can buy, which as far as I can tell, contains salt, pepper, and some other secret homey ingredient, but certainly nothing stronger than paprika. Throw a sausage on top of all that and maybe a spot of beef gravy, and you are eating traditional Dutch." Krista didn't respond, so Clara assumed she was pondering the spice packet and its ingredients.

"What's that?" Krista asked when it was finally time to bring the pot over to the table.

"It's hutspot! What do you think we've been doing for the last hour?"

"I don't know. As far as I can tell, you just peeled hella potatoes and then we gossiped for 40 minutes."

"You are so weird."

"Right," she said, "like I'm the only weird one in this relationship."

"Well, you're at least weirder than me... freak," she muttered under her breath and then chuckled.

"Yeah, right, *I'm* weird," Krista laughed, "but you're prego and living in a country where the language is clearly based only on spitting. Plus, from what I have seen, you only eat baked goods—and some weird potato dish that looks like it has already been eaten."

"Hey, you are going to love this."

"Whether or not it tastes good, it still looks like it has already been processed once."

"Yuck, that's gross. And don't talk about throwing up, I haven't really been sick and I don't want to start."

"And my talking about it is going to make it start?"

"It might! You have an abnormal influence on people."


dertien


"I can't deny that this is quite the lifestyle we have," Krista commented when they boarded the train the next morning. They had a full day of exploring planned and a pleasant and comfortable train ride with coffee and chocolate croissants for breakfast just ahead of them.

When they arrived in Vlissingen, the very last stop on the southwest coast of the country, they deboarded and immediately spotted a seafood stand selling fresh fried calamari and shrimp. They devoured an order and then ordered a second and took it to a sunny picnic table next to the ocean. The sandwiches they packed for lunch were still in Clara's daybag.

"With all this," Krista asked, "is there anything that you miss?"

Clara smiled, "It's pretty nice here." They sat in silence gazing around them. "And simpler," she added. "It's weird. I find myself speaking more quietly, thinking a bit more before I talk, even speaking the words more slowly, not that they couldn't understand if I spoke at a normal speed. It's just different. It's nice. I feel like," Clara spoke carefully, "I know myself better here... Is that possible?"

After an extended pause Krista spoke, "So nothing?" she repeated.

"Well, you," Clara declared, "and sometimes I do kind of

miss Reno."

"Wait, what?!" Krista turned to her in horror. "Did you just admit that you *missed* Reno? And in the same sentence as missing *me*? I'm going to give that a hearty tsk. Pathetic."

"Well, we went so many times, and there's a casino here, but you have to pay to get in. Isn't that crazy? To have to pay to get into a casino?" Krista was still staring at her, though her facial expression had now transformed into more of a glare. "Don't you think?" she repeated.

"Don't change the subject," said Krista. "Who misses Reno?" she sneered. "At least miss Vegas or Tahoe or some place a little less ghetto."

"It's not that ghetto."

"It's hella ghetto."

Clara laughed. "I miss that."

"What?"

"Hella."

Krista shook her head. "You're so weird."

Clara smiled and shrugged.

"And if I didn't want you to continue living here with all my heart, I would give you a list of about a hundred things that are way more awesome and pineable than *Reno*. Dear Lord, Reno. What an insult to NorCal."

Clara laughed and shrugged.

They wandered around Vlissingen, and then Middleburg after that, before getting on a train heading east toward home. They rode peacefully, both looking out the window and observing the changing Dutch countryside. They were now on the lookout for an interesting small town to stop off in for dinner.

"There's a ton of water here," Krista noted, "but it hardly ever seems to be moving. Do they have problems with flooding?"

"They certainly used to. I'm not sure if it's much of a problem anymore. That's why there are so many canals. They control it, so the water level is basically unchanging."

"Goes!?" Krista suddenly cried out, noticing the sign at

the station of the city they were pulling into. "What a ridiculous name! Who goes to Goes!?" Krista laughed. "The Dutch... weeeird people, I gotta say."

"I'm sure it's not pronounced like that. Dutch pronunciation is much more extraordinary than that. It's probably something like... goose, except instead of the *g* sound, it is more like an *h*, but in the back of your throat."

"Like a goose in the back of my throat? And you're gonna stand by that explanation?"

"Shut up."

"How do you know, anyway? It's not like you speak Dutch."

"I speak some," Clara said defensively. "I'm trying at least," Clara murmured.

"You really are?"

Clara nodded with a proud little smile.

"Well, I'll be. Haven't you just become one of a kind over here in Hollandia."

"Wow, the highest of compliments. I move across the world by myself, pregnant, and I achieve something others have when they shoot from the womb."

Krista smiled. "Ghoose."

Clara shook her head, "Less g, more throat, and let the s whistle in your teeth a bit... Hoose."

"Goose."

"Again."

"Again," whined Krista, "You let it whistle in your teeth," she muttered, "more throat."


viertien


When it came time to take Krista to the airport, Clara did everything in her power to remain positive and cheerful until Krista walked through security towards her gate. To her surprise, she didn't burst into tears immediately. Krista's confidence made Clara feel like she actually was settling in.

After sending Krista off, she had an urge to sit and watch the planes come and go. It was a bit strange, yes, but they had a viewing platform, so it might be kind of romantic in a Nicholas Sparks kind of way.

She headed upstairs and found the viewing platform basically empty due to the soggy rain clouds hovering above. She found a bench and sat down to watch.

It was nice. With each takeoff and landing, she wondered about the passengers and where they were at in their lives.

Were they coming? Going? Visiting family? Living a work-obsessed life? Just arriving home, or taking off for good, running away from everything they had known?

Her visa situation was becoming dire, now that Krista was here and gone she could readily admit it. While she was fairly sure that they wouldn't hunt her down and throw her in a Dutch prison for spending more than 90 days in the country without a new visa, she was also sure that it wouldn't help her situation if she actually wanted to stay long term.

She sat back and put in her earbuds. It was difficult to think properly with all the jet engines in the background.

She swayed a waltz along with Janne Schra, the singer of Room Eleven, her new favorite Dutch band and means of peaceful canalside relaxation.

*Could she* just leave Schengen temporarily? There really wasn't any good reason why she couldn't. It's not like she would do this forever, she would have to figure out some way to earn an income and become a permanent member of society if she did want to stay—cautious budgeting could only get you so far. If she couldn't make it work here, she would be heading back to the U.S. pretty quickly.

Or she could get divorced. That would definitely improve her financial situation.

She began to make a mental list of places where she could take a nice little vacation: Morocco, Tunisia, Turkey, Russia, though she might need an even stricter visa for some of those places. It might be a little hot in Tunisia or Morocco. What about Suriname or South Africa? India was a possibility.

Perhaps going on vacation—a vacation from her current extended vacation—was just what she needed. If she left and went on a little vacation, maybe she could reexamine her life yet again and decide whether or not to move on, or...

Well, who could blame her for wanting to stay in The Netherlands?

When the train pulled back into the Breda station after her brief trip to Noord-Holland, she realized that she didn't want to go on vacation; she wanted to be here. She'd rather stay for years confined to this little town than have a week in any of the exotic countries she'd considered.

On her way home from the train station she paused for a minute at the Grote Markt, the main plein where the market was held each week. She looked across the square just in time to see a couple biking by, holding hands. It all felt rather bittersweet.

She had been nervous and scared to come here, but there had been a pull. She hadn't known where the pull was coming from, or what it was specifically pulling her towards, but she hadn't felt scared of it, she had felt hopeful, and she had been right. It was based upon nothing but a story about her great aunt, yet somehow it had been right.

She loved Breda. This little city was the haven she'd always been looking for. Of course she missed her friends, her family, and some of the finer things of life in Northern California, but how could she ever think of going back now that she had *this* beautiful home? She was now standing in front of it looking up in admiration as if standing in front of the gates of heaven.

She loved it; she loved it so much that she was starting to feel that pressure in her chest—good pressure, like the feeling you got from falling in love.

How could she be in this place, where she was a complete foreigner, a complete stranger, and still feel so at home?

She looked up into the huge, white clouds, rolling by at an enormous speed. This had to be her answer. It hadn't been a vacation that she needed after all, she had needed a home, and here it was standing in front of her.

Perhaps she was finally where she belonged, and in fact, citizenship might be what she ought to be thinking about after all.

$$C_M$$

That afternoon her doorbell rang and she hurried down, wondering who could possibly be there.

"Lars!" she yelled shrilly when she opened the door and found herself looking up at a tall, brown-haired Dutchman.

"Claartje!" he greeted her, "How are you?"

"I'm great! But you're back, how was your trip?"

"It was great!" he cried, "Just great!"

They spent the whole evening chatting, laughing and eating. They talked about his trip and the differences between California and The Netherlands. She explained her great aunt and how she had come to have a home in Breda. Lars asked what she was doing in terms of a visa and she sadly described her 90-day dilemma. To her surprise, Lars revealed that he had a friend who was an immigration officer.

"Actually, Claartje, you might be able to stay in the country by means of your great aunt. Obviously your grandmother is the key figure, but Ilse may help your case. I didn't realize you still had family in the country."

"Really? You think it could help?"

"Well, if you'd like to stay-"

"Yes, I do, I do!"

Lars smiled gladly. "Well, then we'll have to see what we can do. I'll give my friend a ring and see what he thinks."

"Thanks so much, Lars!"

Lars showed her hundreds of pictures and she showed him some of her pieces. He was both stunned and intrigued by the mural she had begun to paint on her wall. She could tell by his hesitance that the idea of painting a giant scene on one's wall was *not* normal, but she didn't care. He seemed to like what she was doing. He even went as far as asking for one of her charcoal drawings to take home for his mother. Apparently Ellie had a soft spot for the plump rabbits that ran around the country, and Clara had a charcoal of two rabbits posed like statues under a park bench in the Breda Central Park that he claimed was terrifically sweet.

He pushed and pushed, but Clara would absolutely not allow him to give her money for it. The fact that he'd offered—and pushed—thrilled her to no end and gave her great optimism for the future, so much that the very next day she brought her confidence and her easel outside and sat on the side of the Singel to paint.

The freedom was exhilarating. It was a perfect day and the light shimmering down the canal towards the drawbridge was magnificent.

She spent the whole day out working on the piece, and by the end of the day, she was pleased to admit that she had created a somewhat impressive work of art. She was so proud of herself that before she went to bed she set up the easel near the front window of her downstairs "studio." Of course, she didn't put it on display, but she angled it just so. If anyone *happened* to be looking in, they would certainly be able to see the new painting.

The next day Clara was back out on the canal with her easel. She sat for a while, simply enjoying her newly embraced confidence. Eventually, she pulled out a nearly finished piece that she hoped to conclude that day. It was one of the first pieces she'd done in Amsterdam. She had sketched in pencil and then painted it into color once she had moved to Breda. It was quite amazing how far she had come.

Clara looked up from her painting to see a boat glide through the canal in front of her. An old man stood at the wheel looking down the canal. He was shirtless, and had a tan, bald head encircled by a fringe of white. His wife was sprawled on the navy blue cushions in the front of the boat, and although she wore sunglasses, Clara knew from the way she rested her head on the striped throw pillow that her eyes were closed.

Life was serene here, and so much more bearable in general. A few months ago she was living in Sacramento with her husband and working in an elementary school within two miles of her childhood home. She was born in Sacramento, so she knew it like the back of her hand. She had favorite restaurants and cafés where she could meet old friends. She had a beautiful house. However, passion, confidence and joy had come only in waves, and infrequent waves, at that.

She looked down at her lap at her flowing summer dress, and the two thin scarves she had chosen for today, both woven colorfully around her neck, and the changes floored her.

"Excuse me, ma'am?"

Clara looked up to see a woman slightly older than herself, dressed casually, clearly a tourist, with her stocky husband standing behind her.

"Do you speak English?" she asked, "Are you an artist?"

Clara smiled. The woman was doing very well at speaking loudly and slowly for a "foreigner."

"Yes, I'm an artist," Clara replied, stunned by how quickly the words came out of her mouth.

"Oh, tremendous, I just love your work. I hope you don't mind, but my husband and I were just walking, and well, we were lost actually, and then we saw you and you looked so peaceful and we saw that you were painting-"

"Actually," her husband interrupted, "we were wondering if that piece is for sale? Or if you have a studio shop?"

Clara was shocked, but hoped that this didn't show on her face.

"Well, er, I." *Think quickly, think quickly*, her brain grinded. "I don't really have a studio open to the public... yet."

"Oh, I see," the woman nodded along, "Is this piece for sale, though? It looks like you're nearly done."

"Yes," Clara replied, unable to help herself. There were so many emotions coursing through her body. "It's nearly finished, and it is for sale," she smiled.

They talked for a while longer; her painting was exactly what they were looking for, a piece of artwork to take home, one that captured a piece of the priceless way of life here in The Netherlands. Photographs just didn't capture it like paint on paper, they said.

They decided on a price and agreed on a meeting place for the following day. Clara wanted to finish touching up the piece, and she also wanted to find a suitable container for the woman to use for the trip back to the U.S. The price that Clara quoted them was reasonable for a new artist, but much more than what a street vendor would have asked. It was enough so that if she sold regularly, she could make a living.

As the woman turned to go, she questioned Clara once more, "By the way, if you have any others, please bring them tomorrow, I would love to bring a piece back for my sister as well."

It was then, still sitting on the edge of the canal in the presence of her first client, that she realized what it all meant. Her future was mapped out. She had a home, she would have a child, and now, two days from her 32nd birthday, she had a dream career. She was an artist. This income could make her an entrepreneur, and as an entrepreneur, she could obtain a visa to stay in The Netherlands. After so many years it was all coming together. If she planned this right, and kept at her artwork, selling even one or two pieces each week, she should have enough income to support herself and her daughter and to stay in The Netherlands as long as she liked. God bless her grandmother for this house, and her Aunt Ilse for standing sentinel for so many years. Without them, nothing would be possible.

The next morning she met the nice woman at a café nearby. A tiny part of her didn't want to give away this painting that she had been working on—or at least building up to, for such a long time—the first successful sale of Clara Jean Mason.

From then on, each day she trekked out with her easel and brushes or charcoals and a canvas. She loaded it all in her colorful canvas bag, which became more and more smudged with paints and pastels each day. She didn't mind; every time she looked at it, it just made her smile. Her dream was coming true. Each day she woke up so excited to go out and create that she thought she would burst if she didn't let some color flow from her fingertips. It was exhilarating to feel this inspired, like having the sun shine on your face that first summer day, except somehow the light was shining not on her face, but from it. She had never known it could be like this, never imagined life could be so grand.

In stories, there is always an instant when success first seems possible. Not just a drop of success, but one of those big, life-changing, lifelong goals that had so little chance of being accomplished.

A month later, as she sat at the park café with her sketchpad balanced on her growing belly, she couldn't help but smile at the turns her life had taken. A month before, she had sold two paintings; last week she had printed business cards and sold one more, and this morning her website had gone live—the very same day she'd filed for divorce. Against all odds, Lars' friend had come through. The day after she told him about her situation, his friend called to discuss the possibilities, and just days later Clara received notice that she had a temporary visa extension while her immigration status was under consideration.

*Wow.* What a far cry from where she'd been that spring.

Clara watched from across the park as a bride and groom were photographed near the pond. The bride was older, probably 35 or so.

Clara liked the way things worked here. Everything was taken at a slower pace. It didn't matter that a woman was getting married at an older age. She was happy.

Soon, the photographer and happy couple had made their way right into the café where she was now enjoying a cup of tea. They took pictures at the tables and framed in the white paned windows; at one point the photographer was even crouched next to her chair, hoping for an optimum angle so the sun glistened just right off the bride's light blonde hair.

Halfway through their session they stopped for a drink. The bride and groom each ordered a small beer and the photographer got a small coffee. The proprietor of the park café offered them each a drink of Jägermeister as a congratulatory gift, and they both accepted graciously. They sat a few more minutes before taking off again across the park in the direction of the old castle. She assumed they were headed there for more pictures; the picturesque drawbridge would have made it into her wedding album without a single person at all.

## vijftien

Then it happened, the moment that every woman wants. Her man came running back. She was standing in Capitol Park in Sacramento under a redwood and he was running toward her shouting her name. He wanted her, and he was so sorry for what had happened.

She was amazed. This never happens. Besides movies and books, she had never heard of it happening.

When she woke up, the feeling of nausea in her stomach was excruciating and she ran dizzily to the bathroom to throw up.

*I just woke up*, she thought. Six months later and she was back to this. She rested her face pitifully on the cool white plastic toilet seat. After everything, she was back to dreaming of him. *How revolting*. She tried to shake her head, but it made her dizzy. She threw up again and put her cheek back down on the toilet seat.

After a few more sessions, she lifted her head, pushed her hair back from her face, and got directly in the shower. She felt awful in every way possible, mind and body.

The next day, Clara woke up to dreariness. The following day was the same, as was the next. Finally, she decided she'd had enough and persevered, umbrella in hand, to an exhibit opening at a small museum nearby. On the way home she hit up her local fruit and veggie store. She had meant to go to the market instead, but the chill outside was getting to her.

"So much rain," she commented to the woman behind the counter as she asked for her leeks and broccoli for soup that night.

"Yes," the vendor replied, "we were having a warm year, so humid."

*Strange*, Clara thought to herself. The man at the museum she had spoken to had said more or less the same thing.

"Back to normal," he replied when she commented on the downpour outside.

*And humid?* She was beginning to think she had been experiencing a slightly skewed view on what it was like to live there.

By the end of the week, the sun had altogether set on her optimism. Daylight savings time had occurred and the darkness that ensued was almost unbearable. It felt like morning all day and she was *not* a morning person. The haze was never entirely swept away, the light didn't fully shine on the forever dewy grass, and the moment she thought it might be time for midday, the darkness crept back in and it was night.

She spent much of each day alternating between glaring out the window at the rain and glaring in at her cold, nearly empty apartment. Both no longer met her expectations. All the inspired decisions, the independent path she had chosen, they were making less and less sense with every drop of rain.

*What was logical about living alone in a foreign country in the winter?* It was entirely illogical when she had nothing and no one. She turned to glare out the window. Escaping this slump was impossible.

She made it out for a walk and some fresh air, but she was struggling. It was one of those days when it was a constant struggle just to get through. The many-headed beast of life had her fighting to keep her hair out of her eyes, struggling to walk without tripping, failing to find the bread store, working hard to keep her chamomile tea down—just struggling.

She turned left onto a hopeful looking street and found that she was back on the Singel, nowhere near the place she thought she was headed. As she took the curve toward home, the wind hit her face with such a force that she reactively turned away from it. Putting it at her back, she shivered violently. She was alone and battling life on the same streets she had relished exploring just a month earlier.

She ducked into the first café that she saw and found a seat as close to the little stone fireplace as possible. She sat alone, surrounded by near darkness.

It was crazy to think that she once thought brown cafés such as this were cozy and happy. Sitting all alone on a cold, hard, wooden bench in a dimly lit room surrounded by dark brown wood in every direction—she could hardly stand to hold back the tears. The despair was nearly overwhelming her. It came at her and from her, the loneliness and emptiness seeping out everywhere, making the smoke-stained wood bleed gloom.

She was beginning to wonder if every path really had a rainbow at the end. Perhaps it was simply one big circle of failing and trying to rise up—no end, no real beginning, just working to overcome obstacle after obstacle.

*If her visa failed and she was forced out, would she be able to start again? Just how many times could you start over in life?* She had to imagine she was about at her max. It was like running a car completely out of gas. It's not training for the car; the car doesn't get any better at running on fumes. She certainly wasn't getting any better. In fact, she seemed to be doing a worse job every day. She had the vaguest of memories of success, but that too, was slipping away. She hadn't sold a piece for two weeks, *hell*, she hadn't even painted that week.

Over the following days the gray skies seemed to suck the life out of her just as the wind took her breath and the rain soaked her to the bone. The little warmth that she carried disappeared in the effort to recover all her struggling senses.

And then there was her baby. It was like her child was

rejecting her. She threw up day after day, and cried in between.

*First trimester's the worst... yeah, right.*

Dr. Booij continued to say that everything was fine, although she wondered if her wise doctor could feel the aura of despair surrounding her every time she stepped in the door. On her last visit Clara had been asked who would be with her for the birth, and she hadn't known how to respond. She mumbled something noncommittally, knowing Dr. Booij wouldn't press, and then went home to cry in a corner.

To make matters worse, Lars' friend the immigration officer was calling with problems every few days. It seemed there was one person in particular that could remedy all this— her mother. It would enormously help her situation if they could understand the status of the generation in between Clara and Ilse. Her homework for this week was to get her mother to call him, a task which she was not looking forward to.

About her only comfort was her mural, though that, too, she was starting to despise. Day by day she planned, drew, and painted on her wall. Her first strokes of paint had been monumental and symbolic somehow, like the remaking of her life. Now the only purpose they served was to keep the minutes passing by. Sometimes she painted in strokes that were slow and deliberate, sometimes when she was angry or sad, it became faster and layered. The layers of paint became thicker as she became more pregnant.

Eventually she couldn't physically bear standing at the wall for the long hours. Her tiny step ladder had been abandoned long before. She was glad that she had at least more or less finished the tracing before she retired completely to the lower half of the wall. With time, she retreated further and spent her evenings after the sun had gone down sitting on a pile of bedding or pillows on the floor—drawing, painting, outlining; letting her mood and her mind wander as it liked. She listened to music constantly. It was the only way to hide the silence around which her life was based.

Her wall had become a huge Dutch street scene. Dark

silhouettes became figures out of nowhere. She sat on the wooden floor under a pile of blankets as they appeared one after another. It was as if the figures were in the forefront of her mind, willing themselves to escape onto her wall, into the Dutch world in which she'd once flourished.

It was somewhat similar to her other pieces, but rather than the usual meandering and wandering and bustling pedestrians, there was instead a woman, dancing freely, arms spread, face turned up to the heavens—or rather, the enormous, white Dutch clouds. Near the darkly flowing canal stood a young girl, waving with a smile. Window shopping in the alley of the quaint Dutch street was a proud mother, holding the hand of her young daughter, both of them dressed in colorful skirts and brightly colored tops.

There were no men at all, she realized and coughed out a laugh—the first in a long time. She continued unchanged or moved by the discovery. She had no need for men right now. They could cause her nothing but more pain and grief.

At first, it was so easy. She had stepped inside the romantic world of old houses and gently glowing street lamps and fallen in love. Most people would say that the most difficult part is getting your foot in the door, getting inside and meeting real Dutch people, like Ilse. She had come to find that it was the later step that was the hardest. Stepping inside was but a step, while becoming a real part of it, this was next to impossible.

On Thanksgiving she sank down onto her scuffed hardwood floor with tears in her eyes. She'd decided she had very little to be thankful for, having dined on a turkey and Swiss sandwich alone an hour before. She made to add a layer of deep blue to the passing canal, but then set down her brush and went to work with her fingers, trying desperately to make the bubbling movement of the water appear tranquil. It was not possible; it only looked angered. The waters got darker as the winter weather penetrated Clara's warmth further and further.

She stepped outside one day to find big, fat snowflakes

falling down from the sky. She was now almost eight months pregnant and ate whatever she wanted whenever she wanted— her only solace as of late. The snowflakes made her cry of course. Holding it together was too much to ask of a pregnant woman who hadn't grown up in a place where such a phenomena existed.

The mystically giant flakes were larger than she imagined possible, as if there had been so much moisture in the air and so many chilly bits wanting to fall onto Breda that they'd made the leap together. It was enchanting.

## zestien

Later Clara saw that this was her turning point. The first snowfall shook her out of her noose of despair and placed her gently back into the reaches of normal society. That day she walked through the city park in absolute placidity. She was crying, yes, but that was to be expected, she had finally realized. The quota of tears per month for a pregnant woman who was alone was very simply higher than that of any other woman. After a cup of warme chocolademelk, she meandered slowly back to the park to admire the inch or so of snow that had accumulated.

In the park, just outside the entrance to the sculpture garden, she became unexpectedly possessed by the spirit of her unborn child—or so she thought—and thus staggered clumsily down onto the ground to make a snow angel. She had never made one.

It wasn't as much fun as she thought it would be. She thought it would be more soft and powdery and fewer wet leaves. She did her best all the same, and then spent the next five minutes trying to get up.

While she rested between efforts, she thought about Jack. She managed to consider the situation with a somewhat neutral frame of mind, a first for her since their breakup. As much as she despised Jack, she now knew that it wouldn't last forever. She also understood that she couldn't let her bitterness spread to others. She didn't like the thoughts that passed through her mind when Jack was mentioned, and she didn't like the idea of letting her thoughts bleed into the thoughts of others, especially her daughter's. She resignedly decided she would try to start mending the bridges in her mind, just so her child could have a chance of knowing her father—if that was what she wanted.

Eventually she hoisted herself up and then set off towards the main square, the Grote Markt, in the light snow. She strolled through tiny alleys, across major bicycle, car, and pedestrian thoroughfares and down quiet pedestrianized streets. She began to notice that everywhere around her were little bits of holiday decor. As she reached the main shopping street, she was soon amongst a hundred others, despite the snow, and she was fascinated to see that everything was decorated for Christmas and every store was advertising Christmas sales. Their spirit and enthusiasm was shocking.

Dutch Santa looked a bit odd, she noticed, after an ad featuring a tall man with an extra long and thin white beard caught her attention. He wasn't plump either, maybe a tribute to the many tall, thin Dutch people.

Was this how things worked? People in the U.S. were a bit overweight, so their Santa was too? Or was it the other way around? She giggled to herself. Were the people fat because they wanted to be more like Santa?

It was an interesting idea to ponder, as was how her mood had transformed so completely in the span of a day.

As she continued down the shopping street, she soon realized that their "elves" were different as well. They were dressed very similarly to a court jester, pointed shoes and all, with curly black hair and black skin. The stuffed doll versions of these *helpers* weren't the worst part, it was the random costumed Dutchmen that made her feel uneasy. They had the outfit and the shoes and the black wig, and their faces painted black with a very disgusting-looking paint. *Was that supposed to be soot?* It was a little traumatizing. She would have to ask

Annemarie about it later.

On her way home from the shopping street she saw cyclists everywhere bundled up to make their evening commute. It seemed the winter weather made absolutely no difference at all. As long as they had their two wheels intact, they were biking.

## zeventien

Over tea with Annemarie the next day Clara learned the ins and outs of the Dutch winter holiday season. This was not Santa at all, but someone entirely different. Sinterklaas, the starring figure for Saint Nicholas Day, "arrived" in The Netherlands each year—by boat, interestingly enough—and now the holiday season was in full swing. He brought goodies for the children on December 6, rather than on the 25th as her Santa did. Annemarie stumbled a bit when asked about Piet, Sinterklaas' helper. Clara got the feeling that the story had been touched up over time.

As soon as she got a grasp of the holiday, Clara let her instinct take over and she fell right into her usual holiday spirit. Although it was going to be just her for the holidays, she baked as if she'd be having a dozen people over for a holiday party. Chocolate star cookies, several kinds of fudge, brittle, and toffee—in no time, her kitchen counter and her small dining room table were covered in holiday goodies. Her house smelled constantly of peppermint and chocolate and cinnamon, and she couldn't have been happier about it.

She also began to think about how she would decorate. She hoped that they left things decorated until December 25, but she supposed she'd have to wait and see. For days she contemplated whether or not she would get a tree, but then realized that if she wanted one it might be difficult to find. She hadn't noticed any trees yet. She was now getting pretty good at peering out of the corner of her eye to check as she passed by all the bright, open windows in the evening.

Her wonderings were answered when she caught sight of a strapping Dutch mother who had propped a rather large Christmas tree on her bicycle, branches flinging everywhere. She was steadily walking her bike down the outer edge of the bike path. The most amusing part of the situation was her daughter, who was on her bike about fifty meters ahead. The pre-adolescent girl was irritably looking back at her mother, quite annoyed that she was having to wait.

Clara walked home from the grocery store with yet another box of powdered sugar. It was already dusk although it was still only mid-afternoon. The hour the sun now set was unspeakably early. Funny she hadn't thought of this when she was basking in the 10 p.m. sun during the summer.

She found herself walking more and more slowly each time she passed one of the many tanning salons. Not only did she now fully understand their abundant presence, but she was getting a bigger craving each day to stop in for 10 or 15 minutes—just until she was warm and toasty and giving off that lovely summer burnt skin smell that had so frequently occurred during Sacramento summers. She shuddered and shivered simultaneously, hating it and wanting it. She realized the sun was weaker in the north, but the timid quality of the Dutch sun was absolutely ridiculous. Thankfully, she was once again in love with the Dutch brown café culture—hot chocolate and real whipped cream, flickering candles on every table and often a blazing fireplace.

One day Clara found a pleasant surprise at the market. There was a stand selling something called *oliebollen*. The fried balls of dough, basically spherical doughnuts, were about four inches in diameter, warm, sprinkled with powdered sugar, and basically the best thing that she had ever tasted.

That evening, since it was Wednesday, she decided she would be the one to make the call and ended up talking to her Dad about doughnuts for nearly 20 minutes. It seemed that he remembered her grandmother making oliebollen, Dutch doughnuts, for the holidays every year. She had only stopped after she'd moved from her house to a smaller place with much less of a kitchen. He said she would make dozens and give them out as Christmas gifts to neighbors and friends. Once they became cold, he explained, she would cut them open and stuff them with cream or apple filling. Clara thought she remembered that there had been several kinds of oliebollen at the market that day, so she promised her father that she'd scope it out and get back to him. Secretly, she planned to buy a few and pack them up to send home for the holidays. She had to imagine, despite the shipping time, that they would still be pretty amazing reheated in the oven and sprinkled with fresh powdered sugar. Her mouth watered just thinking about it.

Sure enough, the next morning when she practically sprinted to the market—if a penguin could sprint, that is—she spotted the cart right away, only this time there was a line down the market aisle. She spent a few minutes peering around people's shoulders trying to decide if she wanted cherry stuffed or apple stuffed or raisins or a sack of a dozen plain that she could snack on for the rest of the week. She made small talk with the busy fryer, hoping to find out exactly how long the cart would be parked there and the hot and fresh fluffy balls of goodness available. In the end she decided on one apple-stuffed and one plain. He promised to be there on and off until Christmas, so there was no use stocking up. Fresh was undeniably better.

She got home and called her dad right away, letting him know the many varieties and the upcoming oliebollen cart schedule. When she got off the phone, she went to her coziest chair by the window.

It was December 5, the night before Saint Nicholas Day, which she'd been anxiously awaiting like a child. It was both a winning and losing situation, really. The anticipation made her feel excited and interested, but the loneliness always hit a little harder on an important day, making the day itself kind of a letdown. That evening she made a nice hot cup of tea and with a sigh, went back to staring out her window and longing for friends.

Just down the street, she saw a door open and out came Santa Claus, or rather, Sinterklaas. An immaculately dressed Sinterklaas was sneaking up to the front door of one of the houses across the street. He set a bag of presents on the step and knocked on the door before running back down the street. The door opened and in the light of the streetlamp, she saw two small faces fill with joy as they saw the bag of presents sitting there before them. They looked up and down the street, but Sinterklaas was nowhere in sight. Clara smiled as she recognized the look of delight on their faces.

After a few moments their father picked up the bag and they all went back inside, shutting the door behind them and leaving the street dark once again. Just as Clara was about to turn her attention to a sketchpad, Sinterklaas emerged from his house once again. She laughed as the busy fellow headed back down the street. He approached the house he had just visited but continued past it to the next house where he repeated the act. Another bag of presents was left on the steps, followed by a knock on the door before he ran away down the street. It appeared he was the designated Sinterklaas for the year.

Again and again he returned, bustling back to his house each time in order to preserve the surprise and keep the magic alive for the children of each of his neighbors. Clara wondered if he had his own children or if this was how he played a part in the holiday. Perhaps they were older and didn't believe anymore. Or maybe, she pondered, he was a dad and his kids were busy—occupied for the moment or supervised by their mother, playing unknowingly as their dad was the hero of the night on their street.

Yet again the light from a loving family home flooded onto the street to reveal no one, the secret intact. She realized that there were tears, happy tears, running down her face. It was a pleasure to witness such a tradition.

## achttien

Although the Dutch families in her neighborhood went all out celebrating Saint Nicholas Day, they still managed to do Christmas as well. She saw trees and lights go up all around, including one wildly decorated houseboat complete with reindeer and a sleigh on the roof.

She thought about getting herself a Christmas gift— mostly because she likely wouldn't be getting much from anyone else, but she'd always enjoyed giving presents much more than receiving them.

Perhaps a new computer would be both functional and exciting. Her laptop was slowly zapping itself to death, probably something to do with the funky adaptor that she had it connected to. *But what was she to do, order a laptop from the U.S. or buy a Dutch laptop?* The whole thing seemed to abstractly symbolize her efforts at rescuing what used to be her life. *What type of plug would she buy? Should she stick with what she knew... knowing that eventually, she would go back to it all? Or should she dive forward into the bizarre world of two round pegs?*

The most obvious solution was a full restart. If she really wanted to rid herself of the horrible muck that had been building up over time, a full restart was in order, but somehow, after all she'd been through, she still couldn't fully manage it.

Jack had picked out this laptop for her, she remembered. It seemed for now that he would always be there to haunt her. Thus far she just couldn't push him out of her head for good.

It was like an experiment of sunk cost, she sometimes thought, what she did right before what she did wrong. Some days during this holiday season she couldn't help but recall the good memories. She thought about the way it felt when he hugged her, the precise spot where her forehead pressed against his chest when she leaned into him, and the way he would laugh when she told a funny story from school.

On snowy winter weekends it was almost as if she needed

the bits of love that she'd once felt. Her heart wanted to remember a time when she knew, just *knew*, that she was the one that he was in love with. Even if it was painful, her heart needed to sporadically recall those times to get through, to feel that she might be able to do it again... fall in love.

## negentien

Clara woke up on December 24 with a huge hole where her heart should have been and the most horrible sick feeling in her stomach. It felt worse even than her worst day of morning sickness. She was completely alone at her favorite time of year.

It's not like she expected anyone to come spend the holidays with her. She was the one who left, after all, but that didn't mean it didn't hurt. Somehow, she still wasn't prepared for the reality of it.

*No one around,* she mourned, *just me and my Christmas sweatpants...* reindeer all over them.

She turned on Christmas music and let herself fall into the trance of Martina McBride singing *White Christmas.* Just before noon she gave in and put on *It's a Wonderful Life,* just like she did every other Christmas. Like every other Christmas, she both tenderly and laboriously watched each scene. Like every year, she began to cry as it got worse and worse.

*Might as well.*

If she could make it to the end all on her own, then at least it would show that she had perseverance.

It started to snow around noon. The fat flakes made her smile through the tears. It was almost worse than being in the Sacramento Valley where it never snowed at all. Here the beautiful flakes showed their faces, but there was no one to enjoy it with.

With only a somewhat excessive amount of tears, she made it to the end of the movie. When the Christmas bell rang and the final words were spoken, she began to sob.

The doorbell rang at four in the afternoon. At first she was only shocked, and then she prepared for the worst. Eviction, a serial killer, sewer so backed up that her toilet would never flush again... There were so many possibilities for Christmas Eve disasters alone. She considered not answering the door at all. It was highly doubtful it could be anything positive.

She looked down at her reindeer pants and baggy, sparkly red sweater and decided to just bear it. It was almost dark and soon she would have made it through an entire Christmas Eve day alone. She unlocked the deadbolt and pulled the heavy door open. There was a sucking sound as the seal broke and the rush of icy winter air flowed inside.

Standing at her door was Delia, and behind her, there he was, the man of her dreams. Standing at her door was the man of her dreams and the man of her nightmares. Jack.

twintig

Unfortunately, he was the man of the dreams of her past, and the man of the nightmares of her present. Clara's mind was perfectly blank. She could not think of any possible action to take, nor any words to be spoken.

Her heart pounded as she stared at him standing there at her door, literally waiting to be let in. She was not ready for this, wasn't ready to face him, to talk to him, to see his facial expressions, hear his jokes, see him smile. She turned back to Delia, but knew that she wasn't seeing her sister at all. She had turned her head but not her thoughts. Clara had been working so hard to forget him, to hate him, or at least let him go. She had worked so hard trying to dwell on the annoyances and the reasons that she was better off, but he looked so innocent there in front of her, so young and youthful, all the charm of being relaxed in life without the wear and the bitterness that she had—without the edge. His only edge was a slight tendency toward laziness, towards taking it too easy. But really, now that she saw him again, was it laziness? Or just... stresslessness?

Had she overreacted on that day so long ago? When she'd flown the coop? His face was so smooth, so unlined without all that worry and hate and stress. How badly she wanted that. How she had wanted him—wanted him back.

It was all happening too fast. There were so many emotions, so many thoughts running through her head that her delicately built world was simply spinning. The pregnancy didn't help. She could almost feel the hormones gushing out of her pituitary gland.

*Was that where pregnant lady emotion came from?*

Wherever it came from, it was gushing out, filling up her bloodstream with another 1,000 ways to be irrational.

*Dear God, she was a crazy pregnant woman. Was this what it was like for everyone?* She felt something else too, something a little more, like her ovaries doing a little cartwheel, maybe a roundoff—it had been *so* long.

*After all this time, how could she still be attracted to him?*

This man, standing in front of her—someone she had loved for so long, had made love to, had married... someone who had stood beside her when they were looking for jobs and paying off student loans and fighting with her mother about their lifestyle. Back then, they had been on the same side.

There, standing in front of Jack and Delia, she felt a warmth spread over her—the warmth that she would feel if she had someone on her side, if she had a partner, a love. *Her true love...*

Her true love had come back. She turned to look at him and their eyes met. The love, the tenderness, the excitement that they had felt; it was all there. She and Jack had chemistry, there was no denying it. A buzz was shooting in rays around the room, in and out of the doorway. It was all still there.

And then, she felt something else, something from within her, or more specifically, something that was inside of her. The baby gave her a hard kick.

*Was it a sign?* She believed in signs.

She felt herself relax, and out of her depths of loneliness came a smile. A real smile decorated her face and Jack smiled back. He saw the smile and took a step towards her. Before she knew it, she was wrapped in his arms, and her body weakened, truly weakened, at the knees.

*He came back.*

Her smile faltered.

He came back because he had left.

*No!* she screamed inside, but his arms were already around her. They were like a prison that she couldn't decide if she wanted to break out of.

She remembered then that he hadn't left—it was worse than that—he had kicked her out.

He had wined and dined her, and screwed her, she noted, cringing, and then he had told her to leave. He had decided that she wasn't going to be a part of his life anymore, and that she did not belong in their home anymore. That it was not her house.

Feelings of anger sped through her, from her arteries and to her veins until it surged into her heart and overtook her previous lapse in judgement. Piece by piece she remembered all the shit that she had gone through and that he had put her through. She hadn't left the country because he had told her to, she left because she had felt like there were no other options. Her life had been sucked away and her hope exhausted. Leaving had been the only option left that she had been able to stomach. She had gone searching for another world because she'd been desperate to get away... and because that's what you do when someone breaks your heart.

Still, Clara was in his arms. She wondered quietly if he'd felt the change. Probably not.

"Hey, sis!" Delia began her greetings just before Clara had the chance to maul Jack and shove him back out the door. "We're here!"

"Why, exactly, are you here?" Clara asked. There was a tightness to her voice, but she was nervous because she felt like she didn't have control of her emotions. She was very worried what would come next.

"I'm only here because it's illegal to smoke weed in my country." Delia chuckled heartily at her own joke.

"What?"

Clara's look must have been something, because Delia smiled broadly but looked a little frightened. She stepped inside and shut the door before turning to face Clara again.

"Just kidding, Sis. I'm here for you, babe. And look who I brought! A little Christmas present for my big sister!" Delia winked at Clara. "But I guess you already noticed that!"

Jack let go, and Delia wrapped her arms around a motionless Clara, somewhat from the side and somewhat from the back.

"Why do people keep hugging me from behind?" Clara asked without any basis whatsoever. "Geez." She threw off her sister and turned to walk away. If a human-sized tulip had been at her front door, she would have been less shocked and dumbfounded than she was right now. And what was with Delia? She was being even weirder than normal.

To her unpleasant surprise, Clara soon found herself sitting in her living room with her sister and her ex-husband, the latter two drinking eggnog while Clara sipped a cup of tea.

"And I'm telling you, Clare-"

*Since when did Delia call her Clare?*

"The guy that was seated in between us on the plane snored louder than Dad—snored louder than Dad plus Jack!" She smiled at Jack and punched him playfully in the arm.

"Wow." Clara responded dryly, probably her fourth word since the door had been shut behind her unwelcome guests. "Why are you here again? I mean, I'm surprised that you're not with Mom and Dad."

"Like I could handle another Christmas New Year combo with them!" cried Delia. "Bo-ring," she sang, "and how often do you get to spend the holidays in Europe? That was something I wasn't willing to miss."

Clara next turned towards Jack, slightly fearful after her

last near-forgiveness episode. She raised her eyebrows questioningly at him.

"We just missed you, Clarie."

*Damn it! How did that warm voice just make her melt? Wasn't she smarter than this!? And* Clarie, *the sound of it was orgasmic.*

Again, the baby kicked, this time serving as a reminder to wake up and remember the dreadful morning eight and a half months before.

"Oh." Clara replied in the driest tone she could muster in her volatile state of hormonal imbalance.

"I'm going to get us some of that faaabulous Dutch cheese." Delia chirped. "You know they don't call it Gouda here, Jack. They just call it 'cheese.' Isn't that funny?"

*Why was Delia acting so weird? All cool, and "fun" and... flirty? Is that what it was? Whatever it was, it was bizarre, that was for sure.*

"A lot of help you've been," Clara growled at Delia as she walked away towards the kitchen, "bringing *him* here." She glared at Jack. "Wish you'd both go home," she mumbled.

"Oh, don't be too hard on her, Clarie."

Clara gritted her teeth as he continued relentlessly to use her old pet name.

"She just feels bad about everything and she wants to make up for it."

"Huh?" Clara asked, "What does she feel bad about?"

"NOOOO!"

Clara heard a yell from the kitchen where Delia had been cutting cheese and apparently eavesdropping. She tripped and stumbled on the doorframe as she entered the room, but Jack continued, leaving Delia either unnoticed or ignored.

"She introduced me to Jane," he continued on blandly, "so she feels kind of responsible."

Clara turned to look at Delia with a look of fire. She huffed in fury. Delia closed her eyes tightly shut as if she hoped she could blink and make the whole scene disappear.

"You!?" Clara choked at her. If this didn't make her go

into premature labor, she doubted that the baby would ever come out.

Delia bumbled and stumbled over her words but said nothing real. In less than ten minutes she was out the door on her way back home. No tears were shed; Delia was probably happy she'd made it out alive.

Clara had tried to force Jack to go with her, but he simply wouldn't go. His absolute refusal had been astounding.

In the back of her mind, it was slightly reassuring that Jack wouldn't be traveling with Delia. Clara still couldn't handle the mental picture. Jack, Delia and Jane, chatting it up, becoming friends.

*When had this happened?* She wanted to ask, but was afraid of the answer. She might find out more than she wanted to know. Even after all this time, she knew it would do nothing but harm to find out more about his affair.

*Damn it, what was happening?* her conscience roared. *How was he here, in* her *home? Jack!* She thought it like an expletive. *Jack!* Acting all lovey-dovey like he hadn't been a treacherous bastard just months, maybe even days, before.

She had been doing so well.

*How could she have let herself lapse back to this stage? Jack and unhappiness.*

She could admit that she had dreamed about this. When Jack wasn't there it had been easier to dream about him coming back, to wish that he would search her out and beg her to forgive him. It had been easier for her to think that she wanted him to want her back. But this man sitting in front of her had done so little to deserve her wanting him that it was almost laughable. He had cheated on her once, and she had forgiven him—not because he had proven himself or because he had begged her; she had just gotten over it—as if she had no other options... as if this happened to everybody.

She had been spineless, letting him off when he had cheated.

Now this Jane, a woman he had openly chosen over her, and Jack was somehow still here in her house. He was still with her, thinking that he had a chance at being the third member of this family.

*Definitely third, never second,* she thought evenly. He surely lost that position.

She couldn't—couldn't possibly just let him... come back?

She raged against the mere notion nearly every moment, but there was a random fragment, a rare split second of an instant when she heard Delia's demon words in her head, talking about a perfect little family.

*Delia.* This, too, was an expletive. *Was this all because of Delia?*

Delia, who had been fighting for Jack all this time, had introduced him to a friend; Delia, who had never been on Clara's side, ever, not since elementary school when they had been placed on competing tee ball teams.

The idea of settling for anything after all the effort and hard work she had put in here seemed just blasphemous. She went to her bedroom and slammed her door like a child.

*Geez, Clara!*


## één en twintig

Clara woke from a horrible night of sleep and groggily stumbled to the front window the next morning. As of yet there was no sign of Jack. Maybe he had died in his sleep. She pulled back the curtain—snow on Christmas morning. She sighed. How nice it would have been to be able to enjoy it.

"What is it, Hon?"

*Nooooooooooo!* she screamed inside her head. "What?" she snapped, turning to look at him. "What is it that you want, *Jack*?" She was proud that she spoke his name like an expletive as well. "Do you really want me? Or something else? Our old life? Our Tuesday night tv watching? Guacamole Thursdays? Sex? I'd have to imagine that you're getting that with Jane."

Unbelievably, he chuckled. "Guacamole Thursdays..."

Clara's jaw dropped.

"I just want you to give me a chance, Clare. Let's see if we can work things out—for this one." He placed his hand softly on her belly. "Thanks for telling me, by the way," he laughed. "Thank goodness Delia's watching out for our little family."

Clara couldn't speak she was so frustrated. *Yeah, Delia had helped this little family out so much.*

Jack walked back to the kitchen and returned with two mugs.

"Hot chocolate?" he offered.

She took it, but hated herself for it. *Why couldn't she just be stronger?*

She settled into the couch and he sat down right next to her, leg to leg, and placed his hand warmly on her left knee.

"I missed you, doll," he smiled.

Clara frowned into her hot cocoa. He had never called her doll. Ever.

"It's been almost a year," she said to him, "You didn't miss me for a year?"

"Ha!" he laughed, "Don't kid yourself. I missed you every single day. How couldn't I, love?"

Clara scowled, he never called her *love* either. Ever.

"Man, I couldn't believe that you skipped out like that. I didn't know you had it in you, really."

*Now this,* she thought angrily, *this was Jack.*

"You are going to make me go into labor!" she howled, "and I'll be damned if you're here for the birth after all this time that I spent completely and utterly alone!" She emphasized the word alone. "Get out!" she screamed, "No, actually, just go *away!* Go away and don't come back. I can't keep dealing with this over and over again."

"What do you mean over and over again?" he asked, "It only happened once."

Her eyes were locked open, horrified. "Don't you think that was enough?" she spoke in an eerie and manic voice. She turned to look at him and saw nothing of the man she had married. This was over. It *had* to be over.


## twee en twintig

The next day it was three o'clock in the afternoon before she came to terms with the fact that yes, she was awake, and yes, this was really the state that she was in—feigning sleep for almost four hours as she waited for her *husband* to finish packing and leave. *Whatever happened to those divorce papers, anyway?*

After another minute, she realized that it was Tuesday— market day and her favorite day. In a matter of seconds, she was up and out of bed. She pulled on leggings and an oversized pregnant lady shirt and only heard Jack call out from the open bathroom door as she pulled the front door shut.

"Where are you going!?" he called.

"Market!" she yelled through the closed door, so thankful that she had made an easy and quick escape that she realized too late that she had forgotten both her key and a bag for her market goods.

*Shit.* She couldn't go back, he would definitely want to tag along, and the hell if she was going to let him ruin her precious weekly market trip. It was sad enough that she had already missed out on nearly the whole day—the sun shining from a beautiful blue sky filled with those big, fat, fluffy Dutch clouds tumbling gently across the landscape. Four or five inches of snow covered everything sitting still. She stopped at the apex of the curved bridge over the Singel for just a second, staring up at the endless sky over the white Dutch cityscape. It was so easy here to just forget your problems—even with an insane husband at her house and a sister recently booted out the door. Maybe that's how she managed to survive here in the first place. Unimaginably vast blue skies and peacefully drifting water had a soothing way of smoothing over life's rough spots.

She plopped down on a bench to readjust her colorful scarf. She thought about putting in her headphones for the walk, but just then a busy Dutch mother clinked past on her bicycle. The tiny baby in the front seat couldn't have been older than six months, and on the back, two kids sat facing each other on the back rack, clapping hands and singing. As they slowed and the mother bore down on her pedals to cross the bridge, she heard their sweet voices.

"Tumpity, tump, tump, tumpity, tump, tump, look at Frosty go."

She smiled peacefully despite her situation. This soundtrack was good enough, she decided, and placed her hand on her stomach.

She jumped as she felt something slide around her.

"*Oh,*" he cooed, daring to put his hand on her belly again, "How's my little Patriot?"

*Ugh. Patriot? Yuck. Who was this guy?* With some of the things he said, she couldn't even *be-lieve* she had ever been in love with him.

"*Your?*" Clara glared back at him, "What was that?"

"You know I'm not going to let you raise him here," he smiled back creepily.

*Creep. How had he caught up? Couldn't he just get lost in the loops and old streets and fall in the canal like any other tourist?* He would have in Amsterdam, that was for sure.

"Get off me," she replied, pushing his hand off her stomach, "and don't ruin my market day."

Laughing cheerfully, he followed her over the canal and into the city center.

*My city center,* she muttered moodily to herself.

Krista was right, she had changed. She had never been this blunt before. It kind of made her proud.

As the day with Jack got worse and worse, she longed to lock herself in her studio with a blank canvas. Normally she soothed her agitation with art, and she just wasn't getting the daily therapy sessions that she needed to maintain her sanity.

Back at the house, while he rambled on about the Giants

season, she reached under her chair and pulled out a sketchpad. Maybe she could at least do a bit of charcoal work—just to keep her fingers moving. He continued talking, as if this was something she had enjoyed when they were together. *As if.*

She reached into the charcoal leftovers tub sitting on her windowsill. She didn't have much, enough to do one or two. Even the paper in the sketchpad she had was running low. Talk about being unprepared in a time of need—not that she had expected him to show up on her Dutch doorstep.

She began sketching away, blackening and shading nothing in particular as he prattled on about Lincecum and how many double-doubles he ordered at In-N-Out.

*Blah. Blah. Blah.*

For two more days it went on like this. She counted her blessings daily that he had a job he had to get back to. She took him all the way to the airport personally, simply to ensure that he got on the plane and left her country.

"Bye," she said bluntly when they'd reached the security station for his gate. She hoped it would end at that, but he smiled gently and smoothly stepped toward her.

"Well, Clara," he spoke softly in her ear, "I really hope to see you soon." He pulled back and smiled at her, but she didn't trust it.

"Ungh." She just grunted back at him, half thankful that her giant belly was in between them so he couldn't get so close, and half saddened that she couldn't protect her child from being so close to him.

He pulled her close again and kissed her on the cheek. He hadn't tried to kiss her lips, which was smart, considering she would have socked him if he had.

"Clare," he repeated. "Just think about it…"

*She wouldn't,* she reaffirmed in her head, *she would* not!

"This is our only chance to have a family," he continued, "I know it's been rough for you, and I know I've been terrible," he acknowledged, "but all that can go away."

Her breathing was quickening. She couldn't take this. Her

hormones couldn't handle it and her heart couldn't take it. She needed him to step away. She needed him to go right now, but he went on, and her arms were weak. She couldn't get herself to lift them to push him away.

"The baby never has to know," he whispered.

His breath on her ear made her shiver in a way that it shouldn't have. He shouldn't be doing this. He shouldn't be muttering sweet nothings into her ear.

"It can just come into the world knowing its parents love each other."

Involuntarily, she felt her neck relax and loosen and then her cheek was on his. *Nooo!* She wanted to scream, but she couldn't. Her throat was dry.

She wanted love so badly. It ached. He was suddenly kissing her and she was kissing him back. Her arms were around him and there were tears running down her face.

And his.

Maybe he did really want her back. Maybe he did want her and their daughter. Maybe she was wanted, after all. As horrifying as it was to admit, he pulled away first.

When he turned and walked through the gate into security it was so strange—like he had never kicked her out and never hurt her. The thought of him leaving was horrible. All this time she thought she was ready—independent, all set to be on her own and take care of herself—and here she was, back at square one. She stood at the departures gate alone with tears running down her face.

For the slenderest of moments, she wanted to go after him. The urge to run after him was there, deep inside her. She would board the flight and take him back. He would pull her over and she would cuddle into his neck as she drifted off to sleep for the long flight.

He would order her an orange juice, with ice, and a water, and remind her to stay hydrated. All the feelings existed within her. She could take him back and with that take it all back—the life that was once hers, the house that was almost, the...

But while the tears streamed down, her feet didn't budge. This wasn't how her story should end. It couldn't end this way.

*It couldn't.*

She stood there for a long time, wondering how she really felt. She suddenly had no idea.

She ran a love scene through her mind a million times. He came back, she was angry; she took him to the airport, and then decided she just couldn't live without him.

She stared at the door until the image began to blur. She could do it. She could walk away from him. *Couldn't she?*

The thing was, she had wanted this, in a way. She had wanted to be the one who succeeded, the one he came back for, the woman who got it all—the man and the redemption. Now he had come back, and she was just steps from the redemption, but again, her feet wouldn't budge. You didn't get freedom if you were pining.

She was ready; she was so far past ready that she had begun to confuse herself, that's what this was. She was done with him just like he was done with her. She turned and walked towards the train station.

She had done it. She had walked away from him. All of a sudden, there was buzzing all around her. An alarm was going off and a flashing red light was spinning on either side.

*What the hell was going on?*

Next she realized that everyone was looking at her. No one else was concerned about the buzzing or the flashing, but they were looking at her like she was wearing a clown suit— or maybe an American flag t-shirt.

"Excuse me, Miss," a handsome young security guard extended his hand kindly, "where would you like to go? All gates are this way." He smiled, pointing his hand to an entirely different area of the airport.

"Oh," said Clara, staring back at him, still a bit shaken by the fact that she was the one who had caused the buzzing and the flashing.

"Can I help you with something, Miss?" He was

obviously now taking in her tear-streaked face and red eyes. "Are you trying to find the queue for security?"

"Oh," she paused, trying to remember where she had been trying to go, "Oh, no," she said finally, "thank you."

Confused and embarrassed, she wondered what secure door she had just tried to enter. "Um, wait, the train station?" she asked.

The security guard smiled and extended his hand to the right.

"Thanks," said Clara.

She hustled off in the right direction and turned the corner around a pillar, hoping to get away from the staring eyes as soon as possible. As she rounded the corner she ran smack into someone.

The someone was of course, Ian.

drie en twintig

If anyone was going to see her try to bust out of Schiphol through an emergency exit, it might as well be Ian.

"Uf," Clara smiled involuntarily, "Hi!" she almost shouted.

"You Americans!" he yelled back at her.

Yelling at her as usual, it seemed.

"Always running into things," he ranted, "never paying attention to what is in front of you or around you."

She smirked at him, but he went on.

"Clumsy? Aggravating? A nuisance? Must be American!"

"Hey-" she said, "Aren't you going a little far?"

"You just ran headlong into me without the least apology."

"Sorry," she grumbled. "So, what are you doing here?"

"What are *you* doing here? I am at the airport," he sneered. "Obviously I am either going somewhere or coming from somewhere."

His tone caused her to lean back in surprise. *Was he*

*serious? This wasn't just another* dumb American *joke?* If so, she hadn't seen him this irritated since her first month in Holland.

"Well," she shot back, "*I'm* not coming from anywhere or going anywhere." In her voice she could hear the defensive edge forming. His eyes looked bloodshot and his cheeks flushed, like he had just run a mile, though at the same time, she could have sworn she had just seen him shiver.

"Then get out of the way! Why are you at the airport? Get out of here! All these blasted people running everywhere, changing trains, going *shopping!* This isn't a mall! This isn't a rail hub! It's an airport! Get the hell out! Go home!"

Now she really couldn't believe what was happening. He was angrily waving his arms as his voice raised.

"Go buy your deodorant and your Mexx jeans somewhere else!"

"Are you drunk?" she asked, wondering whether she ought to be nervous about being hit by a flailing arm.

"No, I'm not *drunk*, you bitch!" he yelled.

She gasped, and immediately tears came bursting from her eyes.

"You-" she choked, but before she could even think of the proper term for someone who yelled this at her, a shy foreign woman who was almost nine months pregnant, he was gone. He strolled out the door without a glance.

"Wanker!" she yelled after him, although she didn't know exactly what it meant.

"Shhhh!" hushed a tall, dignified, middle-aged Dutchman.

She took two steps outside and collapsed in shudders on the first open bench on Schiphol Plaza.

She wasn't sure what to do next. This might just be her breaking point. She had been waiting for too long, trying for too long, pretending she was someone she was not. Or maybe trying to be someone she just simply couldn't be.

*I could leave right now*, she thought.

She could go back home and forget she ever experienced this sliver of new life, a slight lapse in her always mediocre judgement, a lapse that allowed her to think that this life could be hers.

Her other option was to go the other way entirely—let her judgement and common sense leave forever and really take advantage of what Schiphol had to offer. She could board a plane to anywhere. Surely there was a city or town in the middle of nowhere where she could teach English and live for nothing. She had nothing tying her down. Women had babies in every city around the world every day. She was nothing special.

Eventually she stood and moved up the stairs to the outside observation area. She stared out at the planes as she had done once before, some starting to move, some busy with preparations for the next flight, some just waiting.

She looked out at the dozens of planes dotting the grounds. It was so easy to watch them go, one by one, their slow departure from the terminal always leaving a gaping hole, a tunnel into the airport. It was a pathway that so many people walk down fearlessly, although just minutes later, it would lead to nowhere.

The plane's slow trek towards the runway, sometimes on its own power, sometimes being pulled, maybe even pushed... You would think that something so powerful could move on its own, but not always. Sometimes the small movements are the hardest.

She watched each plane sit at the top of the runway— waiting, almost thinking—about the flight it was about to make across the world. It made her want to run to the edge of the fence, to be as close as she could possibly be to the moment of takeoff—to all those people who had already made their decisions, already chosen their life.

*What was she doing here? What did she really want?*
She hated Jack for this.

She had decided. She had been set, or at least, she thought she had. Then her husband, yes, he was still in fact her husband—like he would ever get around to actually signing the divorce papers—had to show up and make her question her life. Worse yet, he made her question herself and whether or not she needed him.

*She didn't need him.*

Simultaneously she felt the ache, the good and the bad. She felt the pain that shot through her heart, her stomach, through her brain, through her elbows and her big toe for heaven's sake... a feeling of horror that she would never forget, the feeling that coursed through her as she read that note. The note where his sweet and straight fourth grade cursive defied its own being. She shivered at the memory.

Her name had been written on the front of the envelope. He had even used an envelope. For once, she allowed the details of the incident to pass through her, stinging details that she had been trying to ignore for months.

*How could he?*

He had sealed the envelope, an unusually pedantic choice for such a lackadaisical bastard. She remembered thinking for the tiniest second that it was some kind of a gift—a nice card or a kind note telling her that he loved her or that he was proud of her and what she had accomplished.

*How could he?*

She had gotten a paper cut when she opened the envelope. It was just a paper cut, but she should have known. When she opened the envelope to pull out the note inside, she immediately saw the gold lining on the top edge of the inside. It was a leftover envelope from their wedding invitations. Years later, and they still had boxes of them sitting around. Usually she used them for special graduations cards or for wedding gifts. Apparently, he thought this was an appropriate use.

*Clarie,*

*I don't think this is working anymore. I have plans for my life, and you are not a part of them. Could you do me the favor of leaving by the end of the week.*

*I'll be at Jane's until you are gone.*

*Best, Jack.*

His blows were premeditated. Each cut, like a line in a poem, one by one, so that there was no misunderstanding.

*Could you do me the favor of leaving by the end of the week.*

There had been no question mark. It was not a question, nor was it a request; it was a command. And Jane. He hadn't even hidden it. Her name was Jane; he was there now, and he would be there with her until Clara was gone. Out of *his* house. Not *our* house. *His* house.

And *Best*? Was there really a lower blow than that after being married for nine years? Best is what you write on a postcard to friends that you don't know well enough to put love, or even cheers. She would have preferred "Cheers." At least then she could have laughed. She hated the British, cheersing over every little thing.

Instead, she got "Best" as the final goodbye from her husband.

At the time, she had read the note something like five times to make sure she was not mistaken, but there was no mistaking it, he was done with her. He was done with her then and she was done with him now. He was here for her now and she was there for him then. It was so confusing.

At times in life there is complete freedom of choice. Life seems hopeless with not a chance in the world of success, and one obvious and simple choice appears and stares you in the face, but the only way you can think to go is any way but that one.

She couldn't think of anything else to do, so she just sat there on the observation deck and cried. It was really too bad it wasn't raining. Rainy days were already depressing, but it wasn't even raining during her time of trial. It had misted earlier, and now the sun was shining, so it was a glistening afternoon. Not only was she crying on a non-rainy day, she was crying on a shimmeringly sunny day. No one was getting wet, everything surrounding her was sparkling and she could only cry alone over her lost love.

After a while, she wandered over to arrivals. She wondered indifferently whether or not there was still a train back to Breda, but since she had not a clue what time it was, she let the thought breeze right out again.

This was somehow possible in airports. They let you exist in a bubble with no time at all and a constant buzz of others all around you, causing you to feel completely alone, but at the same time, one of many. Everyone was headed somewhere, doing something, but at the same time, doing nothing.

*How did we ever get ourselves into this?* she wondered, *flying all over in ridiculous silver bullets in the sky—moving around, defying home, family, and any sense of belonging at all. Who do we think we are anyway?*

She approached the arrivals gate, where she at least got to see more of what she thought she wanted and needed—tons of love and so many homecomings. In her current state it felt so good to feel the energy of so many people all standing on their toes trying to see their someone finally arriving.

Another hour and she was standing at departures, half dreaming, half mourning. She could still leave for somewhere exotic and new and different. She always had that option, and the more she thought about her last nine months of mistakes, distraction sounded like the perfect anecdote to her pain. There were flights to Paris and flights to Moscow. There were flights to Sao Paulo, Cairo, and Dubai, plus those to Izmir, Nador, Antalya, and Kos—all places she couldn't point out on a map if someone asked her to. She may have sat there for hours, staring at the screen, watching flight after flight slide their way up the screen until finally, it was their time. She saw people wait in agony and in delight, and she saw so many people hug that she could almost imagine that her turn was coming, too.

Some were more angry than sad. They were mad that their other was leaving—their lover, mother or father, partner, brother, sister. They would stand, arms crossed in protest, revolting against the fact that their someone was leaving them. They would be unnecessarily cruel as they waited, not speaking, barely looking at their other, and unforgivingly turning away when the other tried to comfort them, tried to make them see the positive.

Clara knew though. She knew that they would soon be feeling the regret. In just a few minutes, they would be angry with themselves. Once that someone had stepped through the automatic doors for the last time, they would be mad that they hadn't given in, horrified that they hadn't said goodbye, and mostly, they would be sad, because now that the someone was gone, they were just alone, and that was worse than anything else.

Sometimes, just at the last minute, when they first began to glimpse the loneliness, they would snap to their senses and run up to the automatic doors and cry out.

*Goodbye!* they'd yell. *I'll miss you!* Or *I love you.* Or just, *Thank you!*

Sometimes they would realize so late that they would have to run down the hall to the right and knock on the glass— just so they could smile and blow a kiss through the smudged, double-thick security glass.

"Goodbye," they would say, never just mouthing the words even though the other could obviously not hear them. They always spoke the words aloud, as if it might help make up for their pathetic and bitter display just seconds before. Whatever they did, their someone would always smile and their shoulders would relax in relief.

*Goodbye. I love you,* she would see their lips respond. She wondered if they were speaking aloud as well. Probably. Somehow love made people blatantly unaware of their actions.

It was long past prime commuting hours when she finally got on a train back home, so it was almost empty. She shared the car with one quietly chatting couple. Out the window a lone biker rode swiftly down the clean path. In the distance she saw a small group of ponies resting together on the chilly evening. She followed the biker's path as it continued through the countryside and passed just feet from a sad-looking brown pony. She closed her tired eyes for just a second and woke as they were pulling out of a station. She was almost home.

The train emerged into the countryside and she was dazzled to find a fresh layer of snow covering the ground in all directions, the moonlight reflecting romantically off it. The view was completed by frozen canals trimming the edges of each field. Better yet was the next field, filled with long since unsheared sheep. It was now decorated with a perfect maze of sheep tracks in the snow. Beautiful. She wondered if she would ever relive this moment or recreate this sight. She took out a sketchbook, thinking she could and would certainly try.

She was told that the land here was passed down father to son in strips, which gave the fields the shape that they so often had. A large area of land was separated in long, thin sections, sometimes with a house on the outer edge near the closest road; sometimes there was no house at all.

All in all, the narrow strips of land seemed to work well for the fields of flowers. All throughout the journey she watched the pieces of land pass by, remembering the times she had admired the brightly colored tulips decorating her view. One particular leg of the journey out of Amsterdam down the Randstad had always been her favorite, the passage between Haarlem and Leiden on the way home from Amsterdam. She could very nearly ride that route all day long and be perfectly content. A life with flowers was so much more enjoyable than one without. How odd that now it was fluffy white sheep. Clara found herself smiling at the sheep huddled in the moonlight. Perhaps it was all worthwhile, after all.

## vier en twintig

An eerie wind was attacking Clara's windows that evening when she got home. It was like a storm had been brewing but not until now had it decided to strike. Although she was happy to be warm and inside, the sounds and creaks made her feel uncomfortable in her own home—or perhaps that was what Jack had done. Eight months getting to know the country and after four days of Jack she felt like she didn't belong in her own life.

As if the clouds heard her, she immediately noticed that the rain had turned to a thick slush. It was sleeting. Cold, wet, frozen matter was smacking her window as if daring her to come outside.

She dropped down into her chair, letting out a huff of air as she did so, and groped in the magazine rack for something to read. The first periodical she pulled out was *Sports Illustrated.*

*Damn it, Jack.*

He'd been there for seconds and still marked his territory all over the place. As a matter of fact, right then Clara was fairly certain that she could smell urine.

*Filthy men.* If they weren't peeing all over the place, they hardly knew what to do with themselves.

She took aim and readied herself to violently throw the magazine towards the garbage can 30 feet away in the kitchen. She felt slightly validated that her hormonal symptoms seemed to be manifesting as irritability and man-hating. It pleased her. She chucked the magazine towards the kitchen, but the cover flung open and it flew in the wrong direction about 10 feet, nearly hitting a vase of dead flowers from the week before. After noticing the vase of flowers, she hauled herself up out of the chair and went to dump them out. On a dreary day like this dead flowers could only hurt the situation.

On the way back from the garbage she saw the magazine, but was basically unable to stoop down and pick it up. She spent a solid minute kicking it slowly but steadily over to the kitchen garbage, cursing Jack and his sperm with every oomph of effort.

She sat back down in her chair by the window a few minutes later, slightly out of breath but pleased that at least she was hating Jack once again. Maybe she *was* at home here. It was just more difficult when the evil specimen was standing in front of you with his arms around you, kissing you.

*So* like a man.

The wind seemed to pick up again the moment she turned to stare out. Huge raindrops were slamming against her window as if someone were dousing the side of her rowhouse with buckets of water. This weather was terrible.

She shivered and thought of her bed, but her stomach was growling. She wanted a Turkish pizza so badly it was painful. She glared out at the sleet and let her mouth water as she imagined the spicy sambal sauce and yogurt mingling on her tongue.

An hour later she'd managed to make up some food—doused, but with sriracha—and she was back in the same position in her chair. Since she was now sweating up a storm, for whatever reason, she had her heels resting on the windowsill and was pressing her feet up against the cool glass. A young Dutch man walked by and she scowled at him. She could put her feet in the window if she wanted. As an afterthought, she realized that he was probably more interested in her underpants, which were surely displayed in her present, spread-eagle position in her bathrobe.

*Men*, she thought to herself. *Filth.*

## vijf en twintig

The next morning her bell buzzed annoyingly early in the morning and Clara was forced to emerge from her warm and comfortable bed far sooner than she would have liked. She donned her bathrobe and a stocking cap and scarf, shivering, and went to the door to accuse whoever it was of waking her.

She swung the door open and found Ian standing in front of her. Amazingly, this was not the most surprising aspect of the morning. Ian was bundled up, standing in two or three inches of snow in front of two more shivering visitors, Krista and Clara's mother.

"Clara, I'm here!" her mother cried out immediately.

"What?" she stared back, ogling. Both her mother's words and presence weren't registering as possible. *Was this the third time she'd had surprise visitors?*

"Look at me!" she cried, "In Holland!"

*Heaven help us*, Clara thought to herself.

She tried to say it as nicely as she could, but unfortunately it came out a little strong. "But why?"

Krista let a laugh slip out and even Ian had a hard time hiding a smile.

"For the baby and for New Year's! Now move. We've got to come in. It's freezing in this country. No wonder my mother wanted to move to California."

Although Clara was uber pregnant, her mother didn't seem to have a problem edging her out of the way to get inside, though she did pat the belly on the way in.

"But Mom, the baby's not due until the second week of January."

"I know! It'll be a nice visit. I booked it on-the-line." She stressed each word separately as if spelling it out for Clara.

"Oh?" said Clara, allowing Krista and Ian to see her look of complete skepticism.

"Krista helped me, we Googled it."

"Oh?" she repeated, eyeing Krista angrily. *Krista?*

As Clara's mother went ahead with a self-tour of the house, Krista came over and began whispering frantically in her own defense.

"It's better with me here though, right?"

Clara continued to frown.

"You can't deprive your mother of seeing the birth of her first grandchild! Come on!" she shout-whispered. "We can handle this. I'll help keep her in check."

She did love how Krista said *we*. It made her feel taken care of, even if she didn't have a husband. Clara sighed, knowing she'd lost her ground. If it meant that Krista would be here with her at the end, then she could live with about anything.

Krista noticed the change in Clara's expression and chippered up a little. This made Clara feel better as well. At least Krista had grasped just how traumatizing it was for Clara to have her mother show up on her doorstep, unannounced, in a foreign country. Though after Jack, this was nothing.

"And Ian," began Krista with a smirk—he looked up when he heard his name, "will entertain her with clever British wit."

"What?" he said loudly, "wit?"

They both burst into laughter, knowing that there would be more laughing *at* Ian than with him, in the end.

"Should we go listen to your mother criticize your home?" asked Krista, gesturing to the ceiling where they could hear echoes of Mrs. Mason pacing quickly back and forth around the room.

"Sounds like she's moving furniture," added Clara, "Let's."

"Excuse me, Clara?" Ian spoke for the first time of his own accord. "Could I speak with you for a moment?"

Krista shot Clara an inquisitive glance and Clara shrugged. "Sure," she replied, and waved Krista up the stairs.

"I would like to apologize for the things I said to you," he began formally, "I didn't mean to…"

"Engh," Clara waved him off, "Like I said, bitch is hardly profanity in the U.S. of A." He remained unconvinced, and to her surprise, took a step toward her.

"I had, a short while before, had an encounter with my ex-wife, and it did not go well at all. I wanted to spend the holiday with her and the girls, you understand."

Clara was surprised to hear emotion in his voice. Maybe he liked being able to talk to her about his life.

"I just miss them so much, and I had some gifts for them and she wouldn't even let me in the house!" he screeched.

*So this is how it was going to be…* Clara watched him pine for his perfect little nuclear family. Her only friend in the country, and in the end, he was in just as bad of shape. *Maybe worse*, she thought, thinking back to the way his eyes were swollen and bloodshot the day before. Even today, they were still slightly swollen and appeared to be on the verge of drooping closed. She remembered his arms, swinging and flailing around him as he cursed her out.

*Had he always been like this? The bitter humor just strong enough to hold him back short of the arm-flailing threshold?*

He had tried to go back to her once again, and again, she had refused, declined the love of someone who clearly loved her and her children *so* much. Clara wondered what kind of a monster this woman was, but then she remembered that she had done just about the same thing. She wondered if Ian's wife had let him kiss her before she told him to go. She shuddered at her own memory.

"Clara? Clara?" Ian was saying her name, pulling her out of her thought trance.

"Clara!" her mother screeched from the stairs, "*Where* is this baby going to sleep!? You don't even have a crib!"

Clara turned to her mother, shrugging lightly at Ian to let him know that all was well with her. He had enough problems to worry about.

"I have a bassinette, Mother."

"A crib?"

"No, a bassinette."

"Is this how it's going to be, young lady?"

"What?"

Krista laughed, and Ian laughed, and Krista winked and left the room, calling after her, "You must be hungry Mrs. Mason. Would you like something to munch on, or would you like to freshen up first? Anything to drink while we're up?"


zes en twintig


"A *what!?*" Clara's mother came running in from the other room.

Clara had just been explaining to Ian that she'd recently found a midwife.

"You *can not* give birth to a child at home." Her mother looked around in disgust, "especially not *this* home!"

"What's wrong with my home?" demanded Clara.

"Well, for a start, it's not a hospital! What, should I help you tear up some sheets while I'm here? Help pre-pare for the birth!" she sputtered.

"One-third of the children born in this country are born at home with the help of a midwife."

"Yeah, and I'll bet about one third of those take their last breaths with that same midwife."

"Mother!" Clara gasped.

"Geez, take it easy, Mrs. Mason."

"One third of home births don't *die*," argued Clara.

"Oh, Clara. Be reasonable. I didn't really *mean* it to be factual."

At this response Krista burst out laughing. "Nice one, Mrs. M!"

"What?" asked both Clara and her mother.

"Uh, never mind," said Krista.

"I already have a midwife chosen," said Clara. I got her name from a friend of mine, Annemarie, and she has helped deliver hundreds of babies."

Clara's mother turned back towards her. "What do you mean *helped*—so they don't do it on their own?"

"Geez, mother."

"Well," continued her mother, "make sure you have the number for an ambulance close by. You'll probably," she stressed, "need it."

Clara and Krista exchanged looks—Clara's appalled and Krista's pleased. She was obviously enjoying the mother-daughter feuding that was going on.

"Okay, Mom… I'll be sure to have the ambulance number nearby. Where do you think we are, anyway? There's a couple hundred thousand people in Breda. It's not exactly rural, and it's definitely not undeveloped. This city was founded in like 1250."

"What?" said her mother.

"Aren't you just a font of Dutch history," Krista teased Clara.

"Well, how would I know that?!" argued Clara's mother, "It's not like you tell me anything! You hardly speak to me. *Krista*," she enunciated, "invited me here. I doubt you ever would have made the effort."

Krista smiled as Clara's mother walked over to give her a hug. Clara scowled and turned to Ian.

"Anything you want to chip in?"

Before Ian had to get involved, Krista stepped forward and led Mrs. Mason to one of the chairs in the living room.

"Come now, Mrs. Mason. This conversation is getting to be too much for you." As Mrs. Mason allowed Krista to lead her to a chair, Krista turned back to Clara and shot her a look, throwing her head first toward Ian and then to the door. Clara took full advantage, grabbing him with one hand and a parka with the other and quietly slipped out.

"Let me get you something to drink," Clara heard Krista say as she silently shut the door and headed down the street.

"What's this all about?" Ian asked.

"We're getting takeout," declared Clara confidently, "and air."

"Oh, right."

"But first a cup of tea," she inhaled deeply and patted her belly.

It was nearly dinner time when they got back to the apartment. After a rejuvenating cup of tea, they had enjoyed a slow walk around the Singel, Clara waddling and Ian following behind, slightly befuddled at the proceedings.

As they approached the house, Ian called out from a few feet behind her. It was amazing that she could waddle faster than he could walk.

"We forgot dinner!"

"Nah, don't worry about it. Krista will take care of it."

As they approached, they could smell Krista's cooking before they got the front door open. It smelled both spicy and meaty. Clara wondered how Krista had gotten her mother to agree on a meal with those characteristics.

Clara walked into the house and looked towards the

kitchen. Krista peeped out and smiled at her, and Clara noticed that she looked surprisingly relaxed after having spent the last few hours holed up in a house with her mother.

"Hey Clare!" Krista called out.

"Clara!?" shouted Mrs. Mason in a voice that could only be described as jovial. "I'm so glad that you're back, Honey! Krista and I have been having the most magnificent fun."

"Magnificent, eh?" Clara muttered, but Krista shot her a look, and she shut up. She took it she was expected to thoroughly appreciate the transformation Krista had brought about regarding her mother's personality and attitude.

"That's great, Mom," Clara smiled, trying to push the fakeness out of both her voice and facial expression. "What did you do?"

"Well, Krista and I talked about you a lot..."

This time it was Clara who shot Krista a look, both curious and confused, but Krista smiled back serenely.

"Then we walked to the most lovely market..."

"The market?" responded Clara, quite surprised, "You went out and came back? That's great. Which one?"

"It was on a *huge* square and since it was such a nice day, Krista thought we ought to enjoy the day before doing our shopping... We got a glass of wine," giggled her mother.

"A carafe, actually," said Krista quietly as she eased around Clara's enormous belly to get some plates out of the cupboard."

Clara smiled. *They* did *have a nice day.*

"And then we went to the market to get something fun for dinner," her mother went on, "and we found this *sweeeet* couple with their own little vegetable and spice stand."

It was then that Clara noticed that her mother still had a glass of wine in her hand. Leave it to Krista to get her mother drunk. There's an effective way to break the tension.

"They were from *Suriname*," explained her mother. "That's in the north of South America."

Her intonation reminded Clara of the year she'd taught second grade.

"They had the most interesting foods there."

Clara's mother was facing away from them, talking animatedly with her hands, the one holding the wine glass included.

"They had peppers and tropical fruit, and this chicken dish that was like chicken salad, but with a tomato paste that had just a *liiitle* bit of a kick. They let me try a few bites and wow, it just popped!"

The hand motion that went with "popped" was hilarious. Clara could only imagine the facial expression that went along with it.

"It had a little something called *car-ree*."

"Curry, Mrs. Mason," added Krista. "With a *u*, remember?"

"Yes, that's right. Curry…. Just delicious… So that's what we're making!" she ended and turned to give Clara a smile.

"Curry!?" shouted Clara in amazement.

"Curry?" asked Ian with a wary look.

"Yum!" said Clara, "That actually sounds really good."

"Don't act so surprised," muttered Krista.

"Sorry," replied Clara, "and thanks." They both turned to look at Mrs. Mason, who had now finished her glass of wine and was draped in a comfortable chair in the living room across from Ian. Her head was propped up on one arm and her legs draped over the other. Ian looked extremely uncomfortable.

"What a *wooonderful* place, Clara."

"Thanks, Mom," said Clara cheerfully.

"Oh!" shouted her mother, "and guess what!?"

"What?" asked Clara, very honestly intrigued.

"We decided that while we are here, we're going to throw a holiday party!"

"What?!" Clara nearly shouted, turning on Krista.

"Don't worry," waved Krista casually. "It's all under control."

Clara thought about it for a second, let her hormones

rebalance, and then conceded with a shrug. After all, with Krista here, she could hardly think of it as a struggle. No wonder she had depended on her all these years. She just made life so much easier.

After a delicious, albeit a little spicy, dinner of Surinamese chicken curry, all three women went to bed, and Ian took the last train home to Amsterdam. To Clara's surprise, he said that he would be returning for the holiday party.

The next morning Clara again tried to sneak out for some fresh, motherless morning air before anyone woke up. Unfortunately, when she got downstairs to the kitchen, she found it was already bustling with activity. She tried to slip back upstairs, but the squeak of the floor gave her away.

"Clara!" her mother called, "Are you going to the museum again...? Art isn't human you know, Dear."

"What?" asked Clara.

"The museum," said Krista knowingly, "She's wondering if you have to stop in at the museum to get some work done— you know, like you did yesterday," she added with a raise of her left eyebrow.

"Oh, well, yeah. I think I'll stop in there and then stop by the market for some groceries for this party we're going to throw.

"Great!" called her mother. "I'll come too."

"Wait, what? Why?"

"How 'bout Clara meets us at the market? What do you think, Clara? Mrs. Mason? Then she can get a little work done before we have to start the party prep."

"Well, okay," said Mrs. Mason. "I suppose we could meet you there. Krista and I will brainstorm some recipes!"

Clara smiled and turned for the door. "Great!" she called. "Thanks, Krista," she whispered. "You're the best."

"You're welcome," said Krista. "But remember that I can't get her drunk every day.... and I want some time with you, too."

"I know," Clara whined, "I just *really* need these breaks,

you know?"

"Fine." Krista sighed. "Plus," she began again loudly, "Clara needs to stop by that special British store to get some of that freak pudding for Ian. He's coming, too," she taunted happily.

Krista smiled devilishly at Clara, Mrs. Mason's head snapped towards them with wide eyes, and Clara stepped outside and pulled the door shut with a loud bang.

"So what's going on with this Ian?" she heard her mother ask curiously.

*Damn it, Krista.* Well, she supposed she had it coming. Krista had been letting her off pretty easy.

A few hours later she was sprawled out on the chair in the living room while her mother was in the kitchen baking with Krista.

"More toffee!" Clara yelled out.

"Uh, I think that's it Clare, you've pretty much cleaned us out."

"Oh…" she paused to think. "Well, how long does it take to make more?" she barked.

"Um, I don't know… 40 minutes?"

"Well," she said with a cackle, "you'd better get going then."

Ian, who had shown up earlier in the day to escape the loneliness of his own home, got up and walked to the other room, presumably to a location where there were fewer hormones floating in the air.

In the end, it was mostly a party for the four of them. Annemarie came with her husband, and two other women from Clara's yoga class stopped by, but it turned out that Clara didn't know all that many people in Breda and most were already booked for the evening.

The party was a complete success all the same. Clara was practically passed out from the amount of sugar and butter she'd eaten and Krista had pulled a surprise bottle of cinnamon jenever out from some unknown locale. Ian, Krista, and Clara's mother all partook in the surprise beverage.

Clara had found the energy in her to turn on her laptop and start a slideshow of pictures from her last eight months. They were now watching the Keukenhof album on random repeat.

"My Lord, the flowers," she heard her mother mumble grandly in an awestruck tone. "I wish I could have seen them."

Clara had never seen her mother like this before. She would even admit, if prompted, that she was enjoying her mother's company, something that hadn't happened in a long time.

"You should name her Tulip!" sang her mother suddenly, "That would be lovely..."

"Mom, are you drunk? I'm not going to name my daughter Tulip."

"But you're living in Holland. It's like Tulipland!"

"Especially if I'm living in Holland."

"How about Tulpa!" threw in Krista.

"You're not helping," muttered Clara.

"This vanilla is just delightful," she enunciated the word and put a little extra sway to the middle syllable.

"I thought it was cinnamon," said Clara.

"It was," Ian laughed, "but then Krista pulled a bottle of the vanilla out of the back of your coat closet, so we switched to that."

Clara turned to look at Krista in awe. "How did you even get this many bottles back here without me noticing? We've only been there together!"

"You get distracted," smiled Krista.

"I think I'll bring back the vanilla and the cinnamon," rambled Clara's mother, "and I'll serve them at my next book club event." Clara wasn't sure, but she thought she then heard her mother hiccough. "And I'll buy some of those caramel waffles. And... What else? I'll have vases of flowers at the tables—tons of tulips and those black ones that are so interesting."

"Black tulips and liquor for a book club... what book are you going to be reading, Mrs. Mason?" asked Krista.

"Oh, probably something really serious. It's hard to find a light-hearted book nowadays. If I didn't have my Danielle Steel to read on the side I don't know what I'd do."

Clara and Krista laughed.

"Who's-" began Ian, but Clara interrupted. That impromptu speech was something she definitely didn't want to hear. "Is Danielle Steel really light-hearted?" asked Clara.

"You know what I mean," declared her mother.

Clara leaned toward Krista, "Do I?" she asked playfully.


## zeven en twintig

Clara booked a reservation for the Anne Frank House for the next day, and her mother, who had just read *The Diary of Anne Frank* for her book club, spent the afternoon in tears, unable to believe how the tiny rowhouse was able to make the young girl's story feel so real.

While her mother listened, shocked, to the video account by Anne's father, Clara observed her mother and chatted quietly with Krista, at one point even walking over and putting her arm around her mother. She had been enjoying herself the last few days. It was nice to spend time with friends and family.

That afternoon, while Krista went wandering around Amsterdam, Clara took her mother out to the ocean, hoping to talk with her peacefully while her guard was down and her emotions high and sympathetic. In the end, it was her mother who did most of the talking.

"Your father seems to think you've never been happier." She paused, seemingly pondering this thought, considering the likelihood that it was true.

This was nice because it gave Clara time to think about it as well.

*The happiest she'd ever been? Was that possible?*

It was still difficult, of course. Honestly, she knew hardly anyone, and she didn't speak the language, although she was trying. Still, living in another country was never easy. Of course, easy certainly wasn't synonymous with happiness. Her life with Jack had been quite easy. The day to day grind was really just a light rub with the finest sandpaper. Maybe all she had needed all along was a life that took some effort—some tasks that kept her nose to the grindstone and her hands dirty.

She had come to think of happiness as a sort of linear continuum. Like a constantly shifting machine, it moved back and forth, taking into consideration stress, work, love, the weather. She chuckled at her philosophical musings and her constant pondering. She never thought she would spend so much time just *thinking.*

They stood in the harbor watching quietly as a large sailboat floated by, slowly making its way toward the intricate system of canals. It was a huge sailboat, oceanworthy for sure.

"So," her mother began again, "He also seems to think you're here to stay." Still her mother didn't look at her, didn't turn toward her.

Clara's head dropped a half inch or two and she quickly turned back to look at the water. The man piloting the boat looked up at her at that moment. The look on his face was almost inquisitive, as if he had heard her mother's question and was waiting to hear her response as well. He adjusted his cap, a motion so typical of a Dutch sailor that it caused the corners of her mouth to curl up. A second later he turned back to his craft, adjusting it ever so slightly to guide the tip into a small canal that would take him into the city. She wondered if he was on vacation or if this was somehow his work, his life. Sometimes anything seemed possible here.

"I don't know," Clara finally responded. With a deep breath, she continued, "Maybe…"

She felt a shiver run through her. It wasn't as if she hadn't been considering the idea, but she hadn't ever considered it aloud, in the presence of her mother.

Her mother said nothing.

"Next year, I think your father and I will come for Christmas…if that's alright," continued her mother.

"Of course," Clara murmured. She gave a shaky nod. What a strange turn of events.

They stood together and watched the sun go down. It cast a glow of orange over the marina and the surrounding harbor, the clunk of the rigging creating the peaceful heartbeat of harbor life. They began to walk back towards the train station just as the light was disappearing. Clara led her mother back to the spot where they would meet Krista outside the station, and a stream of light-hearted chatter surrounded them the whole way home.

Tomorrow seemed like it would be just as nice of a day. Maybe she was on a lucky streak, but Holland seemed to have a wonderful effect on all parts of her life.

## acht en twintig

Clara felt a strange aura of sadness surrounding her mother's departure. She would miss her mother, and this was a feeling she hadn't experienced since she was a girl.

She had enjoyed the visit. Compared to her last quiet months, it was nice to have people there when she woke up, have someone to talk to and someone to eat breakfast with.

Her mother had sobbed. She had been utterly devastated that the baby hadn't come while she was there. Secretly, Clara thought that Krista planned it that way. They hadn't even stayed until the due date, but left the day before.

After two weeks of acting as tour guide, Clara went back to life as an anonymous expatriate. She got up and walked slowly around the house, recounting the unbelievable memories from the last several days, weeks, and months. She was amazed that these huge changes could even take place in a lifetime. Her life had been so stable, so concrete, that there had been virtually no change at all for years. She could never have imagined that she would be in this place at this point. She would never have believed that her life could be so different.

She paused at her small, makeshift office desk. On it sat

the papers from her mother that made the house hers. That, too, she hadn't thought possible. She moved to her upstairs observation window slowly, allowing herself to groan with every single step that she took.

*Sooooo fat*, she laughed to herself. *Soooooo very fat.*

All along she had known that this stage was inevitable, but it was still shocking and traumatizing and bewildering all the same. She couldn't see her feet. She couldn't remember the last time she had been able to see them.

She sat at the window for several hours, sketching and staring. She could get used to this life, viewing the world from a comfy chair at a perfect second-story window in The Netherlands. She'd been thinking about what was to come; soon she'd have a baby here with her. Though she had been up 15 or 20 times to get food and snacks, she had done some good thinking.

She could now admit to herself that she sometimes thought of Jack, the man she had assumed would be her husband for life. She sometimes even found him in the background of a charcoal sketch, strolling through an alley or sitting on a cement step smoking across the canal from a café that she was painting, though he hadn't smoked in years. She wondered if this would ever end, if his background presence would ever go away. It was haunting—not his presence, but the idea that the thought of him would always be in the air. If she accepted that he might never go away and that she would always feel him there in the background of her life, it didn't hurt so much. Understanding their relationship, both past and future, was far more about her than him. Being able to think logically about it made for less pain for her overall, she hoped.

Patting her nearly exploding body, she expected that with time she could get there. She just hoped it wouldn't be too visual, at least not in those glass blue eyes. She wondered about her daughter's traits and whether she would be more like her mother or her father.

When she and Jack had first gotten married, she remembered wondering the same thing but from the opposite angle. She had been thinking affectionately about Jack's blue eyes and the curls he had as a baby. Now, she found herself wondering if they would perhaps be her eyes, her hair, her nose.

*Would she find herself waking up every morning and looking into Jack's eyes?*

As much as she had liked the sparkle, she wasn't sure if she could handle that. She tried to imagine it, her daughter, because she was still sure it was a daughter, with *her* brown hair in thick tufts sticking out in all directions. Thick, heavy, and a little dry, but she'd get used to that.

That night, Clara couldn't sleep. Apparently her pregnancy poison was irritability and restlessness with a side of distraction and hot flashes. By midnight she had her laptop back on, and 15 websites open on 15 different tabs in her browser window, plus another window with her email, her Facebook, her LinkedIn, and the Twitter homepage—which she had no idea what to do with.

She was also chatting with Krista and playing a game of spider solitaire. By 2 a.m. her computer's reaction speed had gradually slowed down to a halt, and since then she had spent the time yelling at Internet Explorer, Microsoft Word, Windows, and any other application that she could think of, threatening to switch to Apple if they continued to act up. It was officially her due date and she was very aware of it.

When she finally realized that she just wasn't going to sleep, she moved back to her chair by the window. She reached backwards to grope the magazine rack for a little something to read. Once she realized she had nothing in terms of magazines as a possibility, she slid her chair around slightly and moved to scanning her bookcase. It was fairly easy to find a classic, but at this time of night it was hardly comforting to read stories with pathetically happy endings and marriages that lasted forever. What she really needed was a novel that was short, exciting and had large print—like the ones her grandmother used to read. Her current mood also most desired a plot that centered on the male lead being blown to bits by an empowered woman with a laser gun. She supposed that this type of novel would be hard to find in large print.

She eventually settled on organizing the bookshelf rather than reading, but once she got every book dropped dramatically onto a pile on the floor, she found that she couldn't really reach down to pick them up. She picked up the one on the top of the pile, which happened to be written by Clive Cussler, but almost immediately became too bored and tired, and thus decided to simply sit crankily by the window and wonder why the hell she had a book by Clive Cussler.

After a call from Krista during which Clara ranted for 45 minutes and Krista did nothing but laugh continuously, Clara crawled from her day chair and moved into the bedroom for another few hours of tossing, turning, and farting— presumably.

*This baby had better be good.*

Dreaming about sweet hazel baby eyes, Clara woke in the middle of the night with a searing pain in her gut.

*Oh, no,* she thought. *Here goes.*

She took a few deep breaths and waited for the next round. She passed the time by texting Krista.

*There she blows!*

Krista ought to appreciate that. After yet another painful pass she called Marieke, who arrived in what felt like minutes.

*What a fast biker,* thought Clara. Even in labor she was amazed by the Dutch. By 9 a.m., the midwife was helping Clara get comfortable.

Impossibly, Ian was there by 10:30. Clara had no idea how he'd even found out she was in labor, but she didn't mind as long as he stayed completely out of the room for the entire process.

Four hours later, she'd made no progress at all. She was getting very tired and hungry.

"Ian!!!" she yelled towards the door, open just a crack. "Whip me up some curry! I'm hungry." She'd had about all that she could take, and Ian could likely at least provide some entertainment. She heard some shuffling and then his voice.

"You can't have curry now!" he exclaimed officially, but then deferred to Marieke. "Can she?"

"Nee hoor," said Marieke firmly.

"What?" asked Clara.

"Of course not!" said Ian.

"Is that what she said or is that what- Ahhhh! Damn it!"

"No, you cannot," said Marieke calmly as Clara continued to howl.

She heard Ian running away back down the hallway. At the moment she was tremendously jealous of all those with a penis.

When it was almost time, according to Marieke at least, she again felt the need to chat.

"Ian!"

"Uh, what?"

"His voice came from a place shockingly close, perhaps just outside the door."

"What are you doing?" she asked.

"Um…"

"Are you sitting at the door waiting for me to give birth? Because that's just weird."

"I cannot do this!" he belted out. "Your mother made me promise to be here. Krista sent me a text early this morning-"

Clara actually laughed. She even felt a little sorry for him. Talk about buckling under feminine pressure.

"…telling me to get my arse over here-"

"Wait, what?" Clara froze. *Had he just said, 'arse'?*

"Uh, she wrote that you were exploding! Which is highly inappropriate, and then…"

"You're drunk!" Clara howled.

"I'm not," he tried to articulate.

"You are! You Brits are always drinking! Drunk Brits everywhere! Worse than an American college campus!"

"Hey," he barely spit out the words, "You are the one that wanted me here."

"Maybe sober and for support, but now you're just- Wait. A. Minute…" She turned to look at him accusingly through the crack at the hinge of the door, "What are you drinking? You're not- you had better not be drinking my post-birth Dutch liquor!"

She couldn't see his face, so she waited, entirely impatiently and yelping through another contraction, for his response.

"Are you?!"

"No?" he replied in thick British English.

"It's time, Clara," said Marieke.

"I would... I would never," Ian stammered.

"You did!"

"Push now Clara," Marieke was tapping her knee, trying to get her attention.

"What am I supposed to drink for my post-birth celebration!?" she shouted. "I haven't had a drink in nine months and allllll anyone talks about is this damn Dutch jenever."

"I'm sorry, Clara," he cried, "I was nervous!"

"It's really time, we've got to get her out, push now. Push Clara."

"You!" she accused, in between her screams of pain, "*You* were nervous."

"All that screaming," he exclaimed, almost begging now, "I didn't know how to handle it... I just thought I'd have a quick nip."

"What!" she shrieked, all a part of her struggle. "You thought you'd have a *what*?"

"...and then I got a bit carried away, and now I admit, I'm a bit muckibus-"

"Stop!" she yelled, "I can't even understand what you're saying!"

"Okay, let's push again, Claartje."

"Don't worry. You can get it in abundance here."

"I don't care! I was saving it. It was a gift! Krista got it for me especially for this moment. It's the jenever that you serve when you're announcing that you are pregnant and are going to have a baby."

"Well that just supports it then," he said, "it's not even the appropriate jenever for this point in time."

"It's what I wanted. And you drank it all."

"It's basically just Dutch gin. It's nothing special."

"Push! Clara! Ian, perhaps you should leave."

"Fine!" She looked at Marieke with determination before continuing to scream at Ian. "It was miiiiine! That's why it was special. Now take my gin and get ooooout!"

"Fine!" he yelled, shutting the door firmly.

As if a part of the conversation all along, once he left, Marieke turned to Clara. "It's actually not like gin at all," she said matter of factly. The name is what's most similar."

Clara dropped back on her bed and huffed out a long and full lungful of air.

"It's a girl," said Marieke.


negen en twintig


"Hey, what day is it?" Clara asked.

"Uh, Tuesday," Ian responded, "Tuesday, the tenth of January. Ada was born on the ninth of January."

"Great! Croissants are four for €1 today at the Super de Boer."

"What!?"

"Croissants. Yum, cheap, go."

"What are you saying? You can't eat croissants."

"Why can't I eat croissants!?" She turned to glare at him but peeked suspiciously out of the corner of her eye at her midwife.

"She can eat croissants," said Marieke.

"But- shouldn't she be eating carrots and spinach... brussel sprouts and such?"

"Now, they are four for €1, so get at least eight, no 12. Ada might like them, too. Wait," she stopped as she realized what she'd said. She was still a little delirious from the day before. "Eight, unless you might eat some, then get 12.

Marieke? Do you want some?" She continued to ramble without waiting for a response.

"No, just get 12. Then we'll definitely have enough."

Ian turned to the nurse and inaudibly asked something. Clara thought she heard the word *sleep*.

"Not enough," Marieke replied quietly.

"I'll just... go for the croissants," he said, turning towards the door.

"12!" she yelled at his back, "Cheers!" she trailed off as her head hit the pillow.


### dertig

Clara looked down at Ada in her white bassinette. She was such a good baby. Clara almost wished she were more difficult, at least a challenge, but she just gazed upward peacefully with those pale blue eyes, probably thinking, *What are we going to do next, Mom?*

"Well," Clara responded to her gentle thoughts, "I could use a cup of coffee."

After tucking Ada into her cute European buggy, they walked together down the quiet cobblestone street into the center. Ada was now more than a month old, and today was the first day you could really *smell* spring. Although the rainy days were still frequent, the sun now stuck around until at least 6 o'clock and the air was fresh and seemed to breathe life. Soon, the flowers would come.

They stopped at Clara's favorite European delicacy shop and a breeze of warm air met them at the door. It was so nice to be out in the world again. She inhaled the perfect aroma of freshly-made chocolate swirling around her.

"This," she smiled at Ada, "is what *lekker* is." The woman behind the counter chuckled to herself. "Lekker," she smiled and agreed.

When selecting a dessert in a foreign country, Clara found it important to utilize all the senses in order to make the best possible choice. It usually took her a good half hour, but she *always* chose right, whether it was chocolates or croissants, warme chocolademelk, stroopwafels, suikerbrood, or warm appelgebak in gezellig brown cafés.

Today was chocolates, tiny, delicate, and perfect. She chose one that was cappuccino filled and another with a pistachio center. A third was filled with hazelnut cream, a coffee bean placed lightly on top.

Upon selecting the finest chocolates to go along with her coffee, she pushed Ada to the park where they would be spending the day together watching the amazingly plump rabbits. She got comfortable on the bench and stared admiringly down at her perfect daughter.

"I hope you're not feeding her chocolates," Clara heard from behind her. "She's too young for chocolates. She'll get that obese children's diabetes like all the American children have. You'd better take care."

Clara rolled her eyes and smiled as Ian sat down next to her. She hadn't known he would be joining them, but she didn't mind.

"My ex-wife used to feed my daughters chocolates."

Clara looked over at him, wondering how his life turmoil was progressing.

He scowled, "That woman... not good for anyone." With that he leaned over and softly kissed the top of Ada's head. "She's lovely," he sighed, and rested his arm on the park bench behind Clara's shoulders.

Clara let a slow smile spread across her face. She looked down at her daughter and reveled in her happiness. How glad she was that she had come to The Netherlands. Like Ilse, her heart belonged here, and it would be her daughter's home, too.

CM

## Epilogue

That spring, the same day the Keukenhof opened for the season, Clara hosted a gallery opening. Everyone was there: Ada, Ian, Marieke, Ilse, Ellie and Lars, Annemarie and her family and new baby, even Ian's daughters. No one from Sacramento was there, but that was okay, she had a life here now, too.

Finally, she was doing it on her own, without pressure or unhappiness, just a bit of mouthy British assistance, a few sparks of interference on Wednesday nights, and lots and lots of flowers.

"So Ada," Clara began, "I knew a girl once who got it all. She had a wonderful and vibrant life, work she loved, a beautiful daughter, her independence, and he came back—the one who broke her heart! Can you imagine that? They never come back. And better yet, when he *did* come back, she stood strong. She might have been confused at a point, I admit. But in the end, she knew herself, she knew what she wanted, and she also knew that she didn't need him anymore. She got to do what every broken-hearted woman wants to do. She got to choose. And she chose right, mind you. She chose herself and her own life…"

"Smart girl…" she murmured as she brushed her index finger on Ada's rosy cheek. "Everybody needs to start over once in a while. It's okay. Even when you're at a crossroads, you know which direction you want to be going and you pick your place like you pick your music—half because it's good, and the other half, because it represents the person you want to be."

The End

For Clara, it's Holland.
For you, it could be anywhere.

# Acknowledgements

There were many people who helped me throughout the writing and editing process, all at very different stages. First, I'd like to thank Vanessa Vander Wilt. For whatever reason, her cheerful words of encouragement were instrumental in the initial realization that I could and would write a novel. My mother and my sister, Karen and Natalie Willers, shouted words of motivation from start to finish. They also read quickly when I called to tell them to hurry up. I'd also like to thank the folks over at Figgy Pom, Teresa Pargeter and Eric Lee, and fellow writer Allison Joy, for the feedback they provided. Still to be included are Melissa Oeding, Wendie Doyle, Anthony Caer, and all the friends and family who supported me and were excited for me. You can't imagine how important you all were during the writing of this book, my first.

I'd also like to thank my parents for raising me in a world full of books. Without this world of real and imaginary I could never have become the person I am today.

Last of all, although it might sound strange, I'd like to thank every person that has ever made music. There's no way to thank every artist that helped me survive the writing and revising process. Music really is the best muse.

Patricia Willers is from rural Minnesota. By way of Guadalajara, Mexico and Leiden University, she currently resides in Davis, California where she is a teacher.

*Wandering Canalside* is her first novel.

Made in the USA
Coppell, TX
20 August 2021